# BLOOD

"In twenty-one days you will die," promised the priest. "You will die violently. What came out of you has now returned to you. You must now face the ghosts your past deeds have raised. The instrument of your death will be a young boy who lives in the West. . . ."

## PRAISE FOR MARC OLDEN'S PREVIOUS THRILLERS

# SWORD
## OF
# VENGEANCE

## MARC OLDEN

JOVE BOOKS, NEW YORK

SWORD OF VENGEANCE

A Jove Book / published by arrangement with
the author

PRINTING HISTORY
Jove edition / June 1990

ISBN: 0-515-10370-5

Jove Books are published by The Berkley Publishing Group,
200 Madison Avenue, New York, New York 10016.
The name ''JOVE'' and the ''J'' logo
are trademarks belonging to Jove Publications, Inc.

PRINTED IN THE UNITED STATES OF AMERICA

10  9  8  7  6  5  4  3  2  1

*For Diane, as always*

To really be vitally alive, to truly feel life's offerings, is to know the highs and lows, the exhilaration of the mountaintop and the descent to the valley, and to accept and enjoy not one but both. Life's highs are most invigorating; there is also fertileness to be found in the lowest valley. . . . Any effort aimed at altering this natural law would be futile.

—DAVID CHOW and RICHARD SPENGLER,
*Kung Fu: History, Philosophy, and Technique*

**Te.**   Chinese for the interaction of yin and yang, or the result of life's positive and negative forces acting upon each other. Sometimes called The Power.

---

**Bushi.**   Japanese warrior who followed the code of Bushido, stressing honor, loyalty, duty, and obedience.

# One

## Manila

In thirteen years of setting fires, Leon Bacolod, the arsonist, had killed thirty-seven people.

He himself had suffered neither injury nor arrest. He credited his good fortune to the Virgin Mary, a deity he worshiped with a marked and excessive attachment.

A small, twenty-one-year-old Filipino, Bacolod had boyish good looks, greased crew-cut hair, and a cleft palate that made eating and swallowing difficult. Before setting a fire, he would make a floral offering to Our Lady at Quiapo Church. Here he also said a rosary in front of the Black Nazarene, a life-size image of Christ in blackwood carved by Mexican Indians in the seventeenth century and brought to Manila by a Spanish galleon.

Religion was Bacolod's passion and refuge. His faith was ecstatic and satisfying.

On a humid March night he walked out of Quiapo Church, fingering a bamboo rosary and wearing the gray peaked cap, light gray shirt, and dark gray trousers of a Taaltex Industries security guard. He carried a shopping bag from Rustan's, a popular Manila department store, where he'd recently been a guard until dismissed for sticking small items down the front of his pants and walking out of the store with them.

There was a small flesh-colored bandage below his chin.

He'd shaved three times today. Shaved his legs too. And his forearms. Even the backs of his hands.

Inside the shopping bag was a half-gallon tin of gasoline, a pair of rubber gloves, a pack of Gauloises cigarettes, and several books of matches. The bag also contained a blue dress, black ankle-strap shoes, a padded bra, a red leather purse, and a black nylon wig.

In a red 1983 Datsun, Bacolod drove south on Roxas Boulevard, following Manila Bay out of the city, passing the bright lights of deluxe shoreline hotels and the Cultural Center, which sprawled across seventeen hundred acres of reclaimed bay land. With its museums, exhibition halls, and theaters, the center was practically a city in itself. Imelda Marcos, then governor of Manila, had built it at a cost of untold millions. Bacolod revered her nearly as much as he did the Virgin.

When a Muslim restaurant owner claimed that Mrs. Marcos never gave away anything she didn't take from someone else, Bacolod put him out of business with a fire, which also took the life of three Vietnamese busboys. A year later he torched the home of a Marcos political opponent, a quadriplegic who, with two small grandchildren, had died in the blaze. Bacolod had watched the fire from a Chinatown flat he shared with a dwarf whore, the two of them eating guava and drinking sugarcane juice. The arsonist's loyalty to his country and its leaders was unconditional.

His criminal behavioral pattern, however, was erratic. It had no fixed or regular course. He worked for landlords and other businessmen who hired him to burn down their property for the insurance. On the other hand, when seized by the craving to set a fire, nothing could stop him. He could offer no rational explanation for his actions.

His mother had been a prostitute with no interest in a child, especially one cursed with both a cleft palate and epilepsy. She had disappeared after dumping him in a home for disturbed children, where he was raped by older boys until he'd poured kerosene on the ringleader and set him afire. Leon Bacolod had left the home obsessed with fire. And with a strong urge to destroy.

The very thought of starting a blaze would give him the shivers. On these occasions he became sexually aroused. Absolutely randy. The dwarf whore, Huziyana de Vega, had warned him about men who had literally fucked themselves to death. "Wouldn't surprise me," she said, "if one day you came and went at the same time."

She could also make him laugh about his cleft palate. His speech problem was caused by his cock, she told him. It was so large, it pulled his tongue off-center.

Leon Bacolod left Manila's outskirts and entered the countryside shortly before eleven P.M.

Away from the city, the temperature dropped suddenly. The cool night air, with its smell of wild orchids and rain-drenched bamboo forests, was quite pleasant. Colorful butterflies danced in and out of the glare of the headlights. Bacolod smiled when a giant silver eagle, claws and beak tearing at a dead python beside the highway, took flight at the Datsun's approach.

The roads were still wet from yesterday's monsoon. Driving, however, wasn't a problem because Bacolod had the countryside to himself. No more worrying about metropolitan traffic with its clogged streets and out-of-control drivers. Manila's motorists were a loony lot, driving about in crackpot fashion and scaring the shit out of anyone in a car or on foot. Miracle workers, Huzi called them, claiming it was a miracle when they didn't hit anybody.

Bacolod drove past ramshackle huts, a Chinese cemetery and the ruins of churches and convents destroyed in the Pacific War. The only traffic he encountered were two cyclists and a jeepney, one of the reconstructed U.S. World War II jeeps used as private buses.

Ten minutes later he turned the Datsun left off the highway and up a dirt road on a mountainside covered in towering pines. Bacolod hit a pothole immediately. The jolt lifted him out of the seat and snapped his head forward.

"Goddammit!" he shouted. The slightest damage to his car pissed him off. He was continually customizing the Datsun, tinkering with its motor and washing the car several times a week. A small scratch on the finish was enough to leave him furious.

The car radio was tuned to a baseball game coming from Rizal Stadium. Bacolod would have preferred jai alai, which like all Filipinos he followed passionately. But the new government had shut down the game, claiming it was corrupt. All the casinos had been closed for the same reason.

He hated the new government, and he especially hated Mrs. Aquino, the stiff-necked old maid who ran it. On the surface she appeared to be an angel come down to earth, a fucking goody-goody. Bacolod, however, knew himself too well to believe that anybody was totally pure. Mrs. Aquino was a politician. Therefore she could only be a cheat and a put-on, a wooden penny posing as a diamond.

Just inside the towering pines, the Datsun's headlights shone on a sign reading FREE TRADE ZONE—TAALTEX INDUSTRIES—3 KM. Bacolod chewed his bottom lip. Three kilometers. He dropped a hand from the wheel and cupped his scrotum.

He followed the dirt road through the forest and up the mountainside, tensing when he entered a small tunnel. Tensing because of the bats hanging from the tunnel ceiling. Clusters of them, with pointed ears and folded, tapered wings and clawed hands and feet. Bats now caught in Bacolod's headlights, suddenly flying in his direction, scaring the shit out of him as they flew past the car and out of the tunnel to a hidden and preselected feeding ground known only to them.

Heart pounding, Bacolod shoved the gas pedal to the floor.

Seconds later he was on the summit, in the night air, and driving onto the black asphalt of a parking lot overlooking an extinct volcano. He had arrived at the Free Trade Zone, twenty-two acres isolated behind brick walls topped with barbed wire.

The Free Trade Zone (FTZ)—home of Taaltex Industries, an American-owned electronics factory where silicon wafers were cut into chips and bonded to circuit boards.

Taaltex Industries, which had been drawn to the Philippines by investment subsidies, tax exemptions, a ban on unions, and, above all, by an unlimited supply of young female workers willing to accept wages and working conditions unacceptable to male workers.

Bacolod thought of his fire. He began to get an erection.

Though the parking lot was almost filled, he found a space without any trouble. He simply waited while one of the night foremen, a dignified, somewhat pompous Filipino, pulled away in a battered Renault and headed into the tunnel for the trip down the mountain. Then Bacolod took the foreman's reserved spot in front of a low, moss-covered concrete wall ringing the parking lot.

Reserved parking was limited strictly to management. Signs pointed this out in English, Spanish, and Tagalog, the most commonly used Filipino dialect. Didn't it bother Bacolod to be in violation of company policy? Not in the least. Like any guard on night duty, he parked where he damn well pleased. And got away with it, providing he was gone before the day manager, a loathsome little Muslim prick, made his appearance.

Shopping bag in hand, he stepped from the Datsun and locked the door, making certain it was secure. In his six months as a security guard for Taaltex Industries, Bacolod's car had been robbed twice. He'd lost a tape deck, a pair of lizard-skin boots, a black leather jacket, and a small jade statue of the Virgin that had been glued to the dashboard. Someone had also walked off with a personal computer, which Bacolod himself had pinched from Taaltex Industries.

Everything but the computer had been given him by Huziyana de Vega. Losing her gifts had left Bacolod miserable. The thief probably had been a fellow security guard. Who else had access to every inch of ground up there? Security guards were all over the FTZ.

Property losses aside, Leon Bacolod enjoyed this job. It was an improvement over past occupations, which included stealing headstones from graveyards, scraping off the inscriptions, and reselling the stones at reduced prices. What pleased him most about the FTZ was the country air and slow pace, neither of which existed in the city.

On the mountaintop there wasn't the problem with crowds you had in Manila, where the population was over eight million and climbing. Filipinos shied away from birth control. Blame this on a strong Catholicism and the customary Asian desire for the insurance of a large family in old age. As Huziyana de Vega said, Filipinos believed in family planting, not family planning.

In the darkened parking lot, Leon Bacolod stood beside the Datsun and squinted at his watch, a Patek Philippe with a gold case, gold band, and jeweled hands. Until last month he'd never owned anything so beautiful in his life. The watch was his twenty-first birthday present from Huzi. She'd stolen it from one of her customers, a visiting Hong Kong businessman. Borrowed it, one might say, after slipping him knockout drops via an exceptionally passionate kiss.

The back of the case featured an inscription in Cantonese. Some romantic bullshit from the businessman's wife. Bacolod planned to have it removed one of these days.

Eleven-thirty P.M.

Mustn't be late. This was the big one. The most critical fire of his life. The soft-spoken and graceful Chinese who'd hired him had made that very clear. No mistakes, he'd told Bacolod. Miscues or errors in judgment would not be tolerated.

The Chinese had said, "You have promised me a proper job and I expect nothing less." Bacolod was being threatened, of course. Warned in that shifty, roundabout way the Chinese had of doing everything.

Which left the high-strung arsonist slightly uneasy. It was no secret that the soft-spoken Chinese belonged to Hong Kong's major Triad.

Triad. The most powerful criminal society in the world.

When it was your enemy, the world was made of glass. There was nowhere you could hide.

In agreeing to set the fire, Bacolod wondered if his tongue hadn't outraced his brain. Was he about to be put to bed with a shovel? For a minute or two he seriously considered walking away from the soft-spoken Chinese. True, Bacolod had the qualifications for this assignment: He was an experienced arsonist and he could enter the FTZ without arousing suspicion. On the other hand, he wasn't ready to draw his last breath just yet.

In the end he decided to accept the offer. The money was a big factor. "You'll be paid in American dollars," the Chinese said. Coveted Yankee dollars, not Filipino pesos.

Both Bacolod and Huziyana de Vega were free spenders, pissing away money as though it grew on trees. She lavished gifts on him, kept herself in new clothes, and bought expensive medicine for a defective pituitary gland, the cause of her dwarfism. She also paid bartenders, cab drivers, and tour guides for furnishing her with clients seeking the unaccustomed in erotic adventures.

And there was her drug habit. One of her regulars, a curator from the Museum of Philippine Arts, had introduced Huziyana to speedballs. The tiny whore now smoked the blend of heroin and cocaine almost daily. Bacolod hated the stuff. Two drags on one cigarette and he'd gotten sick to his stomach.

Marijuana was good enough for him. The best smoke around—Kona Gold, Maui Wowie, Puna Butter—was imported from Hawaii but still cost less than speedballs.

With his money Bacolod customized his car, bet on cockfights, and, with seven thousand Philippine islands to choose from, took Huzi island-hopping to get away from congested Manila. He also had special furniture on order. Handmade furniture scaled down to Huzi's Lilliputian size. There was nothing he wouldn't do to make her happy.

They'd discussed a Las Vegas holiday, combined with a side trip to Disneyland in Southern California. And he was thinking about a new car. So when Leon Bacolod said yes to the Chinaman, the money had been very much on his mind. Along with thoughts of the pleasure from setting the fire. Any fire, anytime.

Dealing with the soft-spoken Chinese, however, was a challenge. For one thing, he was evasive. Hard to pin down on anything. Bacolod admired his elegant clothes, manners, and his habit of choosing his words very carefully. He also admired the Chinese's computerlike brain. Bacolod saw him as a deep thinker, the sort who instantly commanded respect.

But arouse the Chinaman's anger and he became as lethal as a snake. That's when he unleashed a hatred without limit. Bacolod knew the informant story, the one describing how the Chinaman had waited fifteen years to retaliate against a Malaysian for betraying him to the police.

Fifteen years. Time enough for the Malaysian to view his betrayal of the Chinaman as so much ancient history. He would have wagered anything that the matter had vanished from the minds of all concerned.

The soft-spoken Chinese, however, never pardoned. Having decided that the moment for revenge had come, he went about it in true Triad fashion. He had acid poured on the Malaysian's eyes, then ordered him hamstrung. These days the informant crawled about Manila's back streets, living from hand to mouth as a blind beggar. And serving as a forceful reminder that the soft-spoken Chinese had an extremely unforgiving nature.

In the parking lot, Leon Bacolod left the Datsun and walked toward the FTZ entrance. A monsoon mist hung over the mountaintop, turning the cool night air drizzly. The damp fog also hid unwelcome visitors, the kind who prowled the parking lot only after sunset. Large, snakelike lizards. Long-tailed black rats. Starved-looking wild dogs. All looking to feast on any garbage, litter, and trash lying about.

On foggy nights the excitable Bacolod couldn't walk across the parking lot without worrying about rats attacking his ankles. Or wild dogs going for his balls. Silly worries, to be sure, since nothing like this had ever happened to him or anyone else working in the FTZ. But as Huziyana de Vega said, Bacolod was quick to get the heebie-jeebies over nothing.

At the FTZ entrance he waved to the gate-house guards, three *Negritos* with the short stature, dark skin, and woolly hair of their tribe. All three were armed with Uzis and eating a late snack of *dinuguan,* pork innards stewed in pig's blood. Country oafs in their first pair of shoes. Yokels who'd come to the big city to rise in the world but who still longed for the eastern jungles where their relatives fought with bows and poison arrows. Bacolod returned their smiles. The bastards gave him the creeps.

Inside the entrance he stopped in the darkness behind the gate house, placed his shopping bag on the ground, and looked around. Not only was it dark, but the Americans, a tight-fisted bunch, had spent precious little on lighting. They relied upon old-fashioned post lanterns, installed by the Japanese Imperial Army when it had used the area as a POW camp. Also illuminating the zone to a small degree was a pale moon, nearly concealed by gray mist.

The FTZ seem deserted but appearances were deceiving. As Bacolod knew, the night shift had been slow lately, and those employees not asleep in the workers' barracks were at home. Which suited him just fine. The less people out and about, the less chance of his being seen setting the fire.

The zone itself consisted of factories, warehouses, barracks for workers' living quarters, and a sprawling electrical transmission station with voltage lines. Scattered throughout the rest of the area were weatherworn machine shops, crumbling sheds, and a pair of sewage pump-houses. Armed guards with flashlights made their rounds, accompanied by Doberman pinschers or German shepherds. The air smelled of sulfur and plant smoke.

From a guard tower on the front wall, a powerful searchlight beamed down on the entrance and parking lot. In the gate house, the *Negritos'* cassette recorder now blared out Madonna's "Material Girl."

Just several yards away from where Bacolod stood in

darkness was an empty square, its red dirt packed down hard by steamrollers. Except for a bare flagpole ringed by mopeds and bicycles chained to wooden racks to prevent theft, the square was empty.

When the FTZ had been a Japanese POW camp, the square had served as its killing ground. Here Allied prisoners were crucified by the commandant, who ordered nails driven into their hands, feet, and skulls. Leon Bacolod, his world filled with phantoms, believed the square to be haunted by souls of dead Filipinos, Chinese, and Americans. There were times when he *definitely* heard their moans on the night wind.

Bacolod shivered. The square made his hair stand on end.

In prewar years the area had been a dairy farm, then a health spa, and finally the country's largest yo-yo factory. Bacolod was an expert with a yo-yo. His involvement with this child's plaything was, in fact, the closest thing he had to a hobby. Through constant practice he'd mastered numerous tricks, to the childlike delight of Huziyana de Vega. He'd also taught himself to use the toy as a missile weapon, an almost forgotten martial skill in the Philippines, where the yo-yo had been invented and was handled with more dexterity than anywhere else on the face of the earth.

Late hour aside, one factory building was in full swing. Bacolod saw light shining through its grimy, broken windows and heard the whine of machine tools and generators. He also heard the grating voice of an Indian floor manager cursing workers in Tagalog, English, and Bengali, the Indian's native language. As Huziyana said, when you work at Taaltex, the shit begins the day you're hired and stops when you drop dead.

Behind the gate house now, Bacolod picked up his shopping bag and walked toward the square. Suddenly he froze and looked to his left. Heart pounding, he listened for a few seconds, then quickly backpedaled, almost tripping over himself in his haste to remain unseen.

In the shadows he fingered the bamboo rosary still hanging from his neck and watched a golf cart enter the square.

In the cart sat two silent guards. Bacolod knew and despised them both. One, Eddie Pasig, was a bony little man and as sarcastic as they come, a thoughtless little toad who constantly teased Bacolod about his cleft palate, imitating his speech and laughing as if this were the funniest thing in the world. Pasig, knowing of Bacolod's epilepsy, had nicknamed him Twitchy.

The other guard was Freddie Bonifacio, a chunky bowlegged Chinese–Filipino, who was Taaltex's best baseball player and fancied himself a ladies' man. He was also Pasig's best audience during any imitation of Leon Bacolod's damaged speech. At the moment these two shits were the last people Bacolod wanted to see.

His eyes followed the small vehicle as it slowly circled the flagpole. And then the cart stopped. An alarmed Bacolod shook his head. Christ, no.

He watched the pudgy Bonifacio step from the cart, spit in the dirt, then pull a pack of cigarettes from a shirt pocket. His back was to Bacolod, now growing more anxious by the second. Growing more afraid by the second.

A sharp gas pain in the arsonist's stomach dropped him to one knee. On the verge of tears, he bit down hard on his thumb until he tasted blood. Then, clutching the crucifix on his rosary, he whispered the Virgin's name repeatedly. If anything went wrong, the Chinese would kill him for sure.

On the other side of the square, halfway between the open area and the women's barracks, stood a small toolshed. That shed was Bacolod's destination; he had to get there as quickly as possible. Crossing the square would save time. It would also prevent him from encountering foot patrols.

Pasig and Bonifacio usually made one swing around the square every forty minutes, then headed their golf cart toward the electrical transmission station. For the past week, as the pair made their rounds, Bacolod had eyed them more closely than usual. In that time he'd seen them avoid detours and delays. He'd seen no surprises. Pasig and Bonifacio, two horses' asses, had been predictable. Until tonight.

Now suddenly they'd broken their pattern for no reason

except that one wanted a quick smoke. Broken their pattern and left Bacolod shaken. Absolutely shaken. He thought of the soft-spoken Chinese. Better to be a mouse in a cat's mouth than be a captive in the Triad's hands. The gas pains in Bacolod's stomach grew worse.

Then he saw the women. Three young Filipinos on the far side of the square. Slim and graceful in their summer dresses, with bare arms and legs showing, the three suddenly stopping, heads together, their laughter a pleasing sound in the quiet night. They were night workers who'd completed their shift and were now returning to their barracks.

Bonifacio called to them. Bonifacio the skirt chaser, who despite a wife and three children was always ready for a bit of horizontal jogging. The Taaltex women stopped and turned to face him. Hands cupped around his mouth, the chunky guard shouted to them in Spanish. Two women dismissed him with a wave of their hands. The third didn't bother acknowledging him. Seconds later all three resumed walking.

Rejection seemed to encourage Bonifacio. He returned to the golf cart, seated himself, and pointed to the women. Grinning, he rubbed his palms together as his buddy, Eddie Pasig, made a U-turn and drove off in pursuit of "the goodies," as Bonifacio referred to women. Leon Bacolod exhaled. Quickly rising to his feet, he crossed himself and thanked the Virgin. Again she had delivered him from his enemies. Then he picked up his shopping bag. Clutching the rosary, he entered the square.

His brain said, *Run. Run to the shed. You know what the Chinese will do if you fail.*

But he forced himself to walk. Walk slowly. Mustn't attract attention. Not while carrying a half-gallon tin of gasoline.

Suppose a guard or someone else smelled the gasoline? Suppose they asked questions? Bacolod's response would be to lie as best he could. And hope to be believed.

Should this happen, he'd have to cancel the fire. Even thinking about a fire once the gasoline had been spotted would be crazy. Bacolod wasn't that thick. He would, of course, have to explain this unfortunate turn of events to the soft-spoken Chinese. And hope to be believed.

He stepped from the square, onto a graveled footpath, and into the shadows. *Now* he ran. Seconds later he reached the toolshed, out of breath, and slightly dizzy. Hand on the doorknob, he looked around, flinching when he heard a dog bark in the distance. But Bacolod saw no one. He entered the small, dark shed and quickly closed the door behind him.

The shed smelled of machine oil, damp sawdust, moldy rags, and human and animal urine. Its cramped space was packed with damaged goods—broken stepladder, out-of-date machine tools, old boots, cracked typewriters, stained coffee urns, empty oxygen cylinders. A junk bin, Bacolod thought. A hideaway for crap.

A single window, minus all glass, looked out on the women's quarters, an enclosure of two-story wooden barracks surrounded by barbed wire and once occupied by troops of the 16th Imperial Japanese Army Division. Lights shone in the windows of those barracks where employees were working the night shift.

One of the barracks was entirely dark. Bacolod stared at it for a few seconds, then reached for the shopping bag. No time to lose.

With moonlight shining on his back, he stripped down to his white boxer shorts, then removed the bra and blue dress from the shopping bag and put them on. Both hands were perspiring; he stopped to wipe them on his shirt. Get too anxious and he could trigger a seizure.

He put on the fuck-me pumps, black nylon wig, and imitation gold-and-jade bracelet. Then a bit of toilet water, some cheap shit he'd picked up from a Chinatown chemist. Taaltex girls couldn't afford expensive scents, so he'd spent only a few pesos for his. A dab behind both ears and a bit on the forearms should do the trick.

Opening the red leather purse, he removed a small hand mirror, compact, and a tube of coral lipstick borrowed from

Huzi. Crouching under the window, he angled the mirror to catch the moonlight and carefully applied lipstick to his full mouth. Next a bit of powder on his cheeks, and a deep brown eyebrow pencil to thicken and darken his eyebrows. Finished, he stared in the mirror at his new face. He smiled. Absolutely smashing.

He hid his uniform and shoes, shoving them under a paint-stained tarpaulin. Wallet, watch, and rosary went into the red purse. He was gambling that his clothing wouldn't be found while he was gone. No choice there. But why risk losing his money and watch? Or the bamboo rosary blessed by his eminence Cardinal Sin, the holiest man in the Philippines.

At the window, Bacolod fingered his beads and with wide, unblinking eyes stared at a pale sliver of a moon. Then, with his back against the wall, he listened to the flow of the waterfalls in gorges surrounding the mountain and waited to catch his breath. Under the dress, his penis was rock-hard.

He left the toolshed whispering the Virgin's name.

# Two

**Manila, 11:45 P.M. the same night**

A troubled Angela Ramos decided that her informant had been scared off and wasn't going to appear. The informant was Elizabeth Kuan, a twenty-four-year-old Taaltex computer operator who claimed to have evidence the company was laundering money for a powerful Taiwanese drug lord known as the Black General.

If the idea of confronting him even indirectly had frightened Elizabeth Kuan, it also left Angela Ramos unnerved. The Black General had clawed his way out of Shanghai's nightmarish slums and the opium-producing Golden Triangle to stand atop the brutal Asian underworld. On the way he had acquired an extraordinary reputation for cruelty and duplicity.

The petite, husky-voiced Miss Kuan, usually seen in the same long blue dress and black ankle-strap shoes, did have reason to turn whistle-blower, however. She'd been raped in the computer room by a pair of male supervisors. Both men had taken Polaroids of each other in the act of assaulting her and were showing them to coworkers. Miss Kuan wanted her revenge.

She'd said nothing to company officials or police about the attack. Sexual harassment by male supervisors, particularly those on the night shift, was common practice.

Women workers called Taaltex the Mattress Company because they were frequently told to lay down or be laid off. And since they couldn't afford to lose their jobs, the women were easily intimidated.

While stiff and a bit pretentious, Miss Kuan was also a woman of profound personal integrity. Taaltex must be punished for defiling her. To do this she had sought out Angela Ramos.

In front of a barred kitchen window in the dark, silent barracks, a perspiring Angela Ramos looked out at a pair of long-abandoned gasoline pumps and lit another cigarette. For the past week she'd been smoking less, not inhaling, sticking with low-tar and forcing herself to take fewer puffs. It was the closest she could come to quitting.

She reached into a pocket of her thin cotton robe and felt the voice-activated microcassette recorder, a gift from her godfather, who lived in Hong Kong. He was a man of sound judgment with an intuitive knack in practical matters. Yesterday he had urged Angela to leave the Philippines for her own safety.

"It's become much too dangerous for you to remain there," he said. "Taaltex has hung a noose from a tree. Now all that's needed is a neck, which could well be yours."

He was about to retire to Florida—polluted paradise, he called it—where he owned an oceanfront condominium in Key Biscayne. Come to America with me, he told Angela, and get away from those wretched villains in that wretched country of yours. You can't be enjoying yourself, he said.

Enjoying herself? Not while she was suffering the consequences of a bitter struggle with Taaltex, consequences that included colitis, shingles, and an irregular heartbeat. Not while she was leading the fight against the company's plan to cut starting wages from $1.25 to $1.00 a day.

Not while she was mounting an attempt to take over a union leadership that was little more than a management front. Or was organizing slowdowns and sit-ins to protest hazardous working conditions at Taaltex. Or was personally attacking management's long-standing policy of refusing to grant holidays, sick leave, or vacations.

She had no husband, no lover, and, while admired by the women she worked with, had few friends. Such relationships demanded sacrifices that were beyond her at this point in her life. She had neither time nor energy for them.

Enjoying herself? Not hardly. She feared Taaltex too much for that. The company had more power than many national governments yet owed little allegiance to anything except itself. Her godfather called such people SANs, stop-at-nothings. "You can't trust them any further," he told Angela, "than you can throw a bull by the prick."

She was in her early twenties, a plump woman with a round face and black hair so long, she could sit on it. Tonight she wore her hair in a waist-length braid, an accommodation to the humidity brought on by the recent monsoon. The braid meant her hair wouldn't curl. She hated curly hair, hers or anyone else's.

At Taaltex her job was to inspect completed circuit boards before they left for the United States, where they were assembled into tanks, missiles, bombsights, and other military equipment. There was no mystery in her work, no uncertainty. Nor was there any prospect of ever being pleased. There was only the prospect of being unceasingly bored.

While Angela feared Taaltex, she hated it even more. There were times when she thought her animosity toward the company might be the only pleasure she would ever have. Her godfather understood. "Cling to your animosity," he said. "Indeed, I don't think you can function without it."

Driven by that animosity, she'd led protests, walkouts, and demonstrations against Taaltex. It was the reason she'd waited tonight for Elizabeth Kuan's evidence linking Taaltex with the Asian underworld. Her animosity was the reason behind tomorrow morning's vigil, which she'd organized and which Taaltex vigorously opposed.

The vigil, to take place in the company square, was in

memory of two female workers who'd died six months ago. Taaltex had killed them both. The women, Nelia and Sara Ramos, had been Angela Ramos's sisters. Sisters she'd raised alone after their parents' deaths and who hadn't lived past their teens.

First to die had been fifteen-year-old Nelia, the youngest. Sweet, cheerful Nelia, whose idea of the finer things in life had been a new motorbike and digital earphones, and who'd tried to get them by working for Taaltex.

To avoid paying maternity benefits, the company forced all potential women employees to take a pregnancy test. Those who tested positive were not hired. A cash bonus was given every worker who agreed to voluntary sterilization.

Impatient Nelia, unable to tolerate delays of any sort, wanted quick money. A week after coming to work for Taaltex, and without telling her sisters, she agreed to be sterilized. But during the operation her urethra was punctured and she died of blood poisoning. A regrettable accident, said Taaltex.

Angela Ramos called it murder and refused to accept Nelia's sterilization bonus of one hundred dollars.

Nineteen-year-old Sara Ramos, a Taaltex employee for five years, died next. Tall, brown-eyed Sara, who was hot-headed and impulsive and who hated any rules unless she made them herself.

Facing rush orders or production deadlines, Taaltex sometimes forced women to work as much as forty-eight hours straight without sleep. Management supplied the amphetamine injections and other drugs which kept the women awake and functioning. Some women, however, became addicts.

A month after her younger sister's death, Sara Ramos's nude corpse was found in a barracks shower stall, where she'd died of an amphetamine overdose. Taaltex said it was suicide brought on by sorrow. Angela Ramos called it murder and blamed the company.

Tears, however, were no cure for Angela's pain. Strength

to bear the unbearable could not be found in grieving. Heaven had taken both sisters from her because it wanted to provoke Angela into opposing Taaltex with all her heart. This was now her karma, her purpose in life, and if she stuck to it, then she would be a match for heaven.

Her godfather now began to play a stronger role in her life. Until recently he'd been closer to Angela's father, a relationship born after the Pacific War when they had met at the Japanese war-crimes trials. A year ago Angela's father, Fidel, had died of stomach cancer, and that's when the man in Hong Kong had begun to take a paternal interest in her.

"Call on me when you need help," he'd said. Look upon him as her godfather. He'd recently come into a bit of money and was now inviting Angela to come live with him in Hong Kong. Not her sisters, just her. He wasn't much on women about the house, he said. Angela would be the exception. That much he owed her father.

With a ticket furnished by her new godfather, Angela flew to Hong Kong and quickly learned she could never live there. The city was a nightmare. It was noisy and horribly crowded, filthier than the Philippines, and the people were too damn tribal for her taste. They were consumed with their families, clans, and sects. Foreigners simply weren't accepted.

In any case, she couldn't desert her sisters. True, the Philippines was a poor country; unless you worked for a foreign multinational, it was all but impossible to earn a living wage. But she loved her country; she wasn't ready to abandon it or her sisters and their dream of one day going into business together.

When her sisters died, her new godfather immediately understood her anger. From his home atop Hong Kong's exclusive Victoria Peak, he at once began counseling Angela in her war against Taaltex. He hired Gregorio "Gringo" Arbenz, a top Manila attorney, as her legal representative. The grotesquely obese but sharp-witted Arbenz traveled everywhere with a carload of bodyguards, collected peacocks, and possessed what Angela's godfather called wicked knowledge. He also didn't come cheap. But as Gringo Arbenz himself had told Angela, I'm worth every fucking peso because nobody was ever cured by kindness.

For a time the fat man's bag of tricks effectively kept Taaltex at bay. He prevented the company from dismissing Angela, then stopped it from demoting her. He quashed an attempt to jail her on trumped-up criminal charges of vandalism and theft. And he orchestrated a media blitz around her, giving Taaltex its most adverse publicity in years. He was also planning to file suit against the company over its role in the deaths of Angela's sisters.

It would seem that the five-foot-five Arbenz, who weighed four hundred and ten pounds and relaxed by playing Scott Joplin rags had pulled off the impossible. His skills had prevented Angela Ramos from being dumped on by Taaltex while turning her into what the Asian press called the "savior of Filipino womanhood." The most corpulent David in history, as one journalist wrote, was on his way to slaying the American Goliath.

But two nights ago the fat man had telephoned Angela at her barracks and said he could no longer represent her. He was resigning, effective immediately. Thoroughly unnerved, Angela demanded to know why. "Talk to your godfather," Arbenz said. "He has the answers. I'm sorry. Truly, truly sorry."

In a temper inherited from her mother, Angela cursed him in Tagalog, Spanish, and English. Calling him a fat-assed shyster, she demanded to know how could he do this to her. Couldn't he see she was killing herself trying to hold down a job and fight the most money-hungry bastards God had ever created? Couldn't he see she was ready to fall apart?

When Angela telephoned her godfather minutes later, he said, "It's the Black General. He knows what you and Miss Kuan are planning, and he's striking back. Forcing Arbenz to withdraw was step one. Step two is dealing with you,

Miss Kuan, and myself. From now on, we'd all better walk softly.''

Angela said that between feeling shitty for cursing Gringo and worrying about the Black General, she was ready to throw up. What did they do now, and how had the Black General found out about Elizabeth and her? How had he found out?

"Nasty piece of work, the Black General," her godfather said. "Crossed paths once or twice, he and I. You've mentioned Elizabeth Kuan to Gringo, and in all likelihood his phone lines are being tapped. And I'll wager you're being watched by a company stooge who reports to Taaltex, which in turn reports to the Black General. This afternoon his people kidnapped Gringo's six-year-old son, then dropped off a note ordering him to stay away from you, effective immediately.''

Angela said, "I didn't know."

"The lad's right ear was enclosed with the note. Further pieces of the boy's flesh are to be delivered daily until Gringo complies with the Black General's wishes.''

Angela closed her eyes. "Mother Mary, forgive me, the things I said to him just now."

Her godfather said, "Bloody waste of time torturing yourself with hindsight. More to the point, the Black General's threatened me as well. I'm to stop supporting you against Taaltex or face the consequences. I've been given three days to see the light. Cheeky bastard. Imagine threatening someone in my position.

"Fortunately I don't have a wife and child to worry about." Her godfather went on. But there was Angela, and should any harm befall her, he would be endlessly despondent. He had come to love her as though she were his own. Nothing must happen to her. Let Angela be victimized and he would fight the Black General tooth and nail.

Angela said she felt awful for having cursed Arbenz and for having dragged her godfather into this mess. He said, "I promised your father, God rest his soul, that I would take care of you, and I intend to keep that promise. As for myself, I go the way Providence dictates, and in any case I shall soon be enjoying blissful retirement in America, far from the intrigue, machinations, and ongoing collusion that make life here in Hong Kong so attractive and repugnant.'' Meanwhile he had instructions for Angela.

Angela said she was going to telephone Gringo Arbenz but her godfather said, ''The bloody hell you will. Gringo's phones weren't clean.'' Did Angela always have to be so obstinate?

When she apologized, he said, ''Forgiven and forgotten. Now let's have some strategy of our own.'' After Angela received Miss Kuan's information on the Black General, she was to hand-carry it to Hong Kong without delay. ''Do not put it in the post. Do not give it to a third party. Do not tell anyone about this information.''

Angela said, ''Won't he be watching you?''

Her godfather said, ''I'm not underestimating the Black General by any means, but in thirty-odd years in Hong Kong I've learned to connive and scheme with the best of them.'' For starters, he intended to pass on Miss Kuan's data to a friend in New York. The friend was a well-known television journalist—quite a good one, actually. Angela's godfather had saved his life some years back when the American had been a policeman. Now was as good a time as any for the favor to be repaid.

Angela asked if the American could be trusted, and her godfather said, ''Yes. Most definitely yes.'' The American's wife and daughter had been murdered by Chinese drug traffickers, not the sort of thing one was ever likely to forget. Besides, the Yankee press loved a bit of tittle-tattle apropos its great men. Expose the Black General and you exposed the Taaltex executive or executives who made this money laundering possible.

Angela's godfather said, ''My American friend, bless him, delights in giving offense to the high and mighty. I figure him for more than a passing interest in a corporation which does business with a drug lord who mutilates children. And if I'm correct in my assessment, his country's interest in this story should stir up interest worldwide. After that it might prove rather sticky for Taaltex and the Black General to take measures against us."

Meanwhile Angela was in extreme danger, he said. She had to leave the Philippines. The sooner, the better.

Angela said, "I'm no Rambo." She wasn't brave and she certainly wasn't happy about the Black General being in her life. But she had a duty to her dead sisters, and as much as she'd like to run away, she couldn't. A couple of weeks, she said. Then she'd think about leaving.

"A couple of weeks may be too late," her godfather said. Every madman had his agenda, and the Black General was no exception. Who's to say he wouldn't strike at Angela within the week?

She said, "I can't leave right now." For one thing, Elizabeth Kuan couldn't get the tapes concerning the Black General's laundered money until a particular supervisor went on holiday. And that wouldn't be for two days. Angela couldn't think of going anywhere without those tapes. Not when she was this close to making Taaltex pay for killing Nelia and Sara. "If you're looking for fish," she said, "why climb trees?" The place to hit back at Taaltex was here, not in Hong Kong.

"So you're choosing to ignore an old man's advice," her godfather said. "Well, your being rather single-minded doesn't exactly come as news to me. Your father always said you were the strongest of his three princesses. You were the fighter and the dreamer, the one he thought could throw a rock at the heavens and hit the stars. No, my love. I won't waste your time and mine by demanding you leave. Nelia and Sara meant too much to you."

But once Angela had those tapes, he said, she was to flee the country and hightail it to Hong Kong. No argument this time. Just get the hell out of the Philippines. Angela would always stick to her truths. And the Black General stuck to his lies. A collision was inevitable.

He said, "The Black General, believe me, is markedly deficient in any tolerance or sympathy for his fellow man.

Unfortunately you've never been the type to let sleeping tigers lie. Still, it's wise to remember that while man can plan, only fate may complete. Take care, dear girl. Do take care.''

In the barracks kitchen, a perspiring Angela Ramos lit another cigarette, then glanced at her watch. It was almost midnight and still no Elizabeth Kuan. Damn that little chink. If she didn't appear soon, a worn-out Angela was going to bed. It bothered her that she hadn't seen Elizabeth Kuan on the factory grounds since yesterday morning, when they'd set up this meeting during a hurried chat in the barracks shower room. Then again, Angela could be worrying over nothing.

She walked away from the window, pushed open the kitchen door, and looked along the dark, empty hallway. No Elizabeth Kuan. Entering the enclosure was simple, provided you were a woman. You only had to walk past one guard manning the entrance. None of the barracks were locked. So where in hell was Elizabeth Kuan?

After closing the kitchen door Angela sat down on the rung of a stepladder and dropped her cigarette under the heel of her slipper. She thought about telephoning Elizabeth Kuan, who lived close enough to stay at home with her family and commute by bus. But the barracks' only telephone, coin-operated and antiquated, was out of order. It had broken down this afternoon and had yet to be repaired, something else that pissed off Angela.

Except for the hum of electric fans in the individual rooms, the barracks was quiet. There were no sounds of girlish chatter, cassette recorders, flushing toilets, slamming doors. The fifty-one women living here were either asleep or too burnt out to do anything except collapse on their beds. Taaltex operated several shifts and forced all workers to rotate day and night shifts every two weeks. The result was an uneven scheduling which ruined sleep patterns, leaving women physically and emotionally ill. Everyone, Angela especially, needed more rest than they were getting.

Her godfather was right, of course. She could be headstrong, even pigheaded at times. But never blindly stupid. Making Taaltex pay for killing her sisters was something she had thought over thoroughly. And she had decided that since she could never deaden herself against the loss of Nelia and Sara, she had no choice but to avenge them.

Which didn't mean ignoring her godfather's warning about the Black General. Maybe it was a good idea to leave the islands while she could. Accept her godfather's invitation to join him in America. Without Gringo Arbenz to stand between her and Taaltex, she faced rough going here in the Philippines. He'd been her safeguard, her protection. Angela had come to like the fat man who played ragtime on an upright piano he'd built himself. Thanks to him she'd become Saint Angela, media darling and folk heroine.

At the stepladder, she absentmindedly rolled an empty beer can back and forth beneath her foot. The floor was littered with trash, cigarette butts, carpenter's tools, and plaster dust left behind by workmen. In addition to paint and turpentine smells, there was also a foul odor Angela couldn't place. At her insistence this room, once used to store furniture, was now being converted into a kitchen. Upon completion it would allow the women to eat here instead of in the main hall, where they were frequently sexually harassed by male coworkers.

None of the other barracks had a kitchen or was scheduled for one. This kitchen was being installed only to accommodate Angela. She'd have to fight to have them installed in the other barracks.

Her barracks lacked a dining area; the women would have to eat in their cramped rooms or in the hallway. And they'd have to take turns cooking. But the women, some no older than thirteen, wouldn't have to be pawed and mauled when they showed up in the main hall at mealtime. Nobody should have to choose between accepting sexual aggression or going hungry. And who the hell could work on an empty stomach, anyway?

Angela stopped toying with the empty beer can and stared

across the room at two refrigerators against the far wall. Where was that horrendous smell coming from? Not even two open windows could eliminate it. At first she hadn't noticed the smell because of paint and turpentine odors. Also, her mind had been taken up with Elizabeth Kuan. Now she was getting a noseful.

Both fridges were new. Each gleamed in the moonlight, their door edges secured with brown sealing tape. Neither was plugged in; the room wasn't yet wired for electricity. As for the odor, it was absolutely revolting. Even shit didn't smell this bad.

Angela, a hand covering her nose and mouth, crossed the room to stand in front of the refrigerators. Jesus. The smell was enough to make her throw up. It seemed to be coming from the one nearest her. From behind the sealed door. The room was starting to stink to the max.

She reached in a pocket of her robe, took out a small penlight, and switched it on. One hand for the penlight, one for the tape. Right about now she could use a surgical mask. Holding her breath, Angela began peeling off the sealing tape, wondering what in the world could stink like this. Suddenly she spun around, almost dropping the penlight. The door to the kitchen was opened and a woman stood in the doorway.

She was a slender woman with a red leather purse in one hand and a shopping bag in the other. The shopping bag was held in front of her face. Her left wrist sported a brace-let, familiar to Angela and anyone else who knew the woman. It was imitation gold and jade, a knockoff of an Italian original. The bracelet was probably the only one the woman owned, since she was never seen wearing other jewelry.

Elizabeth Kuan.

"Turn off the light." The voice from the doorway was a husky whisper.

Heart beating wildly, Angela clicked off the penlight and dropped it in a robe pocket. But before the room went dark, she saw the familiar blue dress and ankle-strap shoes. Elizabeth Kuan, creature of well-established habit. The little chink was late. But as Godfather would say, all was forgiven and forgotten. Arms outstretched, a gloriously happy and teary Angela ran forward to embrace her.

Walking haltingly in the ankle-strap shoes, which he found uncomfortable, Leon Bacolod entered the kitchen and softly closed the door behind him. One step to the right and he was away from the moonlight. Back against the wall, he waited in shadows. The shopping bag was now at his side.

Angela was almost on him when Bacolod flung the red purse to the floor. Then, using both hands, he swung the shopping bag with all his strength, smashing Angela in the face with a half-gallon tin of gasoline.

A shocked Angela, her head bursting with pain, spun around and stumbled forward into the stepladder, knocking it to the floor. Her back was to Bacolod; he swung the shopping bag again, hitting her in the right temple. She fell facedown, her right hand tipping over an open tin of paint thinner toward herself, sending a bright bluish liquid gurgling across the rubbish-littered floor to mingle with her blood and long hair.

Clasping the shopping bag to his chest with both arms, the arsonist stood over the fallen woman. *I expect a proper job, the soft-spoken Chinese had said.* Well, that's exactly what he was going to get. Bacolod didn't like or dislike Angela Ramos. True, she was always bitching about one thing or another. But on the other hand, working at Taaltex wasn't exactly a call to serve God. You had to give the woman credit for having balls.

A proper job. Removing the gasoline tin from the shopping bag, Bacolod held it overhead with both hands, then swiftly brought it down on the base of Angela's skull. He hit her again in the same spot before setting the tin on the floor and inhaling deeply. His heart jumped around madly in his chest; his hands trembled like those of an old man with palsy. Pray to the Virgin that he wasn't having a seizure.

He shook his head violently. Good way to stir up the brain. The shaking sent the black wig sliding down onto his forehead, over his eyes. After adjusting the wig, he crossed the room and crouched down in front of the refrigerator Angela had been interested in. Palm on the floor, he felt beneath the front edge. After finding the key he rose and finished tearing off the tape. Under the tape was a small lock, which had been attached to the door by Bacolod himself. He unlocked the door and pulled it open.

Christ, what a sickening smell. Wrinkling his nose in disgust, Bacolod reached inside for Elizabeth Kuan's nude corpse. The little lady was right where he'd left her. Wedged in the refrigerator and stinking to high heaven. With knees tucked under the chin and arms wrapped around her head, she reminded Bacolod of a fowl ready for roasting.

Last night he had forged a message, signed Angela Ramos's name, and lured Elizabeth Kuan to the main warehouse once used by Japanese troops to dry tobacco leaves. Here, behind empty packing cases, Bacolod had strangled her to death and jammed her body into one of the new refrigerators earmarked for St. Angela's barracks. Why did Kuan have to die? Because the soft-spoken Chinese had said so.

After hurriedly attaching a small lock to the refrigerator door, Bacolod had covered the door edges with brown sealing tape. Then he'd summoned three security guards and, using two hand trucks, had delivered the appliances as scheduled. If this fridge seemed heavier than the others, no one complained.

In the darkened kitchen, Bacolod pulled Elizabeth Kuan's body from the fridge and onto the floor. Rigor mortis had set in. She was rigid, frozen in the fetal position. And the smell. Not only was the little Chinese woman rotting away, but she had emptied her bowels, fouling the inside of the fridge. The bottom of the food compartment was stained brown with her shit. The back and sides were stained red with her blood. All of it was enough to put Bacolod off his food for some time to come.

But thoughts of the fire entered his thoughts, and his balls started to tingle.

More sexually aroused than he'd been all night, a grinning Bacolod poured a thin trail of gasoline around the edges of the room, over windowsills, the stepladder, a pair of wooden carpenter's horses. He splashed some on the door and threw the remainder on a pair of painter's coveralls lying across a cooking unit. Then he picked up a can of turpentine and sprinkled most of it on the walls, taking care not to get any of it on his blue dress. Elizabeth Kuan's dress. The rest he poured on Kuan herself—on her hair, back, and buttocks.

Now for St. Angela. Her long braid, wet with paint thinner, gave Bacolod an idea. Just thinking about it almost made him shoot his juices under the dress. He giggled softly. He was one damn clever fellow.

Using a screwdriver, he pried open a can of turpentine and poured the contents over Angela Ramos's hair, face, and back. Finished, he squatted beside the dead woman and stared at her for several seconds, swaying gently as he softly hummed "Material Girl." Sighing, he reached for the shopping bag and rose to his feet. The fun was about to begin. This is what he'd been waiting for.

He removed the Gauloises and a book of matches from the bag, lit one of the French cigarettes, then folded back the matchbook cover, exposing the matches. One more drag on the cigarette to get it going. Then he tucked the unlit end behind the match heads and placed the matchbook near the base of one wall, a fraction of an inch away from the gasoline trail. He set similar burning cigarettes and matchbooks on a windowsill, on the stepladder, on the edge of an open can of paint thinner and at the door. Five slow-burning fuses. Three-minute fuses. Enough time for Bacolod to remove himself from the barracks before the fire started.

But first . . .

He lit one last Gauloise, inhaled, then leaned over and dropped it on Angela Ramos's turpentine-soaked hair. Tiny blue flames raced along the braid, then fanned out along her shoulders, hair, and face. A fully aroused Bacolod reached under his dress, gripped his penis with both hands, and began masturbating furiously. He came in seconds and stood unsteadily on his feet, swaying from side to side, breathing through his open mouth, and was happy, happy, happy.

Chest heaving, he wiped his hands on the dress, then stumbled toward the door. Suddenly he stopped dead. His purse. He wasn't used to carrying one. Christ, he'd almost left it behind. Where in hell was that damn thing?

Right. He'd thrown it to the floor because he'd been in a hurry to cancel the Ramos woman. In a fucking hurry to get to the fire. One dumb pineapple head is what he was. Which is why he now had to spend precious time looking for the purse. Fumbling around in the dark wasn't easy, but finally Bacolod located the bag.

Bad luck. The purse had landed on top of an uncovered metal toolbox. And opened on impact. Coins, wallet, rosary, keys, *everything* had fallen into the fucking toolbox. Dropping to his knees, a frantic Bacolod worked with shaking hands, scattering nails, bolts, screwdrivers, pliers in all directions in a frantic attempt to recover his property. As he found the various items he shoved them into the purse, fighting back tears because he hadn't allowed for this delay.

*Whoosh!*

The sound came from his left and almost made the arsonist jump out of his skin. Bacolod recognized it immediately and became terrified. He looked over his shoulder to see Angela Ramos's entire body go up in flames. Suddenly he hated her enough to kill her again. Hated her for burning frighteningly faster than he'd thought she would. Hated her because now the whole kitchen was just seconds from going up in flames.

He watched in morbid fascination as trails of orange-blue flames sped from Angela Ramos's corpse and across the floor. Bacolod had counted on the barracks igniting within minutes; it was nothing but old, dried lumber. But he hadn't counted on being here when it happened. Snatching the purse from the floor, he fled the room, slamming the door behind him. He raced down the hall, trying hard not to trip in his ankle-strap shoes.

He was out of the barracks in seconds, pausing only to lock the front door with a copy of the master key pulled from the purse. Bacolod's hands shook; it took him three tries to insert the key. Then, dizzy with fear, he walked past the squat, large-eared guard at the enclosure entrance, ignoring his invitation to share a freshly rolled joint of Lebanese marijuana laced with opium.

Minutes later in the toolshed, Bacolod, wearing shorts and knee socks, crouched near a window and viewed the fire. His latest triumph. For the moment nothing else mattered; all fear was forgotten. Watching the flames left him happy in body, mind, and soul. And when he was happy, there was no time to be afraid.

The blaze swept the barracks with awesome speed. It flashed through the ground floor to burn fiercely on the second floor. Inside the building there was only chaos and horror. Women shrieked hysterically, calling on God and the Virgin for deliverance. No prayer, however, could remove bars from the windows or open the locked door.

Some women leapt from second-floor windows, arms flailing in the air, until they landed shrieking on the rain-soaked red earth. In nearby barracks, wailing women cried out to their doomed sisters. A handful of women raced toward the fire, and all Leon Bacolod could say to that was, *Ain't going to do you no good, little ladies. What will be, will be*.

The barbed-wire enclosure began to fill up with people: with security guards shading their eyes against the fire's glare, with tearful women hugging each other, with factory officials gesturing wildly and yelling orders. Bacolod thought the barking guard dogs added a weird sort of background music. The giggling arsonist gently pulled at his penis. This was a good one. Definitely one of his best.

After putting on his uniform Bacolod picked up the red leather purse and removed his wallet, keys, and rosary. Then he put his hand inside the purse again and experienced one of the worst moments of his life. He became so terrified, he almost passed out. Gasping for breath, he dropped to his knees and began to urinate in his pants. He swayed with nausea and tasted vomit in the back of his throat.

The purse was empty.

He'd left his watch behind in the burning barracks.

# Three

## Taipei, Taiwan

Because he admired their independence of spirit, the Black General collected tigers.

He housed the great cats on his estate, a lavish complex of two-story, tile-roofed buildings connected by gardens and courtyards atop the lush, green slopes of Yangming Mountain. His name was Lin Kuang Pao, and he had taken tigers into his mind and soul.

To study these animals he had camped out in the forests and jungles of east Asia, their native habitat. In Java he had filmed tigers stalking their quarry. In India he had sketched them swimming in wooded lakes. In China he had recorded the moaning and mewing sounds which indicated they were content.

Tigers, Lin Kuang Pao had learned, were solitary hunters whose strong, flexible backbones and powerful hind legs enabled them to pounce swiftly on any prey. They killed by biting the nape of the neck and driving a single, pointed canine tooth into the vertebral column. Death was instantaneous.

A tiger matured at three years of age, consumed up to sixty pounds of meat a day, and disliked great heat. Females mated every two years or so, producing a litter of up to six cubs, only one or two of which survived. At the age of seven months, cubs began to kill for themselves.

Lin Kuang Pao was discerning enough to appreciate selective qualities in other species of cats. The cheetah's quickness impressed him, as did the speed of the lynx, which was fast enough to catch low-flying birds by leaping in the air. And there was the merciless ambition of youthful lions, who, in groups of two or more, moved in on a pride and killed or expelled the reigning males. Next they slaughtered the cubs, then mated with now distraught lionesses and sired their own cubs. Thus the young lions created and perpetuated their own social system while introducing strong new blood. This brutal strength of will was much admired by the Black General.

Other cats aside, tigers remained Lin Pao's favorites. He appreciated their self-reliance; tigers hunted alone, and he found it relaxing to watch them silently pad around their cages. Nor did he tire of their beauty. The yellow-green eyes, hooked claws, and reddish-brown coat with dark, vertical stripes were a magic which continued to obsess him over the years. Like many Chinese, he took a daily glass of tiger-bone wine as a health tonic. None of the Black General's possessions supplied the joy found in his tigers.

In early March he had been presented with the gift of a female snow leopard, captured in the northern mountains of the People's Republic of China. Had Lin Pao turned to those deities he worshiped, or consulted the spirit mediums called *dangki,* as he'd done in the past, perhaps they would have spoken to him of life and the future. And would have urged him to reject this particular gift.

Perhaps they would have warned Pao, who prided himself on being free from the control of others, that the snow leopard was to determine his thoughts and actions for the rest of his life.

The animal had been a gift from a new business associate and could not have been refused without causing said associate a loss of face. Since he was supplying Lin Pao with three hundred kilos of raw opium per week, common sense dictated that his benevolence be accepted. As it turned out, the snow leopard was a splendid-looking creature with long, silky white fur and dark spotting. Truly magnificent, Pao thought. A most appropriate gift.

The new business associate was an Army general from the People's Republic of China, an emaciated-looking man with a skeletal face who had recently been assigned to China's Xinjiang Province. Xinjiang's location on the Pakistan border effectively removed it from Beijing's central authority, leaving the emaciated-looking general free to do as he pleased. Leaving him free to divert division supplies to Afghan guerrillas for use in their war against Russian invaders.

In payment for these supplies he received Krugerrands and gold bars; the sickly-looking general believed gold to be the key which opened all doors. Some of the gold he forwarded to banks in Macau, Panama, and Zurich. The rest he invested in what he confidently saw as an unfailingly profitable venture: a Pakistani heroin factory that produced one hundred kilos of raw opium a day.

The snow leopard had given Lin Pao trouble from the start. Excitable and skittish, she lashed out whenever caretakers came near. In captivity her appetite disappeared, leaving her tired and drawn. Deciding the animal missed the cold mountain air of its native habitat, Lin Pao installed a lavish cooling system in its cage. There was also the outlay for doctors and extra caretakers; this so-called free gift was proving quite costly in terms of patience and money. In the snow leopard Lin Pao had grasped a knife by the blade.

Its presence disturbed the usually calm tigers, who now continually trotted about their cages, eating irregularly and intimidating the caretakers. The big cats, with their ongoing roaring, were no longer a source of peace for Lin Pao. Was the snow leopard an evil premonition? Were sleeping misfortunes about to be awakened?

Lin Pao was Asian. His view of the world blended age-old religious and social customs with common sense, a belief in the supernatural, and fear of the unknown. And relationships with a thousand gods. The result was a deep-rooted conviction that life was controlled by forces more powerful than man.

Was the snow leopard an evil premonition? Were sleeping misfortunes about to be awakened?

Upon observation and reflection Lin Pao was forced to admit that since receiving the snow leopard he had indeed suffered misfortunes. Misfortunes which suggested he no longer enjoyed protection from fate. Misfortunes which might have shaken a weaker man.

Last week he'd ordered the deaths of two Filipino women in Manila before they could connect him to the American corporation laundering his money. On hearing the women had been terminated, he'd been quite pleased. Angela Ramos, in particular, had been quite the little mischief maker.

His people in Manila had finally put an end to her antics. Be thorough and painstaking in your actions, Pao had said to them. So they'd arranged for a fire to hide any signs that the Ramos woman had met with foul play. Result: an official verdict of accidental death. A major problem has now been resolved, the Black General's people assured him.

Enter Angela Ramos's godfather. Ignoring a warning to stay clear of Lin Pao's affairs, he had taken it upon himself to investigate his goddaughter's death. Such initiative wasn't too surprising; a disagreeable and shitty little man, Angela Ramos's godfather was not easily intimidated.

Included in his future plans was a campaign against Lin Pao in the American press, a strategy which could be ruinous to Pao. The godfather had to be liquidated, and the sooner the better. It wouldn't be easy, however. He was a quiet, self-contained man, and such men, like still waters, were deep and dangerous.

Other recent misfortunes for the Black General: in Amsterdam, the confiscation of ten million dollars' worth of heroin by Dutch police and Interpol; in Marseilles, the stabbing deaths of three Triad members by a rival gang; in London, the confiscation by Scotland Yard of a million dollars in arms meant for the Provisional IRA; in Sydney, the kidnapping by rivals of the operator of Pao's largest gambling house.

And in New York, the biggest misfortune of all. A police detective who regularly smuggled Lin Pao's money to secret bank accounts overseas had surrendered yesterday to federal authorities. Unless he informed on the operations of Lin Pao's Triad in America, he faced forty years in prison. The detective had a history of looking out for himself. The Black General, therefore, knew what to expect.

The detective had been born intelligent, resourceful, bold, and greedy, and like most people, he had remained greedy. Two weeks ago he and a friend had taken $1.8 million in Triad money to Atlantic City, where they'd lost almost $1.5 million at roulette and blackjack. Pao's men had executed the friend. But the detective, fearing for his life, had given himself up to DEA agents.

What exactly did the detective know about the Black General? He knew about his drug trafficking and distribution routes in North America; about his gambling, extortion, and prostitution interests in various U.S. cities. He knew about murders committed in the U.S. in the struggle for power among rival Triads. And he certainly knew how Pao's money was laundered. For those U.S. authorities who longed to curtail Pao's activities in their country, the detective was their window to heaven, the answer to their prayers.

The Black General found this blow especially ill timed, coming as it did so closely on the heels of unspecified intrigues by Angela Ramos's godfather. Both could have a devastating effect on his U.S. operation. Both could greatly reduce the importance of his Triad in that country, the most lucrative market in the world. Both could start a violent power struggle by rivals anxious to replace him in the land called the Golden Mountain.

Just the detective's knowledge of the Chinese takeover of New York's heroin trade from Italian gangs made him a pearl beyond price to American police. But did they know how difficult the detective could be? Outwardly quite pleas-

ant and charming, he was actually treacherous and dangerous, a man with honey in his mouth and a sword in his
heart. The Americans would have their hands full with this
one. Their first problem: keeping him alive to testify against
Lin Pao. To that end he was under twenty-four-hour guard
in a location considered to be all but impregnable.

Lin Pao found the Americans' belief in their power amusing. He smiled when told of their boasts: "Nobody comes
within a mile of this guy without getting his ass blown off.
He's safer with us than the president is with the Secret
Service. Our man's going into court and will blow that chink
out of the water."

The Americans were a confident people, embarking on
one course or another with a sure hope and trust in themselves. Within an hour of the detective having entered his
so-called fortress, Lin Pao knew his whereabouts. And knew
how many federal marshals, DEA, and FBI agents were
guarding him around the clock. He'd even known what
foods the detective had asked to be served during his captivity.

The Black General's ties with Taiwan's government had
given him worldwide power. He had only to lift a finger
and death came to a Shan tribesman in Burma, to an investment banker in San Francisco, to a restaurant owner in
Paris, to a federal drug agent in Dallas. Anyone who thought
Pao could not kill the detective was amazingly dim-witted.

Lin Kuang Pao was in his early sixties, a bull-like man
with a large shaved head, flat nose, and a black patch over
an empty right eye socket. The empty socket still ached,
long after he'd lost the eye to assassins hired by a woman
he'd trusted and loved. His left hand, also missing, had
been replaced with a prosthetic device covered by a black
glove. On this wrist he wore a bracelet made of human skin
from the woman whose attempt to kill Pao had also cost
him that hand. He was Dragon Head, leader, of the Triad
called the Hundred Pacer Snakes, named for the Taiwanese
snake whose bite was so deadly that its victims died before
they could run a hundred steps.

He combined extraordinary vigor and stamina with an iron will. A brusque manner hid a keen intelligence and great presence of mind. Arrogant and uncompromising, he despised weakness in others. He suffered from insults more than most people and as a result was capable of exploding with an anger that could be terrifying. Then he would destroy anyone in his path, and there was to be no reasoning with him until the anger had run its course. In Pao's Triad his word was law; his orders were to be obeyed without question.

He trusted no one. In his heart he feared that others might use the violence and treachery he had used against them. He walked alone, never forgetting there were those who would kill him for his wealth and power. Never forgetting that the elephant was killed for his tusks.

There were times when force and violence proved insufficient. Then Lin Pao would call on unearthly powers: on Chinese folk religion with its ancestor worship; on Tao, Buddhist, and Confucian thought. Faced with exceptional difficulty and challenge, he turned to temple deities, to divining blocks, to priests and spirit mediums. Thus his *joss,* luck, had always been good.

The source of his good *joss* was an old Taoist priest who lived alone at the bottom of Yangming Mountain, in a dwarfish temple that was little more than a stone hut. Over the years the priest's predictions had saved Pao from failure. Saved him from reversals and the pain of regret. And given him confidence in the future.

The snow leopard, Lin Pao decided, was quite sinister. It was time to take refuge in the old priest and let him cancel the injunctions of destiny. It was time to let him dispel further misfortunes. A wise man appeased the gods, soothed sleeping dragons, and saw that bad spirits were blown away. A wise man knew that the supernatural and human worlds coexisted.

At dusk an angry Lin Pao left the main pavilion of his compound, strode briskly through connecting courtyards, then crossed a miniature wooden bridge leading to his private zoo. Mindful of his past outbursts, servants and attendants gave him plenty of room. Guards dropped their eyes or simply looked elsewhere. Better to be naked among wolves than to annoy the Black General on this particular day.

At the zoo's entrance, Lin Pao stopped dead in his tracks, his anger suddenly gone. Remarkable, he thought. Truly remarkable. His tigers—the giant Manchurian, the Indian albino, the small dark Bali—all eighteen were quiet. This hadn't happened in weeks. Not since the snow leopard's arrival.

Several of the cats, narrow-eyed and alert, sauntered back and forth in their cages. Others, watchful behind half-closed eyes, lay quietly on piles of straw, their breathing all but imperceptible. Each waited expectantly. Clumps of red meat, the animals' evening meal, lay untouched on cage floors.

In gardens and fish ponds, herons, ducks, pheasants, and cuckoo doves were also silent. The skin on Pao's arms began to tingle. *Something was about to happen.* The tigers and birds knew it. Knew that the unexpected stillness was only the calm before the storm. Suddenly Lin Pao felt vulnerable.

Then he saw the priest. The old man stood in front of the snow leopard's cage, eyes fixed on the beautiful cat and oblivious to all else. His name was Da-chien, and he'd appeared at Lin Pao's house, not when summoned but when it pleased him to appear. It was an attitude that angered Pao considerably.

This time the priest had arrived four days after being sent for. And with no advance notice to Pao. Damn insolent of him. Highly disrespectful too. The sort of behavior the proud, quick-tempered Lin Pao would not take from anyone else. *Anyone else.*

Da-chien was a small, bespectacled man with an immense forehead and a pleasant, low-pitched voice. He wore a threadbare saffron-colored robe, battered sandals, and leaned on a cane. Was he already aware of Lin Pao's difficulties? Pao watched as the priest fingered black beads dangling from his neck and stared at the snow leopard through half-closed eyes. The priest knew. Pao was convinced of it.

The snow leopard lay on its side, head facing the priest and two zookeepers, husky young aboriginals from the Bei Nan tribe. Both aboriginals seemed grumpy, no surprise to Pao. There was the aroma of mixed pickles, fried dumplings, and fish rolls in the air. Apparently the aboriginals had been enjoying their evening meal until interrupted by the old priest and Lin Pao.

Since they had been dining on leftovers from his kitchen, Pao felt entitled to interrupt them anytime he pleased. One of the pair, a bandy-legged, curly-haired little fellow, pouted while continuing to grip a pair of teak chopsticks in a tight fist. *Let him be unhappy,* Pao thought, *but unless he wants to die this instant, let him not speak of his unhappiness to me.*

Crabby dispositions aside, Pao preferred aboriginals as zookeepers. They were hardworking and dependable, as long as they weren't faced with having to make snap decisions. Primitives were not quick thinkers. But what else could you expect from people who until the twentieth century were still head-hunting.

As for the priest, Da-chien, Lin Pao found him to be a moody and humorless little man. A bit too sharp in debate and argument but excellent at gauging the future. Quite headstrong too. Apparently his knowledge of the divine will had made him exceedingly sure of himself.

He gave or withheld counsel as he saw fit and disappeared from his temple for weeks at a time without telling anyone of his whereabouts. He appeared insensitive to any opinion but his own and spoke his mind without fear. Unable to control or intimidate the priest, Lin Pao could only hide the discomfort and apprehension felt in his presence. Around him, Pao only *seemed* tranquil.

There were several matters to be discussed with Da-chien, the snow leopard being the first. Since acquiring this cursed créature Lin Pao had suffered one reversal after another. Let the priest halt this bad *joss*.

Next, the termination of Angela Ramos's godfather and the New York detective. Was it possible to discuss with a holy man one's intention to commit murder? Yes, providing it was done discreetly. Lin Pao would ask only if certain immediate opposition could be successfully removed. Discretion meant saying what you should, not what you can.

Pao's ethics, or lack of them, appeared to be greeted with indifference by the priest, who relayed the gods' verdicts without showing passion, bias, or emotion. "We do as we please until fate descends upon us," Da-chien told him. "Fate, not I, rules the holy and the unholy."

Finally, the most critical matter of all: the secret meeting in Hong Kong two weeks from now between Lin Pao and his enemies.

In a daring move Pao had managed to talk four rival dragon heads into sitting down with him at the conference table. Why had sworn enemies agreed to such an unprecedented conference? Because in less than ten years Britain was to return Hong Kong to the Chinese mainland. Because the Triads were based in Hong Kong and, like others with much to lose, didn't trust China to allow the territory to remain capitalist, decadent, and pragmatic.

Free enterprise, particularly in Hong Kong, was a glorious activity. But free enterprise was possible only in a democracy, in an independent, self-governing Hong Kong. However, an independent, self-governing Hong Kong threatened Beijing's authority and would not be tolerated under any circumstances.

The communist takeover of China in 1949 would always remain one of Lin Pao's most unpleasant memories. Unlike other Triad members, he'd managed to escape death at the hands of the Reds, but only through his cunning and good fortune. The Bolsheviks were bastards. Shepherds of the people, so long as the people remained sheep.

Secret societies had long been politically important in Chinese history. At the time of the Reds' victory the Triads had been closely aligned with the ruling Chiang Kai-shek government. Gang members—military officers, intelligence agents, assassins, drug traffickers, policemen, business-men—had help put Chiang in office. They were also his strong-arm boys, doing the dirty jobs regular party members couldn't or wouldn't do. But with Chiang's defeat by the communists, three hundred years of gang influence in Chinese politics came to an end.

The Reds had established themselves in blood and were to rule in the same fashion. They tolerated no opposition, crushed all individuality, and energetically punished all ene-mies. To no one's surprise the Triads, allies of the despised Chiang Kai-shek, were among the first to be driven from the mainland. Most joined members of the moneyed classes in fleeing to British-ruled Hong Kong. Lin Pao remembered some affluent entrepreneurs arriving in the Royal Crown Colony with complete factories. As for the economic and political freedoms promised China by the Reds, they never materialized. Capitalism, went the joke, was the exploita-tion of man by man. Communism was the reverse.

With life under the Reds subject to chance—or unknown conditions at best—the Hong Kong–based Triads were now diversifying abroad as never before. The eighties found Lin Pao and other dragon heads flooding America with money, putting it into real estate, businesses, luxury homes, and bank accounts. Pao had also stepped up his lucrative drug trafficking in New York; he was one of the Chinese who had taken over the city's multibillion-dollar heroin trade, once exclusively the property of the American Mafia.

In pushing for the Hong Kong conference, Lin Pao in-sisted that gang warfare in America would call attention to this massive infusion of capital. The results would be dev-astating for all. It was difficult, he said, but not impossible to conduct business under close scrutiny. Close scrutiny, however, made the amassing of great profits inconceivable.

The meeting was an attempt to avert gang warfare at a very inopportune time. Gang warfare was the traditional method of settling territorial disputes and old scores. Years ago it had cost Pao his first wife and beloved younger brother. But he was the only man who could talk rivals into considering changes. Even the most provoked enemy was forced to admit that Lin Pao possessed superior intelligence of the brain and heart. His warning could not be ignored. Not with memories of the communist takeover of China still fresh in the minds of many.

"Our future wealth lies in America," he told his rivals. "But hear me well, for unless we consent to reciprocal concessions, we will never realize this wealth. We will be too occupied warring against one another. We will draw the increased attention of the American press and the police. This will cost us money, men, even legitimate invest-ments."

"So I offer a solution. Let us reach an accord, one which allows us to expand in America without destroying each other. This can be done by dividing the major American cities among ourselves. Here. Now. In Asia. Without blood-shed. I see no other way of avoiding senseless and excessive losses. I say to you, my brothers in the ancient societies, that the compromise I propose is no longer a matter of choice."

And if the conference should fail? Lin Pao could only hope such a nightmare never came to pass. But if it did, then his prestige in the world of ancient societies would disappear overnight. His enemies would deem him inept. His judgment would appear suspect to his own Triad, which would immediately turn away from him.

He could not survive such a fiasco and still retain the respect of his men. Failure at the Hong Kong meeting would be punished by death at the hands of his followers, death being the preferred remedy for foolishness among gang lead-ers. At the conference he must lose neither face nor territory. Let the old priest read from the book of fate and tell Pao if the conference would be successful.

Let the old priest encourage him to trust the future.

• • •

In his private zoo, a troubled Lin Pao touched a forefinger to a pulsating nerve in his right temple. Damn that priest. Pao was growing angrier with him by the second, chiefly because the priest had yet to acknowledge his presence. Instead Da-chien remained engrossed in the snow leopard with the intensity of a small boy discovering his penis for the first time. Pao, easily irritated, viewed this indifference to him as insolence. He'd had men killed for less.

Suddenly Pao felt chilled. The weather had abruptly turned nippy. Not what you'd expect in March, when temperatures were moderately warm and the humidity often matched that of summer months. He shivered and thrust both hands up his sleeves. He wore a cotton robe trimmed in gold braid, not warm enough for this startling weather change. A pair of felt slippers failed to keep his feet from feeling icy. His empty eye socket began to ache, a sure sign that foul weather was imminent.

He looked at the sky. True, it was sundown, but night was arriving faster than usual. The darkness and temperature drop signaled the return of last week's strong winds and heavy rains. All the more reason for Lin Pao to complete his business in the zoo and get inside before the deluge arrived. He shivered and found himself longing for the feel of the sun on his body as never before.

To his right, a huge Manchurian tiger rose to its feet and began to pace its cage in long, loping strides. Two cages away, a black-and-white-striped Indian albino swiped viciously at its mate, driving her back into a water hollow. On the edge of the zoo, crows in a clump of bamboo trees hopped nervously from branch to branch and cawed loudly.

Crows. A portent of evil. A sign that something calamitous was about to happen.

At once the aboriginals became skittish. The curly-haired one dropped his chopsticks, then quickly squatted to retrieve them. His partner, a tall, stooped-over man with blackened teeth, rolled his eyes and placed both hands over his ears. Time to conclude matters here, Lin Pao thought, before these superstitious fools break out in tears.

Removing both hands from his robe, Pao stepped toward the priest, willing the old man to purge him of the bad *joss* brought on by the snow leopard. Willing the priest to remove the shadows cast upon Pao's life by the animal. Willing the priest to guarantee Pao's success in Hong Kong.

Da-chien spoke without turning around. Never had his deep voice sounded more imposing or intimidating. Lin Pao stopped in place, heart pounding, mouth dry as dust. He shivered under the first drops of cold rain. And refused to allow himself to be ruled by fear. What a man feared too often came to pass.

Eyes on the prone snow leopard Da-chien, said, "First you will kill this creature. Then within twenty-one days you yourself will die."

He turned around to face Lin Pao, suddenly looking child-like and smiling gently, more relaxed than Pao had ever seen him.

Unable to speak, a stunned Pao stood rooted to the spot.

"You will die violently," Da-chien said. "The instrument of your death will be a young boy who lives in the West. He is a part of your life and from birth has followed you like a shadow. What came out of you has returned to you. You must now face the ghosts your past deeds have raised."

A shaken Lin Pao found his voice. "Do not say these things to me, old man. I warn you. Do not talk to me this way."

"I am neither the doer nor the deed. I am but the instrument. A higher power works through me."

"Old fool, you play jokes on me at a time when I need—"

"I speak the truth. You will die within twenty-one days. I suggest you prepare yourself for death."

"You senile old imbecile. Who are you to tell me to prepare to die? So, some simpleton thinks he can take my life. What is that to me? I have survived many attempts on my life." His one eye bore into the priest. "A young boy, you say."

"Yes. In the West but of the Middle Kingdom." The Middle Kingdom was the ancient term for China.

Lin Pao turned his head toward the cawing crows. "A boy. A mere boy." He shook his head, then glared at the old priest. "And you expect me to fear him?"

Da-chien smiled. "You fear him even now."

It was true. For the first time in years Lin Pao was afraid and hated himself for it. Nothing weakened a man's judgment more. One could never act sanely while terrified. The priest—damn him for being the cause of this dreadful feeling.

Pao said, "Take back your words, Priest. I order you to tell me only of heaven's help. I order you to tell me the truth."

"Heaven has willed it," Da-chien said. "You cannot control your future."

"You control my future, old man. You and only you. Now stop wasting my time. I order you to make my good fortune last. With your blessing I will have everything."

"Until now destiny has supported your every act. And you have felt your behavior to be suitable and proper. Never did you stop to think that what comes out of you always returns to you, that you were creating your own future. You have, I fear, met yourself on the journey of life."

An increasingly fearful Pao said, "Tell me I will triumph and tell me nothing else."

"He who asks questions cannot avoid the answers. Neither you nor I can control your future. Such things lie in the hands of heaven."

A shaken Pao did the only thing he could do: He vowed to challenge fate. He was a proud, resourceful man. A survivor. It was ridiculous to suggest that he could be defeated by a mere boy.

*The boy is in the West but of the Middle Kingdom.* Pao thought, Let the search for this boy begin in New York. Let it begin among the Jade Eagles, a Chinese youth gang Pao used as enforcers and assassins.

The gang included Vietnamese and Koreans but was

mainly Chinese, illegal aliens from Hong Kong's toughest slums. The Jade Eagles. Lin Pao's sword arm in New York. Protectors of the gambling, extortion, and narcotics interests run by his Triad in that city. The youth gang was Lin Pao's judgment and punishment on his enemies in America.

The leader was eighteen-year-old Benjamin Lok Nein, a cold-blooded killer and born leader whom Lin Pao liked and had marked for bigger things. Benjy Nein admired the Black General and took pride in disposing of his enemies. But when the front door was protected against tigers, the back door may let in a wolf. Was Benjy Nein the wolf come to destroy Lin Pao?

Were Lin Pao to take Da-chien's prediction seriously, Benjy Nein could no longer be trusted. All of the Jade Eagles, a dozen members, would have to be carefully watched. Some were no older than twelve, but from such children would come the Lin Paos of tomorrow.

The most likely threat? Benjy Nein, of course. Caution, however, demanded that Lin Pao protect himself against all of the Jade Eagles. A prudent man was his own best ally.

Pao's solution to this particular problem? Accept the priest's words as fact. Without telling anyone, of course. Then call upon the Gong Nam Bat Hop, the Eight Knives of the North. A secret group of assassins within Taiwan's military intelligence, Gong Nam Bat Hop was named for eighteenth-century assassins who had served Emperor Yung Cheng. The Taiwanese government often used them to silence political dissenters throughout the world. And to protect the profitable connection between Taiwan's rulers and drug lords, such as Lin Pao.

Like the old Gong Nam Bat Hop, the modern counterpart brought back the heads of its victims. The old priest's prediction need not come to pass. Lin Pao had only to wait for the delivery of a boy's head and with it the return of good *joss*. At the same time it was important that Pao's enemies not learn of this prediction, for they would grow bolder and more dangerous. Even his men might use this prophecy to their own advantage.

The prediction was an outrage. The more Pao thought about it, the more incensed he became. Who was this dried-up old man to give him just twenty-one more days of life? In making his forecast, Da-chien had shown no respect for Lin Pao's powers, something which could not be tolerated.

Meanwhile the two aboriginals decided they'd seen enough. All signs indicated that the Black General was about to vent his rage. Both now looked at each other and nodded in silent agreement. Better to back off and leave that bastard Pao and the old priest to go at it in private.

They knew of his contradictory characteristics. Knew that his strong discipline hid a frightening instability. Knew what a quick-tempered prick he could be. How *changeable* he could be. A blind man could see that Lin Pao and the priest were on bad terms. If the aboriginals knew the Black General, the priest was in for some rough handling.

As rain pelted the metal overhang above the cages, Lin Pao raised his voice to be heard above the screaming crows and restless tigers and the gathering storm. He demanded that the priest admit he'd lied, but the old man shook his head and said, I speak the will of heaven. You have spit against the sky. You have brought this on yourself.

When Da-chien again turned to face the snow leopard, Lin Pao abandoned his remaining self-control. Restraint was no longer a possibility. The storm, the screeching crows, the howling tigers had unnerved him. A terrified Lin Pao surrendered to an overwhelming urge to destroy the priest.

He rushed across rain-slicked yellow tiles, threw his left arm around Da-chien's neck, and pulled back hard, cutting off the priest's air. Then he lifted Da-chien from the ground and swung him back and forth, sending the old man's sandals flying.

Still applying the choke with his left arm, Pao snatched a chopstick from the curly-haired aboriginal with his right hand and jammed the fragment of wood into the priest's right ear. Into his brain.

With his dying breath Da-chien whispered the name of God and went limp in Lin Pao's arms—resigning himself to death, it would seem. Not that Pao was moved, for at that moment he felt only a wild joy at having purged himself of this old man.

A rain-soaked Pao yanked the chopstick from Da-chien's ear, threw it aside, and released his hold on the corpse. Then he ordered the tall, stoop-shouldered aboriginal to run to the caretakers' hut and bring back a rake. *Run.*

Neither aboriginal moved. Both were too paralyzed with fear. In no mood to lavish forbearance on a pair of dullards, a keyed-up, frantic Lin Pao began cursing. He kicked the tall one in the left leg, which was enough to get the oaf moving.

The tall aboriginal returned with the rake, not so much running as shuffling full tilt. Without a word Lin Pao snatched the rake from him, shoved the aboriginal aside, and looked down at the dead priest. A brief hesitation, then, gripping the handle with both hands, Pao lifted the rake overhead and brought the metal teeth down on the priest's face. The aboriginals turned away.

From the face, Pao went on to attack the arms, chest, thighs. He clawed the flesh each time, gouging deeply, making sure he drew blood. Oh, he could have forced the aboriginals to do it, providing he was willing to beat them black and blue while standing in the pouring rain.

"Take the body to the cage," he said to them. "Quickly! Quickly!" Let the snow leopard be blamed for the old man's death.

Shading his good eye from the driving rain, Lin Pao watched the aboriginals grip Da-chien by the ankles and drag his carcass toward the snow leopard's cage. Around Pao, the storm grew stronger. Bamboo trees were doubled over in the powerful wind, and he could feel the sting of the driving rain through his cotton robe. For their protection the animals' cages should be covered, and he'd certainly get around to that. But first let him tie up one loose end.

Lin Pao turned his head slightly, cupped both hands to his mouth, and barked an order. Instantly two guards, slim Paiwan tribesmen in ponchos and conical straw hats, raced across the small wooden bridge and into the zoo, kicking their way through puddles until they reached Lin Pao.

Pao whispered to the Paiwans, then watched them slowly walk toward the snow leopard's cage. The tall, stoop-shouldered aboriginal had just opened the cage door, flinching when he saw that the snow leopard was on its feet, teeth bared, back arched. Rain-wet hair plastered to their skulls, the aboriginals worked fast. One gripped the priest's wrists, the other his ankles. No need to respect the old man now. His soul had left the body and gone to a better place. Just sling his remains inside and be done with it. Which is what the zookeepers tried to do.

They threw Da-chien's corpse into the cage, barely missing the snow leopard. Startled, the animal leapt aside and dove for the opened doorway. Both zookeepers panicked. And so did Lin Pao, who pointed to the cage and yelled, "Secure the door! That damn animal wants to kill me!" Pao was afraid. Very, very afraid.

Heads lowered against the rain, the aboriginals worked frantically. One fumbled for the keys clipped to his belt, while the other reached for the cage door. Neither saw or heard the Paiwans.

Both guards swung Ithaca 12-gauges from under their ponchos and fired from the hip, hurling the aboriginals forward and slamming them against the snow leopard's cage. Their deaths meant that now only Lin Pao knew the priest's prediction, and while Pao was thinking this, the snow leopard leapt through the open doorway and raced toward him.

The guards fired simultaneously. One missed the speedy snow leopard completely, shattering tiles and spraying Lin Pao with water. A blast from the second guard broke the animal's back and flung it to the ground. Disabled and dying, the snow leopard continued to move. Stomach down, it clawed at the wet tiles and with its last strength inched through the blood-darkened water. Toward Lin Pao.

Dizzy with fear, Pao backed away as the Piwans stepped between him and the snow leopard and killed it. Pao's breathing and heartbeat seemed out of control. He pressed his hands against his temples to stop the wild twitching but could do little about the throbbing in his brain. Only when his heartbeat slowed did he drop his hands.

*Free.* He was free. He repeated the word to himself several times. *Free.* In control of his life once more.

For no one but he knew the old priest's words.

A shivering Pao walked past the Piwans to stand in front of the snow leopard's empty cage. Closing his one eye, he inhaled the animal's scent and listened to the rain pounding the metal overhang. From the moment he had acquired it, the snow leopard had detested him. Why?

Well, the animal's feelings about anything no longer mattered. What mattered was that in killing it, Pao had secured a reprieve from fate. Or had he merely eliminated a single link in the chain of destiny?

He opened his eye, breathed deeply, and reached out for the bars of the cage, squeezing them with all his strength. He was the Black General, and his destiny had always lay within himself. Always. The boy who would kill him had much to learn.

Lin Pao turned to face the Piwans, and in a strong, sure voice he told them what he wanted done.

# Four

## New York City

Governor's Island is one of three small islands lying just south of Manhattan in New York harbor. Visits to the island, which is home to the U.S. Coast Guard, are limited strictly to open-house weekends during warm-weather months. Individual tours are forbidden. Group tours are permitted only when you write in advance to Coast Guard authorities on the island.

The island received its name in 1698, when the New York Assembly set the land aside ''for the benefit and accommodation of His Majesty's governors.'' In addition to housing the colony's governors, it has also served as a game preserve, a sheep farm, a racetrack, and a quarantine station for immigrants. With its wooded areas, Colonial cottages, and nineteenth-century homes, Governor's Island remains the one New York City locality that most resembles a country village.

Other sights include Fort Jay and Castle Williams, fortifications built to protect nineteenth-century New York from attacks by the British Navy. Lining the ramparts are scores of cannon, none of which were ever fired in battle. The British threat never materialized. Gun usage has been limited strictly to target practice and commemorative occasions.

Governor's Island continues as a protective shield, but under conditions known to only a few. Witnesses in federal criminal cases, particularly those involving organized crime, are kept in protective custody here.

After trial testimony in Manhattan Federal Court, some witnesses are placed in the Justice Department's Witness Relocation Program. This involves new identification, a new home in America or abroad, and, on occasion, plastic surgery. Also called the Alias Program, the relocation plan is not without its critics, who claim that the protection of witnesses can be inadequate. Criticism has also been leveled at witnesses who, while under government protection, continue to commit such crimes as bank robbery, stock fraud, arson, rape, and murder.

The Witness Relocation Program will continue, however. No amount of criticism or controversy seems likely to bring it to an end. Offenders will receive immunity in exchange for testifying against their associates. And certain ethical questions will be ignored or go unanswered.

The program will continue because cooperating witnesses remain the leading source of information in solving crimes.

It was late afternoon when Frank DiPalma stepped onto the front porch of a two-story brick manor house on Governor's Island and allowed himself to be searched by two U.S. marshals. "I'm not carrying," DiPalma said. They knew he wasn't and they knew who he was, but he was patted down, anyway.

One of the marshals was a young, broad-shouldered Puerto Rican without much neck. He wore a brown bombardier jacket, acid-washed jeans, and black cowboy boots with silver-tipped toes. He gripped a Czech Scorpion machine gun with one hand, barrel resting on his shoulder, and he practically boogied into position behind DiPalma.

His partner was a lean, middle-aged black with brown eyes that looked friendly but weren't. He wore a three-piece gray flannel suit and a double-breasted beige trench coat with a cotton plaid lining. He did the inspection with a

Beretta Model 12S machine gun dangling from his right shoulder. In winter's final days both marshals were hatless and wore black leather gloves. Neither went in for idle chatter. DiPalma thought the Rican looked like a defendant, while the brother looked like a CEO.

Frank DiPalma was in his mid-forties, six feet and bulky, with hooded eyes, gray hair, and a flat-faced ugliness made attractive by self-confidence. His wife—it was his second marriage—said his vaguely sinister appearance was sexy. As a New York vice cop, he'd put in his twenty years, then retired with a lieutenant's pension and a slight limp, a reminder that crime, in Raymond Chandler's words, was not a fragrant world. For the past three years he'd been employed by a major television network as an investigative reporter.

He'd come to Governor's Island to talk with his ex-partner, a New York City detective named Gregory Van Rooten, who was now a protected witness. To avoid prison, Van Rooten was informing on the American operation of Lin Pao, a Chinese drug trafficker known as the Black General. As a rule, contact with informants was limited to family members and attorneys. DiPalma had gotten around this rule. Or rather Van Rooten had gotten around it for him by telling the Justice Department, "When I don't get my way, well, you don't know what this does to my disposition." What he wanted was a private meeting with Frank DiPalma. And he wanted it now.

DiPalma wasn't welcome on Governor's Island. The FBI and DEA didn't relish protected witnesses talking to the press. The less known about Van Rooten, the better. The media knew nothing of his arrest, and the feds wanted to keep it that way. Now along comes Frank DiPalma, ready to blow the case sky-high, or so it would appear.

DiPalma was asked to "cooperate," to voluntarily and of his own free will refuse to meet with his ex-partner. His reply to that was Why the hell should I? Then would DiPalma be willing to sit down with the U.S. Attorney and talk about it? Not really. Would he like to have dinner with the U.S. Attorney? No again. The meeting with Van Rooten was on. If DEA or the FBI had a problem with that, the man to speak with was the witness himself.

The final telephone call to DiPalma came from an icy-voiced Hispanic woman claiming to be an FBI spokesperson. She was barely into her rap about how uncooperative he was being when he interrupted. He said, "I think I love you. I just saw my pants move." She slammed down the receiver.

DiPalma wasn't going to be pressured, and he wasn't going to ruin a police investigation. As a cop, he'd had his share of run-ins with glory-seeking schmucks. So he telephoned U.S. Attorney Logan Peale and promised to keep quiet about the upcoming meeting with Van Rooten. The meeting was personal, strictly a private matter. It wasn't going to end up on the tube.

Peale said, "Your wife?"

DiPalma thought, Great, the whole fucking world knows. He let the question go unanswered. Good enough, Peale said, but you know how uptight Republicans can be. Meaning certain Feebs and DEA people saw DiPalma not as a former cop but as a civilian. The worst kind of civilian. A fucking journalist, no less. On the scale of human life, only lawyers and child molesters ranked lower. Face it, DiPalma was the enemy.

But as long as the feds needed Van Rooten, he'd get his way. Bet your last money, honey, that the meeting between DiPalma and his ex-partner was going to come off. It would come off because Van Rooten knew a lot about Lin Pao, the man who now dominated the heroin trade in New York. Handsome Gregory held all the cards and knew it.

DiPalma knew that no matter how much information Van Rooten came up with, Lin Pao would never stand trial in America. The Black General's political connections in his home base of Taiwan were strong and enduring; it would be a cold day in hell before he was ever extradited. Bet the ranch that Taiwan's leaders would see Pao dead before letting him walk into an American courtroom.

But take away the Black General's American operation, his biggest money-maker, and you could damage the bastard no end. Chop down the money tree and watch the big boys in Taiwan panic. Van Rooten, if he talked some good noise, could kick Lin Pao off the Golden Mountain.

As DiPalma knew from his own investigations, the Mafia was fading. Aggressive federal prosecution, good undercover work, and first-class informants had all paid off. However, no sooner were the Italians packed off to federal correctional facilities than they were replaced by new players. Smart, tough, ambitious players.

Increased immigration, legal and illegal, gave the Chinese a larger base than their rivals and therefore a faster rate of expansion. In the areas of drug trafficking, extortion, prostitution, and gunrunning, the Chinese were taking an increasingly large piece of the pie, branching out of Manhattan's Chinatown and across the country, into Philadelphia, Boston, Dallas, Houston, Oregon, Los Angeles.

Asian organized crime was giving the FBI fits. One bureau source had told DiPalma that more than two dozen agents were being pulled off Mafia cases and reassigned to Chinese cases. Did the feds need Van Rooten? Did rectal thermometers cause brain damage to Iranians? DiPalma's ex-partner was dog shit, but as an informant, he could write his own ticket.

The bureau source said, "Couple weeks ago, your boy Van Rooten freaked out. Did some coke, pills, booze, you name it, and off he goes, him and a fellow officer, one Detective Sergeant Olonzo LaVon, the two of them with a million eight of Lin Pao's money. Couple couriers stoned out of their fucking minds. They were supposed to take the money out of the country to Panama and leave it in a certain bank. Instead they boogie on down to Atlantic City and proceed to gamble most of it away. Uncool. Very, very uncool."

"I would say so, yes," DiPalma said.

"If Officer LaVon could be with us now, I'm sure he would agree. Found what was left of him over on Staten

Island a week or so ago—hands, feet cut off. Eyes gouged out. Never did find the guy's dick. The lesson to be learned here is: Do not fuck with the Black General's money."

"Wonder why Greg freaked out before making a big run like that. The man's not totally stupid."

"My father once told me there's two kinds of women in the world: goddesses and doormats. Van Rooten got caught by a goddess. Freaked out over the bitch, Chinese singer, name of Taroko. Your boy always did have a bad case of yellow fever. Couldn't keep away from those Asian lovelies. Couldn't keep away from women, period. Anyway, Taroko's supposed to be one of the most gorgeous women God ever made. She's a superstar in Chinese communities, whatever the fuck that means. Draws big in Atlantic City. Brings in Chinese gamblers by the carload. Talk about your high rollers. Casinos love those slant-eyed little fuckers."

DiPalma said, "You're saying a woman brought Greg down?"

"Did she ever."

"Van Rooten burned by a woman. I think the word we're looking for here is irony."

Van Rooten had been assigned to Manhattan Vice, which loaned him to federal task forces for undercover narcotics work. He was good-looking, with an easy charm and an offbeat sense of humor. But as DiPalma came to learn, Van Rooten used people, women in particular. He'd wring them dry until nothing was left, then dump them in a hurry.

His first words to DiPalma had been, "I'm not giving up one fucking piece of myself to be like anybody else."

DiPalma had thought, Just what the world needs, another loudmouthed overachiever. But he'd liked the guy's style. You had to like a man who wanted to be a cop bad enough to walk away from a father whose business grossed almost five billion dollars a year.

Gorgeous Greg. Amiable and likable until you got to know him, and then he turned out to be a snake. DiPalma thought, He's young, he'll learn. But it was DiPalma who'd learned. And what he'd learned was that Van Rooten was not like other people. The man heard a different drummer. And he was not of unblemished character.

His skill lay in using women, and there wasn't a cop in Manhattan who didn't envy him for it. Wives, mistresses, daughters, and female associates of drug traffickers. Van Rooten exploited them all with a religious ardor, winning convictions and commendations while collecting more ass than a toilet seat.

He'd also collected nicknames. Ronald Romance, the Gynecologist, and Freddie Furburger were a few. DiPalma called him Shark Eyes, because Van Rooten was the best at giving you a hood's cold-blooded, unfeeling stare. Call him what you will, the man made things happen.

Van Rooten began by doing everything right. He listened to DiPalma, imitated his example, and walked a straight line. DiPalma couldn't recall another young cop with this talent for working undercover. Van Rooten was a born player, an actor who'd found the perfect role. DiPalma, who'd gone through a few partners in his time, began to think that Van Rooten was the one he'd been looking for all his life. Together they had more balls than a pool table.

The only rule in undercover work was, anything goes. You were free to lie, cheat, betray, to do whatever had to be done to bring down the bad guys and penetrate their organization. The end justified the means. Feel free to dispense with morality. Don't think twice about shortcutting your way to wherever you want to go.

Undercover cops, DiPalma learned, were con artists, snake-oil salesmen who survived by twisting the truth. He also learned that since lying was the one thing keeping you alive, well, you just stopped worrying about it. An undercover cop's life hung by a thread; one wrong word and you could end up with your eyes shot out, or your dick sliced off and shoved down your throat. Lying was the least of your worries.

Undercover work did have its up side. Hell, in some ways it was a great life. Where else could you live out your macho dreams, the same dreams glorified by the press and TV crime shows every day of the week.

But if you weren't careful, undercover work could drag you down. The criminal life had its glittering prizes; the straight world couldn't touch it for sex, drugs, money, and power. And where else were you free from rules, guidelines, and morality, from any and all restrictions? In the underworld you did as you fucking well pleased, and the world had better get out of your way. Seductive? Yes, sir. But as DiPalma had warned Van Rooten: *Don't cross that line. Cross it and you can never step back*.

DiPalma's warnings, however, failed to stop Shark Eyes from losing all interest in the nine-to-five world, in family and friends, in a normal life. He came to believe the masquerade, to like it. And that's when he became just another cop who was no longer able to recognize his own lies. The Asian underworld in particular seemed to fascinate him. Its women became his passion.

DiPalma had been the first to sense when his partner's little compromises became big compromises. One big compromise concerned a protected witness, a forty-year-old Chinese named George Hin, who'd been supplying guns to youth gangs in Chinatowns all over the country. After helping to put some people away, Hin and his family were given new identities, then relocated in Arizona. Six months later, on Christmas Eve, two masked gunmen shot Hin to death on his front lawn in a Phoenix suburb. Van Rooten had been very friendly with the Hin crowd. Too friendly, DiPalma felt.

Then DiPalma received a tip from an informant, a low-level Harlem pusher named Honey Fortune who got off dishing cops. Honey said, "Your boy gave him up." Van Rooten had sold Hin's address to some very bad people. Price: $250,000. But before DiPalma could move on this information, somebody did a Jimmy Hoffa on Honey Fortune. Honey disappeared and was never seen again. Without his testimony, DiPalma had no case against Van Rooten.

Then came the matter of the Black General's son. Julie

Kurt, a cigar-smoking Manhattan call girl who preferred Chinese customers because they paid well and were partial to sexual experimentation, repaid DiPalma for discouraging a Venezuelan pimp who'd threatened to slash her face if she didn't join his stable. According to one of her regulars, Lin Pao was on his way to America. Coming to the Golden Mountain on an errand of mercy, Julie Kurt said.

He wanted to pay a final visit to an only son who was dying. The boy, a student at Harvard Business School, had been riding his bicycle when he'd been hit by a drunk driver, a Boston fireman named Seth McDaniel. Traces of cocaine were also found in McDaniel's bloodstream, and he'd been suspended pending a departmental hearing and a civil trial. Meanwhile Pao's son was given less than two days to live.

Working with DEA and the Boston police, DiPalma set a trap at the Boston hospital for Pao. The trap failed, however, because Pao never showed. Someone, a cop, had tipped him, Julie Kurt told DiPalma. Van Rooten? Julie Kurt said, "I don't have a name, but I'll ask around."

A week later her body was found in the courtyard of a Gramercy Park high rise, Julie Kurt having jumped, fallen, or been pushed from the balcony of her twenty-second-floor duplex. Suicide, ruled the coroner's office. A month later McDaniel, on bail and awaiting trial, disappeared on his way to an alcoholic counseling session in downtown Boston. He was never found, but informants told DiPalma he'd been kidnapped, drugged, then flown out of the country to Taiwan, where Lin Pao had hacked him to death with a chain saw.

DiPalma now refused to work with Van Rooten under any circumstances. He also tried to have him brought up on departmental charges. An angry Van Rooten said, "What the fuck makes you think you know what you're talking about?" If DiPalma wanted war, fine. Van Rooten didn't need a teacher anymore. Besides, he'd been carrying DiPalma, who was starting to show his age. From now on DiPalma could make it on his own. Van Rooten said, "I'm as good as you ever were."

He resented, fucking resented DiPalma going behind his back to Internal Affairs, trying to get him brought up on charges. It was a shitty thing to do to a partner. If DiPalma could prove Van Rooten had crossed over, fine. Otherwise, get fucked. Van Rooten wasn't going to forget this. One of these days it would be payback, he said. Get-even time. Count on it.

DiPalma's main FBI source said, "You'll love this. Taroko, the woman who broke Van Rooten's heart, she's Lin Pao's mistress. I mean, is that weird or what? Apparently she was working him on Pao's orders, while he was falling in love with her. Then she ups and dumps the dude. Kicked a hole in that sucker's heart. Ronald Romance took it hard. He ain't giving us much on her, but we're working on him. He already feels the heat; now all we got to do is make him see the light."

Shark Eyes. The man who wouldn't know the truth if it fell from the sky and bit him in the ass. So why had DiPalma agreed to meet him? Because instinct said Van Rooten was being righteous when he'd telephoned to say that a woman named Jan Golden was in danger.

Van Rooten said, "It's my fault it's happened, but all I can do about it is warn you. Can't talk about it over the phone. Better to have a sit-down. Face-to-face, you and me. Two of us alone in the same room. Should be interesting."

Jan Golden was DiPalma's wife and Van Rooten had been having an affair with her.

On the front porch of the manor house, the black marshal said to DiPalma, "You know the drill." DiPalma nodded, then took off his hat and topcoat, handing them over for inspection. Seconds later they were returned. Then the black marshal held out his hand for DiPalma's cane, saying you can pick it up after you finish inside. *Kendo,* Japanese fencing, and *arnis,* Filipino stick fighting, were DiPalma's passions. The cane was his favorite weapon.

Hand-carved from black oak, it was topped by a thick silver knob embossed with exquisitely detailed dragons. He'd gotten it in Hong Kong. A nurse, Katharine Shen, had given it to him when he'd gone there to extradite a Chinese heroin trafficker, Nickie Mang. Nickie had been operating out of Manhattan's Chinatown and was a sociopath, a loony tune who poured gasoline on his enemies, then touched it off with a burning match. He'd invaded DiPalma's Queens home, taken his first wife and nine-year-old daughter hostage, then shot them to death.

Thirteen years ago in Hong Kong.

A humid, rainy August night. A drenched DiPalma, gut-shot and with a shattered left arm, lay in putrid ditch water just off an empty highway between Hong Kong Island and Kai Tak Airport. Light-headed from loss of blood and with Nickie Mang very much on his mind. Nickie Mang, who'd just been taken away from him by four Chinks with shot-guns.

Now they were in a beige Chrysler and it was pulling away, DiPalma forgotten because he was history. But in the downpour he crawled out of the stinking ditch and onto the highway, never taking his eyes off the Chrysler, steadying his .38 Smith & Wesson on the chest of the prone, late Sergeant Arnold Yeh, of the Royal Hong Kong Police Force, the little driver who'd been in on the ambush and whom DiPalma had shot through the right eye.

A groggy DiPalma emptied the Smith & Wesson at the Chrysler's taillights. And hit the gas tank. A fraction of a second later he felt the shock wave. Heard the *boooom*. Felt the heat sear his face as the Chrysler exploded into a jumbo fireball, lighting up the night and turning into fiery pieces of metal clanging along the rain-slicked highway. Nickie Mang departing this world as a crispy critter.

Ten days later in a Kowloon hospital, DiPalma attempted to walk for the first time since Nickie Mang's people almost took him out. Disaster time. Unable to handle the crutches, he lost his balance and dropped to his knees. The pain was blinding. He thought, Can't do it. Won't ever be able to do it.

When he turned to crawl back to his bed, surprise. Nurse Katharine Shen blocked his way. Crawl toward the window, she ordered. Or roll toward the window. But you're not going back to bed, she said. DiPalma said, Get the hell out of my way. Knock me down, she said, but you're not going back to bed.

DiPalma said he wasn't ready to walk, that maybe he'd never be able to walk. Being on his back was just fine for the moment. He resented being a cripple, resented being out of control and dependent on others. She was the nearest target, so why not take it out on her? Tough lady, this beautiful Katharine Shen. Didn't budge, didn't cry, didn't lose her cool.

Arms folded across her chest, she stood looking down at him. DiPalma got the message. He pulled his crutches toward him, hating her for making him do this, but he pushed himself to his feet and limped toward the window, ten feet away. Shit, it felt like ten miles. Ten agonizing miles and he wanted to quit almost as soon as he'd begun. But he wasn't going to give her the satisfaction, so he kept going, until dizzy, exhausted, and sick to his stomach, he reached the window, reached the sun. For a few seconds he stood there with the sun's warmth on him, hearing pigeons cooing outside on the ledge, feeling the firmness of the floor beneath his bare feet, feeling his face grow hot as the tears started to flow, and he looked over his shoulder, not ashamed that a woman was seeing him cry, not now. Katharine Shen was crying too.

He would relive that day in his mind many times, always remembering that had he remained on his knees or returned to bed, he'd never have walked again. Nor loved again.

DiPalma returned to New York without knowing that his affair with Katharine Shen had produced a son, Todd. She'd then married Ian Hansard, a smug little English banker given to irrational rages and who'd been nothing more than a selfish schemer. It was the murder of Katharine and Ian Hansard by Japanese ultra-rightists that had brought Di-Palma back to Hong Kong and face-to-face with his son.

By then Todd was twelve, a tall, thin boy with a sad-faced, sloe-eyed beauty that bordered on the feminine. His eyes were astounding—one a deep violet, the other an extraordinary blue. His moods were equally as contrasting. He was pleasant one moment, moody the next; his energy level alternated between low and hyperactive.

There was no accounting for Todd's ability to speak Japanese, to see into the future, to practice *kendo* with an ability which DiPalma himself could only envy. Forget the kid's size and youth. With a wooden sword or stick in his hand, Todd was lethal. Absolutely lethal. He could out-fence adults competing on championship levels. Pissed these so-called champions off, but so what? DiPalma, one of the best *kendoists* on the East Coast, had trouble fighting the kid.

Spooky? Very. But then, Todd was unique. A very uncommon child. How uncommon was something understood only by DiPalma and Jan. Todd was uncommon because he was sometimes possessed by the soul of Benkai, a savage and cold-blooded sixteenth-century samurai with phenomenal fencing skills. DiPalma had always been a hardheaded realist. So he'd resisted the idea that his only son was an incarnation of a cold-blooded feudal killer. No way, he'd told himself. No damn way.

But on a warm Tokyo night a burly *yakuza* thug with a *balisong* knife had trapped Jan and Todd in a deserted blind alley, and DiPalma had been an eyewitness to what had happened next. Too far away to help, he'd tossed his cane to Todd, then watched helplessly as the *yakuza* moved in for the kill. Todd and Jan were dead, DiPalma told himself. For them to survive, Todd would have to fight off an experienced killer several times his size. And that wasn't possible.

But it was. Todd *was* invincible. *Invincible.* And merciless. He dominated the *yakuza,* breaking his arm and leg before executing him with a ferocious strike to the throat. What DiPalma had seen with his own eyes, he'd been forced to believe. Just as he was forced to accept that he'd never truly know his son. Todd was unknowable through reason. He was beyond human understanding.

In Japan, DiPalma had destroyed Benkai's four-hundred-year-old sword, which had been in Todd's possession. The weapon had been forged by Muramasa, a brilliant but unstable swordsmith. Those who possessed a Muramasa blade were said to be unable to live without killing. With Benkai's sword no longer in existence, DiPalma told himself that Todd's demons had finally been laid to rest.

But lately the boy seemed troubled and restless. Even tormented. At night he slept fitfully, tossing and turning, sometimes crying out and waking up soaked in his own perspiration. DiPalma and Jan now had difficulty communicating with the boy. These days he kept to himself and spoke only when spoken to.

An uneasy DiPalma wondered if the *thing* inside Todd was about to appear once more. If so, then what?

Todd and Jan. DiPalma loved them both. But both were being drawn away from him, making DiPalma very aware of his limitations.

The manor house. DiPalma entered a large room on the second floor, thinking, Greg's done it again. Shark Eyes hadn't let anybody stick him in some crappy barracks on the island, where witnesses shared a communal kitchen and bathroom and got to sleep on bunk beds and smell each other's farts. For him it was first-class all the way. Which is how he'd ended up in a building formerly used by the Coast Guard as officers' quarters.

Coat over one arm and hat in hand, DiPalma stood with his back to the door and looked around the room. Snug and comfy, to say the least. Low, spruce-beamed ceiling, ladder-back chairs, cherrywood cabinets, and verse samplers hanging from the walls. An electrical heater glowing in a corner on the polished oak floor. Atop a small pine table beside a canopied four-poster bed, a Sony shortwave radio was tuned to an all-news station. Behind DiPalma, someone in the hallway locked the door. He was alone with Gregory Van Rooten.

The rogue cop was in front of a window staring at the circular-shaped, red sandstone walls of nearby Castle Williams. He was a lean man in his mid-thirties, just over six feet, with thinning brown hair blow-dried to appear thicker, and a handsome, full-lipped face which seemed incapable of deceit. As always, he was decked out in high-priced items. Today it was a tan cashmere sweater, yellow silk shirt, black slacks, and black Gucci loafers. Diamond rings glittered on both hands, while his left wrist sported a gold Rolex. He could have been standing on the sun deck of his Malibu beach house, torn between working on his tan or ordering stained-glass windows for the garage.

Nervously tapping a windowpane with his forefinger, a chain-smoking and unshaven Van Rooten watched sea gulls fly across Buttermilk Channel, the waterway separating Governor's Island from Brooklyn. Finally he aimed the forefinger at the gulls and said, "Bang, bang." Then he faced DiPalma and smiled.

The smile hadn't changed, DiPalma thought. It was the usual love-me flash of teeth coming from a man who'd once tried to have DiPalma killed. On the other hand, Van Rooten himself had changed in the months since DiPalma had last seen him. He'd put on weight. His tan was fading, his face was rounder, and under the pricey sweater DiPalma spied a growing paunch. The hand holding the cigarette trembled slightly, and there were frown lines across Van Rooten's forehead. His eyes weren't so threatening anymore. The man was scared. He was hearing footsteps and trying hard not to look over his shoulder.

Neither man offered to shake hands.

Van Rooten cleared his throat and said, "Well, well, if it isn't my favorite Zen Fascist. Still active in the wild and wacky world of the martial arts? I told the guys on the door about your cane, about how you can really kick ass with that thing. Not that I was worried about you opening my skull or anything. But I do feel better knowing they took away your little toy. Gives me peace of mind, know what I mean?''

Eyes almost closed, DiPalma leaned his head to one side. ''You want to tell me about Jan?''

''Uh-oh. Here it comes, boys and girls. The famous DiPalma *ray*. The look that's supposed to make perpetrators shit in their pants and promise to write their mothers more often. That's the trouble with you, Frank. You're like safe sex and three-piece suits. Totally predictable.''

''You said she was in danger.''

''Lighten up, crime fighter. Next ferry back to Manhattan doesn't leave for an hour or so. I won't keep you past your bedtime. Can I get you a drink? Dewar's, Remy Martin? Oh, that's right. You don't drink. Bad stomach from that time in Hong Kong when they almost punched your ticket.''

DiPalma looked over his shoulder at the door. Yes, he was ready to leave. Leave before he did something pointless and ill advised. Like pull out Van Rooten's eyes.

Van Rooten said, ''I wasn't shitting you. Jan's in trouble. Now chill out. You don't like me, I don't like you. That ain't about to change. But hear me out before you walk. I think you owe it to Jan.''

DiPalma's voice was a husky whisper. ''You don't tell me what I owe my wife, understand?''

A subdued Van Rooten nodded in agreement; the big dago was not just mouthing off when he addressed you in that tone of voice. If anyone could inundate you with bodily harm, it was Frank DiPalma. And if anyone could catch you at your little tricks, it was that same Señor DiPalma. Van Rooten was going to have to be more forthcoming as to why he and the big dago were having this little chat. On the other hand, can one be truthful with a man when you've been schtupping his wife?

DiPalma said, ''You want to cut the shit and tell me why you really got me out here?''

Van Rooten thought, Well now. He looked down at a hooked rug under his feet.

DiPalma said, "I hate it when you think you're being clever. Is Jan really in danger?"

Van Rooten nodded. "Unfortunately, yes. And you're right, I want something from you. Something for myself. Coming to you for a favor is one thing I swore I'd never do. But right now I don't have much choice."

He looked at a door to his right. DiPalma followed his gaze. A second later Van Rooten rose, walked to the door, and opened it. The door led to a small, narrow bathroom with a floor tiled in a black-and-white diamond pattern. DiPalma thought, *I've come this far, so why not.* He walked toward the bathroom.

After both men were inside, DiPalma watched Van Rooten shut the door and flush the toilet. Then the rogue cop turned on the bathtub and sink taps. Finally he jumped in the air once, twice, landing flat-footed each time. The quick and easy way of fucking up unwanted wiretaps.

Van Rooten dropped his cigarette in the toilet, closed the seat cover, and sat down. "They tell me my room isn't bugged. Said I could trust them on this. Right. Pardon me if I go through life peeling my own banana. Okay, let's talk about Jan."

Chewing a thumbnail, he stared down at the floor. "I hear you two aren't living together anymore. She's moved out. For what it's worth, it's over between us. Her idea. Second lady who's dumped me lately. You'd think I had shit on my teeth or something. Anyway, the feeling in certain quarters is that Jan knows things about Lin Pao she shouldn't."

DiPalma aimed a forefinger at Van Rooten. "You're saying that Lin Pao might kill Jan because of you. I want to know what the hell you told her that's got her jammed up."

Eyes still on the floor, Van Rooten said, "Nothing. Not a goddamn thing. No reason for me to. Unfortunately somebody thinks I did. Look, I'm being up front with you because I don't want to spend the rest of my life looking over my shoulder. I know you. Jan gets whacked, and if you think I was involved, shit, I'm history. Doesn't matter where they relocate me. You'd hang in there till you found me, and then I'm a dead man. For once in my life I'm being right-eous. No lies this time, I swear it.''

DiPalma said, ''The only time you lie is when your lips move.''

''Give me a break, all right? Hear me out before you start breaking my ribs. To start with, it's not Lin Pao who's after Jan. It's one of his friends. Somebody who doesn't want people to know he and Pao are, shall we say, real good buddies.''

''A name.''

Van Rooten smiled at DiPalma. ''We're talking heavy-duty, partner. This here man heads the A list. By the way, he's American, not Chinese, and Taroko tells me he's been doing business with Pao for a long, long time. She thought I'd be shocked. I was and I wasn't, know what I mean? Superior investigator that I am, I checked out Pao's friend myself. He's dirty, this guy. Super dirty. And that's where you come in. It's gonna take somebody like you to do battle with this guy. Whatever else you are, my man, you are one good cop. Official or unofficial, it don't matter. We both know—once a cop, always a cop.''

Still smiling, Van Rooten hugged himself and rocked back and forth on the toilet. ''Man, oh, man, this is gonna be good. You going after him. By the way, don't turn your back on the Puerto Rican downstairs, the one on the door. Jive-ass son of a bitch name of Chacon. Pao's friend is paying him to keep an eye on me. Means Chacon can be bought. Jesus, is he one ugly spick. If he ain't proof that people fuck dogs, I don't know what is.''

Van Rooten started rocking faster. ''Frank DiPalma. Gray of hair and gray of mind. But a good cop. Goodgoodgood cop. I may be down, hotshot, but I am definitely not out. I'm gonna make you a big man. Gonna win you the Pulitzer prize or whatever the fuck they give you when you do it right in your business. Get this guy, man. Bring that sucker down.''

''I'm waiting for a name.''

''Nelson Berlin. My father.''

''Jesus, you don't ever stop, do you? You expect me to believe Nelson Berlin's working with Lin Pao? You're pathetic, you know that?''

''And I thought Italians were smart. You probably look in the bowl before you flush. If you leave me anything in your will, don't let it be your brain. Look, we both know the problem with bad guys ain't making money. It's hiding money. Laundering it. Keeping it away from the cops and the tax man. Lin Pao ain't no different, Jack. He needs all the help he can get in this area, which is where my old man comes in.''

Van Rooten stopped rocking. ''Nelson Berlin and Lin Pao. I mean, old dad ought to be ashamed of something, but dirt bag that he is, I don't think he's ashamed of a fucking thing. I suppose you could say I provoked Taroko and she let slip some things she shouldn't have. Anyway, my father's the one who's got taps on Jan's phones, and all I can say is, watch your ass, 'cause my old man is a barracuda.''

An idea began to form in DiPalma's mind. And out of it came a question that had to be asked. ''Say you're being righteous about your father and Lin Pao. Then your old man is going after Jan because he feels she might pass stuff on to me.''

''You ain't as dumb as you look. Go to the head of the class, amigo. He knows you've got marriage problems, but whether you or Jan are still in touch, that he doesn't know. Meanwhile it's easier to watch her than it is to watch an alert and astute ex-cop who's also a big-time TV reporter. Fuck around with a reporter, and shit, you've got World Wars Three and Four on your hands, and my old man doesn't want that. Not if he can avoid it. So Jan's the easier target.''

''She hasn't told me anything about Lin Pao. Or you,

either, for that matter. You really got a hard-on for your old man, don't you?''

"King-size, my man. King-size. Since I got popped I've seen him more times than I have in maybe ten years. Fucking tears of joy run down my leg every time we meet.''

People who hate their fathers, DiPalma thought, were destined to lead fucked-up lives. Shark Eyes detested his old man with a passion. Detested him enough to drop the family name and go with his mother's maiden name instead. According to Van Rooten, daddy wasn't too keen on him either. As Van Rooten told DiPalma, Old Dad thinks being a cop is an occupation unfit for intelligent people.

There were times when DiPalma wondered if either father and son had learned much from humans. Both men had a desire to be admired. Both felt they had the right to be selfish. And both had a brutal vanity.

Nelson Berlin did not possess a sympathetic or benevolent nature. His reputation was that of an annoying little bastard who bought losing companies and turned them into winners by firing hundreds of people and cutting operating expenses to the bone. His Cameron Corporation did billions in sales each year from hotel, insurance, electronics, and candy businesses. Berlin also owned stock in the network DiPalma worked for, and sat on the board of directors. Rumor had him planning a hostile takeover, the thought of which had network personnel shitting in their pants. Berlin's tight-fisted ways and his height—he was only five-feet-five—had won him the nickname the Poison Dwarf.

DiPalma said, "Why tell me about your father? DEA, FBI, either one would love to hear what you've just told me. Assuming you're still interested in keeping your ass out of prison.''

"You leave the *federales* to me. Old Greg knows how to keep them turned on. My old man, however, has to be handled just right or not at all. Very well connected, my old man, connected from the White House on down. Knows everybody, I mean everybody. Lays big bucks on the Republicans, Democrats, blacks, gays, feminists. Covers all the bases.''

Van Rooten rubbed his unshaven chin. ''You don't get his kind of money without knowing who to buy. But I can't see him buying you, or making you back off. You got the stones to take him on. You're the best cop I ever knew. Shit, you're the best I know. There're times when I wish things could have been different between us. Ain't shit I can do about it now. But I can see that my old man gets what's coming to him.''

DiPalma said, ''Some people say you gave yourself up because you knew you were about to get popped. You heard footsteps, champ, so you made the best of a bad situation. You stopped off in Atlantic City, you and Detective LaVon, had a last fling with Lin Pao's money, then you turned yourself in before the feds came for you. LaVon wasn't so lucky.''

''So that's how you see it, me making the best of a bad situation. How close was I to getting popped, may I ask?''

DiPalma said, ''Two weeks ago DEA raided the home of a Chinese businessman on Long Island, one Samuel Chai. They turned up one of their confidential intelligence files connecting Chai to Lin Pao. Your fingerprints were on that file. They also found DEA evidence bags, used to hold confiscated heroin. And they found the combination to the U.S. Attorney's safe, where the drugs were stored. Your prints were on all of it. I'd say your tit was in the ringer, wouldn't you?''

Van Rooten grinned. ''How 'bout I tell you the elves left that shit in Chai's house?''

''I wouldn't believe you if you said you were in this room with me.''

''I see. Well, pay attention, because I may ask questions later. For one thing, when I take the stand, I'm going to talk about confiscated narcotics and guns ending up back on the street. About cops who check license-plate numbers with the motor vehicle bureau; then tell the bad guys if the cars following them belong to cops or civilians. DEA, FBI, nobody's gonna be happy, either, when I start singing my little song.''

DiPalma said, "When you're in a hole, stop digging."

"What's that supposed to mean?"

"Means lying about cops isn't going to help your case any."

"We'll see who's lying, hotshot. You might ask yourself how I came by that intelligence file, the confiscated narcotics, and the safe combination. But that's neither here nor there. For sure, a lot of people besides Lin Pao would love to see me gone from this world. Well, fuck 'em where they breathe, I say. Lin Pao, cops, feds, my old man. I'm going to dick every one of them. And love doing it."

DiPalma thought, *I just bet you will.* Meanwhile, what the hell was DiPalma's next move? Part one of Shark Eyes's little song was easy enough to check out. Do a sweep on Jan's hotel room and office for bugs. If any turn up, find out who put them there.

DiPalma's sources of information were first-rate, but he hadn't heard squat about Berlin and the Black General being business partners. Still, what did Van Rooten have to gain by lying at this point in his life? He had to know that DiPalma would check for taps on Jan's phone. No taps meant Van Rooten was lying about everything. The man had to know that.

Meanwhile DiPalma wanted out of the bathroom. Its smallness was too confining. And too noisy. The running water was starting to get on his nerves. Also, DiPalma didn't smoke anymore, not after what had happened to his stomach in Hong Kong. So he didn't appreciate Shark Eyes's fondness for the weed. Van Rooten had just opened a new pack of Winstons. Great.

Cigarette dangling from a corner of his mouth, Van Rooten stood up. "You're starting to look a little green around the gills, big guy. Maybe it's time we repaired to the next room. Before we go, gonna give you a couple things to work on. Gonna give you something that says I ain't jerking you around."

DiPalma loosened his tie, thinking, *Why do I get the feeling I'm this guy's personal pit bull, and he's getting ready to turn me loose on the world?*

Van Rooten said, "One thing: You can act on what I've just told you or you can walk away from it. But if something happens to Jan, don't say I didn't warn you. And providing you can hang in there against my old man, you might come up with another prize-winning story. Who knows, you could be the white knight who stops him from taking over the network. Do that and those white-collar assholes you work with will love you forever."

"Finally, when my father learns you're sniffing around his affairs, he'll deal with you in one way or another. If that don't work, then he'll bring in Lin Pao, and when that happens, you might feel more comfortable in the room down the hall. I could use the company."

Van Rooten lifted the toilet-seat cover, dropped his half-smoked cigarette in the bowl, and let the lid fall. Then he immediately lit another. "Listen up, big guy. Two weeks from now some very heavy Triad leaders are going to have a sit-down in Hong Kong. Lin Pao's putting it together. The purpose is to divide up America the Beautiful without the Triads killing each other. Ask around about this meeting. See what you come up with. You might also check to see if my old man's planning to be there around the same time. I'm giving this to you before I pass it on to the *federales*. Let's see what you do with it."

Taking the cigarette from his mouth, Van Rooten stared at the lit end. "By the way, when you sweep Jan's hotel and office and find the bugs, check out Dave Stamm. He's head of security for my old man."

"I know him," DiPalma said. "Worked together once or twice when he was assistant regional FBI director. He still wearing cheap rugs?"

Van Rooten laughed. "The worst. I leave it to you to deal with him regarding the matter of eavesdropping on your wife without a court order. Now, there's something else—'' Van Rooten stopped talking and held up a hand for silence. He listened.

DiPalma heard it too. Someone was in the next room. Male voices. Two, maybe three. He looked at Van Rooten, who seemed more frightened than ever. The rogue cop whispered, ''Son of a bitch, it's my father.''

Seconds later he said, ''Mintzer, my lawyer's with him. And that cocksucker, Chacon.'' He looked at DiPalma and said, ''Means my old man knows we're meeting. Shit.''

Van Rooten leaned closer, lips to DiPalma's left ear. ''Manila,'' he whispered. ''Taaltex. China. My old man's sister. He did it. His own fucking sister.''

Van Rooten pushed past DiPalma, shoving him into the wall, then opened the bathroom door and stepped into the main room, shouting, ''The fuck you doing here!''

DiPalma heard Nelson Berlin shout back in a surprisingly deep voice for such a little man. Heard him yell, ''You've been talking to DiPalma, haven't you? I told you to stay away from that bastard. I want to know what you two have been talking about, and I want to know now, you understand?''

DiPalma stepped into the main room.

# Five

## Chinatown, New York City

Shortly before nine P.M., sixteen-year-old Peter Chen and fourteen-year-old Bing Fong, both members of the Jade Eagles, entered a massage parlor on Elizabeth Street. Each wore a fatigue jacket, jeans, running shoes, and a bulletproof vest. Each also wore a black canvas backpack containing two kilos of white heroin.

The slim, thin-faced Chen and the chunky, cross-eyed Fong were cousins. Born in the same Kowloon slum, they'd entered America illegally together and were closer than brothers. As Jade Eagles, they'd killed eleven people.

Both were ignored by the massage-parlor receptionist, a small, fiftyish woman who was a dental hygienist by day; and by the guard, a balding Chinese bodybuilder who appeared in gay porn films produced in Hong Kong. Receptionist and guard sat at a metal desk, eyes glued to a black-and-white television set broadcasting a Chinese variety show.

Peter Chen led the way up a creaking, narrow staircase, taking the stairs two at a time, a hand resting on the butt of a 9-mm Browning tucked in his waistband. It was good to be back in Chinatown, among his own people and away from the *gweilos,* foreign devils. The massage parlor—in fact, the whole run-down building—belonged to the

Hundred Pacer Snakes, who controlled the Jade Eagles. Which didn't mean Chen and cousin Fong shouldn't be on their guard.

Last week gang members Sam Liu and Elvis Chan had left Chinatown with three kilos of China white for the Slicky Boys, a Washington D.C. black crew. Within hours of leaving New York, Sam, Elvis, and the heroin disappeared from the face of the earth. The Triad had been forced to replace the three keys, plus give the Slicky Boys eight free ounces as a goodwill gesture to make up for the late delivery.

Meanwhile there'd been no sign of Sam and Elvis. The two had never reached Washington, nor had they surfaced anywhere else in America or abroad. Peter Chen naturally assumed the obvious: Sam and Elvis had ripped off the Hundred Pacer Snakes, an act of monumental stupidity, since the secret society wouldn't rest until it found them. Dumb, dumb, dumb, said gang leader Benjy Lok Nein to Peter Chen, his second in command.

Then something happened which caused Peter Chen and Benjy to reevaluate their theory concerning Sam and Elvis. Two days ago, newspapers reported that a Coast Guard patrol boat had found the nude, headless corpse of a young Chinese male floating in Long Island Sound. The corpse's hands had also been removed, making it impossible to identify him by his fingerprints. But according to police, the dead man's abdomen bore knife scars from past wounds, and there were tattooed eagles on his chest and arms.

Peter Chen and the other Jade Eagles knew his identity, even if police didn't. The headless corpse was Joey Liu, a gang member who'd just celebrated his fifteenth birthday and hadn't been seen since he'd gone to Long Island to visit his girlfriend. All Chinese had an intense distrust of authority. Crimes committed in Chinatown, no matter how serious, were rarely reported to police. Which was why authorities would never learn Joey Liu's identity from the Jade Eagles.

Benjy Nein was the first to speculate on a possible connection between Joey Liu's murder and Elvis and Sam's disappearance. As Benjy told Peter Chen, maybe Sam and Elvis hadn't been a couple of stupid shits, after all. Maybe somebody was deliberately killing off the Jade Eagles. Peter Chen asked if Benjy thought it was a rival youth gang. A worried Benjy thought a long time before answering, then said he wasn't sure.

On yesterday's drug run to Toronto, Peter Chen and Bing Fong had been more vigilant than ever, looking over their shoulders and trusting no one. Now more than ever, it was wise to be on guard, to stay loose and be observant. To be mentally responsive and perceptive, as *dai low,* elder brother would say.

But the run wasn't over until the white powder was handed to Elder Brother, who now awaited Chen and Bing Fong on the second-floor office of the massage parlor. And who didn't appreciate people who arrived later than expected.

Like all Jade Eagles, Peter Chen feared Elder Brother. Every youth gang had its *dai low,* with each receiving the awe and reverence due any supreme power. Most were martial-arts instructors able to command respect through fighting skills, personal magnetism, or measures that gang members like Peter Chen knew to be violent and unkind.

The Jade Eagles' Elder Brother was a thirtyish, baby-faced Taiwanese named Ivan Ho, a lean, muscled man with short black hair and bulging, myopic eyes. He was a former Hong Kong police sergeant who favored black clothing, wire-rimmed glasses, and was a skilled full-contact fighter in three Southern kung-fu systems. He also possessed an amazing cruelty and was a pathological liar, making it impossible to determine his true emotions.

On behalf of the Hundred Pacer Snakes, Ivan Ho recruited members for the Jade Eagles, trained them in the martial arts, and served as gang enforcer. Gang members took their orders from him and had no contact with the Triad. Any communication regarding Triad matters, from instructions to money, was between Ivan Ho and one Triad member. With only two men directly involved, men sworn to secrecy,

American police had found it impossible to establish any connection between the Jade Eagles and the secret society.

Ivan Ho did not hesitate to punish or penalize. Peter Chen hadn't been a Jade Eagle for long when he and the gang had been ordered to watch Ho penalize fifteen-year-old gang member Eddie Louie, who was also Ho's nephew. Nephew had been talking to the wrong people, Elder Brother said. Watch the show, he told them, and that's what they'd done. Watched him slit Eddie Louie's tongue, then put on work gloves and strangle Eddie Louie with barbed wire. Regard this as your training, Ivan Ho had said to them. Training that was expected to produce moral and mental improvement.

Ivan Ho selected only the most energetic and fearless youngsters for gang membership, choosing boys between the ages of ten and seventeen. He preferred immigrants, considering them tougher than American-born Chinese. His puppies, as Ho called recruits, came from the slums of Hong Kong, Kowloon, Taipei, and Singapore. His favorites were the Chinese from Vietnam, youngsters who'd learned violence in that war-ravaged country and who'd do anything without fear or hesitation; who had no family, clan, or allegiance to Hong Kong. Who had nothing to lose and were very, very dangerous.

Ho provided gang members with apartments, cars, money, and guns. Get arrested and you could count on lawyers and bail money. Betray Ho or the Jade Eagles and you were dead.

On behalf of the Triads, gang members extorted money from businesses, guarded gambling houses, trafficked in drugs. They also collected protection money from stores, restaurants, discotheques, movie theaters, massage parlors. They served as muscle for Triad loan sharks, silenced offensive journalists and community activists, and warred on opposing gangs. The more immigrants, the more gang members. And the more gang members, the more violence in Chinatown.

The Browning now in his right hand and hidden behind

his thigh, Peter Chen stepped from the staircase and into a shadowy hallway. Ahead of him a small, gray Chinese mopped the floor with a mixture of disinfectant and water from a battered bucket. His efforts, however, did little to remove a permanent stench of urine, cigarettes, and alcohol. At the sight of Chen and Fong, the old Chinese flattened himself against a plywood wall and averted his eyes.

Without slowing down, Chen glanced at a young, pretty whore who stood in the doorway of her room listening to a middle-aged Chinese man she'd just serviced. Chen knew him to be the married owner of Chinatown's two largest restaurants, a man who refused to pay his waiters a salary. Their income came entirely from tips, which they were forced to share with him.

The girl couldn't have been more than sixteen. She had waist-length black hair, wore a purple robe with white satin high heels, and appeared shy. Chen was definitely attracted to her. He knew most of the girls, but this one was new to him. She was probably one of the dozen Taiwanese teenagers smuggled into the U.S. this week by a ring of Mexicans down in Texas, guys who made a fortune bringing in anybody, terrorists included, for a price.

Tonight, after he took care of business, Chen was going to party with that little girl. The new ones were his favorites. They were anxious to please, easy to dominate, and, as a Jade Eagle, he didn't have to pay. You could do what you pleased with the new ones. It was best to get to these girls early, before drugs, liquor, or AIDS fucked them up forever. But first Chen and Cousin Fong had a date with Elder Brother.

At the end of the hallway Chen and Fong stopped in front of the last door on the left. Chen took a deep breath, then used the butt of the Browning to tap on the door three times. He waited, then tapped once more. Then he silently counted to ten and tapped twice more.

Inside, a male voice asked in Cantonese, "Did you have an interesting trip going and coming?" Chen and Cousin Fong smiled at each other. Elder Brother. Waiting for them.

And telling them all was well. Had he said, Was your trip interesting, Chen and Fong would have fled from the massage parlor as quickly as possible. The white powder had to be protected at all costs. As Elder Brother had repeatedly told them, compared to the white powder, their lives were absolutely worthless.

Chen opened the door and stepped into the small room, the massage parlor office, which contained a battered desk, wooden folding chairs, a metal filing cabinet, and a small brown leather couch. A single, grimy window looked out on a sooty air shaft. But to Chen and Cousin Fong the room was a palace. It was in Chinatown, where the cousins felt safe.

Ivan Ho, Elder Brother, was alone. Sitting on the edge of the desk, one hand on a king-size cassette player and smiling. Dressed in black, as usual. Suit, shirt, tie, silk pocket handkerchief, lizard-skin boots. He seemed pleased to see them.

"No problem, *dai low*," Peter Chen said. "The Toronto guys were on time and didn't give us a hassle. Four keys, just like they promised."

Ivan Ho stood up. "Nice work. Now, I think you puppies are entitled to a little fun. Put the backpacks on the desk. Anything suspicious happen? I mean, did anyone follow you or try to rip you off?"

Chen walked to the desk, placed the Browning near the telephone, and removed his pack. "No, *dai low*. After what happened to Joey and Sam and Elvis, we were pretty careful."

Ivan Ho nodded.

Chen, helping Cousin Fong out of his pack, said, "We were ready to take out anybody who even looked at us sideways. We were careful. Really careful." Then, for the first time, he stared at the floor. "Hey, what's this?" They were all standing on pale green oilcloth, which covered the floor from wall to wall.

"Room's being done over," Ivan Ho said. "You have to admit it needs it. Paint, new furniture, even a new fridge.

Electricians came in today and worked on the wiring. Oilcloth's for the painters. They're coming in early tomorrow. Right now, you guys take it easy. You're in Chinatown now. You're home.''

Ivan Ho picked up the receiver, dialed a single digit, and then spoke in Cantonese to the receptionist, telling her what he wanted. Chen interrupted him. The new girl, he said. The one in Room 4. Ivan Ho smiled and said, She's yours. Make her happy, my little puppy. Then he continued speaking to the receptionist, but he did snap his fingers to get Chen and Fong's attention, then pointed to a pair of mattresses rolled up against the far wall. The Jade Eagles grinned at one another.

Minutes later the door to the room opened and two young whores entered. One was the pretty teenager Chen had requested. She carried a tray containing a bottle of Remy Martin and two glasses. The other girl, a round-faced teenager in pink slippers and a black see-through shorty negligee, carried a small silver tray. Stopping in front of Peter Chen, the round-faced girl bowed her head and held out the tray to him. It contained several thumb-size glass vials of cocaine and crack, along with glassine envelopes of heroin and amphetamines. Party time.

Ivan Ho pressed a red button on the boom box and it came alive with LL Cool J rapping that he needed love. Ivan Ho said, ''My puppies, I think you can take it from here.'' He winked. Seconds later he was standing in the doorway, waving to Chen and Cousin Fong, and then he was gone, closing the door softly behind him.

Peter Chen, naked on a mattress in the center of the room, opened his eyes slowly and looked left in time to see Cousin Fong vomit into a brown metal wastebasket. Glassy-eyed, slack-jawed Cousin Fong, his squat, naked body gently rocking back and forth on the edge of the desk, his mattress at his feet and covered with half-eaten pizza slices, empty Big Mac containers, bits of Hershey bars, empty glassine envelopes, and cocaine vials and fresh beer stains. Naked

Cousin Fong, who'd said he was never fucking going back to Hong Kong because life was too good on the Golden Mountain and who was now puking his guts out.

An exhausted Peter Chen closed his eyes, yawned, and cupped his scrotum. He'd fucked the shit out of Joan, the new girl who'd been in America only two days and was terrified of Chen because she knew he was an important person with the Jade Eagles. But she followed orders, which is all Peter Chen wanted her to do. He only had to hit her twice.

He felt wasted. Good but wasted. The booze, drugs, food. And the fucking, not to mention the thirteen-hour drug run to Toronto and back without sleep. All of it was finally getting to him. Time to crash, to nod out for a few hours, then wake up and party some more with Joan.

He forced his eyes open. Where the hell was Joan, by the way? And where was Mabel, Cousin Fong's girl? Chen's eyelids were starting to weigh a ton. He wanted Joan beside him. Now.

He heard Cousin Fong drop the wastebasket, then tumble off the desk and land cursing on the floor, all of which Chen thought was the funniest thing he'd ever seen, and he just had to laugh. Cousin Fong laughed, too, and neither heard the door to the room open just wide enough to allow two nude figures to slip into the room. One closed the door without making a sound.

It was Peter Chen who looked at the door, saw the bare legs coming toward him, and smiled. He pushed himself onto his elbows, saying, Get the hell over here, thinking of the pleasure Joan had given him and looking forward to enjoying her again. He was slamming the mattress with the palm of his hand, yelling Joan's name, and that's when the naked figures, hard-muscled men who rushed across the oilcloth, leapt on the cousins and strangled them to death with their bare hands.

One man turned up the volume on the cassette player. The other walked to a closet, removed a chain saw, and returned to stand over Peter Chen's corpse. Both had years of experience in Taiwanese intelligence and as members of the Eight Knives of the North. So both knew that wiping the boy's blood from their naked bodies would be less expensive than cleaning their clothing. It was also less time-consuming than changing attire. And it definitely reduced the possibility of leaving behind incriminating fibers or buttons.

Sad to die so young, thought the man with the saw. Seconds later he began slicing off Chen's head.

# Six

Because of the nightmares, Todd did not like to sleep. Hours of *kendo* and *arnis,* practiced alone and in secret for the most important task of his life, left him exhausted but still unable to rest at night.

Until recently he'd had no trouble sleeping. He'd go to bed tired and usually awakened refreshed. Now he slept fitfully and never without nightmares, apparitions, or the chilling forecast of omens. Sleep had become the dominant terror in his life, a look into a hell that hid the unfinished tasks of past lifetimes.

Life, Todd knew, was karma. One's actions in this life determined one's destiny in the next. His current suffering could only be blamed on his past. His reaction to the nightmares would determine his future.

Last week he had been alone in his father's Brooklyn Heights apartment when he'd wake up screaming from the most ominous of the nightmares. His skin had tingled with an unnatural heat, and there'd been a throbbing pain in his throat. Blood had trickled from his left eye. Todd was again becoming possessed by Gongoro Benkai, sixteenth-century samurai and bodyguard to Lord Saburo.

Fifty-year-old Benkai, a stout, bearded, muscular man who was dark-skinned and ugly enough to be called Land

Spider behind his back. Whose eyes had a wolflike brightness that followers of black magic believed came from eating
human flesh; who fenced with such fanatical skill that few
doubted he was the son of *Shinigama*, Lord of Death-Desire,
and the fox, that creature which could invoke demonic possession at will.

Benkai, who had killed sixty men with the long and short
swords. Who had also killed with the aid of the Iki-ryo, a
ghost that sprang not from the dead but from the living.
Dark and malignant thoughts—blood lust, vengeance,
hatred—could send this evil spirit from a man's mind and
into the world to destroy. In a Japan where all believed in
demons, ghosts, specters, and phantasms, Benkai's remarkable swordsmanship could only be due to the invisible
and deadly Iki-ryo.

Benkai's honor demanded that he serve the *daimyo*, his
lord, with an undivided loyalty. It was a loyalty which could
continue past the grave. Because of it, Todd was now being
terrified by an evil in his dreams, an evil that had begun
with an act of treachery four hundred years ago.

## Ikuba Castle, Japan. August 1585. Two A.M.

*The rain had just ended, leaving the night hazy and
humid. Benkai and the woman were alone in her lavish
quarters of polished oak floors, lacquered redwood chests,
wind chimes, and painted folding screens. They sat facing
each other across clean straw mats, each holding a drinking
bowl of green tea.*

*The woman was Saga, Lord Saburo's most prized con-
cubine. She was seventeen, small and elegant, with fash-
ionably blackened teeth, shaved eyebrows, and fragile
combs of engraved oyster shells fastened in cocoons of black
hair. Benkai found her cruel and committed to the immediate
gratification of her most petty desires. Quick to speak her
mind, she could be oxlike in her obstinacy. She was noto-
riously ill mannered toward everyone except Lord Saburo*

*and her uncle, Nitta Kiichi, commander of the Saburo's military forces.*

*The forty-year-old Kiichi, a broad-chested man with deep-set eyes and an extremely small mouth, was a cold social climber with a talent for fawning over anyone he felt could advance his career or put money in his pocket. Few were as dogged in their pursuit of self-interest as the polite, smooth-talking military commander. Such men, Benkai felt, were for sale to the highest bidder.*

*Benkai and Kiichi were enemies. The ill will between them had begun when Benkai had outbid Kiichi for a slave girl. When Benkai refused to sell her to Kiichi, she was stabbed to death by a killer who was never caught. Benkai suspected she'd been murdered on Kiichi's orders. A proud man, Kiichi would rather see a woman die than lose her to someone else.*

*Benkai and the daimyo's chief general had also argued over the castle's defenses. While Kiichi had insisted they were strong enough, Benkai had urged Lord Saburo to strengthen them at once. For hundreds of years Japan had suffered from civil chaos as warlords fought to become the country's supreme military ruler. The fighting was still raging throughout the land. No man's life or property was safe.*

*Lord Saburo rejected Benkai's advice, choosing instead to side with Kiichi. Which did not stop Kiichi from accusing Benkai of embarrassing him in front of the daimyo. The word* honor *was not mentioned by Kiichi; to do so would have meant challenging the Land Spider to a duel, and Kiichi was not yet ready to meet his ancestors. He was also not one to forgive or forget. Sooner or later he would have his revenge.*

*Meanwhile Kiichi's position at Ikuba Castle was quite secure. He supervised Lord Saburo's spy system, collected badly needed tax money, and ran a disciplined army. And he was married to Saburo's sister. His influence with the daimyo was greater than that of Benkai, which did not stop him from hating and fearing the bodyguard.*

*Benkai felt strongly that Lord Saburo had not been well*

*served by Kiichi's advice on the castle's defenses. Weak and lecherous, the forty-year-old daimyo, a fat and totally hairless man, was in need of strong walls. He had been foolish enough to make an enemy out of Toyotomi Hideyoshi, the most dangerous man in Japan. Despite an emperor and royal court at Kyoto, Hideyoshi ruled the country as shogun, military dictator. Dwarfish, brilliant, and a born leader, Hideyoshi's ambition was to make a single country out of China, Korea, and Japan.*

*Japan was to be his first conquest. Using his army, a massive spy system, and his considerable charm, Hideyoshi was attempting to bring all daimyos under his authority. Saburo, among other warlords, was refusing to recognize Hideyoshi as Japan's sole ruler. He'd gone even further and was now plotting to kill the Crowned Monkey, as Hideyoshi was called. It was a risky scheme, one which Benkai knew could easily backfire. The code of Bushido, however, did not allow the bodyguard to waver in his loyalty. Right or wrong, he was obliged to live and die for his lord.*

*Saga's quarters. Benkai had come to hear the concubine tell him of a plot to murder Lord Saburo. A plot devised by traitors living in Ikuba Castle.*

*Benkai said, "Why not give this news to your uncle?"*

*"Because my uncle's youngest son is involved," Saga said. "Uncle would do his duty and punish the boy, but I wish to save him the shame of bringing this news to the daimyo. I do not want my uncle to know this information has come from me. I implore you to warn the daimyo."*

*Benkai said, "How did you come by such hazardous news?"*

*She said, "From my slave, Ichiro." Ichiro was the blind musician who had overheard men talking in the stable where he slept. Certain men who had been hiding from the rain and who were careless with their words. A slave, as Benkai knew, could not approach the daimyo. Ichiro could pass along what he'd heard only to his mistress.*

*Benkai thought, It would have been wiser for her to speak*

of this to her uncle. Wiser and much easier. She cares only for herself. Why should she weep if Kiichi's son is a traitor?

Watched by the concubine, Benkai brought his bowl to his lips, tasted the tea, and frowned. Then he looked to his left, at a blue screen painted with golden cranes and pine trees. Mosquitoes had gathered in front of the screen. Mosquitoes drawn by someone hidden behind the screen.

Benkai stared down into his bowl. The tea's surface was cloudy. Poison.

A trap.

He threw the bowl aside and leapt to his feet, long sword in his hands and held overhead in a two-handed grip. A single stride brought him to the screen, where he brought the sword down in a powerful cut, slicing through the rice paper and cleaving the skull of a crouching ninja, a lean man dressed in black.

Saga screamed, "It is too late, Land Spider. You will never reach your lord in time. He belongs to the ninja now! To the ninja!"

Ninja. Clans of assassins and spies skilled in the martial arts, espionage, blackmail, murder. Men and women in black whose strength, agility, and stamina made them superb athletes and flawless killing machines. Whose superior training caused many to view them as supernatural. Whose trade, ninjitsu, was stealth, or the art of invisibility. Ninja meant "stealers in."

As the dead man fell onto the torn screen, Benkai turned and slashed the stomach of a charging ninja wielding a long hardwood staff. Three ninja, who'd entered through the open window, dropped to the matted floor and raced screaming toward Benkai. The bodyguard, short sword in one hand, long sword in the other and with the rage to kill roaring in his blood, ran to meet them.

He severed one attacker's arms at the elbow, buried the short sword's blade in the unprotected armpit of a second, and when the third attempted to wrap a chain around Benkai's ankles and yank his feet from under him, the bodyguard *leapt over the chain and landed on the floor, instantly thrusting the point of his short sword into the attacker's throat.*

Keen to destroy the conniving Saga, Benkai spun around and took an arrow in his left eye. The pain was excruciating. Unbearable. He staggered backward, then stopped. He was still under attack. And half blind.

Drawing on a maniacal inner strength, Benkai willed himself to remain on his feet, to ignore the violent agony in his skull. The way of the warrior was death. A samurai's life did not belong to him; it belonged to his master, and to give up this life for his master was the samurai's glory.

By the light from paper lanterns and flickering pine torches, Benkai counted the remaining attackers. Four ninja. And Saga. He saw the open space in the floor where the concubine had hidden the stealers-in. He saw their weapons—blowgun with poison darts, swords, a chain with a weighted steel end, hardwood staffs. And a hankyu, the half bow used to shoot the arrow into his eye. None was the equal of his Muramasa blade, a weapon which hungered after men's lives. A weapon which compelled its owner to kill.

Saga, a metal-edged war fan in one hand, pointed to Benkai. "He bleeds. He is no demon. Kill the Land Spider and I will see that you are paid double what you have been promised. He must not reach Saburo."

Benkai heard shouts from the courtyard and the guards' quarters, from the ramparts and from the floor below. The dreaded ninja, with their unseen and unknown methods of death, had infiltrated the castle. They could only have done so with help from the inside. Curse those who had betrayed Ikuba Castle.

Such intrigue was beyond Saga. Someone far more cunning than she had plotted this treachery, and that someone could only be her uncle. Even as he tasted his own blood, Benkai vowed that Kiichi's betrayal would not go unpunished. In this life or in lives to come, Kiichi would pay for what he had done this night.

Benkai tore his mind from the arrow in his eye. There

*was no time to remove it or to care for this most serious of wounds. His honor demanded that he get to his lord at once or be rejected forever by all the gods and his ancestors.*

Hurling the short sword aside, a screaming Benkai threw himself at the four ninja. Without turning around, he thrust the long sword to his rear, into the stomach of one attacker, then withdrew it and, in one long slash to his left, cut the throats of two opponents. Pivoting right, he knocked aside a hardwood staff in the hands of the last opponent, then brought the long sword down in one powerful stroke, splitting the attacker from right shoulder to left hip. The last four ninja had been killed in just three seconds.

Now he pressed the point of his long sword into the throat of a weeping, terrified Saga. He said, "Kiichi?" She nodded repeatedly.

Benkai beheaded her with a single stroke.

It was dawn when Benkai, the arrow still in his eye, knelt facing a barred oak door in Lord Saburo's quarters and prepared to commit seppuku, the cutting of the stomach, the ritual suicide that was the defeated warrior's escape from disgrace.

Four castle guards watched as he removed his long and short swords from his sash, placing both weapons on the floor to his right. Saga's bloodied head remained tied to the sash by her long, dark hair. Benkai opened his kimono, baring his chest and stomach. Several yards away from him, the oak door trembled under the pounding of a battering ram wielded by shouting, cursing ninja.

Led by Kiichi, the ninja had slaughtered Saburo's officers, leaving the garrison troops leaderless. Dressed as Saburo's troops, several ninja then moved freely around the castle and its grounds, killing as they pleased. The result was panic. Now unwilling to trust their comrades, the more frightened of Saburo's soldiers had barricaded themselves inside a barracks and were refusing to fight.

With or without Saburo's total forces, the battle for Ikuba Castle was lost. The fortress was now in the hands

*of the traitorous Kiichi and the Koga ninja, a clan pow-
erful enough to rule its own province. Outside, the castle
was surrounded by thousands of Hideyoshi's cavalry and
foot soldiers, an army which never had been defeated in
combat. Ikuba Castle was completely encircled, its defend-
ers doomed.*

*Seppuku was the only way that Benkai could avoid capture
and retain his honor. Suicide was preferable to the disgrace
of falling into the hands of a hated enemy. Only minutes
ago, under a gilded ceiling luxuriant with sunken panels of
painted seashores and waterfalls, Benkai had assisted Lord
Saburo in the* daimyo's *seppuku.*

*To cut open one's stomach called for a courage and
composure possessed only by a true warrior. Saburo had
not been such a man. He was weak, and Benkai knew it.
It was a certainty that the* daimyo's *courage would fail him
at the last moment. Which was why Benkai had shown his
master one final kindness.*

*As a tearful Saburo reached for the long ceremonial knife
with a shaking hand, Benkai quickly beheaded him, preventing the* daimyo *from shaming himself in front of the
guards by a show of cowardice. As* kaishaku, *second and
executioner in the ritual suicide, Benkai could end his lord's
agony whenever he saw fit.*

*Now, as the oak door shook under the pounding of the
battering ram, Benkai prepared to close his eyes to this
world. Giri, duty, commanded that he kill Kiichi. It would
not be possible to do so in this life. But existence was eternal.
Both he and Kiichi would have many lives to come. Benkai
would now open his own abdomen, hoping that when the
gods saw the purity of his soul, they would once more bring
him and Kiichi face-to-face. If it took a thousand lifetimes,
Benkai was determined to return blood for blood, evil for
evil.*

*Behind Benkai, someone called his name. He looked over
his shoulder to see Asano, commander of the household
guard, take two steps forward, stop, and bow. The burly,
brooding Asano was Benkai's closest friend. Weeping si-*

*lently, the guard volunteered to be his second, to end his agony. The bodyguard nodded once. He was growing weaker. The pain in his head was unbearable. He swayed, ready to pass out.*

An instant later the oak door shattered. But the bar and hinges held. Benkai heard Kiichi urge the ninja to capture him and Saburo. It was Kiichi who screamed that he would have his revenge on Benkai for killing Saga.

The door flew off its hinges, and masked ninja rushed from the smoke filled hall and into the richly ornamented daimyo's quarters, knocking aside cedarwood folding screens, ivory carvings, and hand-carved redwood furniture. Kiichi was at their head. When he saw the kneeling Benkai, he shouted, "No honorable death for you! Blood for blood! Your life for Saga's!"

Benkai reached for the Muramasa. His strength was almost gone. Unless he lifted the blade, Kiichi would be the instrument of his death. A shameful, dishonorable death. And then he saw a screaming Asano rush by him, sword raised, attacking Kiichi, who was the better swordsman by far. Asano, who was sacrificing his life so that Benkai could end his own life with honor.

As the ninja silently watched Kiichi and Asano fence with all their skill, both men yelling to give themselves courage and make their spirit strong. But it was Kiichi who ended the match in dramatic fashion, charging Asano and faking an attack to the head, then ducking low and bringing his blade across Asano's stomach.

When Kiichi turned to look at Benkai, one of the masked ninja stepped forward and placed a hand on Kiichi's shoulder. He ordered Kiichi not to attack Benkai. A friend had just given his life so that Benkai could die honorably. The guard's sacrifice must not be in vain. Kiichi tore his arm free and rushed toward Benkai. Three armed ninja blocked his way. One menacingly raised a hand sickle, causing Kiichi to back up toward the door.

Ignoring the ninja, Benkai gripped the arrow with both hands and broke off the shaft, leaving the arrowhead in his *eye. Tossing the piece of bloodied wood aside, he picked up Saburo's long knife. Benkai's face was tight with pain, but he refused to cry out. Except for Kiichi, all watching had admiration for the bodyguard's courage.*

*Benkai said, "I will show you how a true warrior dies, willingly and at a time of his own choosing. And with my last breath I vow to return and punish he who has betrayed my master." He stared at Kiichi, who drew himself up and attempted to hold the bodyguard's gaze and in the end was forced to look away.*

*Then, without hesitation, Benkai picked up Saburo's long knife and, holding the handle with both hands, plunged the blade deep into his left side. He trembled but remained silent as he slowly drew the knife across his stomach to the right side, and in a show of courage beyond anything ever witnessed by the ninja or Kiichi, the bodyguard brought the blade slightly upward, in the cut called jumonji, one which only the most brave of samurai would ever consider doing.*

*Pausing for several seconds, he gathered all of his strength, then yanked the knife free, jammed the blood-red blade in his mouth, and fell facedown to the matted floor.*

*As astonished ninja watched unbelievingly, the skies darkened and lightning flashed wildly across the almost pitch-black sky. The castle was suddenly lashed by a cold rain and large hailstones, followed by an earthquake, which killed men and beasts and buildings. Fires and plague followed close upon the earthquake, and in less than forty-eight hours a third of Hideyoshi's great army was dead. The Iki-ryo, that most evil of spirits, was said to have exacted its revenge for the death of Benkai, the first of many such payments to be claimed in years to come.*

*Later Kiichi would sleep only in a lighted room, in a bed ringed by armed guards. Corridors in his castle had "nightingale floors," elaborately sprung floors that "sang," or squeaked, when stepped on, warning of an assassin's approach. Castle ceilings were hung with weighted nets, ready to fall down on Kiichi's enemies. There were trapdoors opening onto pits bristling with poisoned bamboo stakes, twisting corridors deliberately leading to dead ends, hidden springs that tripped off poisoned arrows. All designed to protect him against the return of Benkai, the Land Spider.*

Two years after he had betrayed Ikuka Castle, Kiichi, too, died by his own hand. He did not, however, choose the warrior's death of seppuku. He swallowed poison. It was, he admitted to a concubine, his only escape from Benkai and the Iki-ryo, both of whom came to him in dreams and gave him no peace.

*The unfinished tasks of past lifetimes.*

In his bedroom, Todd sat at his desk and finished tying his shoes. A digital clock in front of him read 11:09 P.M. He had to hurry. He must be in Chinatown before midnight. There was no question of anyone preventing him from going out at this late hour. His father was having dinner with a friend, and his stepmother, Jan, had recently moved to a hotel.

Todd stood up, walked to the closet, and crouched down. Reaching inside a brown leather boot, he removed a belt. He held it up in one hand and touched the small dark buckle. He began to shiver as though freezing. The buckle was made of metal from Benkai's Muramasa blade.

Todd slipped the belt through the loops of his jeans and fastened the buckle. Eyes closed, he stood unsteadily on his feet and trembled. Then, perspiring and breathing heavily, he dropped to his knees beside the bed, clutched at a pillow, then fell back on the floor. His body went rigid, and then his back arched and he collapsed. He lay quietly, and when his breathing had become normal, he pushed himself to his feet.

Walking to a window, he stared at the darkened East River and the lights of the Brooklyn Bridge. He stood without moving. His young face was impassive, his eyes unfeeling.

Then he left the apartment to begin the journey that would bring him face-to-face with Kiichi.

# Seven

DiPalma had come to Chinatown to repay a debt.

He was in a Mott Street restaurant, having dinner with Chief Inspector Martin Mackie of the Hong Kong Police Force, and the only other Caucasian in the late Sunday night crowd. Mackie had picked the place. The more Chinese in a restaurant, he told DiPalma, the better the food.

There'd been no crowds outside on the sidewalk waiting to get in. No plastic mock-ups in the window of food served inside. "Hopeful signs," said Mackie, who'd come directly to the restaurant from Kennedy Airport. In fluent Cantonese he'd asked the manager for a window table and the services of the best waiter on duty. A short conference on the menu, then he'd ordered beef with asparagus in brown bean sauce for himself and, for DiPalma, thin noodles in beef broth and a pot of green tea. Mackie rarely left any chance for refusal or denial.

Like all Chinatown restaurants in DiPalma's experience, this one was short on elegance and atmosphere. It was small and dark, with black Formica tables, ceiling fans, and a sawdusted floor. The patrons ranged from old Chinese grandmothers in long silk shirts to blue-jean and sneakered teens with crew cuts and tattooed forearms. Same crowd you'd find in my neck of the woods, Mackie told DiPalma.

All speaking and cursing in Cantonese, Shanghainese, Mandarin, and Thai, Mackie said, with Granny talking the foulest of anybody.

Martin Mackie was in his late sixties, a slender, long-faced Englishman whose ragged blond mustache hid a scarred mouth acquired in a Kowloon gun battle. In Hong Kong he worked with ICAC, the Independent Commission Against Corruption, which investigated police corruption. He was intelligent, tenacious, and because he detested loose ends, he wholeheartedly applied himself to the task at hand, refusing to back off until it was finished.

In time he came to believe that police work made a man rigid and narrow-minded if he wasn't that way already. What a bitter and fastidious little mister I turned out to be, he once told DiPalma. Never could rise above being outrageously self-righteous and dull, he said.

DiPalma had met him thirteen years ago in Hong Kong while recuperating from wounds suffered in the Nickie Mang shoot-out. As often happened with cops, a common profession had yielded an instant friendship. So when it was learned that friends of Nickie Mang were going to make a second try at killing DiPalma, Martin Mackie had gone to see Mang's people and warned them in no uncertain terms to drop the idea.

There'd been talk that Mackie himself might be killed for daring to threaten a Triad leader on behalf of a foreigner, even a fellow policeman. After all, the Triad leader had to save face, which meant dealing with this foreigner who'd killed several of his men. It was a Hong Kong DEA contact who later told DiPalma about the compromise that had saved his life.

The compromise: DiPalma would be allowed to live. But the price of his life was to be a small service to be performed by Martin Mackie for the Triad leader at some future date. If DiPalma was curious about the price of his life, he hadn't approached Mackie about it. For his part, the Englishman had volunteered nothing.

It was better that way, DiPalma decided. Hong Kong

police suffered from a systematic and organized corruption that had allowed the Triads to flourish for years. DiPalma decided there were things about the Englishman he was better off not knowing. Which is also why he hadn't bothered cross-examining Mackie thirteen years later when he'd telephoned to say he was coming to New York because he needed DiPalma's help.

In the Mott Street restaurant, DiPalma said to Martin Mackie, "A matter of life and death, you said."

"Mine, unfortunately. I've been warned to stop investigating a certain Manila factory fire or face permanent removal from this earth. The fire destroyed the Taaltex electronics plant some two weeks ago. Forty-five women burned to death. One was my goddaughter, Angela Ramos."

"I know about the fire. But I didn't know Angela Ramos was your goddaughter."

"You seemed to have heard of her."

"My wife, Jan, admired her. She thought Angela was a special woman for taking on the factory bosses in what seemed to be an impossible fight. The media here was just starting to pick up on her before she died. You saying the fire wasn't accidental?"

Martin Mackie said, "It was arson designed as a diversion. Forty-three young women burned alive to cover the murder of Angela Ramos and a computer operator named Elizabeth Kuan."

DiPalma said, "Who ordered Angela's killing?"

Martin Mackie said, "Lin Pao, a name familiar to all of us." Elizabeth Kuan had been about to give Angela Ramos a computer tape detailing Lin Pao's money-laundering arrangement with Taaltex Electronics, the American multinational. That's why Elizabeth Kuan and Angela Ramos had been killed.

DiPalma, thumb stroking the silver knob on his cane, said, "It's a small world," and mentioned a recent meeting with Gregory Van Rooten. Van Rooten, he told Mackie, had strongly hinted that his father, Nelson Berlin, was up to some dirty tricks in Manila. The same Nelson Berlin who owned Taaltex Electronics.

DiPalma looked through the window and across Mott Street at a noisy video-game arcade crowded with teenagers. He said, "Nelson Berlin and the Black General."

Mackie nodded. "The subject of more than a few rumors circulating throughout the Far East. The American captain of industry and the Triad leader. No official connection between the two, which doesn't mean they aren't in bed together."

"Lin Pao's threatened to take you out?"

"That he has. The bastard's become quite evil-tempered lately. Everything seems to have turned sour for him. Bad *joss*, we call it. He's lost gun and drug shipments. Lost some of his people in run-ins with rivals. One of his Sydney gambling houses got hit, and that cost him a bundle. I understand he was almost killed by a snow leopard he kept in his private zoo. Appears all his chickens have come home to roost at once. Never was the most stable of individuals. He would prefer I let this business of Angela and the fire remain undisturbed. That is something I cannot, and will not, do."

Martin Mackie reached for the teapot. "Anyway, I'm here to impose on you if I may. I figure if you can help me look into this fire, I might just live a little longer."

DiPalma said, "You mean Lin Pao wouldn't dare kill a journalist."

"That's how I see it, though you can never tell in which direction his crafty little mind will turn."

"Speaking of crafty little minds, you didn't have to fly ten thousand miles to ask my help.'"

"Meaning?"

"Meaning let's have the rest of the story."

Mackie sighed, reached into an inside jacket pocket, and removed a white envelope, which he handed to DiPalma. DiPalma peeked in the envelope but did not touch the contents.

Mackie said, "The watch is a Patek Philippe. It was found

at the fire, in the barracks where Angela and the others perished. Still in good condition. I was told it was protected from the flames by a toolbox. I managed to buy it from someone in the Manila Police Department.''

''You didn't tell me you'd been to Manila.''

''Didn't I? An oversight on my part, I assure you. Yes, I was there. Stopped by on my way here. Looked around, asked a few questions, and in general made a nuisance of myself before being asked to leave. It's all being covered up. The arson, Angela's murder, the Triad's relationship with Nelson Berlin. The Philippines is every bit as corrupt as it was under the Marcoses. Everything's being done to protect the foreign multinationals because they bring in the hard currency, you see. Thank God I have a bit of money put aside.''

DiPalma wondered how much money Mackie considered a bit. He'd heard of one Chinese police sergeant who'd left Hong Kong and retired to Canada with six hundred million American dollars. Any Hong Kong cop who wasn't stinking rich by retirement time just wasn't trying.

DiPalma fingered the second item in the envelope, a torn half of an American thousand-dollar bill. He could almost predict Mackie's next words.

The Englishman said, ''The man holding the other half of that bill is willing to turn over the tape containing the details of the money-laundering arrangement Lin Pao has going for him at Berlin's Manila factory.''

DiPalma said, ''You made contact with the guy. So why didn't you bring out the tape yourself?''

''Because, as I said, the rich own the Philippines now, just as they did under Ferdinand Marcos. Because they want this matter closed rather than have it scare off foreign multinationals. Because I was searched quite thoroughly before being allowed out of the country. Since I suspected this might happen, I decided it was wiser to leave the tape with the man who owns it. He'll hand it over at the proper time.''

''And just who is this man with the tape?''

''Raul Gutang. Works in the Taaltex computer department. Sought me out. Claims to be quite upset at what happened to Angela and the girls.''

DiPalma said, ''How much are you paying him for the tape?''

After a long time Mackie said, ''You'll find out, anyway, so I might as well tell you now. One hundred thousand American dollars.''

DiPalma thought, Now that is definitely a bit of money. He said, ''How did you get the watch out?''

Mackie smiled. ''Edgar Allan Poe. You know, hide in plain sight? I simply put it on my wrist and wore it out of the country. No one looked at it twice.''

The watch, he said, had been found in the barracks, where obviously it didn't belong to any woman making a dollar a day, or to any security guard, making only a bit more. A Manila cop remembered a robbery report filed by one George Mei, a Hong Kong businessman who claimed a similar watch had been stolen from him by a prostitute. A dwarf prostitute.

DiPalma tried not to grin. ''A dwarf prostitute?''

''Name's Huziyana de Vega. Lives in Manila's China-town with a Taaltex security guard named Leon Bacolod. Huziyana has denied any association with Mr. Mei. Came down to his word against hers, so nothing was ever done about the watch.''

''Think Bacolod left the watch in the barracks?'' DiPalma asked.

''As a security guard, Bacolod could come and go as he pleased. He has no record of arson, but that doesn't mean anything.''

''Means if he's a torch, he's a damn good one.''

When Mackie had been in Manila, Bacolod and the dwarf whore had been on holiday, so Mackie never got the chance to interrogate them. As for the computer tape, Raul Gutang hadn't been paid as yet. He had half the number of a Zurich bank account containing the one hundred thousand. The second half of the number was on the bill in DiPalma's hand. One half was no good without the other.

DiPalma said, "So you want me to go to Manila, check into the fire, and pick up the tape."

"Yes."

DiPalma stared down into his noodles. Mackie said, "By the way, what brought you and Van Rooten together? I was under the impression there was bad blood between you two."

When DiPalma said, "It's personal," Mackie nodded and patted his mustache.

DiPalma thought of Jan, the woman who was a mixture of darkness and light. Who was driven, self-centered, singularly ambitious. And who was kind, loyal, vulnerable. She'd helped DiPalma over the rough spots when he'd entered broadcasting. If he owed his television success to anyone, it was to her.

But he had to live with her dark side, her sexuality, something that in the past had led her into dangerous relationships with dangerous men. She knew these feelings could be destructive, and since her marriage she had fought against them. Both she and DiPalma had hoped this part of her life was in the past, that she had finally suppressed her dark side.

But then she'd become involved with a man who'd brought out that dark side in her once more, a man who could only drag her down. Not just any man, but Gregory Van Rooten. DiPalma wondered if Jan had ever been his to lose.

Yesterday he'd gotten the word from Buddy Bosco, a wireman who worked for the telephone company and moonlighted for a select few clients on the side. Buddy didn't come cheap, but he kept his mouth shut. It cost DiPalma a bundle to learn that Jan's suite at the Hotel Perigee on West Fifty-sixth Street in Manhattan was bugged. The sickly-looking, nail-biting Buddy, who didn't trust phones and preferred delivering reports in person, said he'd found ultra-miniature mikes in the phones, a bedroom closet, and sewn inside pillows on a living-room couch. He'd left them there.

Did DiPalma want he should find out who'd bugged the

room? DiPalma said no. Buddy Bosco had shrugged, spun on his heels, and walked away clutching an envelope of hundreds. Buddy preferred cash. Meanwhile, score one for Van Rooten. Jan was being watched by Nelson Berlin. Maybe on the orders of the Black General.

In the restaurant, Mackie said to DiPalma, "I'm about to pack it in. Retire to Florida. I have some beachfront property in Key Biscayne. Also own a seafood restaurant there and have an investment in a fishing fleet, among other things. Now's as good a time as any to begin enjoying my golden years."

There was a strain in his voice which hadn't been there seconds ago. DiPalma eyed him carefully. Mackie, concentrating on his food, used chopsticks to scoop rice from a small bowl onto the plate containing his beef. "Bloody Triads. They practically own Hong Kong. I'm getting tired of fighting them. Damn tired of it."

He put down the rice and chopsticks and said that there was currently an official police purge against homosexuals on the force. In Hong Kong such a purge was a serious matter, since the laws against homosexuality were barbarian to say the least. Buggery was a crime punishable by life imprisonment.

And as expected, the police purge was being conducted with typical British arrogance and bloody-mindedness.

Mackie said, "Lin Pao's behind it, of course. He's used his influence with the police force, which is considerable, to bring about this witch-hunt for gays. The whole point is to tie my hands, to stop me from looking into Angela's death."

Martin Mackie was a homosexual. That he was also an outstanding policeman wouldn't keep him out of prison if the fag-bashers were determined to get him.

Mackie said, "I've been asked the name of fellow officers or colony officials who are gay, and I've refused to cooperate. Now, you and I both know the Hong Kong police force is more than a bit corrupt, and I have made my share of compromises. But I'm no informant. I won't betray gays

I've served with, nor will I rat on any gay members of Hong Kong's ruling class. I've a bit of honor left, and I'd like to cling to it, if I can.''

He said that if DiPalma looked into the Manila fire and publicized his findings, it might just give Angela the justice she deserved. The communists, who were getting ready to take over Hong Kong, didn't like negative publicity of any kind. Especially negative publicity that might keep away American business technology and cold cash, both of which were badly needed. DiPalma's involvement alone could mean an end to the fag-bashing.

Martin Mackie, waiting for DiPalma's reaction, eyed him unblinkingly. When DiPalma finally put the white envelope inside his jacket, a relieved Mackie slumped back in his chair and looked out at Mott Street. He said, ''Did you know that Lin Pao owns this restaurant? Fact is, he owns this entire block. Every doorknob, pane of glass, and stitch of carpet.''

DiPalma said, ''I understand Pao owns the biggest casino in Las Vegas.''

Mackie nodded. The ownership was hidden behind a maze of companies, but yes, it was true. Pao's money had also found its way into American films, fast-food franchises, automobile dealerships, and soft-drink bottling companies. The Black General was the soul of business.

Mackie said, ''Then there is the other Lin Pao, the one who seems to enjoy destroying anyone who stands in his way. That's the Lin Pao who's let it be known that Van Rooten isn't going to live much longer. Speaking of violent men, I can pick out a half dozen or so of Pao's Triad members in this restaurant. Seen their ugly faces in Hong Kong a few times. Daresay they recognize you too. Can't be too happy about my talking to the American press.''

DiPalma said, ''You hear anything about a big meeting coming up in Hong Kong between Triad leaders?''

''I'm impressed. Did this come from Van Rooten?''

DiPalma nodded.

Mackie said, ''Yes, we've heard rumors about a so-called

super meeting. But that's all it's been so far, just rumors. We're still looking into it. Lin Pao's supposed to be the organizer. Apparently he feels it's better to work things out at the conference table than shoot it out on the battlefield. Theoretically he has a point, what with the communists about to take over and the Triads forced to look for greener pastures. Criminals can grow rich here in America, providing police attention's kept to a minimum. The idea of compromise by Triad leaders has been kicked around for years, but no one's been able to pull it off.''

''Van Rooten says it's a go. Says it's definitely going to happen.''

''We'll have to look into that. I suppose if Lin Pao is to parade among his peers as the great bloody statesman, he first has to kill Van Rooten. Pao has to show he's at least in charge of his own house. Anything else of note from your Mr. Van Rooten?''

''He mentioned something about Nelson Berlin, Berlin's sister, and China. Said Berlin did it. What the hell did he mean by that?''

''I would suppose he's saying Nelson Berlin killed his sister when they were in China during World War II. Trouble is, this is old news as far as rumors go. And there's been no evidence to back it up. In any case, another man was executed for the crime.''

''Was he guilty, this other guy?''

''The Chinese apparently felt he was. They executed him. He was an American, by the way. A godforsaken missionary. I'd like to ask your Mr. Van Rooten what he knows about his bloody father's role in Angela's murder.''

DiPalma picked at his noodles. ''You have to wonder how a Nelson Berlin ends up in business with a dirt bag like Lin Pao.''

''China. The war. No rules. Anything goes. A war is a most exciting time.''

Mackie leaned back in his chair, eyes half closed, remembering. ''Met Angela's father, Manuel, in the Philippines just after the war. I'd gone there in 1947, with the

British team attending Japanese war-crime trials. Manuel Ramos was assigned as my driver and personal aide. He eventually became my friend. Stayed in touch over the years, we did. Felt quite honored when he asked me to be godfather to his first child. Ah, those first days after the war. Truly the best of times and the worst of times. One day we're hearing testimony about the Japs eating the flesh of Allied prisoners and the next day we're as drunk as lords on cheap rum and out in the hills digging for buried treasure the Japs were supposed to have had hidden away. Everything I know about Asia stems from those rather hectic two years with Manuel. Marvelous times. Bloody marvelous times.'' Mackie leaned closer to the window. "I say, over there. Looks a bit like Benjy. By God, that's who it is. Benjy Lok Nein.''

DiPalma looked at a crowd of teenage Chinese boys that had gathered in front of the video arcade. Mackie pointed out Benjy Lok Nein to him. Sixteen years old, husky, and handsome in a studded black leather jacket, jeans, running shoes. Leader of the Jade Eagles, a Chinese youth gang with a much-earned reputation for violence. Lin Pao's little tigers, Mackie said. Pao points, and they do the clawing and biting. Benjy's quite the lad, Mackie said. A born leader, killer, extortionist. Also an accomplished martial artist, not to mention something of a ladies' man.

Mackie said, "Years ago we put him in a holding cell with an adult. Just overnight, you understand. But the adult decided that a pretty young boy like Benjy was heaven-sent, so he decided to rape him. Bear in mind that the adult was a hardened criminal, a very large and sadistic hardened criminal. Well, the next morning, the guard looks into the cell and this hardened criminal is lying on the floor dead with a broken neck. Benjy, meanwhile, is lying on his bunk, hands behind his neck, peacefully staring up at the ceiling. He was asked what happened. His reply was he'd been asleep and had no idea what had happened. Of course, we couldn't prove a damn thing. Truth is, Benjy had broken the bugger's neck.''

DiPalma said, "Looks like a meeting's about to get under way."

"The Jade Eagles. Toughest lot in your Chinatown. Benjy's the biggest villain of them all. Every Hong Kong street kid's heard of him. They dream of coming to America and following in his footsteps. Well now, what have we here?"

DiPalma said, "What do you see?"

"If I didn't know better, I'd swear they've been waiting for this chap to show up. That rather thin lad who just joined the party. The one in the light-colored leather jacket. Jesus, they're all hanging on his every word. Never thought I'd live to see the day when Benjy submitted to anybody. He's doing everything but tugging at his forelock and kissing that little bugger's ring." Still staring through the window, Mackie said, "New lad's smaller than most of them, but the way they're listening to him, you'd think he's an incarnation of Buddha. I say, isn't he—"

DiPalma recognized him too. Before Mackie could finish the sentence, DiPalma was on his feet and heading toward the door. The boy to whom Benjy and the others were listening so intently was Todd.

# Eight

It was past midnight when Todd led Benjy Lok Nein and three Jade Eagles into the dirty, shadowy basement of the Elizabeth Street massage parlor owned by the Hundred Pacer Snakes.

Ivan Ho, backed by a broad-shouldered Triad member in a dark green leather cap and matching coat, watched the youngsters line up, facing them across a battered, abandoned pool table. His attention was drawn to Todd, whom he'd not seen before. *Odd little duck,* Ho thought. *Doesn't seem nervous at being around us tough guys. Carries himself like some kind of prince. But he shouldn't be here, since he isn't a Jade Eagle, and that's something to take up with Mr. Benjy.* Ho instantly disliked the boy. The little bastard seemed too fucking sure of himself.

For several seconds no one spoke as Ivan Ho and Todd stared at each other. Benjy zipped his jacket, then placed his hands palms-down on a pool cue lying on the dusty table. Seconds later he slowly began rolling the cue back and forth. Another Jade Eagle reached into a table pocket, removed the cue ball, and tossed it from hand to hand.

Finally Ivan Ho grew tired of waiting and said in Cantonese, "Benjy, you want to tell me why you brought this new puppy to the meeting without clearing it with me first? I don't like the way he eyeballs people. Too disrespectful. Get your little friend out of here before I hurt him. Then you can tell me why you insisted on getting together at this time of night. What's this big emergency you couldn't talk about over the phone?"

Benjy, still not looking up, continued toying with the pool cue.

Ivan Ho said, "Benjy, I'm talking to you. You wanted a discussion, so let's discuss. But first the new puppy goes, and I mean now."

Todd, also speaking in Cantonese, said, "I ordered Benjy to bring you here."

Ivan Ho frowned. "What did you say?"

Todd continued staring at him.

An angry Ivan Ho ran a hand through his short black hair, looked up at the ceiling, then whispered to the broad-shouldered man on his left. The man grinned. Elder Brother was about to put on a show. Punish and penalize. First the little boy with the woman's eyes, then Benjy. Benjy and his little friend had to be reminded not to play jokes on Elder Brother.

Ivan Ho, eyes bulging more than usual, aimed a forefinger at Benjy. "Your little friend's too dumb to know better. But you have no excuse. You drag me over here in the middle of the night because he tells you to? If this gets around, people are going to say I can't control you guys. Then I lose respect here in Chinatown. I won't be able to show my face on the streets. So now I got to teach you to have reverence for your older brother. And you will never, do you understand, never again bring a stranger to a meeting without my permission."

Todd said, "You are not worthy of respect. You have betrayed those who trusted you. Sam Liu, Joey Liu, Elvis Chan. You helped murder them."

Ivan Ho's head snapped back as though he'd been struck in the face.

Todd inched along the pool table to his right, with Benjy

and the others clearing a path for him. When he reached the end of the table, Todd stopped. He said, "Last night Peter Chen and Bing Fong were murdered upstairs. You will tell Benjy and the others why you are betraying the Jade Eagles."

Fists clenched, Ivan Ho nodded several times and forced himself to breathe deeply. Had Todd physically attacked him without warning, Ho would not have been upset. But strong verbal attacks, particularly when true, always left him momentarily overwhelmed. The reaction stemmed from childhood, when schoolmates had taunted him because his crazy mother had strangled his two sisters after first biting out their tongues.

Now, as he faced Benjy's little friend, Ivan Ho reminded himself that he didn't have to be pushed around by children anymore. Now he could deal with them as he fucking well pleased.

He spoke to Benjy. "I'd heard you'd found yourself a little playmate. A real pretty boy. What's the matter, you don't like girls anymore? I thought you liked girls, Benjy."

Ho removed his jacket and tie, then handed them to the broad-shouldered man. He said to Todd, "So you're blaming me for what happened to Sam and Joey and Elvis and the rest of the boys. Well, for openers, the Jade Eagles' business don't concern you. I don't have to account to you for nothing. Next, I don't like being accused of murdering my own people. It's bad for my image. I had nothing to do with what happened to the boys."

Todd said, "You're a liar."

Ho grinned. "Well, we'll see about that. You and me, we're gonna put on a show, and when it's over, you are gonna be one sad little puppy. You won't ever call me a liar again. You got my word on that."

Still grinning, Ho rolled up his sleeves. He'd almost finished when a small man with gelled hair, gold front teeth, and wearing a fake fur jacket ran into the basement, rushed up to Ho, and whispered in his ear. When the man finished,

Ho nodded and the newcomer positioned himself beside the broad-shouldered man in green leather.

Ho said, "Seems we have a little problem. Woo, here, tells me that a few minutes ago he was in the Golden Pheasant and he sees some TV reporter leave in a hurry and run out in the street after you guys. You managed to lose him, and I suppose I should be thankful for that. I hear he ran down Mott Street, yelling, 'Todd, Todd.' Guess that's you, little brother."

Ho turned to Benjy. "See what I mean when I say keep away from strangers? This little bastard you brought here is connected to Frank DiPalma, and if DiPalma starts poking around our affairs, we got problems. How do we know that Todd, or whatever he calls himself, isn't a spy? Maybe he plans to join the gang, then expose us to Mr. DiPalma. I think he knows more than he should, particularly about what's happening with our boys."

All of the Jade Eagles, except for Benjy, backed away from the pool table and into the shadows, detaching themselves from Benjy and his new friend. Elder Brother was ready to punish and penalize. It was best not to be too close to his victims.

Ho walked slowly toward Todd. "You and me, little brother. Let's put on a show."

Todd grabbed the pool cue and smashed it against the table edge. Half the cue went flying off into the darkness, landing near the boiler. Eyes almost closed, Todd inched away from the table and toward Ho. The broken cue was in his right hand, low and away from his body.

Ivan Ho had trained in *choy-li-fat*, the fighting style which combined the quick footwork of northern kung fu with the power found in southern styles of fighting. *Choy-li-fat* included training in long and short weapons—staff, spear, trident, cane, knife, war fan, short sword. Ho also carried a butterfly knife in his back pocket. This scrawny boy standing in front of him with a broken pool cue was a joke.

Ho had indeed helped the Eight Knives of the North to kill the Jade Eagles. Orders from the Black General were not to be questioned. If Lin Pao wanted the Jade Eagles' heads hacked off and brought to him in dry ice, so be it. When Ivan Ho had tried to learn why, he'd gotten nowhere. The answer to this strange business lay within the Black General's mind. Those willing to discuss it would only say that Lin Pao was mentally unbalanced about this matter and wanted it finished within twenty-one days.

In the basement, Ho kicked low to Todd's shin. He was prepared to follow that up with the *sow,* the roundhouse punch that was the knockout blow of *choy-li-fat.* But his kick did not land. Nor was he given the opportunity to punch.

Moving faster than any fighter Ho had ever faced, Todd stepped right and struck the kneecap of Ho's attacking leg with a blow so forceful that Ho screamed and grabbed the pool table to keep from going down.

His back was to Todd, who struck him in the right thigh, then in the kidney. Again Ho screamed, spinning around with his back arched and his hands still clinging to the table, and that's when Todd, his warrior's yell filling the basement, drove the thick end of the pool cue into Ho's stomach, folding him in half and dropping him to the floor. A second later Ho threw up.

For long seconds those in the basement could not accept what they'd just seen. No one had ever defeated Ivan Ho. Yet it had just happened, and the defeat had been total. Shockingly unexpected. The only sound in the basement was Ho's labored breathing as he sat on the floor with his back against the pool table, his black shirt and trousers stained with vomit. With both hands he squeezed the muscles above his pained knee and tried to deal with the worst moment of his life. Not only would this moment bring him great shame, but unless he was very, very lucky, it could also cost him his life.

The broad-shouldered man in green leather shook his head disbelievingly. Then he reacted, jamming his hand inside his coat. Benjy, however, was faster. His hands left the pool table, and an instant later he yanked an Uzi from under his jacket. He barked a command in Cantonese and the other Jade Eagles drew pistols. All guns were aimed at the two Triad members, who slowly raised their hands.

Jamming the sharp end of the broken cue into Ho's throat, Todd said, "Are you helping to kill the Jade Eagles?"

Ho nodded.

Todd said, "Tell them."

"Yes, I am helping the Eight Knives of the North to carry out Lin Pao's orders."

"Tell them why."

"I don't know why. I swear on my dead mother that this is true. I know only that Pao fears them. He fears Benjy the most. That's why the others are dying first. Pao wants to isolate Benjy."

"You mean, if he killed Benjy first, then the others would unite to avenge him?"

"Yes."

Todd threw the broken cue on the pool table. He said to Ho, "Tell the Black General that he changed nothing by killing the snow leopard and the priest. He must pay for the evil he has committed in this life, and in other lives as well. The snow leopard was a signal that the gods have turned their faces away from him. Tell him the priest spoke the truth."

Ivan Ho felt his abdomen. The pain was incredible. No one had ever hit him this hard. Not in training, not in full-contact matches, not in gang fights. He must tell the Triad about this boy. The Black General must be warned. This Todd was the boy to be feared. Todd, who fought like a demon. How could anyone, man or boy, fight in such fashion and be human?

Todd said, "Tell Lin Pao that before twenty-one days have passed, Benkai will come for him."

Then he stepped over Ho and walked toward the exit. Benjy, his Uzi aimed at the Triad members, was the last to back out of the basement.

• • •

Upstairs in the massage parlor, Todd knocked twice on a door in the middle of a dim, smelly hallway. After waiting a few seconds he knocked twice more. Behind him, Benjy, the Uzi still cradled in his arms, served as lookout. Benjy also listened for the sound of anyone coming up the stairs. But all he heard were noises from the rooms around him: a cassette recorder playing a George Benson tape, a whore singing softly in Mandarin, a man cursing because he'd come too soon.

Benjy was listening for the Triad members, who were on their way here to kill him and Todd. A telephone call from Ho and a dozen shooters would be through the front door in minutes. The sooner Benjy and Todd got the hell out of here, the better.

Todd wasn't here for sex; that much was sure. Then what was he doing in the hallway when he should have been miles away from Chinatown? Benjy didn't know. All he knew was that he had to stick with Todd even if it cost him his life.

Because of Todd, the gang now knew who was killing them. Fighting back, however, wouldn't be easy. This time they weren't taking on another youth gang, bullying a restaurant owner into giving them free meals, or shaking down some old storekeeper. The Triad and the Eight Knives of the North were heavy-duty opponents, the kind even governments couldn't fight. And add Ivan Ho to the Jade Eagles' enemies, providing Lin Pao let him live after his humiliation by Todd.

Elder Brother was a sick bastard. Even Benjy was afraid of him. Ho wouldn't rest until he'd revenged himself on Todd. Benjy grinned. Elder Brother's respect for Todd had probably risen a bit.

Benjy had seen Todd's secret training sessions. The kid was awesome, his fighting spirit unreal. Benjy couldn't compare him to anyone he'd seen or heard of. The two had worked out once or twice, short sticks and long sticks. Benjy had gotten his ass stomped each time.

He'd also watched Todd work out with a knife and decided then and there never to go after the kid with a blade. Not unless he wanted to die quick, fast, and in a hurry. Nothing, however, had prepared Benjy for what he'd seen Todd do to Elder Brother.

Todd was in another league. Hell, he was from another planet. He was out of his class fighting other kids. Anyone who could beat Ivan Ho qualified as a Red Pole, a Triad enforcer. Benjy couldn't think of a single adult fighter who could stand up to Todd. A thirteen-year-old Red Pole. Put that in *The Guinness Book of World Records*.

Meanwhile the Jade Eagles who'd come to the massage parlor with Benjy were running for their lives. He'd ordered them to warn other gang members about Lin Pao's treachery, then find somewhere to hide. Forget about their old apartments. Everybody had to disappear. Their protectors—the Black General, the Triad, and Ivan Ho were now their enemies. And so were the Eight Knives of the North, creepy killers who scared Benjy shitless.

So why was he still in the massage parlor? Because Todd was a special friend. Todd, whom he'd known for less than two weeks. Who'd made him believe in their friendship, one that had begun over four hundred years ago. Their minds and souls were joined in ways Benjy could feel yet not fully understand. Turn his back on Todd and Benjy was throwing away his own life.

In the hallway, the room door opened and the teenage girl, Joan, stood in front of Todd and Benjy. She wore a cheap cloth coat, white fur hat and boots, and carried a single suitcase. Benjy thought, Very, very nice. Taiwanese by the look of her. An FOB. Fresh off the boat. Benjy would love to party with this sweet young thing.

But she was with Todd, so forget about it. Keep your pants zipped, Benjy boy. How the hell had she and Todd gotten together? She couldn't have been in America more than a few days. Then again, Todd wasn't normal.

Taking the girl away from here would bring the Triad down on them for sure. She was its property, and no one stole from the ancient society and lived.

Why did Todd want the girl? Benjy only hoped to live long enough to find out.

Suddenly he looked toward the staircase. Footsteps. Not a guy casually walking toward one of the whore's rooms but several men running up the stairs. All of them in a hurry. There were no secrets in Chinatown. As long as Benjy and Todd were down here, there'd be no place to hide. Suddenly Benjy was frightened. But then he looked at Todd and his fear eased.

Benjy said, "Let's go," and led the way along the hall, toward a rear window and a fire escape that would take them to the roof.

Behind them, the sound of rushing footsteps filled the hallway. When he heard the crack of gunfire, Benjy stopped and let the others rush past him. He was about to turn and fire when he felt a bullet hit his back.

# Nine

Frank DiPalma lived on the top two floors of a Brooklyn Heights brownstone, which overlooked New York Harbor and the southern tip of Manhattan. He preferred the peace of Brooklyn to the pretentiousness of Manhattan, a place, he told Jan, where the waiters called you shit head and expected a twenty-percent tip.

The brownstone was located on Cranberry Street, an area with the charm and coziness of a New England town. It had been built during Lincoln's presidency and was in a landmark district. Nothing in the area could be demolished or changed without the Landmark Preservation commission's consent.

We're safe from real-estate developers, Jan told DiPalma.

DiPalma's duplex had high ceilings, a spiral staircase, and four white-stone fireplaces. The top-floor bedroom, his reason for renting the flat, offered a spectacular night view of freighters, tourist boats, garbage scows, and sailboats passing under the lights of the Brooklyn and Manhattan bridges. Since Jan had left, DiPalma spent nights alone in the bedroom, sitting in a rocking chair and looking at the lights of Manhattan, where Jan was now living.

It was almost six in the evening when the plump, fifty-five-year-old Mrs. Velez, his Dominican housekeeper, knocked on the bedroom door and said, *La señora está aqui*. Jan was back. At the same time Mrs. Velez announced she was leaving for the day. She was returning to Manhattan to help clean a Wall Street brokerage house before going home to cook for a husband and six children.

The job at the brokerage house had prompted Mrs. Velez to become a small, but careful, investor. It had also convinced her that she was an authority on the stock market, an assumption DiPalma felt free to question. His portfolio of blue chips had been put together by experts, leaving him free to ignore Mrs. Velez' fiscal counsel. Then came last year's crash, correctly predicted by Mrs. Velez almost to the week. DiPalma had lost almost fifty thousand dollars and now wondered if he shouldn't be listening to Mrs. Velez, even if her financial know-how was based on the contents of office wastebaskets.

On her way out of the flat, Mrs. Velez ignored Jan, whom she'd disliked from their first meeting two years ago. *La señora* was too clever, too easily bored, too intent on having her way, and, perhaps worst of all, too skinny to really please a man. It wasn't Mrs. Velez' place to say these things to Mr. DiPalma, so she expressed her opinion by snubbing Jan whenever possible while being endlessly polite to DiPalma.

When Jan showed up this evening after being away two weeks, Mrs. Velez let her in without a word. Then she announced Jan's presence to DiPalma and left the flat, wondering why he didn't kick his wife out on her ass. A man and his wife should think together. Mrs. Velez could only wonder how much longer Mr. DiPalma would continue playing the fool around this skinny bitch.

DiPalma walked into the living room, where he found Jan looking into the fireplace, a cigarette in her long fingers. She was a tall, long-nosed woman in her late thirties, with green eyes and auburn hair, recently touched up to hide the first signs of gray. She wore a cream-colored blouse, a long rust-colored suede skirt, matching boots, and a wide tan belt. A cameo brooch was pinned at her throat. As DiPalma drew nearer, Jan tossed her cigarette into a dying fire.

She turned to face him. "When do you leave?"

"Day after tomorrow," DiPalma said. "We fly to San Francisco, then nonstop to Manila."

"We?"

"Todd and a couple of his friends. It's a long story."

A long story. Last night Todd had shown up with a teenager hooker and a baby-faced Chinese kid who carried an Uzi. According to Martin Mackie, Kid Uzi worked for Lin Pao and had whacked eleven people. DiPalma was all for kicking the hooker and Kid Uzi out on their Oriental behinds. But Todd had wanted them to stay, and stay they had.

Jan shivered. "You're saying Todd's been possessed by Benkai again."

DiPalma rubbed the back of his neck. "I'm the hard-nosed cop. Twenty years working vice. Seen it all, done it all, right? If someone were to come up to me and tell me about a kid who turns into a four-hundred-year-old samurai warrior, I'd call him feebleminded and would hustle the bastard off to the rubber room. But, Christ, it's true. Other than you, who the hell else can I talk to about this?"

Closing her eyes, Jan thought of what happened the last time Todd became Benkai. Two years ago she'd had an affair with a Japanese film director who'd turned out to be one very lethal individual. He'd been the protégé of a wealthy Japanese businessman whose industrial espionage ring had stolen hundreds of American business secrets. Together they had been responsible for several murders. Jan had involved herself with a madman.

She'd discovered one or two other things about the director and the industrialist she shouldn't have. Frank, the good reporter and good cop, went on to discover even more. Possessed by Benkai's spirit, Todd had killed to save their lives. And he'd done it with a cold-bloodedness that had made Jan sick to her stomach. Unable to control the ancient spirit that had overpowered him, Todd had even attempted to kill Frank.

In the living room, Jan said to DiPalma, "When Benkai appears, someone dies. Don't let it be you. For God's sake, don't let it be you." She hurried to him, and he took her in his arms. "I love you," she said. DiPalma held her close and kissed her hair. And since he wanted to believe her, he said, "I love you, too, Jan." He remembered his father's words: *You love a woman or you know her. There is no middle way.*

In life as well as in love, DiPalma rarely saw a middle ground. As a teenager, he'd attended high school and worked in his father's produce market, while being the starting center on the school's football team during a thirty-game winning streak. Two years of college bored him to the point where he notified his draft board to call him up so he could get his army service over with.

Looking for excitement, he worked his way into the Criminal Investigation Division and was assigned to Berlin. Most of his cases involved Southern boys who were too lonely, too bored, and too fucking stupid to stay out of trouble. DiPalma worked on drug crimes, sex crimes, on thefts of Army property. On psychos who killed their officers and white racists who firebombed black bars. Moderation did not appeal to the criminal military mind. DiPalma survived only by making himself feared and respected.

He returned to New York after finishing his tour, having grown to dislike Southerners and the army's criminal-justice system, which he considered out-of-date and one-sided. He married a girl he'd known fifteen years and who'd written him twenty letters a month during the eighteen months he was out of the country. With only his army experience to offer prospective employers, he joined the police force, where during his twenty-year career he killed six perpetrators and lost three partners, as well as his wife and daughter. Because so many people died around him, he was called the Albatross and Mr. Departure. Among Hispanics, his street name was *Muerte,* death.

His specialty was narcotics, which in time he came to
see as more than just a growth industry. It was unstoppable
because it was unbelievably lucrative. Americans were
spending more money on illegal drugs than on food, sex,
medical care, new clothes, cars, education. All over the
world, traffickers were killing cops, district attorneys, and
judges when they couldn't bribe or intimidate them.

For DiPalma, that wasn't the worst of it. The worst was
learning that American intelligence agencies were assisting
traffickers with guns, money, and information—and doing
it for the same bullshit reason they did everything else,
namely national security. Law enforcement was fighting the
drug war while the CIA was promoting it by backing the
traffickers in return for intelligence and political influence.
DiPalma, who'd lost his wife and child to traffickers, decided there was no percentage in continuing to fail consis-
tently. Since compromise was out of the question, he retired
from the police force with a detective lieutenant's pension,
thirty-four commendations, and a left leg shredded by a
shotgun blast and reconstructed with muscles from his right
buttock.

He got a job as a television crime reporter through the
influence of a New York senator, whose seventeen-year-
old daughter had had a problem until DiPalma had burned
the negative and all copies of a porn film she'd made with
a black boyfriend and other home boys while high on angel
dust. What DiPalma lacked in media experience, he made
up for in honesty, wit, and, according to the fan mail from
women, sex appeal. He drew on past sources of information,
which included wise guys, politicians, men he'd served with
on DEA and FBI task forces, foreign diplomats, Latin
American call girls, Justice Department lawyers, and three-
card monte dealers. The results were high ratings, big bucks,
awards for journalistic excellence, and a spacious office he
rarely visited, since he preferred working the streets.

He refused to dye his hair for the camera or take speech
lessons to eliminate the Brooklyn in his voice. Nor would
he wear horn-rimmed glasses and a vest and smile on camera

unless he fucking felt like smiling. He'd walked out of meetings rather than discuss the proposed changes. Then the network honchos quickly came to see he didn't need them, so they left him alone. And also came to want him all the more.

At the network he'd met Jan, who'd been in charge of all series and made-for-television movies in New York. A failed marriage and a career as a failed actress had pushed her into becoming a producer. She was good at her job, but did she enjoy it? "I'll give you a definite maybe on that," she told DiPalma. "Someone once called filmmaking a kind of hysterical pregnancy. In any event, as long as educational standards remain low, I think I'll continue to get by."

They fell in love almost on sight, enjoying what Jan called a desperate madness. Beneath her ambition and ego she was vulnerable and quite kind. She was honest, with passions that leapt from love to hate and back again. By her own admission, her biggest failing was persisting in her mistakes, especially where they concerned men. DiPalma found her irresistible.

Her advice on dressing for the camera and dealing with network executives made him slightly more relaxed in a world in which he could never truly be at ease. It was his turn to help when a network vice president threatened to fire Jan unless she started sleeping with him. At DiPalma's suggestion she agreed to meet the vice president at a Madison Avenue hotel where the network kept a luxury suite.

DiPalma showed up in her place, setting his licensed .38 Smith & Wesson on the coffee table within reach of the vice president, whose eyes went exceedingly wide at seeing the piece. DiPalma thought, A fucking civilian who's never seen a loaded gun in his life. Shouldn't be hard to raise this guy's consciousness. DiPalma said to the terrified vice president, "Let's talk about Jan."

DiPalma also agreed to talk with Jan's ex-husband, Roy Pesta, who had an expensive cocaine habit and wanted Jan to help pay for it. If she refused, he was going to throw acid in her face. Even without nose candy, Roy had a quick temper; during his one year marriage to Jan he'd broken her nose, ribs, and left thumb. Not too surprisingly, she took this latest threat seriously. But DiPalma said, Pay him and you'll never get rid of the bastard. He'll come back every time he's strung out, or dealers get on his ass to pay what he owes. DiPalma said, I'll talk to him.

A Houston Street apartment that Roy Pesta shared with an unemployed dancer named America Coco was a pigsty with broken windows, dog shit on the floor, and no furniture. Tanned, handsome Roy Pesta, who once knew every headwaiter in Manhattan and could shuffle a deck of cards with one hand, was living the consequence of too much flake. Flake had also made him unruly, if not downright dangerous.

He gave DiPalma the finger, saying, "Split that between you and my fucking ex-wife." Then he cursed Jan, told DiPalma he hated dagos, and finally unzipped his fly and urinated perilously close to DiPalma's shoes. When DiPalma called him an asshole, Pesta attacked him with a rusty waffle iron. DiPalma, using his cane, broke Pesta's right wrist and gave him a hairline skull fracture. Which still didn't stop Roy Pesta from coming out ahead on the deal.

His lawyer and DiPalma's lawyer sat down, and when they finished, the best DiPalma could get was a deal calling for him to pay Pesta's medical bills and kick in five thousand dollars besides. Forget self-defense, DiPalma's lawyer said. America Coco's ready to go into court and swear you attacked Pesta without provocation. Nor did it help matters that DiPalma was sleeping with Pesta's ex-wife. DiPalma paid the five thou, which got Pesta and America Coco to Houston, where one Sunday afternoon Pesta, wired on crack, grabbed a screwdriver and stabbed America Coco eighty-eight times.

If Jan was inexplicable and sensual, DiPalma was faithful and earnest, a persevering man forced by his nature to pursue the woman who fled from him even while she lay in his arms and told him she loved him. She warned him of her restlessness, that she was fighting with herself every moment of her life. DiPalma, she said, was the first man she'd met who was stronger than she and this was either the best or the worst thing that had ever happened to her.

DiPalma said, "Do you love me?"

She said, "Yes, I feel safe with you. I wish I could promise I'll never hurt you, but I can't. God forgive me, but I can't."

Remembering that in love there was no middle ground, DiPalma asked her to marry him, and when she said yes, he told her that he had known no greater happiness in his life.

In his Brooklyn Heights living room, DiPalma handed a Dewars on the rocks to Jan, who gripped the drink without taking her eyes from Todd. She and the boy sat together on a velvet-covered sofa, Todd talking quietly while a silent Jan hung on his every word. "Let Todd tell his story," DiPalma said. The kid had lived with this thing for over four hundred years, so who knew it better.

DiPalma sat in a wicker armchair as Todd told Jan of the connection between himself and Lin Pao. The boy spoke of when he had been Benkai and his greatest enemy had been Kiichi, military commander for Saburo, Benkai's lord. Kiichi had betrayed Saburo, causing his magnificent castle to be destroyed and its inhabitants to be slaughtered.

Kiichi had also murdered the captain of Saburo's guards, a brave and honorable man named Asano. Asano, Benkai's closest friend, had been reborn in this life as Benjy Lok Nein, a young Chinese. A slave girl belonging to Benkai and murdered four hundred years ago by Kiichi in a jealous rage had come into this life as a Taiwanese girl named Joan. The gods had decided that Todd, Benjy, and Joan must now revenge themselves upon Kiichi who in this life was called Lin Pao.

As warriors, Todd and Benjy must fulfill their duty to Saburo and punish Kiichi for his treachery. Honor demanded that they pursue the cause of loyalty until the gods were satisfied. The gods would not be satisfied, Todd said, until those sworn to protect Saburo had avenged him.

Joan's duty was to herself. She must learn correct judgment, to do what was right without hesitating. Revenging herself on Kiichi would enforce her sense of what was morally correct. She would develop a concern for right reason and the courage to exercise correct judgment.

DiPalma said the three youngsters would be accompanying him to Manila, where he was to get proof that Nelson Berlin was washing money for Lin Pao. And he told Jan about his promise to Martin Mackie: that he would look into the Manila fire which had killed Angela Ramos and dozens of other Filipinas.

Jan said, "And my hotel suite being bugged is a part of this?"

DiPalma nodded. "Yes. Berlin thinks Van Rooten told you about him and Lin Pao. As you know, Van Rooten and his father don't like each other, so it figures Greg would try to stick it to his old man."

Jan looked into her drink. "Gregory told me nothing. I wouldn't know Lin Pao if I tripped over him. When it comes to Nelson Berlin, I know he's a short little man who's a lot taller when he stands on his money. I also know he's a prick to work for. Look, don't get me wrong. I'm well aware that Gregory's a son of a bitch who used me to get back at you. I could slit my wrists every time I think about it. But he never took me into his confidence. Believe me, if I knew anything that could give him sleepless nights, I'd gladly pass it on. By the way, when do I get to meet Benjy and Joan?"

DiPalma said, "In a few minutes. They're upstairs. Benjy's resting in Todd's room, and Joan's got the guest bedroom. Benjy was shot last night by some of Lin Pao's men. Bullet creased his back but didn't penetrate his body or break any bones. Todd's nursing him."

DiPalma thought about last night, about him chasing Todd, Benjy, and the others down Mott Street. It had been no contest; the kids were doing it on young legs and Di-

Palma's wheels weren't what they used to be. Ahead of him, the kids turned right off on Elizabeth Street, taking the corner with the speed of an Olympic relay team. By the time DiPalma reached the corner, Todd and his crew were nowhere to be seen. An exhausted DiPalma felt half dead, which, for a middle-aged man, was half true, unfortunately.

At three in the morning, when Todd returned home with a wounded Benjy and a young Chinese girl, DiPalma was waiting for him. Waiting for Todd to explain why he'd been hanging out with Benjy Lok Nein, who killed people on behalf of Lin Pao. Todd's eyes were blazing. Explanations could wait, he said. Benjy needed care.

Todd took Benjy to his own room, then turned him over on his stomach and slid his thumbs along Benjy's spine until the bleeding in Benjy's side stopped. Then Todd took roots and bark from a suitcase beneath his bed, boiled them, and applied it to Benjy's wound. He brewed *kuko*, a tea he'd successfully prescribed for DiPalma's upset stomach, and forced Benjy to drink two cups. Only after Benjy fell asleep did Todd sit down and talk to DiPalma.

On the surface, the tale of Benkai and Kiichi was too implausible to be believed. But the story was coming from Todd, meaning DiPalma had no choice but to believe it. Just as Todd had no choice about being possessed by Benkai. DiPalma's son needed his help. So did Jan and Martin Mackie.

Jan said to him, "I knew something was up when I got your telegram this morning saying to call you—and to use a public phone. You never were one for practical jokes. You're doing this because of me, because I was stupid enough to get involved with Greg."

"I've got to go to Manila," DiPalma said. "They're tapping your phones, and that means things could get heavy unless I put an end to it. Also, Todd's my son. I can't let him face this thing alone, and he won't let *me* go alone, so there you are. Besides, if I can dig up some dirt on Nelson Berlin and Lin Pao, I'll have myself one hell of a story."

Jan frowned. "The English cop. The one who helped

you in Hong Kong. Did he ask you to check into Angela's death?''

"Yes."

"Meaning you would have gone to Manila even if I'd had sense enough to stay away from Greg, and Todd had remained Todd."

A smiling DiPalma shrugged. "No middle ground, remember?" He stood up. "Want to look in on Benjy and Joan?"

She said, "You go on. I want to ask Todd something."

When DiPalma had left, she said to Todd, "Will all of you return from Manila?"

Todd took her hand in his and shook his head.

A terrified Jan closed her eyes and thought of asking him which of the three would die. But she decided she didn't want to know. It was her way of keeping Frank alive a little longer.

# Ten

Shanghai in the 1930s was China's largest city and, for armchair travelers, a symbol of the intrigue, conspiracy, and romance to be found in the Mysterious East.

The Chinese, however, saw a different Shanghai, one symbolizing the dark side of foreign intervention; where foreign armies protected foreign business interests, children worked thirteen-hour days in Western-owned factories, and park notices stated that dogs and Chinese were not allowed.

In this Shanghai, American-owned factories operated with Chinese slave labor, and expatriate Moscow countesses worked as prostitutes and spies. Opium dealers, gunrunners, and British bankers engaged in the impassioned pursuit of money. Deformed beggars, communist zealots, and teenage streetwalkers lived with impossible dreams.

Shanghai. A kaleidoscope of people, wealth, degradation, and scheming. Queen of the Orient and Whore of China.

The city's epic status began with the Opium War of 1842, when China attempted to stop Britain from flooding the country with opium. Britain won the war, forcing China to hand over Hong Kong and open five Chinese ports—Shanghai among them—to British traders. America, France, and Japan demanded similar ''concessions''—banking houses, import-export concerns, military bases. All concessions, consulates included, were exempt from Chinese law.

A hundred years later Shanghai had become China's richest and most sophisticated city, a mixture of East and West. Westerners had built their own skyscrapers and fortresslike compounds—arrogant, ugly buildings erected on a broad boulevard facing the Huangpu River.

Except for the Chinese portion of the city, each foreign zone was ruled by its occupants and protected by its own troops and police force. Troops, marines, and police guarded the largest single foreign investment in the world. England's stake in Shanghai alone exceeded four hundred million pounds.

Foreign economic control left most Chinese dismally poor and subject to the most wretched living standards. It also outraged them, turning Shanghai into a fertile ground for revolutionaries, radicals, and political extremists.

In 1921, the Chinese Communist Party was founded on the second floor of a girls' school on Shanghai's Joyful Undertaking Street. At once the party came into conflict with General Chiang Kai-shek, the small, squeaky-voiced leader of the Kuomintang (KMT), China's dominant political party. The KMT pretended to be progressive, dedicated to removing foreigners and creating a modernized, democratic nation. In truth, it was not progressive but incompetent and corrupt.

In prosperous Shanghai, unofficial power lay with the Triads. The secret societies were rich from narcotics trafficking, gambling, extortion, and prostitution, with membership numbering in the thousands. Allies and advocates included diplomats, bankers, society figures. Chiang Kai-shek himself was a longtime Triad member who'd come to respect the unlimited power of the secret societies.

When Chiang decided to take over Shanghai, China's crown jewel, he rejected the idea of using his army. His own men, he decided, were too inept for such an important task. Better to rely on the Triads, which did not fail him. They delivered Shanghai to the little general as promised, butchering and torturing communists, liberals, and striking laborers by the thousands.

Chiang also used this occasion to rid himself of KMT members he disliked or feared. Wives and daughters of the defeated were sold to brothels or the city's factories. No opportunity presented itself to the little general without his noticing it.

As Chiang's hatchet men, the Triads achieved a formal recognition in national politics. Members, who included civil servants, journalists, and intelligence agents, now mixed with ambassadors, bankers, industrialists, and Chiang's generals. Three underworld leaders were made honorary government advisers. One was given the rank of major general. Heaven had brought the secret societies a success beyond their wildest dreams.

Chiang, in turn, did not overlook the narcotics trade. He worked out an arrangement with the Triads that would put millions of drug dollars in his pocket for years to come. In the race for money, the little general would never come last.

Lin Pao was born in a Shanghai dress factory, when his thirteen-year-old pregnant mother was kicked in the stomach by a quick-tempered foreman and abruptly went into labor.

Pao's mother, a thin, dark-haired girl named Kon, gave birth to him at the machine where she worked twelve-hour days. At night she slept under the machine on a filthy cotton quilt. None of the child workers could leave the high-walled, heavily guarded factory without permission.

Kon's family had sold her to the French-owned factory for a five-year period as a slave. The foreman, who'd raped Kon and bitten off one of her nipples, was Chung Sung, a burly forty-year-old former rickshaw driver who also pimped his child workers to the pedophiles among foreign businessmen. He stood to be dismissed should the children fail to produce their daily quota of dresses. Better the little shits die on the job than Sung lose his post, with its profitable sideline of whoremongering.

Holding on to his job meant more to him than Kon's pregnancy. So in her eighth month, when the overworked girl fainted at her machine, the easily provoked foreman put the boot to her and brought Lin Pao into the world.

The worn-out Kon and her new baby were of no use to Sung, who needed healthy workers if he were to continue in his job. Mother and child were quickly sold to Teng Sen, a fifty-year-old clubfooted grave digger who was a drunkard and mental misfit. Teng would exhume his mother's corpse yearly, wrap it in a blanket, then backpack it through Shanghai streets, pointing out the changes since she'd died. He was also a miser who used only three candles a year and fought dogs for scraps from butchers' stalls.

He lived in Old Town, the Chinese Quarter, in a festering slum of low, closely packed wooden buildings, crippled beggars, and cholera outbreaks. Corpses of the poor who'd died from starvation and exposure clogged its narrow streets. Old Town's many brothels were staffed by girls no older than fourteen, most of whom died before they were twenty.

Life with the unbalanced Teng proved so wretched that no girl survived for long. Those who didn't die at his hands either ran away or committed suicide. Kon's hell lasted nearly three years before Teng, in a drunken rage, tore out her throat with his teeth. Her haggard corpse joined the thirty thousand bodies of unwanted babies, hunger fatalities, and murder victims found each year in the city's rivers, canals, and back streets.

Young Lin Pao's life with Teng was no better than his mother's had been. The grave digger treated him brutally, forcing him to work the streets as a beggar, petty thief, and guide to Western tourists who went sight-seeing in the Chinese Quarter at their own risk. He also stole from food stalls and drunks and fought other youthful scavengers for the pick of the city's garbage. When Pao returned home with little or nothing, Teng would beat him unmercifully. The boy, in Teng's opinion, was nothing more than a moody little shit with disrespectful eyes.

By the time he was twelve, Lin Pao had worked three

years as a grave digger, with his wages going to Teng. He was stronger than most boys his age, exceptionally energetic, and determined to rise above the poverty around him. He was also determined to be free of the hated grave digger.

Suspicious and hot-tempered, Lin Pao found it difficult to trust anyone or to control his emotions. He spoke his mind, was quick to pick a fight, and was so defiant that even police feared him. Before long, he came to the attention of local thugs, drug pushers, and Triad members of the Hundred Pacer Snakes. Preferring the Triad to the hated Teng, Lin Pao walked out on the grave digger. But not before exacting his revenge on this insane man who had made his days on earth hell.

Pao mixed weed killer with a pork-and-cabbage dish, Teng's favorite, causing the grave digger and his latest adolescent girlfriend to die agonizing deaths. The girl, battered by Teng, as her predecessors had been, was feebleminded and couldn't be trusted to watch her speech. Better to kill her, Lin Pao reasoned, than tell her of the poison and have her warn Teng.

With thousands of slum dwellers dying each month of starvation, disease, and violence, Pao's two killings went unnoticed. Police eased their work load by listing most Old Town deaths as natural, whether true or not. Teng Sen and his retarded sex slave were ruled to have died of heart failure. Both were cremated and their ashes thrown in a nearby canal.

The Hundred Pacer Snakes put Pao to work as a runner carrying messages, drugs, and money between Triad members. He worked hard, kept his mouth closed and his eyes open. He obeyed orders without question, showed respect for seniors, and promptly established himself as dependable and trustworthy.

Soon after coming to work for the Triad, Pao met his first real friend, a fellow runner who was the bastard son of an opium dealer and a fifteen-year-old chambermaid. Abandoned by his father, the runner, who lived on an old garbage junk in the Whangpoo River, was Son Sui, a small, cheerful boy with a crippled foot and a crafty mind. His energy and love of life, along with his ability to think, attracted Lin Pao.

Though a year younger than Pao, Son was more confident. He made Pao laugh and see the silly side of life. Everything's funny, Son told him, as long as it's happening to someone else. It was Son who gave the almost illiterate Pao the rudiments of an education—tutoring in reading newspapers, giving him his first words of English, and insisting that Pao attend the cinema as a means of opening his mind. He introduced him to Chinese opera, for which Pao would develop a lifelong passion.

Tapping his own head with a forefinger, Son said, "To be clever is also to be lucky. So, my big friend, first make yourself clever, then luck will follow."

Son shared his food, clothing, and garbage barge with Pao, as well as his knowledge of Triad activities and history. Triads, Son told him, were an eight-hundred-year-old system of secret political and martial-arts societies. The name came from the equilateral triangle and represented man, heaven, earth.

Triads began by supporting the poor in their unending battle against the rich. Early membership was composed of farmers, beggars, servants, monks, all drawn together by patriotism. These days, Son said, the secret societies were not too concerned with patriotism. "Our business is business," he told Pao. "Foreigners call us criminals but they know little of China. Is it wrong for a poor man to seek a profit for his labor? And who is to say what that labor should be?

"We are a family," Son said. "Members can always count on their brothers for assistance. But once in, never out."

Until now Pao had kept people at a distance, trusting no one and seeing the world as a place apt to do him more harm than good. But he found himself responding to Son's good-natured teasing and intelligence. For the first time he delighted in the company of another human being.

In the past the crippled, slightly built Son had been the target of bullies who resented his brainpower and ability to read. Lin Pao stopped the bullying with his fists, feet, and teeth, as well as with rocks, knives, and a nightstick he had stolen from a policeman. He was unmerciful in a fight and went to any lengths to win. Shanghai's young thugs soon learned that to harass Son Sui meant confronting Lin Pao and his violent energy.

The two became inseparable. Together they whored and smoked opium, robbed drunken French sailors, and stole the sable rugs used by the wealthy to cover the engines of their parked limousines. Less than a year after meeting, they took a ritual oath to become blood brothers, swearing to protect each other, share their fortunes, and look after each other's children. Each saw the other as a friend worth ten thousand relatives.

July 1937. Japan invaded China, driving Chiang Kai-shek's KMT government into the interior. The heaviest fighting occurred during the first two years. For the remaining six years there were no large-scale battles of any kind. Japan proved unable to conquer China's enormous countryside or to effectively occupy the territory it had overrun. Meanwhile the KMT and China's communists fought each other as often as they fought the Japanese.

By 1939, the Japanese were flooding the north of China with morphine and heroin, both for the profit involved and because they hoped to corrupt the population and weaken its will to resist. Under Japanese protection, the Triads supplied the necessary narcotics.

In parts of China the war appeared to have fought itself out, to have come to a complete halt. Here the opposing armies became commercial organizations, with scheming Chinese and Japanese anxiously trading with each other. In addition to narcotics, the two trafficked in gold, silver, salt, grain, medical supplies, and, of course, guns. This mutually rewarding arrangement involved the Triads and continued until the war's end.

During the war Lin Pao and Son Sui received Triad memberships. At an initiation ceremony lasting three days, blood from a freshly killed chicken was drained into a bowl of wine. Blood was then drawn from Pao and Son's left middle fingers, mixed with the chicken blood and wine, and drunk by the Triad members present as a symbol of blood brotherhood.

Each boy also held a *joss* stick upside down in his hand and repeated thirty-six solemn oaths to the Hundred Pacer Snakes. Each was given a coded number and taught secret hands signals, allowing them to make contact with fellow members in public. Pao and Son Sui were now members of an organization able to give them anything they wanted.

By the age of fifteen, the strongly built Pao had been arrested for armed robbery, rape, and murder but never jailed or brought to trial. His temper tantrums made it difficult for anyone but Son Sui to endure him for long. Pao was especially hard on prostitutes, three of whom he killed in a drunken rage. It was Son who first called him the Black General, after a demon in the Chinese fairy tale who devoured young women.

Because of Pao's ferocity, he was assigned to carry morphine and heroin from Shanghai to Japanese detachments in Wuhan and Nanking, eastern cities that had fallen early in the war. He delivered guns to warlords in the north and brought back gold. And he hijacked medical supplies sent from America, which the Triad sold on the black market.

Venturing out into the countryside was risky business. Travelers faced danger from thieves, armed drifters, warlords, and Chinese and Japanese deserters. Which is why Triad leaders always included Pao among their bodyguards whenever they left the relative safety of Japanese-occupied Shanghai.

Pao was also an effective enforcer. One visit from him and storekeepers, student agitators, and brothel owners rushed to embrace the Triad's point of view. Those who continued to resist, received the traditional Triad warning: a coffin left on their doorstep.

Together Pao and Son Sui dealt with a journalist whose unflattering articles about the Hundred Pacer Snakes had annoyed the Triad elders. Pao strangled the journalist's wife, then watched as Son Sui booby-trapped her corpse. Later, when the husband attempted to move his wife's remains, the bomb beneath her exploded and killed him.

"Someone should have told our journalist friend," Son Sui said, "that life is the source of many misfortunes."

On another occasion Pao, Son Sui, and three men left Shanghai for a nearby village where they were to assassinate the headman, a notorious Chinese collaborator named Du. Du, a small, fiftyish man with a big nose and large feet, was getting rich from the war. His men attacked refugee trains passing near his village, slaughtered the passengers, and stole their valuables, clothing, pets, and even the dead's gold teeth. Du's last train robbery had been especially profitable. His men had killed over two hundred passengers, three of whom had been Triad couriers carrying gold bars.

Pao and several men were on horseback in the open countryside and heading toward Du's village when they were spotted by a Japanese fighter plane. Without hesitating, the pilot strafed the party, killing everyone except Pao and Son Sui. "We'll continue on to Du's village and discharge our duty," Pao had said. "The Triad must never appear weak or lazy."

With only a single horse between them, the two found the going slow. Forced to stop for the night, they made camp in a bamboo forest where they shared a stream with deer and wild pheasant. A fire could attract attention, so they ate a cold supper. Pao took the first watch.

Hours later he was viciously kicked awake and opened his eyes to find himself surrounded by a dozen men brandishing guns, clubs, axes, and pitchforks at him. Like a damn fool, he'd fallen asleep on guard duty and been taken prisoner by Du's men. Son Sui was nowhere to be seen.

At Du's village, Pao refused to answer questions or give

his name. At one point he spat in Du's face and called him an ugly dwarf. Even if he should spill his guts, Pao knew he was a dead man. Better to die without warning Du that the Triad was after him. The Hundred Pacer Snakes would avenge Pao and send big-nosed Du to his ancestors when he least expected it.

Pao paid a painful price for his silence. He was beaten into unconsciousness, then revived and a filthy rag soaked in urine was shoved into his mouth. When he still refused to talk, gasoline was forced down his throat and the soles of his feet were beaten bloody with sticks. The brutal interrogation lasted for two days, during which time he received nothing to eat or drink. Du's men also tormented Pao by cooking his horse and eating it in front of him.

Du said to Pao, "You will talk, tough guy, because tomorrow we'll drill a hole in your hands, run a wire through the holes, and attach the other end to a jeep. Then we will drag you around the village until you beg me to listen to you."

At dawn, Pao's cell door flew open and he was ordered to get to his feet. He'd been awake for hours; he was in too much pain to sleep. His hatred of Du had also helped keep him sleepless. A voice ordered him to stand in the presence of a Japanese officer. Pao, squinting through puffy eyes, saw three Japanese army soldiers, backed by Du and his second in command. Both Chinese were predictable in front of their conquerors, groveling and cringing like whipped dogs.

Pao tried to focus on the ranking officer, a slight man in a khaki tunic, leggings, and sporting a saber. One small, gloved hand rested on a huge pair of binoculars hanging from the officer's neck. Using broken Chinese, he spoke with the arrogance and disdain that had made the Japanese hated throughout China. Fuck you, brother, Pao thought.

The cell's poor light and Pao's damaged eyes prevented him from seeing the officer's face. But he recognized the voice. And his heart beat wildly. *The Japanese officer was Son Sui.* And the men with him were Triad members in

Japanese uniforms. It took all of Pao's self-control to keep his face expressionless.

Son Sui played his role like a good cinema actor would. He demanded, *demanded*, to know why the prisoner hadn't been brought to local Japanese headquarters in the next village. Du started to reply when Son Sui kicked him in the calf. "Address me as Your Honor," Son said.

Bowing his head, Du apologized profusely.

Du resumed making his excuses, but Son cut him short. "Bring the prisoner to your home," Son ordered. "I wish to question him privately and in reasonable comfort. Do you have a telephone?" Son asked.

Du nodded proudly. He owned the only telephone in the village.

At Du's mud-plaster and bamboo home, Son ordered Du's wife to prepare food for his men and to do it quickly. Then he demanded to be taken to the telephone. The headman led them to a back room, determined to be a good host and spare himself the very formidable wrath of the Japanese. In the room, Son closed the door and nodded once at Pao. Then, as Son ripped the telephone wires from the wall, Pao strangled Du with his bare hands.

The two embraced, Son saying that in the woods he'd been off by himself taking a shit when he heard Du's men moving in on Pao. Helpless against so many and lacking a weapon, he could only remain quiet until everyone had left. For the past two days he'd been in Shanghai, organizing the rescue attempt. Pao embraced him again, causing Son to say, "Had I known you'd end up smelling so foul, I might never have returned." Both laughed.

They left the room and walked to the kitchen, where one man cut the throat of Du's wife. Upstairs, they found Du's old mother sleeping in her room, snoring loudly and drooling, her dentures in a glass beside her bed. Pao smothered her to death with a pillow.

In the cellar, a fourteen-year-old maid was discovered making candles from animal fat. Lin Pao insisted on strangling her himself. He was, after all, the Black General and the scourge of women. Before leaving the house, Pao returned to Du's office with a meat cleaver and chopped off Du's hands. Then, with a knife, he carved the Triad's name on Du's chest. A thief deserved to lose his hands. And the world must know that the Triad was neither weak nor lazy.

In the jeep, driving away from Du's village, Pao, Son Sui, and the others ate the food cooked for them by Du's wife. Later Pao and Son Sui sang songs from their favorite Chinese operas. As usual, all ended up listening to Pao sing, for his voice was surprisingly good and he sang with great feeling.

Chongqin, China
August 1944

From a jeep parked near the hospital, Lin Pao and Son Sui had a clear view of the quarrel. It was almost nightfall, and what had been a quiet discussion between two Americans, a man and a woman, was becoming increasingly heated.

The man was Nelson Berlin, a captain in the United States Army. The woman was his sister, Rhoda, a Lutheran missionary and nurse. He was trying to talk her out of getting married. From where Pao sat, Captain Berlin wasn't having much luck. Dear sister seemed determined to acquire a husband. Dear brother seemed to be wasting his time.

Captain Berlin was in his early twenties, a short, stocky man with a large head, big ears, and a deep voice. He wore new olive-green U.S. Army fatigues, a steel helmet, combat boots, and stood legs apart, jabbing the air with a forefinger to emphasize his point. Attached to a web belt around his waist was a canteen, two small ammunition pouches, and a brown leather holster containing a pearl-handled revolver. He was aggressive in his speech and losing his hair. Neither Pao nor Son Sui cared for him, finding the captain to be a bossy, loudmouthed son of a bitch.

A year younger than her brother, Rhoda Berlin was slender and brown-haired, with hazel eyes and a mole near the corner of a wide mouth. Her fatigues were baggy and bloodstained. She appeared tired and not at all interested in what her brother had to say. When Nelson Berlin reached out to touch her, she pushed him away. Lin Pao thought, Sister scorns brother. Interesting, is it not?

Pao finished his cigarette, stubbed it out against the side of the jeep, and lit another. Captain Berlin and the dozen or so Americans with him were bloody fools. Two weeks in Chongqin and they'd learned nothing. They still believed the impossible could be achieved, that the ocean could be drained with a sieve.

The American mission in Chongqin was doomed. If the Yanks didn't know it, Lin Pao did. They were here to talk General Chiang into working with the communists long enough to defeat the Japanese. One more impossible dream. Chiang was obsessed with destroying the Reds, whose growing popularity threatened his power. Communists, he said, were heart disease. Japanese were only skin disease.

Stationed in the northwest and south, the communists were China's most effective combat troops. Chiang, however, had kept them from receiving arms and equipment. American aid was funneled through him, and he gave the commies nothing. The little general was looking ahead. After Japan's defeat an all-out civil war was inevitable. Chiang wanted to weaken his real enemy while he had the chance.

While the Reds lacked pistols and bandages, they had high morale, extraordinary discipline, and the support of millions. Chiang's government, on the other hand, was corrupt, inefficient, and unpopular. Men were press-ganged into his army and roped together so they wouldn't escape before reaching recruitment centers. Chiang's forces hadn't been a serious threat to the Japanese since 1938.

Some Americans believed that a well-supplied communist army could finish off the Japanese. Give them what they needed and end the war sooner rather than later. Berlin's American mission wanted to arm the Reds but couldn't do so without outraging Chiang. When it came to communists, the little general was easily offended.

Built on steep hills, Chongqin was the wartime capital of the KMT and had a refugee-swollen population of more than two million. Early in the war, Japanese pilots had bombed it unmercifully, striking on nights when the moon had turned the Yangtze River into a long, silver finger pointing at the city. Eventually the air raids had stopped, leaving bomb-shattered homes, buildings, and roads that had yet to be repaired.

Chongqin's missionary hospital worked around the clock, treating refugees and wounded resistance fighters. Lin Pao and Son Sui supplied the hospital with badly needed morphine at exorbitant black-market prices. Profit, no matter what the source, always had a sweet smell.

Their most recent morphine run to Chongqin had turned into a longer stay for Pao and Son Sui. The Triad ordered them to remain in the city and place themselves under KMT authority until further notice. Lin Pao found Chongqin to be unbearably hot and smelly. The heavy rainfall also got on his nerves.

Both Pao and Son Sui spoke English and knew Rhoda Berlin. On this basis, Chiang's people assigned them to Captain Berlin as interpreters, drivers, and guides. Pao and Son Sui were also to spy on him and his sister, then report all findings to Chiang's secret police.

Rhoda Berlin was an outspoken critic of Chiang, whom she considered to be little more than a common thief and murderer. She had no respect for him as a military commander; he simply repeated his mistakes from one battle to the next and used his men as cannon fodder. As a politician, Chiang couldn't resist lining his pockets with American aid. America should wake up, she said, and stop swallowing the garbage churned out by Chiang's publicity machine.

If Rhoda Berlin was attempting to bring her brother around to this way of thinking, the secret police wanted to know about it.

In the jeep, Lin Pao and Son Sui were drawing their own conclusions about brother and sister. "He's possessive," Pao said. "Very, very concerned," Son Sui said. Pao said, "One might say the captain was acting like a jealous lover." Son Sui agreed, adding that one must be careful because jealousy often killed.

A briefing by Chiang's secret police had given Pao a bit of background on Captain Berlin. He had a comfortable job in the Washington State Department, safe from bullets, bombs, and the stink of rotting corpses. Yet he'd asked to be assigned to this China mission. The secret police, well informed as usual, said Berlin's chief reason for coming here was not to shorten the course of the war. He was in China to prevent his sister from marrying a missionary. Captain Berlin, the secret police said, was quite fond of his sister. Perhaps too fond.

In front of the hospital, two Chinese soldiers, teenage boys in the captured blue uniforms of Japanese Marines, stood guard. Both were armed with Russian rifles, which were rusty and had no bullets. Around them, women and old men stacked sandbags in sullen silence. Wounded men, women, and children walked or were carried in and out of the hospital. The bickering Americans were of no interest to them.

Lin Pao heard Rhoda Berlin say to her brother, "You've driven me crazy the two weeks you've been here, now please leave me alone. It's none of your business who I marry. I came to China to get away from you." Berlin said, "You don't know him. How can you marry somebody you don't know? I'm leaving in two days," he said. "Please come back with me."

It started to drizzle. Lin Pao looked up at a very dark sky. The gods were pissing down on the earth once more. When he looked back at the Americans, Rhoda Berlin had just pushed her brother aside and was quickly walking toward the hospital. Just before she reached the entrance, a tall, athletic-looking man with sandy hair and long hands pushed through the door. Pao smiled and Son Sui kissed the air.

The man was Thomas Service, the mission doctor Rhoda Berlin was about to marry. Pao watched Service embrace the Berlin woman and look over her shoulder at dear brother. Dear brother was cross. He glared at Service, then spat on the ground and walked away.

"Big brother wants to be lover," said Son Sui.

Pao looked at him, then smiled. Of course.

Seconds later a red-faced Nelson Berlin was at the jeep, climbing into the backseat, where he plopped himself down and sat snorting like an angry animal. His jaw was rigid. Both fists were clenched on his thighs. Suddenly he slammed a palm down on the wet seat beside him. "Get me out of here," he said. "Back to my place. Now, goddammit. Now."

Nelson Berlin wondered if tonight's rainfall would stop before he turned ga-ga. The daily deluge in this part of the world was driving him insane. Back at the hospital, it had started as a light drizzle. Now the city was being blessed with the usual torrential downpour. Noah's ark wouldn't have survived this flood.

Chiang's people had lodged Berlin on a narrow, winding side street, in a small two-room house. It had a concrete floor, a wood stove, and a cold-water faucet shared with a next-door neighbor. The bathtub was an old oil drum; toilet needs were disposed of in a wooden bucket, to be emptied in the street, then doused with running water and disinfectant.

No white man in his right mind would have willingly parked his carcass in this pigsty. But with a war on, what choice was there? China had a king-size housing problem; there was never enough to go around. Berlin's pigsty beat living like a refugee and sleeping in streets, parks, and graveyards, where some bozo would slit your throat the minute you closed your eyes.

He shared the house with his chink watchdogs, the ghoulish-looking Lin Pao, and his gimpy little sidekick, one Son Sui, whom Berlin called Chop Suey. These two rice eaters, both of them younger than Berlin, looked as though they'd pull your heart out for a penny. They carried revolvers and had bodies scarred by knife and bullet wounds. Neither could have been any older than twenty, yet were treated by neighbors and townspeople with a deference bordering on servility. There was definitely more to Pao and Chop Suey than met the eye.

Alone in the front room, Berlin sat on an empty packing crate and refilled a teacup with vodka. Outside, the rain pounded against the shutters and leaked through the tile roof in half a dozen places. Berlin ignored the two chinks who were in the next room, sitting on low stools and eating God knows what. He'd nicknamed them Laurel and Hardy.

Laurel, the little one, was very good at fulfilling requests. American cigarettes, Milky Way bars, gasoline, new tires, clean socks. Ask and he managed to dig it up from somewhere. As for Mr. Pao, he was not the sort you'd want to meet in a dark alley. Berlin didn't trust him as far as he could throw a piano.

This was Berlin's first trip to China, and if there was a God in heaven, it would be his last. Nothing in *National Geographic* had prepared him for what he'd found here. China was hell on earth. The sooner he removed himself from this cesspool of a country, the better.

Berlin detested every inch of this rice-loving, slant-eyed paradise. Hated the people, who were two-faced, undependable, and among the cruelest on God's earth. Hated their singsong way of speaking; their crowded, filthy little streets; their disgusting habit of spitting whenever they damn well pleased.

Hated the fishy-smelling food and the smell of night soil, which was everywhere. Berlin was living on army K rations, tinned Spam, chocolate bars, and Cokes without ice. Not exactly haute cuisine, but it beat what the natives were shoving down their own throats.

His father, a wealthy New York hotel owner, had pulled

strings and gotten Berlin a commission plus a cushy Washington job. Had it not been for Rhoda, he'd never have set foot in China, where chances of getting his butt shot off were very good indeed. Two weeks in this piss hole was more than enough, thank you very much.

He'd seen children starving to death, men with their jaws shot away, old women arrested for cannibalism because they had no food. He'd seen prisoners being tortured in Chiang's secret prisons. If their future was ghastly, Berlin's was a promise. He planned to sit out the war in comfort, then join Dad in the hotel business. No reason why Berlin shouldn't make his first million before he was thirty.

How could Rhoda stand China? Stand it? Jesus God, she thrived on it. Long hours at the hospital, teaching Bible classes at the mission school, and still finding time to practice calligraphy. Rhoda the Great Wonder, Dad used to call her. She still was.

Berlin missed her terribly. Two years without seeing her face, hearing her voice, smelling her woman-scent. A day hadn't passed without him thinking of her. In two years she'd written him once, a postcard telling him she was getting married. One shitty postcard which tore him apart.

He loved his sister. Loved her with an unholy passion he could not control. It was a love without reason, a fever in his soul. He'd long since closed his mind to shame and guilt. It was enough to deal with the pain of not having her. To feel about Rhoda as he did was to be on a horse that was running away with him.

Two years ago he'd told her of his love. She'd wanted to treat this confession as a joke, but she knew better. The way his hands brushed her body, seemingly accidentally. The times when he just happened to open the bathroom door when she was in the tub. And his spying on her when she was getting into her clothes. The overprotectiveness regarding boys who were interested in her. Berlin's confession of love brought forth a promise from a tearful Rhoda to pray for him. She would ask the Lord to send down his grace on Nelson so that he'd stop thinking of her in *that way*.

Reverent Rhoda. Morally upright Rhoda. Churchgoing and God-fearing. She was going to call on Jesus to lead Nelson onto a brighter, higher path. She also wasn't going to say anything to Dad, who might not understand. But Nelson mustn't ever speak to her again in that fashion.

A week later he'd gotten drunk and tried to force himself on her. Shortly after this she'd left the country with some China-bound missionaries. Not a word to Dad or Nelson. Just upped and took off. For years she'd thought about doing the Lord's work in other lands. Circumstances, it seems, had forced her into going ahead with her dream.

When Berlin had shown up in China, his sister didn't welcome him with open arms. He didn't want to hurt her. He'd tried to make that clear. All he wanted her to do was rethink this marriage business. Think before marrying some poverty-stricken Bible-banger who didn't have a pot to piss in.

Did she really want to grow old in China? he asked. Back home she could be a rich woman. The old man was expanding the company into other states and also going into different businesses, such as a small candy company he'd purchased just before Nelson left for China. Berlin couldn't wait to team up with his father. Rhoda could work with them. Her future was in America, not China.

In his small Chongqin house, Berlin held up the vodka bottle. Empty. Damn it all to hell. He threw the empty bottle against the stone wall, sending broken glass flying in all directions. Started to cry too. Always crying over Rhoda. Was he drunk? Probably. He sure as hell was trying to get drunk. He opened his third bottle of vodka and looked around for the teacup.

He must get Rhoda out of China. Back to the good old U.S. of A., where she'd see the light. Get her away from that bible-thumper and the rest of those psalm-singing Holy Joes she hung around with.

Like Berlin told Rhoda, he had a bit of influence around

here. The Americans were giving Chiang money, guns, silk
stockings for his women, and penicillin for his pals when
they got the clap. So let Chiang do something for Nelson
Berlin. Let him close down Rhoda's mission if she didn't
return home with her brother. The Chinks already suspected
Rhoda of being anti-Chiang, so why wait to send her packing?

Why did America support Chiang, whose only skills were
double dealing and trickery? Even Nelson Berlin had come
to see the little bastard for what he was, a fast talker who'd
stab his own mother in the back and was detested by most
of his own people.

So why back him? Because the U.S. didn't know the
truth about Chiang and, for the most part, didn't want to
know. Americans were always in need of heroes, and that's
what Chiang's propaganda machine said he was. He also
had prominent and significant friends in the White House,
the State Department, and the armed forces. Attack the little
turd and they came after you tooth and nail. The quickest
way to end your career in public service was to attack
Chiang.

Nelson Berlin didn't care if Chiang lived or died. He did
care about Rhoda. The trick was to talk her into returning
to America for a vacation. A month or two in the States,
in the real world. After that, who knows? One thing for
sure: Berlin usually got his way. By fair means or foul, he
usually got his way.

In the other room, Lin Pao watched Berlin drink vodka
straight from the bottle. After swallowing the clear liquor,
the American hung his head and began to weep. Pao smiled.
Captain was putting on quite a show. First man swallows
liquor, then liquor swallows man.

Pao watched a very shaky Captain Berlin stand up, kick
his helmet, and send it rolling across the wooden floor.
When the American began to curse Thomas Service, Pao
shook his head in mock sorrow. Jealousy turned a man into
a fool.

Suddenly Berlin stumbled, staggered forward, then fell

on his face. He lay still, not moving. Lin Pao and Son Sui stared at him while continuing to eat.

Minutes later Berlin moaned, and after a great effort rolled over on his back. "Want to see my sister," he said.

Pao, using chopsticks, continued feeding noodles into his mouth, never taking his eyes from the American.

Berlin sat up quickly. "Now, you fucking bastards. Wanna see her now. You two slant-eyed wonders understand English?"

Lutheran Mission Headquarters. Rhoda Berlin sat on a wooden folding chair near a ground-floor window and stared out at the heavy rainfall. Thomas Service stood massaging her shoulders. They were alone. Coworkers—doctors, nurses, teachers—were on hospital duty, conducting Bible classes, or catching up on badly needed sleep.

She'd told Thomas about her latest conversation with Nelson, of his threat to close the mission if she didn't return to America with him. Thomas Service smiled. "Whatever happens is God's will," he said. "Your brother has nothing to do with it. The mission was here before he came. If it be the Lord's will, it'll be here long after he's gone."

Rhoda could only agree. Suddenly she wasn't afraid of her brother anymore. Thomas was right, we're all in God's hands.

She watched the rain pound the windowpane. Outside, the empty mission grounds were a mess. There was no drainage to speak of, so water ran off into every available basement on mission property. The Lutheran bucket brigade, Chongqin chapter, would be out in force tomorrow.

Through the downpour and darkness Rhoda could just about make out the antiaircraft gun located twenty feet or so from the window. God, did she hate that thing! Its presence on mission grounds symbolized all she despised about Chiang and his gang of thieves.

Claiming China was fighting for her life, the KMT had forced the gun on the Lutherans. Mission authorities had protested, claiming they were here to save lives, not take them. Protest ignored. The gun was installed on mission grounds, to remain there until the last Japanese invader had been thrown back into the sea.

The gun was Czechoslovakian, rusty and broken, and once in place had been neither fired nor manned. It sat there, an ugly, gray pile of metal spotted with bird droppings and abandoned by everyone except mission orphans, who used it as a giant plaything. That was the Chinese way. Everything for appearance's sake, even if it turns out wrong.

On the other hand, Rhoda knew the Lutherans had gotten off lucky. Chiang's thugs could have closed down the mission, grabbing the chapel, the orphans' dormitory, the mission school. And, of course, the hospital. The KMT's sticky-fingered toughs threw a crooked shadow wherever they went.

Behind Rhoda, Thomas Service bent down to kiss her hair. She smiled at him over her shoulder. Only seven weeks until their wedding. Seven weeks until they were man and wife. That day couldn't arrive fast enough for her.

He was everything she wanted in a man. He was a Christian, kind and hardworking, and he respected her wish to remain a virgin until their marriage. Doctors, nurses, and evangelists at the mission agreed that Thomas Service was the best doctor in southern China, if not in all of China.

He'd helped her adjust to this harsh land, which she was just beginning to love. When she arrived, Rhoda wasn't sure she'd last out the week. The flies, mosquitoes, and rats drove her crazy. She thought she'd faint when she saw her first leper. All around her, Chinese were dropping from cholera, smallpox, typhus, and diseases too numerous to count.

And there was the war. Dear God, the victims. Men, women, and children by the hundreds passed through the hospital each week, bodies savaged by bullets and explosives. Rhoda, who'd never traveled abroad in her life, had contemplated catching the first plane out of Chongqin.

Thomas Service changed her mind. He loved the Chinese and served them with his whole heart. His father and mother, both Lutheran evangelists, had founded the Chongqin mission. They'd worked here until killed in a 1940 Japanese air raid. Both were buried side by side on a hill overlooking a harbor where tugs pulled lines of junks piled with cargo.

Raised in China, Thomas Service had been attending medical school in Oregon's Reed College when war broke out. "I came back," he told Rhoda, "because I couldn't have lived with myself if I hadn't." He'd been offered a Navy commission, with a Stateside assignment. Eventually this would have been followed by a lucrative practice stateside.

He told Rhoda he'd had a premonition that his parents weren't going to survive the war. One more reason for being with them while he could. After his return they'd had three years together. Coming back to China was the wisest thing he could have done.

China had been good for Rhoda too. She was needed here. She'd combined her love of nursing with her desire to spread God's word and was never happier. In China she was free from Nelson and his unnatural feelings.

When she'd first told Thomas Service about Nelson, he'd said, "That's his prison, not yours." Now, as the rain began to come down harder, he embraced Rhoda and whispered, "Nelson's not a part of our lives. Put him out of your mind. Think of us. We'll marry and work in China until we die, then be buried on the hill beside my parents."

Rhoda rose from her chair and put her arms around his neck. "Good. Then we can all get up in the morning and have breakfast together."

They laughed, and as thunder cracked she kissed him and heard a sound over the thunder, a shout that became a shriek, and Rhoda turned to see her brother standing in the doorway, the pearl-handled pistol in his left hand.

As good spies, Lin Pao and Son Sui had to do their duty. So they ignored Nelson Berlin's order to stay with the jeep. Instead the two, in conical straw hats and U.S. Army ponchos, followed the drunken American as he staggered onto the mission grounds. The harder the rain fell, the more Lin Pao wondered if such terrible diligence on his part was necessary.

Tracking the tipsy captain wasn't easy. Rain and darkness all but hid him from the two Triad members. Twice the captain fell down in the mud. Several yards away, Pao and Son Sui waited while he picked himself up and stumbled forward. Waited and got soaked to the skin.

But as Lin Pao knew, all discomfort must be endured on this most unpleasant of nights. The captain was not in full control of his faculties. Therefore it was almost certain that he'd embarrass himself before the night was over. Pao and Son Sui must be near enough to witness this particular occurrence. Such information would be useful to the Triad, which knew how to make a man pay for his mistakes.

Making their way to the antiaircraft gun, Pao and Son Sui entered the ring of sandbags surrounding it. Crouching, they peered over the sandbags at the mission headquarters. Most of its windows were dark. Most, but not all.

Nelson Berlin, hands shading his eyes, stood peering into a dimly lit ground-floor window. What he saw didn't please him, for he staggered backward, cursing and flailing his arms. Then he lost his balance and sat down in the mud. He shook his fist at the building, then stood up and staggered toward the entrance. Stopping only long enough to draw his pistol, he opened the door and stumbled inside.

With Son Sui close on his heels, Pao raced from the sandbag enclosure. There was a clap of thunder as they splashed their way through sizable puddles. Pao's left sandal was pulled off by the mud, but he kept running. The captain must be kept under close observation.

Pao was the first to reach the window.

The Mission Office

Thomas Service stepped toward Nelson Berlin, confident he could reason with him and make him see that Rhoda deserved a life of her own. The tall, sandy-haired man had both arms at his sides, and he wanted Berlin to know he bore him no ill will. He was about to say this when Berlin shot him in the chest, dropping Service to the floor.

Before tonight, Nelson Berlin had used his .45 for target shooting and the killing of one squirrel on his father's Dutchess County estate in Upstate New York. What surprised him about shooting Thomas Service was how easy it had been and how good he'd felt about it. Berlin had never experienced such power in his life. With a gun in his hand he could grasp the world.

Rhoda, weeping and whimpering, sat on the floor with Service's head cradled in her arms, rocking back and forth. Warmed by the vodka and with a power now equal to his longing, Berlin, more attracted to his sister than ever, holstered the .45, walked over to Rhoda, and pulled her away from Service.

When she screamed, he slapped her face. Then he yanked Rhoda to her feet and kissed her, tasting the salt of her tears, cramming his tongue deep into her mouth, and when she scratched his face, he slapped her again. She brought her knee up, but he was too quick for her, turning his hip into the attack and taking the blow on his thigh. It hurt, but not enough to stop him.

Then they were on the floor and he had one hand on her mouth, the other tearing at her fatigue shirt, and then the electricity went off and they were in darkness. Berlin, on top of Rhoda, had her shirt open, but then she bit his hand, so he placed both hands around her throat and started to choke her, hearing his sister gag. When she grew weak, he stopped choking.

She was still alive. He ripped her shirt, slipped a hand under her brassiere, and squeezed one small breast. Dizzy with excitement, he unbuckled her belt, pulled down her trousers and underpants, then raised himself to his knees and took down his pants and boxer shorts. Feeling himself on the verge of orgasm, he entered her quickly, ejaculating seconds later.

Collapsing on his sister, he lay still, until she stirred beneath him. When she whispered, "Dear Jesus," the power within Berlin vanished and he was terrified. So great was his fear that he found it hard to breathe. There was a faint bit of light coming through the window, but the room's darkness seemed to grow stronger, bringing with it a future evil sure to destroy him.

Berlin again pushed himself to his knees, looked down at her bruised, tearstained face, and when she said "Why did you do it?" he knew he never again wanted to hear her voice. Never again wanted to be reminded of this night. So he strangled her to death with his hands, then collapsed beside her and wept.

When Nelson Berlin opened his eyes, Lin Pao and Son Sui were looking down at him.

Pao removed his dripping straw hat in mock deference. "Captain, sir, do you wish to walk away from this unfortunate situation without being punished?"

Berlin nodded his head. Fear had made him powerless. He possessed no judgment of his own. There was simply no way he could trust himself to think sanely. He was ready to give his soul to anyone who would free him from this nightmare.

"I—I want to walk a-away without being p-punished."

Pao crouched beside him. "Then you must do as we say."

"I understand."

Pao shook his head. "You do not understand, Captain, sir. But in time you will. What shall be required of you goes beyond tonight. You need not worry about what has happened here. But when you leave this room, you will owe obedience to certain of my friends. We will serve you, then you will serve us."

"Just help me. Please, please help me. I'll do whatever you say."

"Captain, sir, after tonight you will do as we say for some time to come."

With the surrender of Japan in August 1945, America pushed for a truce between Chiang and the communists. A cease-fire between the two sides, however, was out of the question. Neither wanted to compromise. The communists had an army, territory liberated from the Japanese, and were supported by millions of their countrymen. There was no reason to bow to KMT rule.

For Chiang, bringing Reds into his government was letting a fox into the henhouse. The growing popularity of communism, he reasoned, would eventually cost him political control unless he stamped it out. Compromise would not be in his best interest. Why hand your executioner the rope to hang you with?

A year after the war's end Chiang struck first, attacking communist troops in Manchuria. But he was no match for the Red forces led by the charismatic Mao Tse-tung. Chiang proved a poor general, incapable of leading or inspiring his troops, who defected to Mao by the thousands, bringing American-supplied equipment with them. In a three-year civil war, Chiang was defeated decisively.

He fled to Taiwan, the mountainous island off China's southeast coast, but not before cleaning out China's museums, banks, and military supply depots. His loot included the country's gold reserves, down to the last gold bar. Triads assisted the little general in one of the grandest looting sprees since the Nazis plundered Europe.

Taiwan wanted no part of Chiang. Opposition to the little general, however, was short-lived. He ordered his troops to torture and massacre thousands of Taiwanese until all opposition had been driven underground or out of the country. In a bloody campaign reminiscent of his attack on Shanghai twenty years earlier, Chiang whipped the island into submission. As always, the little general believed he had the right to do anything to anybody.

Southwest China. Here in the remote Yunnan Province, Mao's forces pushed the last KMT troops off China soil and into the area where Burma, Laos, and Thailand's borders converged. This region, home of the Shan hill tribes, produced much of the world's illicit opium and was known worldwide as the Golden Triangle.

Worried that Mao might now attempt to conquer all of

Southeast Asia, the CIA armed KMT troops in the Golden Triangle and planned an invasion of China. The KMT, however, had no plans to fight the red menace. Chiang's troops in the Golden Triangle decided to go into the drug business on a grand scale. Their objective: Take over Southeast Asia's heroin trade. All of it.

The Golden Triangle was a no-man's land. Power belonged to the strongest, and the strongest was now the KMT. Chiang's remnants easily subjugated the Burmese Hill tribes and forced them to increase opium production. Tribesmen were also press-ganged into the KMT Army. Marriages with local women helped the Chinese to gather recruits as well as opium. For the KMT, success in the Golden Triangle paid for the defeat in their own country.

They flooded Southeast Asia with opium that Triad chemists turned into heroin and morphine. Lin Pao was never busier. Operating out of Taiwan and Hong Kong, he carried drugs not only throughout Asia but to Europe and America as well. With Son Sui, he bodyguarded Triad leaders traveling in the Golden Triangle. And they escorted Triad chemists from Hong Kong to opium refineries in the Burmese hill country.

Lin Pao carried bribe money to Thai policemen, who protected drug shipments passing through their country. In Thailand he and Triad members also kidnapped babies or bought them from the parents, smothered the infants, and removed the internal organs before stuffing the tiny bodies with kilos of heroin. Women pretending to be mothers then carried their ''sleeping'' babies across the border into Malaysia.

Pao set up smuggling routes between drug refineries in Hong Kong and Taiwan and Chinatowns in Sydney, San Francisco, Toronto, Amsterdam, Manila, and New York. He smuggled drugs on container ships, in antique tables and soccer balls, in suitcases with false bottoms, in plastic penises carried by German flight attendants in their vaginas. Triad leaders were particularly impressed when Pao successfully moved fifty pounds of heroin from Taiwan to Brazil.

By his mid-twenties, Lin Pao's fighting skills had won him the respected position of Red Pole, the Triad's official enforcer. He immediately justified the trust placed in him by strangling to death a Chinese undercover cop who'd infiltrated the Triad. He stopped rivals from harassing Triad gambling clubs in Hong Kong, organized the kidnapping of a Singapore banker for ransom, and, with Son Sui, traveled to Honolulu to kill a Japanese banker for mismanaging Triad funds.

As Pao's reputation grew, rival Triads made attempts on his life and put a price on his head. The Black General had become a target. In London, the Silver Bamboo Triad demanded that all Chinese smuggling heroin into England must pay them. It must also allow the Silver Bamboos to distribute the heroin. Those who refused were murdered. The Silver Bamboos were waiting for Pao to defy them.

They didn't have to wait long. Pao's indifference to threats was well known. He scorned all who allowed themselves to be intimidated.

One humid July evening, he and Son Sui delivered two kilos of heroin to a Chinese restaurant owner in London's Soho, the city's largest foreign quarter. At dawn the two Triad members left the restaurant, stepped into a deserted Dean Street, and were attacked by six Chinese. The attackers were armed with knives, iron bars, and two Doberman pinschers. The Silver Bamboos intended to make an example of the Black General.

Pao shot one attacker in the head and another in the chest before the Dobermans knocked him to the sidewalk. The gun flew from his hand and the Dobermans were on him at once.

Flat on his back under the snarling dogs, Pao managed to see Son Sui shoot one Silver Bamboo in the stomach, dropping him to the sidewalk. But a squat Chinese wearing a red headband smashed Son's right arm with an iron bar. The gun went flying. Teeth clenched against the pain, Son stumbled backward, clutching his damaged arm. The squat man waddled toward him.

*Little brother was going to die.*

An enraged Lin Pao wrapped his arms around one dog, broke its back, and tossed the animal aside. On his knees, he punched the second dog in the head, knocking it to the sidewalk. Then, leaping to his feet, he drove a heel into the dog's side, cracking its ribs. As the animal yelped, Pao grabbed its studded collar and flung the dog at the squat man stalking Son Sui.

The dog struck the squat man between the shoulder blades, knocking him into Son Sui. Before the attacker could regain his balance, Son Sui jammed the fingers of his left hand into the man's eyes, raking the nails across both eyeballs. Screaming, the man dropped the iron bar. Scooping it up, Son Sui cracked the squat man across the right knee. When the attacker clutched his kneecap, Son Sui backhanded him across the face with the pipe.

Pao charged the last two attackers. One, a large man with a wide face, swung his knife wildly, slicing Pao on the left side of his rib cage. Defying the pain, Pao kicked him in the testicles, punched him in the throat, then smashed him in the face with his forehead.

The last attacker, a thin man with slicked-down hair parted in the middle, screamed as he swung his iron bar at Pao's head. Ducking under the blow, Pao jammed a foot down on the attacker's ankle. Then, stepping behind the thin man, he placed both hands on his shoulders and pulled him down to the sidewalk. Before the man could rise, Pao kicked him in the head.

The restaurant owner summoned a Chinese doctor—a lean, cat-faced man who silently tended to Son Sui's arm and Pao's knife wound. "Leave England at once," the restaurant owner said. "The Silver Bamboos will drink your blood for what you've done to their men. We're all in danger."

Pao gingerly touched his bandaged side, then glanced at

Son Sui. Son Sui smiled and said to the restaurant owner, "My brother and I will leave after we have completed our business."

Two days later the leader of the Silver Bamboos was at home, waiting for his wife to return from a shopping trip, when two London Police constables paid him an unannounced visit. It was their sad duty to tell him that his wife had been found strangled to death on the stairwell in a leading Knightsbridge department store.

As the shocked Triad leader slumped into a chair, the telephone rang, and when he picked up the receiver, a male voice said in Cantonese, "You also have two daughters." And then the line went dead.

As usual, London's Chinese community refused to co-operate with police investigating the wife's killing. But informants tied her murder to the Silver Bamboos' attack on a Chinese enforcer named the Black General, who worked out of Taiwan and Hong Kong. Was the Black General still in England? No one knew for sure.

What the informants did know was that he revenged himself on his enemies by striking at their women. And they knew that the Silver Bamboos had stopped trying to seek tribute from the Black General's Triad.

When Pao was forty, he married Ai-Ling Kung, a beautiful and vivacious singer with a leading Hong Kong opera company. He was now rich and influential, a man whose position in the world of secret societies gave him unlimited power. She was glamorous and famous, his reward for a lifetime of struggle.

Lin Pao had known many women, but Ai-Ling was the most passionate. He was besotted with her. Her lust matched his; in bed she gratified his every urge and hunger. His craving for her was boundless and insatiable. He left nothing undone to please her and gloried in the envy he saw on the faces of other men.

They shared an interest in Peking Opera. Pao's knowledge of this popular musical form was more extensive than Ai-Ling's, a pleasant surprise to her. "I owe it all to little brother," he told her. Son Sui had introduced him to opera when they were boys in Shanghai. Pao confided in Ai-Ling that he sometimes dreamed of singing with a professional company for one night. Unfortunately he lacked the confidence to perform onstage.

He had a collection of musical instruments—flat drum, castanets, cymbals, large and small gongs—and a collection of costumes—embroidered armor, makeup kits used by famous performers, long robes embroidered with dragons and phoenix. Even the thought of music, he told Ai-Ling, was comforting.

When Pao sang for her, she was moved to tears. He had an excellent voice. He could sing the *sheng* roles, masculine parts for old or young men. And he could do the *jing* characters, blustering generals or young adventurers. At her urging, they sometimes sang together, and for Lin Pao these were among the happiest times of his life.

Pao, in turn, lavished money on his wife's career. He financed productions in which she starred, paid critics to give her rave notices, and arranged a contract with a Triad-backed recording company. Her photographs occupied a prominent place in all his homes. So in love was Pao that he willingly gave up several mistresses. Only Son Sui had the nerve to call Ai-Ling what she was, an expensive toy.

They had one child—a son, Hin, who looked so much like Pao that he was nicknamed the Little General. Together with Ai-Ling, the boy became Pao's most prized possession. With a wife and son, a bit of heaven had come down into his savage world. He could only hope that the boy's life would not be as dangerous as his own. Astrologers and soothsayers called in to predict the Little General's future saw only good things. A favorable prediction insured a nice fee and prevented the predictor from having to experience the Black General's fury.

A year after his son's birth, Pao was added to the Triad's ruling council, a position of great honor. He now divided his time between Hong Kong and Taiwan. From these cities he sent forth others to enforce his will in the Golden Triangle, Thailand, Australia, and America.

With the Triad's leader growing increasingly old and unwell, council membership assumed great importance. The next leader of the Hundred Pacer Snakes would be chosen from the council. The current leader favored two men. Lin Pao was one. Pao's sworn enemy was the other.

Both candidates could not have been more different. Pao represented youth and innovation; he believed the Hundred Pacer Snakes should adapt to changing times. His enemy and older rival Chan Fau preferred to do business in traditional ways, without exception or deviation. "Change," Fau said, "is simply a way of multiplying one's idiocy." For Chan Fau it was ever the old tune.

He was a slim, passionless man in his early seventies and so obsessed with hygiene that he washed his hands almost hourly and changed clothes several times a day. With limited ability and unlimited ambition, he fawned over his superiors and praised himself to excess. Pao found him to be a bore, with his tired tales of World War II battles fought alongside Chiang Kai-shek, said to be a distant relative.

Pao saw himself as the future and Chan Fau as the past. Pao favored expansion; why not increase profits by selling heroin directly to emerging gangs, such as the Blacks and Hispanics in America? Why sell only to Italian gangsters?

"Stick with the Italians," Fau said. "If we go directly to Blacks and the Spanish, we risk offending the Italians. Can we afford a war with them in their territory?" Besides, Fau didn't trust the Blacks or the Spanish. "Too new to the drug business," he said. "No tradition. Stay with the Italians, who've proven themselves worthy of our trust."

Pao and Chan Fau also disagreed on Nelson Berlin. Pao favored putting more money into Berlin's company, which now had hotels throughout America, Mexico, Canada, and Hawaii. The American also had acquired other enterprises—cigarettes, electronics, toy manufacturing companies. And he was planning further expansion.

"Too ambitious," Chan Fau said. "Suppose Berlin becomes tempted to steal from us? What happens if he dies or America suffers another great depression? Our arrangement with Mr. Berlin needs no improvement." He saw no reason to give the American additional funds.

Pao disagreed. The Triad wasn't giving Berlin anything, he said. It was improving on an investment that had been made when the Triad had arranged for a wounded Thomas Service to be tried and executed for the murder of Rhoda Berlin. Her brother had immediately repaid the Triad by flying out of Chongqin with four kilos of heroin hidden in his sister's coffin.

Berlin, Pao said, was now invaluable to the Hundred Pacer Snakes, who had laundered millions of dollars through his companies. The American was a good businessman; his expansion could only benefit the Triad. If Berlin needed money, the Triad should advance it.

Expansion, Pao insisted, is life. Contraction is death. He favored more legitimate investments in America and Europe rather than merely banking Triad money and letting it lie idle. Fau disagreed. To him success was large bank accounts, not shopping malls and parcels of real estate. "Let us draw our strength from our glorious past," he said. "The future can take care of itself."

Pao and Chan Fau both saw themselves in the first rank. Between the two, no compromise was possible, nor would either serve in the other's shadow. Their positions were too far apart for concessions.

For Hin's second birthday Lin Pao and Ai-Ling arranged a party at Pao's home in Hong Kong's Happy Valley. The house, a three-story brick building facing the harbor, had been built a hundred years ago by an English army officer who kept a pet vulture and was the first to introduce tobacco enemas to the Royal Crown Colony.

The rivalry between Pao and Chan Fau had brought both to Hong Kong for a prolonged stay. Each was keeping a death watch. The Triad leader lay dying from leukemia and prostate cancer in a Kennedy Road hospital. With just days to live, he was expected to announce his successor momentarily.

Fau awaited the decision in Shek O Beach, where many of Hong Kong's most influential citizens hid themselves behind high-walled mansions. His home was a four-story brick building isolated in a hilltop forest, which he shared with four wives, one to a floor.

Pao kept Hin's birthday party small. Guests included Son Sui, his wife, and their three young sons; along with two of Pao's closest aides, their wives and children. One aide had flown in from Singapore, a show of loyalty much appreciated by Lin Pao. The only disappointment was Ai-Ling's refusal to sing. She appeared edgy. Like one of the tigers in Pao's private Taiwan zoo. Fatigue, she said. She'd been rehearsing long hours for a new role, she told Pao. Would he forgive her this once? Of course.

Since it was a warm April afternoon, the party was held outside on the veranda. Pao had a clear view of nearby Happy Valley Racetrack, where his horses raced beside those of bankers and corporation presidents. But as he held Hin in one arm and pointed with the other, he was not thinking of stables and the winner's circle. He was pointing west, toward America, where Hin would one day attend school. The Black General's son deserved nothing less than the best.

Time to unwrap the presents. Servants had brought a table of gifts outside, setting it down near the front door. As laughing adults and children gathered around the table, Pao handed Hin to Son Sui, the boy's godfather, then took an envelope from the gift pile. He thought, *I have searched for happiness and found it at last*.

The envelope, from Son Sui, was fat with cash. The two men smiled at each other. "Buy my godson an American car," Son said. Pao embraced him. "Brothers always," he whispered. Son whispered the same to him. The blood oath they'd sworn in Old Town was still strong.

As Pao returned to opening Hin's presents Son Sui placed the boy on the veranda floor and stepped beside Pao. "My godson needs a sweet," Son Sui said. Suddenly Ai-Ling stepped through the doorway, scooped up Hin, and hurried into the house. Pao frowned. What an odd thing to do.

But then, Ai-Ling had been acting strangely for the past day or so. Pao's guests and their children were silent. Son Sui's wife leaned in the doorway and stared into the house. When she turned to say something to Pao, the gift table exploded with a roar.

Because Son Sui was between him and the table, Pao survived the blast. Shock waves, however, knocked Pao off the veranda and down on the front lawn. Dazed and bleeding, he lay staring up into a bright sun. His head and left arm were in agony. He felt faint, confused, and was about to lose consciousness.

With great effort he looked toward the house. Part of the veranda had been blown away, scattering gifts, food, and bodies over the front lawn. The door to the house had been ripped from its hinges and was now on the lawn beside Pao. Flames ringed the front entrance. All front windows had been blown out or shattered.

On the lawn hysterical men and women cried out for help. In the air around the house bits of wrapping paper could be seen floating through clouds of black smoke rising from the veranda. Pao pulled himself into a sitting position. His face was sticky with blood. His skin felt cold and clammy.

Ahead he saw a small girl, her face glassy-eyed and numb, sitting at the top of the stairs leading into the house. Her right foot had been blown off and the hem of her dress was on fire. Son Sui's bloodied head lay beside her. His body was nowhere to be seen.

Pao managed to get to his knees but was unable to stand. He was having trouble seeing out of his right eye and the pain in his left arm was horrific. He sat down on the lawn and watched two white-jacketed servants carefully edge through the flaming doorway and rush toward him. Lin Pao stretched out his arms toward them, then fell back screaming Ai-Ling's name. Seconds later he passed out.

A day later Pao regained consciousness in a Kowloon hospital. The explosion had torn off his left hand and he'd lost his right eye. Son Sui had been killed, along with his wife and two of their children. One adviser was dead; the other was alive, though he'd lost both legs. There'd been casualties among advisers' wives and children, but Son's death was the biggest blow. Pao could not hold back his tears. The loss of Little Brother was unbearable. Pao had known no greater grief.

At the hospital, British Police Constable Martin Mackie informed Pao that someone had hidden explosives and a timer among Hin's presents. As six Triad members watched in silence Mackie said Pao was lucky to be alive. Did he, by any chance, know who'd attempted to kill him? Pao shook his head. He had no idea who'd want to do such a thing.

"I'm a simple businessman," he told Mackie. "I deal in real estate, gold futures, and computer monitors." He was also building a temple for the poor in the Wanchai district. The temple would now be dedicated to his brother, Son Sui, whose last earthly act had been to save Pao's life. Martin Mackie smiled and said, "I understand Son Sui was also a member of the Hundred Pacer Snakes."

Pao turned his face to the wall and said nothing.

When the police had gone, Pao sat up in bed and looked at the bandaged stump on his left arm. Then he touched the gauze taped over his empty eye socket and said, "Chan Fau and my wife tried to kill me."

Pao raised his maimed arm from the bed, then set it down again. "My son. Is he with her?"

The senior in the room was Zhang Wu, a small, bony man in his thirties with the intense gaze of a relentless hunter. After a few seconds he cleared his throat and said, "Your son is with her, yes."

Pao's voice was barely audible. "And they are both with Chan Fau?"

"At his home, which is under very heavy guard."

"Did any of Son Sui's children survive?"

"Chung, the oldest boy."

Chung was a solemn eight-year-old who had his father's intelligence but lacked his humor. He was also Pao's godson.

Pao nodded. "See that he is well protected. Guard him around the clock."

"It is being done."

"I wish to sleep now. Wake me in exactly one hour. I shall deal with Chan Fau at that time." After a long silence he said, "My wife's name is never to be mentioned again."

"I understand," Zhang said.

"From this day on I have no wife. She no longer exists."

Zhang Wu scratched a hairy mole beneath his bottom lip and stared at a water pitcher on the night table, wondering if Lin Pao had the strength to fight Chan Fau, and if not, where did this leave Zhang Wu? Chan Fau was not merciful to his enemies.

Zhang Wu was a realist and had no wish to be on the losing side in this war. The Black General was a cripple. Perhaps crippled in mind as well. Hadn't he just been shamed by a wife who'd tried to kill him and run off with his son? Any man's spirit would have been crushed by such a turn of fate.

Zhang Wu looked at Lin Pao and thought, this is not a warrior. Not anymore. Chan Fau, Chiang's old general and cousin several times removed, was now the man of the hour.

Fau and his four wives were extremely well protected in a home that was all but impregnable. Surrounded by a brick wall, it stood alone on a wooded hill and was guarded by scores of armed men. Anyone desiring to drive the old general out of his fortress would need an army and a great deal of luck. It would appear to Zhang Wu that the Black General possessed neither. While he lay injured and feeling sorry for himself, Triad members by the dozens were rushing to Chan Fau's side. Everybody loved a winner.

Zhang Wu, well versed in Triad affairs, was aware that the attack on Pao had brought forth an outpouring of telephone calls from Triad members around the world. Only a few had been for the Black General. The rest had been made to Chan Fau's fortress home, congratulating him on his boldness in going after Pao. The callers had also pledged eternal loyalty to Fau. Zhang Wu had felt Lin Pao to be the better man. Now he was being forced to reconsider that assessment.

Some Triad members believed that Lin Pao had been killed in the explosion. Zhang Wu suspected Chan Fau of indulging in a bit of trickery in an attempt to spread panic among Pao's forces. The old general was not above such bullshit.

In the hospital, Pao lay facing the wall. To Zhang Wu's eyes he was hardly breathing. You'd have thought he was dead. Had this been true, it certainly would have simplified Zhang Wu's life.

Pity the Black General. He didn't look so ferocious now. He seemed smaller, more vulnerable. Where was the Lin Pao of the terrible temper, the man who always got his way? Perhaps this Lin Pao had disappeared with Son Sui's death. The cunning little cripple had been invaluable in Pao's rise to the top of the secret society. But Son Sui was with his ancestors. The Black General would have to learn to be alone.

With Son Sui's counsel to guide him, the Black General might have given Chan Fau a run for his money. Without him Lin Pao faced almost certain defeat. Heaven itself could not prevent Chan Fau from becoming the next Dragon Head.

Pao stirred beneath the blankets and took a deep breath. He sighed and pulled the covers up closer to his face, seemingly preparing for sleep. But when he spoke, his voice was so commanding that Zhang hung on every word.

Pao's words seemed to be for Zhang alone. It was as if he could read the mind of the cold-eyed little man. Without lifting his head from the pillow, Pao said, "Three days from now Chan Fau will be dead and I shall be dragon head."

In a spacious, second-floor study overlooking a rhododendron garden and the courtyard, Chan Fau sat at a teakwood desk painting a silk scroll. It was a *makemono,* a horizontal scroll which unrolled from right to left and dealt with a single subject, in this case Fau's courageous war exploits.

Except there'd been no such exploits. During the war Fau, like other Chiang staff members, had collaborated with the Japanese, stolen American aid for personal use, and sent his men to die in useless battles. As an officer he'd been picky, rigid, and cowardly. His troops had called him the Iron-ass Chicken.

The theme in any *makemono* unfolded like poetry or music, drawing the spectator into the painting as it gradually unrolled. Such scrolls were never permanently displayed. They were kept in brocade bags or wooden boxes, to be viewed on special occasions.

Chan Fau was a good artist. He used brush and ink quite proficiently, applying black shades then light gray before mixing glue and water with a bit of color and adding it to heighten the effect. His strokes were quick, allowing for no second thoughts. As demanded by the ancient art form, he used an aerial view to render perspective and distance. Chan Fau's subject: his daring rescue of Generalissimo Chiang Kai-shek from a burning KMT headquarters building during an air raid.

*Makemono* painting required the artist to become emotionally involved with his subject, which Chan Fau found easy enough to do. With time and distance his personal vision and understanding of the war had become the only valid account. His was the only truth fit to be told.

The scroll was near completion on the afternoon Police Sergeant Peter Yong appeared unannounced at Chan Fau's home. Like all such interruptions, Yong was unwelcome. There was little Fau could do, however, but stop and chat with the policeman, who was also a member of the Hundred Pacer Snakes.

Yong was a slight, nervous man with taut, angular features and a lopsided grin. Chan Fau found him to be shallow and spineless, the type who refused to stand up and fight for anything. Piss on his shoes and he'd thank you for it. His access to police files, however, was invaluable.

Accompanied by two uniformed police constables in khaki drill shirts, shorts, and blue peaked caps, Yong had been let onto the grounds, then escorted into Chan Fau's study. Two bodyguards remained outside in the hallway, backs against the closed door. Yong's two constables stood on the other side of the door.

Yong apologized for the untimely intrusion, but he had to talk to honorable Chan Fau as quickly as possible. And it couldn't be done over the telephone. Definitely not over the telephone. Again he must apologize. With a wave of his hand Chan Fau dismissed the excuses. ''Just get on with it,'' he said.

Attaché case in hand, Yong approached Chan Fau's desk. ''Lin Pao's betrayed you to American narcotics detectives here in Hong Kong,'' he said. ''He's given them information about drug shipments scheduled for the United States and Canada.''

Chan Fau frowned and put down his brush. ''Why? That's cutting his own throat.''

''Not his, yours. You are next in line to be Dragon Head. The losses will be blamed on you. Pao is too weak to fight you himself, so he has arranged for the Americans to do his dirty work.''

Chan Fau nodded. ''Yes. Yes.''

''All confiscated drugs will be considered your responsibility. Your mistake. Pao wants you to lose face. He wants the members to see you as bungling. A poor leader.''

''I see.''

''With the Americans' help, Pao feels he can weaken you. If there are enough losses under your rule, he is sure the members will turn against you. Then he'll step in and save the society. He also wants his son back.''

Chan Fau snorted. ''And how does he propose to get him away from me? As long as I have the boy, Pao knows he must move carefully.''

Sergeant Yong nodded his head repeatedly. ''Oh, he is

aware of the advantage you have over him, honorable sir.
This is why he plans to bring criminal charges against Ai-
Ling. He knows she is here with the boy. He also feels she
cannot defy the courts without putting herself at risk.''

''Explain.''

''He plans to accuse Ai-Ling of stealing from his real-
estate company in order to buy herself a private theater.''

Chan Fau shook his head. ''Everyone in Hong Kong
knows he gave her whatever she wanted because she gave
him the best fucking of his stupid life. No court will go
along with his little scheme.''

Yong shrugged. ''Honorable sir, I can only repeat what
I hear. Judge Niang, whom you know to be a special friend
of Pao, issued the appropriate warrant. I have a copy of it
with me. Ai-Ling will also be accused of kidnapping their
child. She must answer the charges or be a fugitive, and I
don't think she wants that.''

Chan Fau, ramrod-straight in the uniform of a KMT general, impatiently drummed his fingers on his desk. He'd
worn his old uniform to get him into the mood to paint his
''heroics'' effectively. If Pao was here in this room, Fau
would shoot the bloody traitor himself. Yong had been
correct to bring Fau this information.

Fau's wartime experience in drawing up strategy had put
him in good with the Triad. True, he'd failed to kill Pao.
But it would appear the Black General was about to kill
himself. When the society learned of his plans to turn informant, Pao wouldn't live out the week.

As far as Chan Fau knew, Pao was still in the hospital
and somewhat the worse for wear. The Shanghai bastard
who would be king had lost a hand and an eye to Fau's
little surprise package. He'd also lost two advisers, including the clever and always dangerous Son Sui. From Chan
Fau's vantage point, Pao had had the earth pulled out from
under him.

Chan Fau, a professional soldier most of his life, prided
himself on being smarter than most men. He was someone
who took the long view. He'd disliked Pao from the moment

he'd set eyes on him. The Shanghai bastard had been too stubborn, too committed to having his own way. He was also crude, unpredictable, and lacking in all refinement. He was a gorilla, not a fox. Let him do a gorilla's work, Chan Fau decided, and leave the subtle task to someone else.

Since the secret society's leaders had liked Pao, Fau had pretended to like him as well. But the gorilla had not been fooled by Fau's playing up to him. Pao was not the sort to fawn on those who appeared to be admirers. Fau wasn't too pleased at hearing Pao's opinion of him. The Shanghai bastard considered him little more than a prissy old maid and a back stabber and made no secret of wanting to feed Fau to his tigers.

The two men did not live in the same world.

Chan Fau, however, was the fox, and the fox had out-witted the gorilla.

When Ai-Ling had been fifteen, Fau had owned her body and soul. Then she'd had mud on her face and smelled of her father's cows and had never seen a tube of lipstick. Her family had been among a million war refugees who'd poured into Chongqin, where Chan Fau had been attached to Gen-eralissimo Chiang's staff.

Ragged clothing, dirt-smeared skin, and a country-bump-kin manner could not hide Ai-Ling's beauty. Chan Fau hadn't been the only man who wanted her, but he'd been the most powerful. He'd cut a deal with her father, who decided to get what he could for his daughter rather than have her taken away and receive nothing.

The family was given food, an abandoned stable to live in, identity papers, and, most important of all, Fau's pro-tection. In exchange, Ai-Ling was handed over to him. Within six months Fau had grown tired of her and sold the girl to one of his captains for fifty American dollars.

Ten years ago Fau had again crossed paths with Ai-Ling, who'd become quite attractive and ferociously ambitious. During a night together in which she'd revealed a startling sexual bag of tricks, she requested his help. Would he ad-

vance her money to pursue a singing career in opera? She
didn't want to be a shop clerk any longer.

Chan Fau gave the matter a bit of thought while fondling
her ample breasts, then decided to do as she asked. The
money was to be repaid, however, and on his terms. Did
she agree? Of course. Even if it meant divorcing her husband? Of course. The truth was, she couldn't wait to get
rid of the old fart she was married to.

After that night Chan Fau never slept with her again, nor
were they ever seen together in public or in private. She
received his loan through a Zurich bank, the money first
making its way through holding companies in Panama and
the Bahamas. Ai-Ling was now part of a long-range plan.
She was his *sleeper*, his agent in place until he called upon
her.

Ai-Ling's debt and Lin Pao's obsession with Chinese
opera had allowed Chan Fau to lead Pao by the nose to his
day of destruction. The easiest part had been getting the
singer and the gorilla together. Ai-Ling was one of Hong
Kong's most celebrated and desirable women. As Fau correctly anticipated, Pao saw her as a trophy he had to have.

Fau hadn't asked her to marry Lin Pao; sleeping with the
gorilla and spying on him would have been sufficient. Marriage had been Lin Pao's idea.

After thinking it over, Chan Fau had allowed Ai-Ling to
proceed with the nuptials. Why not? She would always be
the hidden dagger pointed at Pao's heart. Meanwhile she'd
have a luxurious life married to a leader in Hong Kong's
most powerful secret society. Like all good plans, this one
involved taking the long view. Why attack your enemy
openly when you could attack him secretly?

In his study, Chan Fau listened carefully to Sergeant Yong
and never saw the two police constables attach silencers to
the barrels of their pistols.

Pistol in hand, each policeman then placed both hands
behind his back. One constable, a small, bandy-legged man
in dark glasses, turned and cracked the door. After whis-

pering to the bodyguards he closed the door and resumed his position.

Sergeant Yong continued outlining Pao's planned treachery, then placed his attaché case on Chan's desk, prepared to document his charges. Eventually there was a knock on the door, which the bandy-legged constable opened again, after first cracking it to see who was on the other side.

Both constables stepped aside to allow Ai-Ling and the bodyguards to enter. She wore a blue *cheongsam* slit to the thigh, straw sandals, and her black hair hung down to her shoulders. She held a quiet Hin in her arms. Her beautiful face looked strained and was without makeup. When the bodyguards had followed her into the room, the bandy-legged little constable carefully closed the door.

At the sight of Ai-Ling, Chan Fau frowned. He hadn't sent for her. She said, "I came as you ordered. And I brought the boy."

Chan Fau rose from behind the desk. What in God's name was going on here? He was about to tell Ai-Ling how stupid she was when the two constables stepped behind Fau's bodyguards and shot them in the head. A shocked Chan Fau collapsed back into his chair.

The bandy-legged constable jammed his pistol against Ai-Ling's neck and ordered her to remain silent. Wide-eyed and terrified, she nodded her head. The second constable locked the study door, then ran across the room and placed his pistol to the head of Chan Fau. All of this happened in less than five seconds.

In front of the old general, a nervous Sergeant Yong said, "I had no choice."

The bandy-legged constable ordered Yong to keep quiet.

Chan Fau sat up straight. He'd regained a bit of his composure, to be expected of one who'd served with the generalissimo and seen his share of action. He quickly assessed the situation. They hadn't killed him, meaning some sort of plan was afoot that would require his participation. *Well, we'll see about that.*

He intended to turn this stay of execution to his advantage.

A bit of strategy and he'd win the day. He was on his own ground, surrounded by his men, and that was a big advantage. It would take more than a pair of cheap gunmen and the spineless Yong to defeat him. He wondered who was pulling the strings on these puppets.

Chan Fau said, "Let me warn you, your plan isn't going to work. You may have gotten in without any trouble, but I can assure you it won't be that easy to get out. I have dozens of armed men in and around the house. How do you propose to get me past them?"

Chan Fau became moved by his own words. Hadn't he just been painting the story of a hero? *His story*. Rising from his chair, he said, "Try to take me from my home and I'll order my men to shoot. Better to die now rather than later. Kill me, however, and you lose your most important hostage. Then you'll have nothing. So you see, you're destined to forfeit the game. I suggest you lay down your arms, then perhaps I'll consider some show of mercy."

The bandy-legged constable ordered Ai-Ling to carry Hin forward and stand at the desk. Then he nodded at Sergeant Yong, who opened the attaché case, removed a hand radio, and gave it to the constable. He switched the radio on, turned his back to Fau, and spoke in a whisper. After listening for a few seconds he nodded and signed off. He smiled at Chan Fau and ordered him over to the window facing the courtyard. "Watch," he said.

Lin Pao sat in the backseat of a dark blue Mercedes parked in a clump of pine trees several yards away from Chan Fau's mansion. Zhang Wu sat on his left. A hand radio lay on the seat between them. In the front seat, two men with automatic rifles watched three trucks roll past them and park near the mansion's entrance. Pao's men were in the trucks.

As guards gathered at the front gate Pao's men leapt from the front and rear of the trucks. They were immediately followed by dozens of weeping and wailing women, who stumbled and tripped over each other. Shouting and cursing, Pao's men used fists and gun butts to shove the women into a ragged line. The women, thirty-four of them, were now between the mansion and Pao's men, who stood behind them with guns aimed at their heads.

The women were young, old, middle-aged. They were healthy and crippled. Some were in their eighties. Others were as young as nine. All were terrified. All were naked.

Some attempted to cover themselves with their hands, while others turned their backs to the mansion to hide their shame. On the mansion grounds, men ran to the gate, some laughing, others urging their pals to come see the show.

Suddenly Fau's men began cursing and shouting. The women were their wives, mothers, daughters. Several guards pulled at the gate, ready to rush outside. Pao's men fired into the air and drove them back.

Sobbing and calling out to their men, the naked women pleaded for help. Some babbled their fear of the Black General. Their men, however, were powerless and could do nothing but watch. While they had the Black General outnumbered, he had their women.

Inside the Mercedes, Pao nodded to Zhang, who then spoke into the hand radio. Seconds later one of Pao's men left the truck and walked to the front gate, waving a white handkerchief as a flag of truce. After speaking briefly to Fau's men he backed away. Fau's men ignored him, staring at the dark blue Mercedes almost hidden by the pine trees.

In the study, Chan Fau nervously fingered the medals on his chest and looked down at the crazy scene in front of him. Naked women at his gate. And his guards doing nothing but standing around. Something quite unconventional about all of this. Fau began to feel afraid.

The bandy-legged man's radio began to squawk. Flicking on the receive switch, he listened. Then he looked at Fau and jerked his head toward the courtyard. Fau's men were laying down their arms. Even men inside the house were coming out quickly, guns held overhead. The front gate was now open.

Heart beating uncontrollably, Fau watched the women being herded into the courtyard by armed men. Two trucks followed them slowly. The women were ordered to halt under the study window. Fau turned away. But the bandy-legged man gently tapped Fau's cheek with his pistol. "Look," he said.

Fau saw his men being disarmed, then directed to sit against the east wall, hands on head. Only then did the Mercedes leave the pine trees and enter the courtyard, stopping near the women.

As Chan Fau watched, there was a sharp pain in his stomach, and even with his glasses on, he had trouble focusing his vision. His greatest trouble lay in accepting the events now unfolding before him. They defied description.

Explain the naked women being herded onto his property. Explain his guards opening the gates, then surrendering to intruders without firing a shot. Perhaps there was no explanation. Perhaps it was an hallucination, a dream which could not be understood.

His mind wasn't prepared to accept these unfavorable developments. Surely some mistake had been made. If Chan Fau could sit down and reason with whoever was in charge on the other side, this strange business might have a satisfactory ending. Just a word or two with the right people should produce an equitable solution. Chan Fau was a wartime hero. Surely that would command respect.

But he found himself staring into the courtyard and whispering, "Why didn't they fight? Why didn't they defend their general?"

Behind him, the bandy-legged man said, "Let's go." Chan Fau, Sergeant Yong, and Ai-Ling were to leave for the courtyard. Little Hin had fallen asleep in his mother's arms.

In the hallway, Chan Fau paused at the top of the stairs. "I must talk to the Dragon Head," he said.

"Did you not hear the news, honorable sir?" Yong asked. "Dragon Head passed away shortly before I came to see you. Doctors did their best but failed to save him."

"Why wasn't I told?"

"Well, honorable sir, that is a matter between you and Lin Pao."

Chan Fau blinked. Suddenly his throat felt dry. Lin Pao. Of course. Fau said, "He and I should be able to come to some sort of arrangement. I must say I'm disappointed in my men for not resisting."

The bandy-legged man said, "The Black General gave them fifteen seconds to surrender. After that he promised to kill their women."

Sergeant Yong said to Chan Fau, "Honorable sir, I am afraid we did the same thing, your men and I. We chose our women over you. Just as the Black General assumed we would. Sad to say, my wife and daughter are downstairs. I'm told that the wives and mothers of two doctors who attended our recently deceased Dragon Head are also in the courtyard."

Zhang Wu ordered the telephone lines in Chan Fau's mansion cut.

Then a leather armchair was brought from inside the house and placed in front of the garden. After laying a tape recorder on the ground beside the chair, Zhang Wu assisted Lin Pao from the Mercedes. Pao wore a green hospital robe, pajamas, and slippers. His one good eye and empty socket were hidden behind dark glasses.

At the mansion's entrance a tense Chan Fau and Ai-Ling watched Zhang Wu lead Pao to the armchair. When Pao was seated, he beckoned to Zhang Wu, who leaned over to listen to whispered instructions, which were then relayed to Pao's men.

All women, except Ai-Lin, were ordered inside the house, to be kept there under guard. Six of Pao's men were also to be posted outside the house. Any woman attempting to escape would be shot. Any guard molesting the women would also be shot.

Had Fau's men resisted, Pao would have immediately killed the women. But as the women entered the house Pao said to Zhang, his new second in command, "Since I want to win the loyalty of Fau's men, it's stupid to degrade their women unnecessarily." Zhang Wu was in agreement. He'd been a fool to underestimate Lin Pao.

In three days Pao had organized a superb countermove against Fau, bringing in men from Manila and Singapore, men whose faces were unknown to Fau. With or without Son Sui, the Black General was going to be an outstanding Dragon Head.

After repeating Pao's instructions to the men in the courtyard, Zhang walked over to Ai-Ling, took Hin from her arms, and brought the boy to the Black General.

Father and son were happy to see each other. In the tension-filled courtyard they hugged and kissed, ignoring everyone else. Removing a small plastic rocket ship from a pocket of his robe, Pao gave it to a delighted Hin, who playfully tapped his father on the chest with the toy. Again Pao hugged and kissed the boy. For a few seconds the only sounds in the courtyard were the cawing of crows flying overhead and Ai-Ling's weeping. Then Pao handed his son to Zhang, who carried him into the house.

On his return to the courtyard, Zhang shouted to the drivers of the two trucks. Both started their motors at once. A nod from Zhang and four guards on either side of Chan Fau dragged him toward the trucks.

Fau demanded to talk with Pao. Demanded the respect due a man of his rank and achievement. Surely Lin Pao wasn't going to refuse to talk. Chan Fau shouted, *"I am due respect, do you understand? Respect!"*

He was ignored.

Ropes were tied to his arms and legs, then to both trucks. Some men, Fau's and Lin Pao's, looked at the ground or turned their faces to the wall. A few closed their eyes and covered their ears. Chan Fau, gray hair askew, spectacles dangling from one ear, was still demanding respect when Zhang Wu lifted one arm, then brought it down in a signal. The trucks pulled in opposite directions, tearing the old general apart.

Ai-Ling fainted.

She was semiconscious when dragged in front of Pao by the same four men who'd tied Chan Fau to the trucks. Pao nodded to Zhang Wu, who ordered her stripped and held down on the ground. Then Pao turned on the tape recorder, now resting in his lap. The sound of Ai-Ling's singing voice echoed across the courtyard.

Pao placed the tape recorder on the ground and with great effort pushed himself from the easy chair. He held out his one hand to Zhang. Removing a penknife from a back pocket, the small, bony man pulled out the blade and handed the knife to Pao.

Ai-Ling looked up at her husband and begged for mercy.

Pao shuffled over to her, his slippers scraping against the brick courtyard. When he reached Ai-Ling, he leaned down between two men and with the penknife slowly drew a cut across her stomach. Ai-Ling's screams blended into the sounds of her singing voice.

The cut wasn't deep. It drew blood but was little more than a long scratch. An hysterical Ai-Ling pulled wildly against her captors, tearing her bare skin on the cobbled courtyard. Pao, cold and unresponsive, looked at her briefly before turning away.

Back in the armchair, he watched as the four men pinning Ai-Ling removed penknives from their pockets. When the blades were out, the men looked at Pao. He nodded.

Forty minutes later the four men, working from Pao's incision, had carefully peeled back the skin from Ai-Ling's upper body in one strip and pulled it over her head. With the exception of Pao, Zhang Wu, and the bandy-legged police constable, all eyes had turned away from Ai-Ling.

The four men who had peeled off half of her skin now stopped to look at Pao. Rising to his feet, Pao flung the tape recorder at them, demanding they get on with Ai-Ling's slow, agonizing death.

# Eleven

## Manila, March

DiPalma, glass in hand, stood on the balcony of his hotel suite watching a helicopter rise from the heliapad adjoining the penthouse six stories above. Seconds later the helicopter banked left over Manila Bay and headed south toward the airport.

On the grounds below, tropical birds squawked as red-jacketed hotel attendants approached their cages bearing the evening meal of fruit and seeds. The sun had almost disappeared below the horizon. In the growing darkness other attendants switched on the lights around four tennis courts and a large swimming pool.

DiPalma returned to his suite, sat down on a couch of upholstered bamboo, and put his feet up on a low hardwood table beside a tray of sweet-smelling *Sampaguita* orchids. He swallowed the last of the bottled water in his glass, then looked at his watch. Almost eight-twenty. The whore was twenty minutes late.

Three hours ago, while checking into a five-hundred-dollar-a-day suite overlooking Manila Bay, DiPalma had said to Federico, the bell captain, "I want company."

Federico, a stout, middle-aged Filipino with a pencil-thin mustache and slick good looks, said, "Of course."

"You acquainted with a lady named Huziyana de Vega?"

A smiling Federico palmed DiPalma's fifty-dollar bill and said, "At what time do you wish to have her appear?"

"Say eight o'clock. Tell her she comes highly recommended by some people in Hong Kong. Money's no problem. If she can make it, I'd be very appreciative." According to Martin Mackie, de Vega would strip naked for her johns, drape herself in paste jewelry, and dance up a storm.

Federico said, "Fortunately she has just returned from a short holiday. I give you my word, sir, she will most certainly visit you this evening." Rich Americans were God's gift to the needy, and Federico, with thirteen children and another on the way, was as needy as any man in the Philippines. He would deliver the little slut to the American even if it meant dragging her there by her dearest bodily part.

DiPalma said, "Don't mention my name. Just say the gentleman in Suite 557 has heard a great deal about her and would like the pleasure of her company. Tell Miss de Vega that if she has to cancel a previous engagement, I'll make it worth her while."

"Sir, I give you my word that Miss de Vega will be in your presence this evening. You can plan on it." He winked.

Since fucking Miss de Vega wasn't on the agenda, DiPalma didn't wink back. He proposed to play with the little lady's mind, nothing more. Psych her out. Confront her with the stolen Philippe Patek watch found at the Taaltex fire. Get her to admit she'd given the watch to Leon Bacolod, the Taaltex security guard who was her live-in lover.

Next he'd sympathize with any guilt she felt over the Taaltex fire. Because if she'd given the watch to Bacolod, this made him a prime suspect in the arson deaths of forty-five women. Say Bacolod had torched the barracks on Lin Pao's orders, and she knew it. This might be weighing on her conscience. Then again, it might not. Remorse was one thing, self-preservation another.

Should he telephone the front desk and hassle Federico? Not just yet. Give the lady until nine o'clock, then reach out for Good Time Freddy. Telephone service in the Philippines wasn't the best. DiPalma had made one call since arriving, and it had been one hell of a strain on his patience and credit card.

He'd telephoned Jan at their apartment to let her know he'd arrived safely. Since there was no direct dialing, the call had taken forty-five minutes to go through. There'd also been a twenty-five-percent surcharge. This in an otherwise comfortable four-star hotel.

Fortunately he'd made the essential calls before leaving America. First he'd spoken to New York Senator Joseph Quarequio, who'd then asked the U.S. embassy in Manila to show DiPalma every courtesy. Not only was Mr. DiPalma his friend, the senator said, but he was a popular New York television reporter as well. Quarequio hadn't won three terms in the Senate by ignoring the press.

Next DiPalma had called Manila personally and spoken with Barry Omens, DEA supervisor for the Philippines. They'd worked on drug task forces when DiPalma had been a cop, once going undercover to pop Sicilian aliens who'd been operating pizza parlors along the East Coast as fronts for heroin smuggling. An expert on organized Asian crime in America and abroad, Omens was three months away from retirement and looking forward to a new career as an investigator with the Manhattan district attorney's office. DiPalma had gotten him the job.

"Your boy Mackie was right," Omens said. "Nobody 'round here wants to know from the Taaltex fire. Forty-five women dead and all you hear is it's bad for business. Locals are terrified the fire will scare away foreign companies, which bring in jobs, hard currency, and technology they can't get otherwise. They want this thing to die a quiet death. Which should put Lin Pao and Nelson Berlin in a fucking festive mood, I'm sure."

DiPalma said, "Lin Pao's man in Manila probably set up the fire. Who would he be?"

" 'Who would he be?' the man says. We're talking about Charles Sui, one very cold-blooded, very smart cookie known also as Charlie Snake. He's the son of Pao's closest friend, or what was Pao's closest friend until the guy got himself killed over twenty years ago. They don't call him Snake because he's neighborly and outgoing, by the way.''

Omens chuckled. ''Ain't one to forgive and forget, our boy Charles, aka Chung. Supposed to be more vindictive than Lin Pao, and that's saying something. Word is he once had acid poured into a snitch's eyes, then had the guy hamstrung. A fucking sweetheart. Pao's his godfather, by the way.''

''So Charlie Snake hired the torch.''

''Bet the ranch on it. Hard guy to work for. Expects a day's work for a day's pay. Fuck up and your dick ends up in his back pocket. Our intelligence says he's one of Pao's most trusted lieutenants. Dude's got a lot of smarts. He's definitely a major player. Wouldn't surprise me if he didn't end up headman one of these days. Runs the Philippines for the Black General and also keeps an eye on people in Australia, New Guinea, Borneo, and New Caledonia. A lot of them report to him. A young guy. Still in his thirties.''

DiPalma said, ''Any bad habits?''

''None. Unless you consider being a tennis freak a bad habit. Starts each morning with a game or a private lesson from a top pro. Goes to Wimbledon every year. I mean, *every* year. Guy flies to Paris, Rome, the States, anywhere Ivan Lendl's got a big match. Eats, drinks, sleeps Lendl. Snake's married, has two kids. Doesn't play around. Just takes care of business and plays tennis. By the way, you want to tell me what you've got going over here?''

''Right now it's personal. But when I can lay it all out for you, I will.''

''Good enough,'' Omens said. ''When you get here, check in if you can. If not, see you in the Big Apple. Man, I can't wait to get back. Nothing you can tell me now, right?''

DiPalma thought, *I could tell you it involves my wife and son, but I won't. I can't.* He said, ''Tell you this. It has to do with putting Nelson Berlin in bed with Lin Pao.''

"You're kidding. I take that back. You don't kid about anything. Jesus, if you're right . . . I mean, we hear stuff about these two all the time, but nobody's been able to come up with shit, and it ain't because we haven't tried."

"Somebody's got something. That's why I'm coming over there."

Omens sighed over the long-distance line. "You could make me a big man. A very big man."

"When the time's right, I'll cut you in."

"Lawdy mama. Am I really going out in a blaze of glory?"

"We'll see. Might need some help when I hit town."

"You have to ask?"

In New York, DiPalma also devised a game plan for Manila, a plan long on desperation and short on brilliance. He apologized to Todd, Benjy, and Joan for not being able to come up with anything better, but there wasn't time for long strategy sessions.

They had to get to Manila before the Triad learned about Raul Gutang, the Taaltex computer operator who had a tape that could tie Nelson Berlin to Lin Pao. Before the Triad decided to move against a dwarf whore who'd stolen a certain watch.

DiPalma was asking a lot of the three youngsters. He'd understand if they decided to back out and not go to the Philippines. None of them did. Todd was committed to the destruction of the Black General. Benjy and Joan were committed to Todd. All three would do whatever DiPalma asked.

"I've been made," DiPalma told the three youngsters. "The Triad's seen me with Martin Mackie. Figure Lin Pao's men will be watching me from the time I leave New York until I return. In Manila I'll check out the Taaltex fire and see if I can shake up Huziyana de Vega. But basically I'll be a decoy. I'm going to make myself highly visible, not that I have much choice. Which means, Todd—and you, Benjy—will have to meet Gutang and get the tape."

Todd said, "We understand."

"Be very, very careful. We don't know Gutang. Don't

know how he thinks, what his game is. We know he wants the hundred thousand Martin Mackie's put aside for him in Zurich, but that's all we know.''

Todd nodded. "I'll have my portable computer with me. That way I can run the tape and have Mr. Gutang explain it to me. If what he says is correct, I'll give him my half of the thousand-dollar bill with the missing Swiss bank account numbers. If the tape is useless, I give him nothing. I will know if he is lying.''

"Good boy. Something else. We travel to Manila separately. Everybody on a different flight. Same airline, different airline, doesn't matter. But we all take different flights. Todd, Benjy, get your hair cut before you go and wear dark glasses on the plane. Benjy, wear a suit and tie for a change. Todd, in Manila you wait for Joan at the airport. Make sure she gets into town all right. With any luck, you guys should reach Manila without being seen. That is, if the Triad concentrates on me. Like it or not, TV's made me conspicuous. I couldn't hide if I wanted to.''

"Could be dangerous being a decoy," Benjy said. "In New York, the Triad might think twice about killing a journalist. *Might*. In Manila, they won't think about it at all. Over there, being a reporter don't mean shit. They want you dead, you're dead.''

DiPalma said, "Won't be the first time somebody's tried to punch my ticket. Anyway, I'll be in one hotel, you three in another. You guys are to stay together at all times. *At all times*. Last but by no means least, Todd's the boss. Everybody takes orders from him. You got that, Benjy?''

"Yeah, sure.''

"Don't yeah-sure me, hotshot. Like you just said, they kill people quicker over there than here, and I don't want my son dying because you went off on your own and did something stupid. You and Joan stay in the hotel until Todd says different.''

Benjy took out his Uzi and sighted down the barrel at DiPalma. "And when would that be, Mr. Famous Journalist?''

DiPalma gave Benjy a hooded look, the one friends and enemies called "the ray." He looked at Benjy until the teenager slowly pointed the barrel at the ceiling. Gently pulling the Uzi from Benjy's hands, DiPalma said, "You can't take it on the plane, or did you bother to think that far ahead?"

Benjy looked down at the floor and shrugged.

DiPalma said, "I assume you have a passport?"

Benjy held up several fingers. "Six. Keep them in different places. I do a lot of traveling."

DiPalma snorted. "I bet."

He looked at Joan. "Problem is getting you a passport, young lady. Can't leave you behind, that's for sure. You wouldn't last a day in this town on your own."

Joan, who knew little English, suddenly appeared frightened. Todd had been translating DiPalma's remarks into Cantonese for her. Now she moved closer to the boy, taking his arm and shaking her head as though disagreeing with DiPalma.

Todd said, in English, "She's afraid you'll leave her here on her own."

DiPalma shook his head. "No way. Tell her we're just trying to figure a way to get her a passport. She's coming with us."

With extraordinary calm Todd spoke to the terrified girl in Cantonese; as he did, she became more composed. Finally she smiled, wiping away her tears with a small hand.

Todd said to DiPalma, "She's okay now. It's important she come to Manila with us." The boy's voice became sad. "She must fulfill her karma there."

DiPalma noticed his son's concern but said nothing. Later he wouldn't be able to remember Todd's words without breaking into a cold sweat. Now he said, "Karma or no karma, she's going nowhere without a passport."

"No problem," said Benjy. "Guy we use in New Jersey can make one up for her in a few hours. But he doesn't work cheap."

"I'm going to leave that to you. Just get the passport. I

don't want to know how. I used to be a cop, remember?
Don't tell your friend in Jersey that you and Joan are going
anywhere. You have money?''

''Man, money's no problem. Got me three safe-deposit
boxes around the city where I keep stuff. Don't believe in
checking accounts, man. Cash is the only way to go.''

From what DiPalma knew about Chinese youth gangs, a
lot of cash passed through Benjy's hands. Triads paid gang
leaders like Benjy as much as five thousand dollars a week.
No wonder he needed a handful of safe-deposit boxes.

DiPalma said, ''Martin Mackie will alert Gutang to expect
Todd and Benjy. One more thing: While we're in Manila,
you guys don't contact me. I'll reach out for you through
a friend, Barry Omens. Remember that name. Barry Omens.
He'll identify himself through a code word which Todd will
understand. Coming back, we'll meet at Manila airport and
leave the Philippines together.''

Martin Mackie did his part. He alerted Gutang to expect
Todd and Benjy, then told DiPalma the computer operator
wasn't keen on handing his tape over to a pair of adolescents.
But for one hundred thousand dollars the Filipino was willing to put aside his aversion to doing business with teeny-
boppers. Mr. Gutang liked money.

As for DiPalma, he liked things to go smoothly even
though he knew nothing ever happened as expected.

Bet on his trip to furnish a few surprises.


Manila. DiPalma, walking with his cane, paced the spacious living room of his suite. After a twenty-two-hour flight
from New York it felt good to stretch his legs. He thought
about watching TV, then decided he was too antsy to sit
down. He looked at his watch. Huziyana de Vega was
almost half an hour late. Should he call downstairs for
Federico?

He poured himself another glass of bottled water and
drank it. His gassy stomach couldn't take anything else at
the moment. Not while he was worrying himself sick over
Jan and Todd.

He wondered if Nelson Berlin would do more than just tap Jan's phones. And there was the meeting between Todd, Benjy, and Gutang, which was very much on DiPalma's mind. If the boys got the tape, would he then be able to get it out of the country? *Paisan,* he thought, between the woman you married and the child you brought into this world, you're carrying one hell of a cross.

The telephone rang and DiPalma snatched at the receiver. "Yeah."

"Federico. Miss de Vega is downstairs with me. Shall I bring her up?"

"Right away. And, Federico, thanks. I really appreciate what you've done."

In the lobby, the bell captain hung up the phone and turned to the three Chinese men who had him encircled. All three wore *barong tagalogs,* the embroidered overshirt popular with men living in the Philippines. Two held revolvers under folded newspapers pressed against Federico's spine and right kidney.

The third, his hand on the shoulder of a terrified Huziyana de Vega, said, "Let's go upstairs."

# Twelve

Shortly before noon, Benjy stepped from a taxi at the corners of Rizal and Recto Streets, the edge of Manila's Chinatown. A folded jacket and tie hung from one arm and his shoulder-length hair had been cut to within half an inch of his skull. He wore sunglasses and carried a small brown leather suitcase.

Ignoring fortune-tellers, beggars, food vendors and sellers of pirated cassette tapes, he climbed into a *calesa,* a horse-drawn rig, and ordered the driver to take him into Chinatown. Entrance to Chinatown was on foot or by carriage. Cars were banned.

"Don't leave the hotel," Todd's father had said. But nothing had been said about making a stop before Benjy got there. One stop. *Who'd know?*

He'd taken the first flight out of New York. An hour later Todd was to follow on a different airline, flying to L.A., then catching a connecting flight to Manila. Joan was to take the first flight to Honolulu and go on to Manila from there. For the moment Benjy was in Manila by himself.

He'd come to Chinatown to buy a gun. Man, did he feel naked without one. Since Benjy didn't know Gutang, it might be a good idea to be packing heat when they met.

Self-assertive and sometimes prone to take the hard line,

Benjy had a dynamic willpower that had won him the leadership of the Jade Eagles, as well as the admiration of Lin Pao. He applied himself wholeheartedly to whatever he was doing and stayed with it until completion. He could also be narrow-minded and vindictive when he didn't get his way.

In the gang his word was law; he knew how to give orders and expected them to be carried out. He was respected for his honesty and unpretentiousness, however, and because he cared about the Jade Eagles. Benjy cared even more about Todd, which is why he wanted a gun.

He'd been a twelve-year-old Jade Eagle when he'd made his first drug run to Manila from Hong Kong. Later he'd carried drugs and money out of Manila to Sydney, Honolulu, Chicago, and New York. He'd come a long way from the nine-year-old Hong Kong orphan who'd taken over a street gang by throwing its leader off an eight-story roof in a fight to the death. Benjy was a survivor, the guy who outlasted everybody else. That's why he wasn't going to meet Mr. Gutang empty-handed.

Some Jade Eagles had told Benjy about Mr. Two, the old Chinese who operated out of Manila's Chinatown. He was called Two because of his two businesses: He ran an herb shop while selling guns out of the basement. His handguns weren't cheap, but he offered a nice selection to choose from. And he didn't ask questions.

Benjy didn't need a college degree to know that guns were a way of life in the Philippines. Blame it on poverty, crime, and some very wacky politics. Catholics, Moslems, and communists kept blowing each other away. And don't forget the private wars between army death squads, gangsters, union leaders, Marcos supporters, and Aquino supporters. Those people who died, Benjy thought, were those people too poor to afford a gun.

He'd never met Mr. Two. Hell, he hadn't been in Manila for two years, which ought to cut down on his chances of being recognized. He'd buy a piece, then get to the hotel long before Todd and Joan arrived. With a gun, Benjy and

Todd at least had a chance of getting out of the Philippines alive.

Thanks to Todd, the Black General's plan to waste the Jade Eagles wasn't a secret anymore. After hearing about it, gang members had gone into hiding or split from New York in a hurry. Some had headed to Canada and Europe. A few had taken off for Hawaii while others had gone to Puerto Rico and Santo Domingo. Suddenly the Chinese boys who'd come to America to get rich were now only interested in staying alive. Did Benjy know what he was going to do after Manila? Fuck, no. He'd just have to trust Todd to come up with something.

Todd's fight with Ivan Ho had been unreal. Out of sight. On a scale of one to ten, score it eleven. Watching Ho get stomped had almost made Benjy come in his pants. Elder Brother was a prick who got off beating up kids. What goes around comes around.

The other Jade Eagles who'd been there had an answer for Todd's fighting ability. He was stoned on angel dust, they said. Or he'd been wired on coke. How else could the kid have turned into Rambo?

Benjy decided, Shit, let them believe what they want to believe. There were some truths that couldn't be told; if told, they would only bring forth confusion. As for his relationship with Todd, Benjy explained they'd met in a Canal Street video arcade and discovered they'd spent time in the same Hong Kong orphanage years ago.

"We're distant cousins," Benjy said. A slight hype, but not entirely false. For hadn't they been brothers in another life?

When Benjy entered the small, cramped herb shop at Chinatown's Plaza Santa Cruz, Mr. Two had just sold a slender bottle of snake musk to a young Indian woman wearing a white-and-gold sari. Mr. Two, a short, gray-haired man with pudgy cheeks and a sad, sensitive face, glanced at Benjy before handing the woman her change.

Turning his back to the counter, Benjy stepped to a low

shelf crammed with bottles of all sizes, shapes, and colors. A green jar marked POWDERED LIZARD caught his eye. Leaning down, he picked it up and studied the label. When the Indian woman left the shop, he placed the jar back on the shelf and slowly turned to face Mr. Two. After adjusting his dark glasses, Benjy strolled over to the counter.

Laying his jacket near the cash register, he placed his suitcase on the floor and spoke in Cantonese. "I want to buy a gun."

Mr. Two, whose real name was Yuan Sen, shook his head. When he spoke, his lips hardly moved. "No guns. I sell herbs. Any herbs you want, I have."

"Wrong answer, old man." Benjy was in no mood for bullshit. He was very tired and very hungry. His back was aching a bit where he'd been shot, though Todd had said it was healing okay. The sooner he finished here, the better. Mr. Two had guns, and Benjy was going to get one if he had to break the dude's arm.

He looked over his shoulder, then at Mr. Two. "Hear me, old man. The meter's running, understand? I'm in a hurry, so don't jerk me around. You sell guns. You know it, I know it. And they're for sale to the right people. People we both know. Now either you take me downstairs or I take *myself* downstairs. Try to stop me and I'll shove some of your bottles up your ass. Am I getting through to you?"

Mr. Two didn't look worried. Rather he appeared composed and unconcerned, as though Benjy were nothing more than a frolicking puppy. "It is not always good to rush things," he said.

"It's not always good to keep me waiting. Show me what you got."

"You mentioned I sold guns to people we know."

Benjy was getting tired of this little dance. It was time to tell it like it is. "Last year you sold Brownings to Sam Liu and Peter Chen. You charged them five hundred dollars each."

Mr. Two sighed and brought his folded hands to his lips. Then, nibbling the tips of his forefingers, he eyed Benjy from behind almost closed eyelids. After a while he left the counter and, arms behind his back, slowly walked toward the rear of the shop.

At a thick metal door he reached inside his shirt, pulled out a key attached to a long gold chain around his neck, then turned and looked at Benjy. Grinning, the teenager followed him.

It was nearly two o'clock that afternoon when Charles Sui answered a cellular telephone in the basement of his opulent home, a former Augustinian monastery in Forbes Park, Manila's poshest suburb.

Sui, a lean, youthful-looking man with sleepy eyes and an icy elegance, had been absorbed in playing Wagner on an organ constructed especially for him. The unique instrument was a smaller replica of the famed nineteenth-century bamboo organ in the two-hundred-year-old Las Pinas Church just outside Manila. Sui played music as he did tennis, painstakingly but with little feeling.

His Triad duties were carried out with the same unmerciful resolution. He cared little about others, treasured his own privacy, and was fanatical about accumulating wealth. After all, he was the son of a legendary Triad figure and the godson of the Black General, sound reasons for being relentless in his ambition.

He wallowed in intrigue and conspiracies, occupying his mind with plots aimed at keeping opponents and associates off-balance. Paranoid and suspicious, he distrusted members of the Hundred Pacer Snakes, as well as his own family. This did not stop him from being demanding or feeling an intense disappointment when they failed to live up to his expectations. If displeased, there was no limit to Sui's anger. Those who betrayed him or did less than their best faced a mighty hatred.

The telephone call to his basement, which had interrupted a *Parsifal* aria, was from Yuan Sen. Mr. Two's habitual drug-induced composure did not hide the irritation in his voice. He demanded to know why he hadn't been told in advance that the Triad was sending one of its young gangsters to buy guns.

"It's customary to alert me before your murderous children appear on my doorstep," he said. "I insist on knowing who I'm dealing with. I insist on it."

Three times a week Charles Sui left his Manila real-estate office at noon sharp and returned home for a vegetarian meal prepared by his wife of twelve years, to be followed by precisely forty-five minutes at the organ. While at his music he wasn't to be disturbed, except for an emergency. Apparently his wife had viewed the lamenting, whining Mr. Two as an emergency. Sui had married a woman incapable of sound judgment.

For most of his working life the herbalist had limited himself to selling magical oils, devil candles, and love potions. Then, ten years ago, he'd inherited a small illegal gun business from an older brother who'd been shot to death by the Moslem wife of a dissatisfied customer. The wife's husband had purchased an expensive pistol, only to have it misfire during an attack on his life. After his death his unforgiving spouse had acquired an additional pistol elsewhere, thus presenting Yuan Sen with a second income and the alias Mr. Two.

But in the gun business he worried about police informants, rip-offs, or being killed for selling to the wrong people, as his brother had been. To avoid these mishaps he preferred to sell weapons to those he knew or who came recommended by people he trusted.

"You're supposed to let me know in advance when one of your boys is coming in," Mr. Two said to Charles Sui. "I find your disregard of procedures disturbing. Am I to assume you intend to allow your homicidal cubs free reign on my life? The one you sent today was a veritable little emperor."

An irritated Sui said, "Are you mad? I've sent no one to you."

What on earth was this pitiful opium addict babbling on about?

Of course. No one had told the old fart that the Jade Eagles weren't being used anymore. The gang knew of Lin Pao's plan to kill them and were now in hiding or desperately seeking a safe haven. Two of them had been found and executed. But the most dangerous of the lot, their leader, Benjy Lok Nein, was still free.

Had Benjy's young friend really bested the enforcer, Ivan Ho, in a scuffle? Sui considered this a rather fanciful tale, particularly since Ho was so adept in the martial arts and an accomplished assassin. How could such a man be defeated by a mere boy?

Charles Sui, meanwhile, had more pressing problems than the perennially sedated Mr. Two. An American reporter, Frank DiPalma, was due to arrive in Manila sometime this evening. Since DiPalma and Martin Mackie had been seen together in New York, Sui deduced that the American was coming to investigate the death of Mackie's goddaughter, Angela Ramos.

At this point Sui had a boundless hatred for Leon Bacolod, the dim-witted little arsonist who had been engaged to kill Angela Ramos. By leaving his accursed watch at the scene of the fire, Bacolod had put Sui at great risk. From the watch to Bacolod to Sui was an easy avenue to follow, had authorities chosen to do so. Fortunately they hadn't.

A police officer aligned to the Triad said the watch had probably been stolen by the dwarf whore, Huziyana de Vega, who lived with Bacolod in a Chinatown slum. She'd recently returned from holiday and immediately taken into police custody for questioning. Bacolod hadn't returned with her. It would seem he sensed that Sui intended to punish him for having done less than a proper job.

The de Vega woman denied having stolen the watch, which was to be expected. She also denied knowing Bacolod's whereabouts. The police had released her this morning, apparently having accepted her variation of the truth concerning Leon Bacolod. Sui, however, was having her watched around the clock. When he was certain the police were through with her, he intended to have the little slut brought to him and questioned severely, if not bloodily, until she revealed Bacolod's hiding place.

He said to Mr. Two, "I've sent no boy to you, nor do I intend doing so in the near future."

The herbalist persisted. "I know he was one of yours. I know a hooligan when I see one. He mentioned certain gang members by name, youngsters you've previously sent to me. Such a bossy little peacock. Demanded I show him only Uzis. Nothing but Uzis."

Charles Sui spun around on the bench, turning his back to the organ. "Uzis?"

"Damn particular, that one. Carrying a fair amount of cash in a money belt, as your little thugs often do. In future I must be told these boys are coming to me. I simply must be told."

Sui closed his eyes. "His name. Did he give you his name?"

"Does it matter?"

Sui was on his feet, cellular phone pressed in both hands. "Listen to me, old man. Did he give you his name?"

Something in the Triad leader's voice frightened Yuan Sen. Mr. Two suddenly became more respectful. "No. He appeared somewhat cautious."

"In what hotel is he staying?"

"I don't know."

"I want you to think, old man. Push aside your opium dreams and tell me something about this boy. Because unless you do, you will not live out the day. I ask you again: Tell me something about this boy."

Mr. Two was quiet. Then he said in a soft voice, "I believe he comes from America. His Cantonese has a slight American intonation and his jacket has an American label. There was a ticket from an American airline in the jacket pocket. He appears to have the brashness that comes with living in America."

"Describe him to me."

As Mr. Two forced his mind to dredge up details concerning the appearance of the boy to whom he'd sold an

Uzi, Charles Sui said nothing, and in the silence Mr. Two remembered that the godson of the Black General rarely issued an order twice.

"He was young," the herbalist said. "Quite handsome. Thinking it over, I'd have to say he was a born leader."

Charles Sui thanked Mr. Two for calling, then immediately hung up. Next he called his office and said he would not be returning that day. Wife and servants were ordered not to disturb him until further notice. He needed time to think.

And later that evening, when informed that the de Vega woman was on her way to DiPalma's hotel, the pieces of the puzzle came together in Charles Sui's mind. He was about to be betrayed to the American by the dwarf whore and Benjy Lok Nein, the boy who'd purchased the Uzi from Mr. Two. The de Vega woman would reveal the truth about the arson deaths of the forty-three women at Taaltex. And Benjy, seeking revenge for the Black General's treachery, was to lead DiPalma to Charles Sui.

Sui ordered the men following Huziyana de Vega to interrogate her and DiPalma. Interrogate them sternly and together, comparing their answers. From the whore, they were to learn the whereabouts of Leon Bacolod. From the American, they were to learn the whereabouts of Benjy Lok Nein, since their simultaneous presence in Manila struck Charles Sui as more than mere coincidence.

Above all, DiPalma must be forced to reveal what he knew about Angela Ramos's death.

After that the American and the whore were to be executed.

# Thirteen

The three Chinese followed DiPalma from the foyer of his suite into the large, plush living room. Two held handguns aimed at his head.

Each Chinese wore the floral overshirts DiPalma had seen on men in the Philippines. Both guns were .22 Magnums with silencers. One was in the hands of a skinny teenager, whose wide-eyed stare DiPalma put down to nerves. The leader—a hefty young man with a thick neck, deep-set eyes, and several gold front teeth—didn't have a gun, but he sneered a lot.

As for Huziyana de Vega, DiPalma guessed her height to be somewhere between three and four feet. She had a large head, a sunken nose, and short, hairy arms. She wore a yellow silk dress, matching high-heeled shoes, dark glasses, and a wide-brim white felt hat. A white beaded bag hung from one tiny shoulder.

DiPalma had an eerie feeling about the way she was dressed. He'd seen it before, but where? And then it hit him: Rita Hayworth in *The Lady from Shanghai*. That's where the look had come from. He also remembered a very bad joke: Better to have loved a short person than never to have loved a tall. Jesus.

He'd heard a knock at the door, followed by Federico

identifying himself, and when he'd opened the door, the three Chinese behind Federico and Huziyana de Vega had pushed their way inside. What the hell was going on here? DiPalma had looked at Federico, who'd looked away. Then he saw the silenced handguns and his stomach turned icy. The gas pains sliced through his insides and his hands started to sweat.

Hit men. Shooters. Suddenly DiPalma became more angry than afraid. Shit, he hadn't been in the country long enough to make a nuisance of himself. Charlie Snake didn't believe in wasting time. Who else could these guys be but Snake's people?

DiPalma thought, Maybe they're only rip-off artists out for a quick score. Maybe the hotel just had bad security—nothing new in Manila. Maybe he'd walk away from this thing minus only a few bucks, credit cards, and the Rolex given him by the network for signing a new contract. Sure.

Muggers didn't cart witnesses around with them. Except there weren't going to be any witnesses. The silenced .22 Magnums said the Chinese were going to take out DiPalma. Huziyana de Vega and Federico weren't slated for long lives, either.

As DiPalma walked from the foyer he leaned heavily on his cane, making himself appear more helpless. Making himself seem less of a threat until he saw his chance. If the Chinese gave him one.

The chance came so quickly, he almost missed it.

In the living room, Thick Neck spat on an immaculate gray carpet and in passable English asked DiPalma if he was alone. Without waiting for an answer, he barked an order in Chinese, which sent the youngest shooter racing off to search the suite. A second order and his remaining shooter—a thin, balding man with a widow's peak of jet-black hair—stepped forward and jammed his Magnum into the left side of DiPalma's neck. Thick Neck's sneer now became more conspicuous.

If the gun against DiPalma's neck distressed him, it positively unnerved Federico. The bell captain began to plead for his life in earnest, mentioning his thirteen children and a widowed father who was going blind from diabetes and depended on Federico.

Then it was Huziyana de Vega's turn. Whimpering, she extended her short arms toward Thick Neck. Rita Hayworth couldn't have done it any better. "Please, my thyroid is troubling me. My heart, it is beating too fast. I must have my medicine." She opened her purse.

Intensifying his pleading, Federico touched Thick Neck, who regarded the unwanted handling as the last straw. He shoved the bell captain into Huziyana de Vega, which sent the tiny whore crashing into a bamboo side table. Her un-shut purse erupted, scattering jewelry over the carpet. Rings, bracelets, waist chains, necklaces, jeweled combs, earrings. The tools of her trade and all of it quite authentic-looking.

Still whining, the little whore quickly set about retrieving her treasure. Thick Neck and Widow's Peak, meanwhile, were temporarily mesmerized by the jewelry. They didn't know it was fake. Their eyes were bright with the thought of plunder and prosperity. DiPalma was momentarily for-gotten.

He went after Widow's Peak first.

Quickly pushing the Magnum away from his neck, DiPalma elbowed Widow's Peak in the face and with the knob of his cane, punched the Chinese in the throat. The shooter's head snapped back and he spun around, dropping to his knees while choking in his own blood.

Thick Neck turned from the jewels, took in the situation, and immediately shoved a hand under his shirt, clawing at his belt. He was pulling his hand from beneath his shirt when DiPalma backhanded the cane across his elbow, shat-tering the bone. Screaming, the chunky man dropped his Colt .45 automatic.

After the initial cry Thick Neck clutched his splintered elbow, gritted his teeth, and closed his eyes, which were still closed when DiPalma struck him in the forehead with the cane. Thick Neck dropped unconscious to the carpet, landing on his back, his legs crossed at the ankles.

Huziyana de Vega now started to scream. Federico added to the noise by repeating the name of Jesus over and over.

The noise drew the third shooter, the young one, who returned to the living room in a hurry. Unsure of himself, he stopped near the open French doors leading to the balcony and took three seconds to think. Then he saw motion and quickly brought his gun up from his side, firing at what had just registered in his brain.

His targets were Huziyana de Vega and Federico, both of whom were running toward the foyer that led to the front door. Federico reached the foyer and disappeared from sight just as a bullet sprayed plaster from the wall where his head had passed a second ago. Huziyana, running on stunted, bowed legs, couldn't keep up with him. The young dude lowered his Magnum and fired at her three times.

Twenty feet away from the young dude, DiPalma dropped to one knee, snatched a silenced Magnum from the floor, and, aiming for the young dude, squeezed off three rounds, hitting him each time, knocking him down and onto the balcony.

Gun still pointed at the downed man, DiPalma rose and walked over to look at him. Crouching, he felt for a neck pulse. There was none to find. He checked the other two Chinese. Widow's Peak, blood still flowing from his mouth, was dead. Thick Neck, however, was still breathing.

Huziyana de Vega hadn't been so lucky. Two of the three shots fired at her had missed; one had shattered a wall mirror, and the other had torn a gouge in a fairly good copy of a Spanish Baroque table. The third had left a small, dark hole in the back of Huziyana's white felt hat and was buried somewhere in the base of her skull. No more tricking in the raw for this little pro.

As for Federico, the suite's open door told DiPalma that the bell captain would live to pimp another day.

DiPalma closed the door, returned to the living room, and dialed security. After hanging up, he walked out to the balcony and stared at the darkening sky. To keep his hands from shaking, he gripped the wrought-iron railing.

# Fourteen

For two days after the death of Huziyana de Vega, a grieving Leon Bacolod sat naked in the bathtub of a cheap rooming house near the University of the Philippines and drank rum from the bottle. His only company was a portable black-and-white television set resting on the toilet.

Dazed and numb, Bacolod attempted to reflect upon his loss, and when his suffering failed to make him any wiser, he resumed drinking until he passed out. His pain knew no bounds.

Awake, he had periods of persistent weeping. Now and then he banged his head into the tiled walls and called for Huziyana. During the two days he sat in his own waste, neither cleaning himself nor leaving the tub.

So strong was Bacolod's emotional level that Huzi's death had injured him physically as well as mentally. On hearing the news, he'd been seized by a blinding headache. Both legs had been attacked by stabbing pains, and his spine had stiffened so much that bending or twisting in any direction was agony. His heart had begun beating at breakneck speed, then just as quickly slowed down, until the beat seemed to vanish. *Huzi . . . how can I live without her?*

From the first he'd drawn his strength from this special woman. Where Bacolod had felt threatened and unsure, she'd been audacious and brazen. She'd lived, dressed, and loved as she pleased, never caring who she upset or offended. Her sexual energy had been compelling, taking him into uncharted territory without stopping to consider the risks. Huzi had been a woman of action, always ready to conquer new worlds.

Oversensitive because of his cleft palate, epilepsy, and lack of education, Bacolod had been an injured bird who'd needed Huzi's protective nature. And while her whoring had initially bothered him, he'd come to accept it, largely because she'd given him no choice in the matter. "You're sharing my life," she told Bacolod. "I'm not sharing yours.

"And never ask me why I whore," she told Bacolod. "I do it because it's the only game worth playing, and because I'm good at it."

On their recent holiday together Bacolod had worked up the courage to tell her that the watch she'd given him had been accidentally left at the scene of the Taaltex fire. He needn't have worried about her getting angry. She'd been understanding, totally forgiving, and had gone out of her way to cheer him up.

When Bacolod mentioned that Charles Sui would kill him for this slipup, Huzi said, "I'll protect you from Charlie Snake. We'll deal with him together."

Bacolod, thumb in his mouth, had placed his head in her lap and smiled. There was no one in the world like Huzi. No one.

It had been her idea that he go to Quezon City just outside Manila and hide near the University of the Philippines. There were plenty of inexpensive rooming houses near the campus, one of the most attractive in Asia. The baby-faced Bacolod would have no problem passing as a student.

He wasn't to contact her. Huzi would call him every other day, in the afternoon, and always from a customer's phone. A week or two at the university, then they'd find a new hiding place. "But for now," she said, "you join those little shits who think they're smarter than the rest of us."

It had been impossible for him to attend Huzi's funeral,

which had been arranged by an aunt, herself a prostitute until her recent retirement. A couple of telephone calls confirmed what Bacolod suspected: Charles Sui was indeed looking for him and would have men at the funeral. If anything, the situation had gotten worse. Sui now had Bacolod's watch. He'd gotten it from the Manila police, who'd confiscated it from the American, Frank DiPalma.

DiPalma. Bacolod was on fire with hatred for this man. Thinking about his name twisted Bacolod's features into a grotesque mask. Had it not been for him, Huzi would still be alive. Bacolod's hatred of DiPalma had become so keen that it threatened to become his only pleasure.

His psychotic mind, distorted by grief and alcohol, refused to accept newspaper and television accounts of Huzi's death. WHORE IN ASSIGNATION WITH AMERICAN JOURNALIST SLAIN BY HOTEL THIEVES. Bullshit. She'd been murdered because DiPalma had tried to use her to get to Bacolod.

The arsonist knew dirty tricks when he saw them. Hadn't the press said that DiPalma worked for the American television network owned by Nelson Berlin? The same Berlin who stood to benefit from the fire at Taaltex Industries. Bacolod was capable of drawing only one conclusion: There was a plot against him. The two Americans and Charlie Snake wanted him silenced forever so that he couldn't tell anyone about the fire.

Well, Bacolod would have something to say about that. He was going to kill DiPalma. If it was the last thing he did on this earth, Bacolod was going to destroy the man responsible for Huzi's murder. DiPalma had admitted killing two of Sui's men but had denied killing Huzi.

Mr. DiPalma, you are a fucking liar, Bacolod thought. Two dead men and a third with a cracked skull and Huzi dead and only DiPalma left standing. DiPalma, who'd admitted inviting Huzi to his suite because, as he put it, he was working on a story. The truth according to Mr. DiPalma. Well, let him say whatever he wanted. Bacolod knew better.

Still in the bathtub, Bacolod swallowed more rum, then placed the almost empty bottle in the tub between his legs.

"I know the truth," he whispered. Oh, yes, he did. DiPalma was responsible for Huzi's death because she'd gone to meet him in his suite. *At DiPalma's invitation.*

Bacolod didn't care why DiPalma had killed Sui's men. He cared about Huzi and nobody else.

He swallowed the last of the rum, dropped the empty bottle on the floor, then let his arms flop over the side. He started to weep again. "Huzi, I love you. Love you, love you, love you."

Then Bacolod remembered DiPalma. Leaning out of the tub, Bacolod snatched a cigarette lighter from the floor, then collapsed back into his own filth. He turned the lighter around in his stained fingers, then flicked back the top and thumbed the lighter wheel into flame. He giggled. Fire held no terror for him, but it would for DiPalma. Bacolod swore this by the Virgin.

That same afternoon, DEA supervisor Barry Omens, a short, forty-four-year-old Irishman with droopy eyelids, stepped from the hotel hallway and followed Todd into a Spanish-style suite, lighting a cigarette and wondering if it had been prudent to get involved with one Frank DiPalma.

Putting it bluntly, DiPalma was currently holding the rough end of the pineapple. Filipino police had detained him in connection with three killings, one of the departed having been a hooker. A dwarf hooker. Talk about weird.

A witness to the killings, a hotel bell captain named Federico Laurel, was missing and therefore unable to corroborate certain portions of DiPalma's story. Whether or not DiPalma would get the chance to tie Lin Pao to Nelson Berlin, who could say? Omens did know this: Involving himself in something this sticky just short of his retirement might strike some people as ill advised, if not goddamn stupid.

In the living room, Todd led him to a Venetian gilt arm-chair, where he sat down, stubbed out his cigarette in an ashtray on a wicker end table, and looked at the three

Chinese kids facing him. Frank's backup. Frank had to be kidding.

Two Asian males, one Asian female. Not one of them old enough to vote, legally drive a car, or see R-rated movies. What the fuck was Frank going to do with this crew, run for student council president? DiPalma was a man who'd set fire to his hair and was trying to put it out with a hammer.

Leaning back in his chair, Omens studied one of the kids, who looked away from him. Omens smiled. My, my, Mr. Bad Attitude himself, Benjy Lok Nein. Baby-faced killer, drug courier, enforcer, extortionist. What was Frank doing running around with this cold-blooded little punk?

And why the girl? She sat in a brown leather chair, eyes glued to Todd as if he were Christ come down to earth. Even Mr. Vicious, our boy Benjy, seemed to recognize the quiet, self-possessed Todd as crew spokesman.

Omens said to Todd, "Your dad didn't want me saying too much to you over the phone. Right now he's a bit paranoid, and I don't blame him. But as I said earlier, he's fine. Senator Quarequio's working on getting him released and has the embassy involved as well. Meanwhile Frank says for you not to worry, to go ahead with everything as planned. He also says to keep in touch with me. Cops don't turn him loose in two days, you guys are to return to New York. He thinks it's too dangerous for you to hang around here."

Omens waited for Todd to come apart, to insist he wasn't leaving Manila without his father, to ask Omens what should be done next. Surprise, surprise. Todd stared at Omens for several seconds, then nodded once. It was a sign of someone very much in control of himself. The kid definitely had his shit together. What was it Frank had said? "Don't talk down to Todd. He's not your everyday kid, not by far."

"I want to thank you for helping us," Todd said. "And I appreciate your going to see my father at police headquarters."

Omens grinned. "Frank said you were smart. You're right. Being seen with your dad at this point in time is risky business. Especially if you plan on retiring with a full pension. I told the agency that Frank's trying to get something on Lin Pao and Nelson Berlin, and he's willing to share. So they didn't come down too hard on me for paying him a visit. Sooner or later, though, I'm going to have to show my people something.''

Todd said, ''Sometime today we're to meet a man who has the information my father's told you about.''

Omens paused in the act of lighting a cigarette. ''When and where?''

''We don't know,'' Benjy said. ''The dude wants to pick the time and place. He's scared. Doesn't trust anybody. Says the meeting goes down his way or there's no meeting.''

Omens took a drag on his Salem, exhaled, and said to Todd, ''I think you'd better plan on leaving without Frank. Not that he won't be turned loose eventually, but don't count on it happening anytime soon. The Filipino government's involved. I had to use a few favors to get to talk with Frank, who clued me in. The rest I picked up by asking around.''

Omens said that the government didn't want foreign corporations scared off, so it was putting its own spin on this thing. Frank would not be allowed to make trouble for the multinationals. Martin Mackie had tried and failed. Mackie's friend, Mr. DiPalma, was also going to fail.

Todd said, ''I'm sure this is why the hotel bell captain cannot be found.''

Omens almost dropped his cigarette. ''How did you know about that? It's supposed to be a big fat secret. The government's got Federico Laurel stashed to keep him from backing up Frank's story. There's not supposed to be any mention of Triads or Lin Pao or anything that might lead to Nelson Berlin. How the hell did you find out about Laurel?''

Todd said, ''Have you spoken to the surviving Chinese, the man my father knocked out?''

Omens smiled and shook his head. ''Kid, you ever think about working with the agency, say, in intelligence? That Chinese, the one Frank hit in the coconut with his cane, seems to have disappeared from the hospital. He was never booked, either. Again, nobody's supposed to know this. If you read the papers or watch the TV newscasts, you'll notice there's only a mention of two robbers. Two, not three.''

Todd looked at Benjy. ''Laurel will say what the government orders him to say. We must get that information on Berlin and Lin Pao, then what the government says will not matter.''

Benjy nodded.

Omens thought, Definitely not your everyday kid.

There was a knock at the door. Omens watched Benjy and Todd exchange looks, then Benjy walked to a white leather sofa and sat down with his hand behind one of the cushions. Omens tensed. He thought, Jesus, it's my turn to get caught in a hotel shoot-out. Then Todd looked at Benjy and shook his head. Benjy relaxed, placed both hands on his knees, and stared down at his hands.

Omens watched Todd walk to the foyer, then disappear. He heard the front door open, then shut, and seconds later Todd returned holding a white envelope. Opening it, he removed a small piece of paper, read its contents, and looked at Benjy, who nodded. If there'd been a silent signal between the two, Omens had missed it. Todd put the paper back into the envelope and placed the envelope in his shirt pocket.

Then, ignoring Omens, Todd spoke to Benjy and the girl in Cantonese. Omens, of course, didn't understand a fucking word, and wasn't meant to. When Todd finished, all three kids took off in separate directions. Joan left the living room, walked into a bedroom, and reappeared seconds later carrying a shoulder bag. Benjy removed an Uzi from behind a couch cushion and walked into a different room. When he reappeared, he was bare-chested and carrying a shoulder bag and a pale blue shirt.

Todd followed him, carrying what Omens took to be an attaché case. The DEA supervisor thought, They've got the drill down pat. Everybody's moving according to some sort of prearranged plan. Todd's plan.

Omens said, "That note was from the guy you're supposed to meet."

Todd said, "Yes."

Omens stood up. If he asked to come along, he'd be wasting his time. Todd didn't look like somebody you talk into doing anything he didn't want to do. Besides, there was Benjy and his Uzi. Omens said, "I'd like to touch base with you. What time will you be coming back here?"

Without replying, Todd headed for the front door. Joan trotted after him.

Omens turned to Benjy, who'd put on the shirt but left it unbuttoned. Reaching in the shoulder bag, the teenager removed a money belt, then hurried toward the door while placing the belt around his waist.

Omens thought, Now what? He tried the Todd question on Benjy. "When are you guys coming back?"

Benjy never slowed down. "We're not. We'll meet the guy, get the shit, then check into another hotel."

Omens said, "You're leaving your luggage?"

"Todd says it'll make people think we're coming back. There's cash in the bedroom. Pay the bill."

*Pay the bill?* Fuck you too. Omens raced after Benjy. He had a few questions for Mr. Vicious. At the entrance to the foyer, Omens stopped and kicked the baseboard. Shit. Too late. The front door to the suite was open. The kids were long gone.

Downstairs in the hotel lobby, Assistant Reservations Clerk Pedro Sison watched Todd, Benjy, and Joan leave the elevator and head for the hotel entrance. Sison, a diminutive Filipino with narrow eyes, continued to watch the three youngsters as he used a hotel phone to dial the number of a cellular phone in a car parked a block away.

When someone answered at the other end of the line, Sison said, "Benjy and his friends are leaving now." Then he hung up and turned his attention to an Italian cellist and his lover, two young men on their first trip to Asia.

# Fifteen

It looked like a small, quiet village, with houses, trees, power lines, gardens, and mailboxes. It might have been a residential community or an untroubled suburb of Manila. Instead this was the Chinese Cemetery, and the houses were the most extraordinary tombs in the world.

These normal-looking homes, with their carpeting, toilets, and air conditioners, were strictly for the use of the dead. In these bizarre tombs survivors received the spirits of the departed and did everything possible to please them. Sunday visits were the occasions to restock refrigerators, change light bulbs, bring newspapers, and hang fresh clothes in the closets. It was not unusual for the living to sit down for a game of Mah-Jongg, with an empty chair at the table for the deceased.

Ninety minutes after leaving Barry Omens at the hotel, Todd, Benjy, and Joan emerged from a taxi at the entrance to the Chinese Cemetery. Three guides watched them approach. Todd asked them for Alfredo Locsin.

Locsin, a lean, graying Filipino with missing front teeth, was the oldest guide. He identified himself and was handed the envelope received by Todd at the hotel. Removing the slip of paper from the envelope, Locsin squinted at it for several seconds, then nodded. After pocketing a hundred-

peso note Todd had placed in the envelope the guide said,
"I wrote this, yes. The man you want to see is waiting for
you. Please follow me."

Walking with a slight stoop, Locsin led them into the
almost empty cemetery, past lifeless homes, ornate Buddhist
and Catholic crypts, fir trees and stunted pines. No one
spoke. Joan clung to Todd's arm and kept her head down,
as though fearing she might see something ghostly. Benjy
brought up the rear, now and then looking over his shoulder,
glad it was still light and that they weren't bopping around
this place in the dark.

In the center of the cemetery, Locsin turned right at a
pair of dragon temples and began striding up a concrete
walk leading to the top of a slight incline. At the top of the
incline he stopped in front of a small, one-story brick house
fronted by a narrow, well-tended garden. The trip had been
made in silence. They'd encountered no other visitors.

Made edgy by the silence, Benjy said, "For Christ's sake,
is Gutang in there or not?"

An annoyed Locsin said, "You think I bring you all this
way for nothing? You think I walk here myself for nothing?" Cursing under his breath, he began his return journey
to the cemetery entrance. Fucking kids. Why did they think
the world began and ended with them?

Eyes on the retreating guide, Benjy said, "I don't trust
anybody who spends all his time around dead people. Todd,
what about it? Think Gutang's in there?"

Todd took a step toward the house, then stopped. "He's
near the window facing the garden."

Benjy looked up at the sky. "Checking us out, right?"
He slapped the left side of his face, killing a mosquito that
had been using him for fast food. Mosquitoes, humidity,
traffic jams. Manila never changed.

Benjy was about to jump out of his skin. Standing around
a cemetery while thinking about that cold-blooded, un-
friendly bastard Charlie Snake was a bummer. The sooner
Benjy hauled ass out of here, the better.

He looked at Joan, who was even more scared and doing

her best to hide it. She was a shy thing, with the darkest hair and saddest eyes he'd ever seen on a girl. Benjy found her very attractive, with a sweetness missing in big-city girls. You felt like protecting her from the big bad world. "Treat her with respect," Todd had ordered. "Honor her." He didn't bother adding, "Don't try to fuck her." Benjy got the picture.

Just turned sixteen, Joan was from Kaohsiung, Taiwan's oldest city, and had grown up wanting to be a secretary. A month ago her father had sent her north to Taipei, to a secretarial school run by a friend of the family. She was to stay with an aunt and return home in four months.

But on arriving at the school's address, she'd found only a bare office, where three men had forced her to sign a contract stating that she owed money to the Hundred Pacer Snakes. A substantial amount of money. Joan's father, owner of a small taxi fleet, was a gambler and deep in debt to the Triad. To stay alive he'd sold her to his creditors. His debt was now Joan's.

To repay it she would have to work in one of the Triad's New York massage parlors. The debt would also include her passage money to America and living expenses while there.

She adored Todd, which left Benjy feeling jealous, but it was nothing he couldn't live with. Apparently she got her kicks waiting on Todd hand and foot. Benjy thought of her as Todd's little poodle, an opinion he wisely kept to himself. Joan saw to Todd's meals, laid out his clothes, drew his bath, and even watched him while he slept. No fucking for them, either. Todd was all business. And everyone around him had better be the same.

Joan was polite to Benjy, but Todd was her lord and master. What else could you expect? Hadn't she been Todd's slave in another life?

Benjy, Todd, and Joanie Sad Eyes. Three people picking up where they'd left off four hundred years ago. Life was karma—and karma, Benjy knew, was unchangeable. Thinking about this had made him wonder what Todd and

Joan found to talk about. The two were always whispering to each other, and Benjy had felt left out. Finally he'd gotten Todd off alone, just the two of them, and asked him what the chat was all about.

At first Todd hadn't answered. Benjy thought, Watch him trash my ass for asking about something that's not my business. When Todd finally did speak, his answer stunned Benjy. ''Death will soon come to Joan. I am preparing her.'' Benjy never brought up the subject again.

In the cemetery, Todd knocked on the front door of the small brick house where Gutang was waiting. Uzi in one hand, Benjy stood behind him, eyes sweeping the deserted cemetery. When the front door opened, Benjy brought up the Uzi and aimed it toward the house.

From the house a timid male voice said in English, ''I am not armed. Come in.''

Inside, Raul Gutang softly closed the door behind the youngsters, then led the way into a small dining room. After closing the shutters he pointed to a circular table. Place settings—dishes, silverware, pewter candlestick holders, fresh-cut flowers—had been pushed to one side, leaving half of the table clear. Todd and Joan sat down. Benjy remained at a window, where he peeked through the shutters before turning to face the table.

At the fireplace, Gutang removed a large brown envelope from the mantelpiece and returned to the table where he stood waiting. He was in his thirties, a thin, gauntly handsome Filipino with black hair, mustache, and a high-pitched voice. There was a tic near his left eye and he used a green handkerchief to mop perspiration from his face and neck. Benjy thought, The dude stinks of fear.

Todd placed his half of the thousand-dollar bill on the table and pushed it toward Gutang. The computer operator flung the brown envelope at Todd, then snatched up the torn bill half. Both hands shook as he removed his wallet, pulled out his bill half, and placed it next to Todd's. They matched. He smiled and looked toward the front door.

Benjy said, "We check what's in the envelope, then you leave."

Gutang said, "Yes, yes. But please hurry."

Placing his lap-top computer on the table, Todd said, "It is good that you have honored your wife with such an attractive house. I am sorry she had to die so young."

Gutang nodded. "She was Chinese. Her family and I thought the house—" He stopped. "How did you know about my wife?"

Todd picked up the brown envelope. "She died in a traffic accident two years ago. A drunk driver struck her car head-on, killing your only child as well. You recently became engaged again."

A shocked Gutang nodded his head. "Elizabeth Kuan. We worked together in Taaltex's computer department. The company doesn't like fraternization between employees, so we had to keep our relationship secret. She was a wonderful woman."

His eyes filled with tears. "They attacked her. Took photographs while they did things to her, the bastards."

Todd said, "She wanted revenge."

"I begged her to forget about vengeance, but she was a very proud woman. So they killed her. I'm not a courageous man, but I couldn't let them get away with it. Mr. Mackie thinks I'm doing this for the money. The money is important, yes. I intend to leave the Philippines immediately. But the money is not everything. Do you understand?"

"Yes. The spirits of your wife and fiancée are pleased with you."

Gutang stopped drying his tears, then smiled. "Yes," he whispered. "They are pleased. Thank you for telling me that. I needed to hear those words."

Todd removed a single diskette from the envelope. After looking inside the envelope and finding nothing else, he stared at the floppy disk. It was double-sided, high-density, and double-track. One thin piece of plastic capable of holding much information.

Opening his computer case, he pressed the power switch,

slipped the diskette into the drive slot, and began to access. Gutang walked to the table and stood behind him. He said, "You're looking at some of the companies created by Lin Pao and Nelson Berlin to handle Pao's money. Some are legitimate businesses, others are shell companies. Do you understand shell companies?"

Eyes on the screen, Todd nodded. "My father used to be a policeman. He has discussed such things with me many times. He will know more about this than I, but yes, I understand much of what you say."

"Lin Pao deals in cash, and this cash must be made bankable before he can put it into legitimate businesses or spend it. This is where Nelson Berlin comes in. He launders the money for Pao. He cleans it up so that it can be used in polite society."

Todd said, "Through Taaltex?"

Gutang pressed the page-down key, bringing a new page on screen. "In this part of the world Berlin does everything through Taaltex," he said. "He uses his Asian hotels. He uses Asian banks, where he keeps personal and business accounts. Sometimes he blends Pao's money with his, then ships it all from a bank here in Manila to banks in Europe and Latin America. After all this traveling, Lin Pao's money is clean. It is now very legitimate."

Benjy said, "Last money run I did for Pao was down to Panama. That cop who just got busted, Van Rooten, he was supposed to take money there before he flipped out. The way I look at it, Mr. Berlin ain't nothing more than a common mule like the rest of us dumb chinks."

Gutang tapped Todd on the shoulder, then pointed at the monitor. "This is a Manila real-estate company in which Berlin has an interest. It's run by Charles Sui, who's Lin Pao's man in this part of Asia. The company does construction, rentals, and building management in a dozen countries. It also arranges for Lin Pao to be paid for his drugs and guns—not necessarily in cash but in things like oil, cotton, tin. This is another way of washing money."

Gutang tapped the monitor. "This man, he is a Brazilian

who lives in Rio de Janeiro. He is in charge of the Berlin hotels in South America. Any illegitimate money sent to him by Lin Pao, he sends back as emeralds."

Todd said, "What is the meaning of these listings for Zurich banks?"

Gutang smiled. "Those are payments made by Lin Pao and Mr. Berlin to President Marcos. The Philippines is an excellent source of cheap labor, something very important to Berlin and other businessmen. We have many Japanese companies exploiting our people as well. God forgive me for having helped them do it. Berlin paid Marcos through Swiss banks, and in return Marcos made sure there were no labor problems. Berlin also convinced Lin Pao to make political contributions."

Todd removed the floppy disk, then switched off the computer. "My father will be very pleased with this information," he said. "Thank you, Mr. Gutang. You don't have to stay here any longer."

Gutang looked around the small house. "My wife was a very decent woman. And so was Elizabeth Kuan. I have lost two very special people. You are right. I honor their memory by exposing Nelson Berlin and Lin Pao. Please thank Martin Mackie for the money."

Todd extended his hand. "I will do that, sir."

"You are very much a gentleman. I can understand now why your father is willing to place so much trust in you. Tell him many women were murdered to keep this information secret. Their souls must be honored as well."

"He will understand."

They shook hands. Then Gutang looked around the small house for the last time and left.

Benjy closed the door behind him, stepped to the nearest window, and peeked through the shutter. At the table, Todd returned the diskette to its envelope and handed it to Joan to put in her shoulder bag.

Suddenly Benjy said, "Holy shit."

He turned to face Todd. "Four guys just grabbed Gutang at the bottom of the hill. Can't be sure, but I think they're

Chinese. Ten to one they're Charlie Sui's boys. If they followed him, they're gonna be interested in us. And if they followed us, it ain't gonna do him any good, either. I mean, who else would be interested in us but the Triad?''

Benjy again looked out the window. ''Fuck, Gutang almost got away. They ran him down in front of the dragon temples. Man, they're really doing a number on the dude. Punching, kicking, everything. Poor bastard. He's gonna tell them about the diskette, that's for sure. He's gonna tell them anything they want to know. How the hell did they find us?''

Removing a brass candlestick holder from the table, Todd closed his eyes. Silently he begged the spirits of the house for their forgiveness, for his being forced by karma to take the candlestick and thus desecrate a tomb.

Opening his eyes, Todd looked at Benjy and Joan, both of whom were watching him intently. Without a word of command he led the way out of the house, past the narrow garden and onto the top of the incline. A hundred yards away, at the base of the incline and near the dragon temples, four Chinese stood over a prostrate Raul Gutang.

Benjy said, ''I think maybe we should get the fuck out of here.''

Todd, eyes on the four men, shook his head. ''Not yet. We can't outrun them with Joan. It's certain they'll come after us. But I want it to be on my terms.''

Speaking quickly, he told Benjy and Joan what to do. As he spoke, one of the Chinese attempted to pull a bloodied Gutang to his feet. The other three, two of whom were carrying sawed-off shotguns, started to walk up the incline toward the youngsters.

Todd turned and ran. Benjy and Joan followed. The Chinese stopped walking and began to run up the incline at top speed.

With Benjy close on his heels, Todd disappeared behind the small house. Joan, running more slowly, struggled to keep up. Behind the house, a short grassy foothill led down to a row of thick, low-growing hedges. On the other side of the hedges stood a huge, gray mausoleum. Beyond it lay more homes built for the dead.

By the time the three Chinese reached the rear of the Gutang house, the girl was the only visible target. She was attempting to squeeze through the dense, thigh-high hedges, which tore at her dress and at times seemed to halt her progress. With great effort she cleared the shrubbery, but not without a price. She'd torn her dress, lost a shoe, and scratched her calves.

Crouching, she examined her legs, then looked up and saw the Triad gunmen racing down the knoll toward her. Rising to her feet, she removed the other shoe, threw it aside, and ran toward the huge gray mausoleum. The gunmen could hear the girl pleading for the boys, who'd apparently gone on ahead, not to abandon her.

Her cries for help informed her pursuers that they were facing a weak and divided enemy. She'd be the first to go down. Then it would be three armed men against only two boys, a very one-sided contest.

The leader of the gunmen, a barrel-chested man in wraparound dark glasses, had orders to bring back the heads of Benjy and his partner. And there was the computer disk Gutang said he'd just given the kids. Charlie Snake should find that very interesting. As for the girl, the leader and his men would amuse themselves with the bitch before killing her.

At the bottom of the knoll, the Chinese, shotguns held high, began pushing through the hedges. Eyes on the weeping girl, the leader smiled. She was limping now. Putting on quite a show. Getting their attention.

The leader was first through the hedges and first to die. He cleared the shrubbery with only minor difficulty, stepping onto parched grass with his back to Todd, lying hidden at the base of the hedges. Candlestick holder in hand, Todd rose and clubbed the barrel-chested man in the spine, dropping him openmouthed to his knees. A second blow crushed the back of the chunky man's skull, killing him instantly.

Several feet away, Benjy lay on his back, body also

pressed close to the base of the shrubbery. The Uzi, with Benjy's finger on the trigger, rested on his chest. Suddenly a sandaled foot pressed down gingerly on his stomach. Another one of Sui's men had just pushed his way through the hedges.

Benjy shot the gunman in the ankle, sending him shrieking in the air, arms and legs flailing. The man—thin, toothy, and smelling of garlic—landed painfully on the grass to Benjy's left. Screaming, he writhed back and forth on his back, ankle pulled to his chest and gripped tightly with both hands. His shotgun lay several feet away and out of reach.

Rising to his knees, Benjy, Uzi in one hand, aimed at the wounded man's chest and pulled the trigger.

The gun jammed.

Behind him, a sharp click made Benjy look over his shoulder. Recoiling at what he saw, he quickly went light-headed with fear. He'd heard a shotgun being cocked, a shotgun now aimed at his head.

The third man, small and hard-eyed, stood in the middle of the hedges, shotgun pressed against his right hip and pointing at Benjy. *It's not Joan who is to die. It's me.* Benjy tensed to take the charge from the short, murderous weapon.

Todd acted quickly. In a fraction of a second he saw the danger to Benjy and hurled the candlestick holder, striking the small man in the jaw and knocking him off-balance. The shotgun fell into the shrubbery. Dazed and in pain, the attacker was unable to stand. He fell sideways into the hedges, then thrashed about in an attempt to get to his feet.

Benjy went berserk. Screaming, he leapt up and threw himself on the man who'd almost killed him. Together they rolled clear of the hedges and onto the grassy knoll. When they stopped rolling, Benjy was on top of his would-be murderer. Weakened by the blow from Todd's weapon, the small man could do little to defend himself. None of his efforts were a match for Benjy's rage.

Straddling his attacker's chest, Benjy hooked both thumbs in the small man's eyes, gripped the ears, and pushed his thumbs down into the skull. When the thumbs had penetrated into the sockets, Benjy ripped outward, forcing the eyes loose. The small man screamed and stopped only when Benjy broke his neck.

For a long time Benjy sat beside the man's corpse, head bowed as he repeatedly saw the shotgun pointing at him. A hand on his shoulder made him look up to see Todd and Joan staring down at him.

Todd said, "One lives, the other dies. It is karma."

Benjy nodded. Yes, karma.

He rose, retrieved the Uzi, and followed Todd and Joan from the cemetery. Behind them, the thin, toothy Chinese sat up and clutched his damaged foot, teeth clenched against the appalling pain. He should have been dead. Benjy had wanted to kill him.

It was the younger boy who'd saved his life. "It's finished," the younger boy had said. "A true warrior does not slaughter the defenseless. Let him live." And Benjy had obeyed. He'd done it grudgingly, but he'd obeyed.

What kind of boy was this who spoke of warriors, who the strong-willed Benjy obeyed without question? The survivor watched the youngsters walk away from him. His eyes remained on Todd until the boy disappeared in the distance.

# Sixteen

Frank DiPalma's time spent in the custody of Manila's police could best be described as lively.

It began when hotel security perceived him to be a psycho who'd dusted two Chinese males, a dwarf whore, and cracked the skull of a third male. Which made DiPalma someone who bore watching. In minutes six grim-looking Filipinos in matching gray linen suits and white leather shoes were in his suite, where they held him at gunpoint until police arrived.

The police, eight uniformed and six plainclothes, came bearing enough firepower to invade Costa Rica. For Di-Palma, what ensued proved to be as embarrassing as anything he'd ever lived through. He was handcuffed and rushed past ogling hotel guests to a waiting squad car, which took off for a station house near Manila Cathedral at Plaza Roma.

He entered the station house to the sound of the cathedral's thunderous organ. It had forty-five hundred pipes, a detective proudly told him, came from Holland, and was the largest in Asia. DiPalma, cuffs digging into his wrists, thought, That's what inquiring minds are interested in, your great big organ.

Inside the station house, he was forced to undergo a strip search, which he didn't like even a little bit. But the cops didn't look prone to tolerate any attitude. Throwing a tantrum could provoke them into getting even tougher. DiPalma was an American and a reporter, and he made more in a week than they did in ten years. All this was reason enough to harass him and make his time in police custody short on ease and comfort.

He also didn't protest when they refused to allow him any outside contact. No telephone calls to relatives, the American embassy, or his television network. Nor could he at this time retain an attorney or speak with reporters. DiPalma didn't have to be a rocket scientist to realize that he was being isolated long enough for someone to put their own spin on the events in his hotel suite. His own worst-case scenario had him being killed in police custody by order of Lin Pao or Filipino power brokers anxious to protect multinationals operating in the Philippines.

When he asked about the charges against him, one Detective Firlaca, a short, fast-talking Filipino with a wispy mustache, said, "We'll tell you when we're ready." DiPalma thought, *One more way of buying time for damage control.* Something told him not to expect widespread support for his claim of self-defense.

The one witness who might have helped him, Federico, the bell captain, apparently had disappeared. At least he hadn't been taken into custody as far as DiPalma knew, nor was his name mentioned during DiPalma's detention. Worst-case scenario number two: Federico was being sequestered to prevent him from talking to anybody. Or Federico was dead. Either way it would be a cold day in hell before he came forward to help DiPalma.

DiPalma's first hours in the police station were spent in an interrogation room, a windowless, lime-green cubbyhole with cracks in the ceiling, metal folding chairs, and a dingy sink with a leaky faucet. Like interrogation rooms the world over, this one smelled of boredom, fear, and old farts and hadn't been painted in years. The room looked like a million—every year of it.

He decided to cooperate. He answered all questions and

made no attempts to throw his weight around. Police everywhere weren't keen on being given a hard time. Smart mouths didn't last long in interrogation rooms.

Conning these guys would be a waste of time. All they had to do was toss his room and check his notes on the Taaltex fire, Nelson Berlin, and Lin Pao. At which point the cops or any other interested parties would have a fairly good idea why he'd come to the Philippines.

He admitted to having arranged a meeting with Huziyana de Vega, but sex had nothing to do with it. He'd wanted to question her about the Taaltex fire, which had killed dozens of young women, among them a friend's goddaughter. DiPalma believed that Miss de Vega might have some idea who'd set the fire. Later he would remember the police never pressed him on this point. Either they weren't interested or they knew how DiPalma had connected the dwarf whore to the fire.

In any case, his decision to tell the truth had been the right one. Twenty minutes into the questioning, he was shown the stolen watch given him by Martin Mackie and found at the scene of the fire. It had been taken from DiPalma's hotel room, along with press clippings on the fire and his notes on Nelson Berlin and Lin Pao. Police, however, made no mention of the notes—or Pao and Berlin. This omission was not lost on DiPalma.

He was asked how he'd come by the watch. From Martin Mackie, DiPalma said. And how had Inspector Mackie come by it? DiPalma said nothing. He knew who Mackie had bribed to get the watch. It was the fast-talking Firlaca, who now stood nervously among the questioners, his soft brown eyes on DiPalma.

DiPalma wasn't sure why he didn't give up Firlaca. The motor-mouth bastard hadn't done anything but give him a hard time. Call it a whim. Or a reluctance to inform on cops in general. DiPalma simply said, "You'll have to ask Mackie where he got the watch."

While DiPalma was wondering if he'd made the right call on Firlaca, there was some action in the hallway outside of the room. Three men with stern, unpleasant faces had arrived to look in on the questioning. Two wore white dinner jackets and black ties. All three wore the expressions of important people who didn't like having their evenings interrupted. Each eyed DiPalma as if he were a pit bull with rabies. He named them Curly, Larry, and Moe.

DiPalma decided they were heavy hitters from the government or the police department, here to see that multinational corporations were being protected. The four detectives interrogating DiPalma, Firlaca among them, were summoned from the interrogation room to confer with the new arrivals outside in the hallway. The door was closed, leaving DiPalma alone in the interrogation room. He was beginning to feel depressed. Very fucking depressed. He had the best contacts imaginable, and at the moment he couldn't reach out for anybody.

A few minutes later Firlaca reentered the room, closed the door behind him, and leaned against it. "Would you like a glass of water?" he asked.

DiPalma patted his stomach. "Gives me trouble now and then. I'd appreciate bottled water if it could be arranged."

"We noticed the scars on your abdomen and leg."

"I ran into some trouble in Hong Kong back when I was a cop."

The detective grinned. "That trouble you had, I think it was a shotgun."

"I think you're right."

"Did you meet Inspector Mackie in Hong Kong?"

"He saved my life when I was there."

"And you're repaying that debt?"

"I repay all my debts."

Firlaca combed his thin mustache with slim brown fingers. "You understand we have a job to do. As policemen, we must follow orders."

"Same thing in my country. To get along, you got to go along."

Firlaca nodded. "Yes." He pushed himself away from

the door and walked over to DiPalma. "How long were you a police officer?"

"Twenty years. Then I retired."

"We were told you won many awards for bravery."

"I had a job to do. I did it as best I could."

Folding his arms across his chest, Firlaca looked at the closed door, then back at DiPalma. "You use a stick very well. What kind of training have you had?"

"*Kendo, escrima*. I've also done a little work with the *chako*."

Firlaca grinned. "*Chako*. Where do you learn that word?"

"From the Filipinos in America who taught me *escrima*. Your people are the best stick fighters in the world, but I don't have to tell you that." *Chako* was Filipino for *nunchaku*, the weapon made of two pieces of hardwood connected by rope or chain.

Firlaca said, "I've been an *escrimador* since I was twelve. Still work out couple times a week. Ten years ago I started thinking I was pretty good. That's when my grandfather challenged me. He's eighty-three. Hadn't picked up his sticks in over twenty years. Beat my ass black and blue. What kind of sticks you use?"

"Rattan. They're light, flexible. Nothing over twenty-four inches long."

"Yeah, twenty-four inches. That's good. Little bit longer isn't bad, but twenty-four inches gets the job done."

Firlaca looked at the door again, then back at DiPalma. The Filipino's voice was barely audible when he said, "They're going to move you around. You understand?"

Suddenly DiPalma started feeling anxious. Moving him around would make it impossible for anyone to find him. This journey to nowhere—this Magical Mystery Tour, as an ex-partner of DiPalma's called it—was a scam dear to the hearts of police everywhere.

Detainees or suspects were shifted from location to location, from here to there and back again, preventing any and all contact with the outside world. DiPalma had done it a few times himself. You bought time until you'd collected the necessary evidence against a perp who was otherwise tough to bring down.

DiPalma wasn't keen on having it done to him, particularly when it could prove hazardous to his health. The Triad, Nelson Berlin's people, or anybody else could spread a few bucks around and arrange for him to be shot to death by police while attempting to escape. Or he could simply disappear into a network of foreign jails, prisons, holding cells, and private jails unknown to outsiders. A lot could happen to DiPalma before his friends finally located him. Senator Quarequio or Barry Omens had to be told his whereabouts pronto.

He looked at the doorway. The other detectives and their gilt-edged visitors were about to enter the room. DiPalma caught Firlaca's eye. ''Barry Omens,'' he whispered.

Firlaca glared at him, then turned and walked to meet his fellow detectives. At the door, he turned and yelled, ''You dumb son of a bitch! Don't try throwing your weight around with me. You're not in America anymore. You're in my country, and over here we make the rules, you understand?''

DiPalma rubbed the back of his neck, thinking, I guess the answer's no on that one. If you can see the light at the end of the tunnel, you're facing the wrong way.

The interrogation continued with an emphasis on what DiPalma knew about the fire. Curly, Larry, and Moe stood against one wall, quietly observing the proceedings while chain-smoking and occasionally exchanging whispers. An hour later one of the three stepped forward, palm upturned. Without a word a detective gave him the interrogation tapes recorded so far, and seconds later the trio was gone. An exhausted, hoarse DiPalma still hadn't gotten his bottled water.

Firlaca was right about his being moved around. Shortly before midnight, DiPalma was again handcuffed and driven to a station house on the edge of the Tondo slums. He was segregated from the other prisoners, drunks, transvestites, pickpockets, and prostitutes being kept overnight in holding cells. No sharing for DiPalma. For him it was private accommodations and room service.

He spent the night on the floor of a small second-floor room used to store riot gear and old file cabinets. Someone found him an old, piss-smelling mattress and a tatty blanket. He was also given two boiled eggs and a cup of lukewarm tea, which he wolfed down in seconds.

With a bit of food in his stomach he relaxed, lying back on the mattress with the blanket folded under his head as a pillow. He thought about Jan and Todd, finding it hard to believe he might never see them again. He'd come halfway around the world to protect Jan and to help Todd destroy Lin Pao. *Or had he really traveled all this distance to meet his own destruction?*

Todd would say it was karma, something from which there was no reprieve. Something you couldn't outrun. Something the highest walls couldn't keep out. DiPalma hadn't yet come up with a word for his present situation, but he knew this much: He was standing in shit up to his eyebrows and in bad need of a straw to breathe through.

Firlaca had been his last chance to get out. Unfortunately the Filipino detective seemed more interested in covering his ass than in doing good works. Turn out the lights, DiPalma thought, the party's over.

When he awoke the next morning, he found more tea and boiled eggs waiting on the floor beside his mattress. He ate, then spent almost an hour reading two back issues of *Hustler* magazine he'd found on top of a file cabinet. Still antsy, he stopped reading and did a few stretching exercises. Now warmed up, he decided to work out. Using a rolled-up copy of *Hustler* as a stick, he ran through some *escrima* moves. He was sweating when he finished, but he felt almost like his old self. Almost.

Twice he was taken from the room, once to use the bathroom, the other time for an interrogation session. The questioning was done by a new team, three cops he'd not seen before. But everything was the same. Questions about the fire. Threats about his going to prison on charges of having murdered a prostitute and her two partners.

His diet of boiled eggs and tea, boring but edible, also remained the same. DiPalma was peeling one of his two dinner eggs when he was given his marching orders. He was being moved as soon as it got dark. The news brought on a touch of paranoia, which quickly killed any appetite he had.

Supported by shotgun-carrying, uniformed cops, the second interrogation team took DiPalma on phase two of his journey to nowhere. They formed a three-car convoy which ran red lights, missed collisions by inches, and kept DiPalma rigid in the backseat. The trip wasn't made any more comfortable by sitting next to a cop whose breath smelled like he chewed his socks.

DiPalma relaxed when it appeared they were staying in the city; he wasn't being taken out to the countryside for a bullet in the head, after all. What's more, the convoy didn't travel too far. After twenty minutes it slowed down in front of a station house opposite a Shakey's Pizza on Mabini Street. DiPalma had beat the odds today. Tomorrow was another story.

He was rushed, not too gently, into the station house, almost losing his balance when someone pushed him from behind, a sure indication his luck was running out. If they felt free to get tough, it meant they didn't give a shit who he was.

Inside the station house, DiPalma, hands cuffed behind him and surrounded by cops, was pushed along a dark hallway toward a room with light showing through a frosted-glass door. One cop ran ahead to open the door. He stood aside as DiPalma, his cuffed hands bleeding, was shoved forward into the room and onto his knees. From behind the desk, a male voice said, "Take off his cuffs."

There were half a dozen men in the room, all of whom stared down at an unshaven, scruffy, and very edgy Di-Palma.

One of them was Barry Omens.

# Seventeen

The hotel room was almost pitch-dark. A troubled Todd, unable to sleep, lay in bed beneath a window overlooking MacArthur Bridge. He felt surrounded by fire. Seconds later he was gripped by an icy cold which left his teeth chattering. Even his heart shook.

He knew what was happening to him but was powerless to stop it. He was about to be possessed by a samurai who had been dead four hundred years. And with this would come a fear of being enslaved by the demon Iki-ryo. Born of evil thoughts, the Iki-ryo was a ghost that sought sanctuary in something as wicked and savage as itself. Todd's fear only magnified the growing danger.

Near the door, Joan slept soundly in a second bed, her body curled under a lavender sheet and facing Todd. Benjy had an adjoining room. In six hours they were due at Manila International Airport for a five A.M. flight to New York. Barry Omens had made the travel arrangements.

Earlier today Todd and the others had met the DEA supervisor at a restaurant near the centuries-old ruins of Fort Santiago on Aduana Street.

"Frank wants you three to leave Manila with him tomorrow," Omens said. "His network is paying for the tickets. You pick 'em up at the Pan-World reservations counter. They'll be there under my name. Frank's being turned loose on the condition that he leaves the country immediately, if not sooner. That's why he's being taken from the station house directly to the airport. He'll be under guard until boarding time.''

Benjy said, "What about his luggage? Doesn't the man get to take his shit with him?''

Omens shook his head. "The cops are picking up Frank's stuff and bringing it to the airport. If he ain't on the red-eye special, he's got problems. They want him out of town yesterday. He isn't being given time to write a postcard or pick his nose. Bon voyage, aloha, and adios.''

Droopy eyes almost closed, Omens leaned back in his chair and toyed with a fork. "Understand something, Todd. Your father's got clout, which makes him somebody's worst nightmare. Even I was impressed. The minute I learned where they were hiding him, I told the embassy. Jesus, you should have seen them move. They didn't waste any time getting on the horn to Senator Quarequio, which really got the ball rolling.

"Meanwhile," Omens said, "I get over to the station house and insist on seeing Frank right then and there. I tell the cops we're supposed to be working together. 'You call this working together, kicking one of my guys around?' I say. While I'm there, somebody from the embassy shows up, and he starts bitching about the way Frank's being treated. Later I find out Quarequio and the vice president telephoned the Philippines ambassador in Washington. Then Frank's network makes the biggest stink. Next thing you know, we got ourselves a war. Frank's friends dropped on these suckers from a great height. It was something to see, believe me.''

Omens tossed the fork on the table and grinned. "When it comes to reaching out, nobody can match your old man. Nobody. That's what made him a great cop. He knew everybody.''

Todd said, "And you have no idea who told you where to find my father?''

Omens shook his head. "Two days ago I get a call from a woman who wouldn't give me her name. She was Filipino, I know that much. Says her piece, then slams down the phone. But I think she was being prompted. Someone was with her, telling her exactly what to say. And my guess is, that someone was a cop."

Benjy said, "What makes you think that?"

"To know what was happening to Frank, you had to be inside. In this case, *inside* means *cop*. The woman said things like, 'They're moving him at 0600 hours and he's being detained without being booked,' stuff like that. That's how a policeman would phrase it."

Omens looked at Todd. "He mention anything to you about any women in Manila? Policewomen, secretaries?"

"No, he didn't."

"That's what I mean. They never let me and Frank have any time alone, so I didn't get to ask who'd made the call. But I got the distinct impression he knew who'd dropped the dime. Speaking of information, you guys get anything good from your meeting yesterday? I mean, you ran from the hotel like bats out of hell."

Benjy grinned and said nothing.

Todd said, "Yes."

Omens tried to make his voice sound casual. "How good is it?"

"It's important," Todd said. "It definitely connects Mr. Berlin to Lin Pao."

Omens stared at the fingernails on his right hand. "Christ, what I wouldn't give to make a case against those two bastards. Been trying to put them in bed together for more years than you've been on this Earth."

When Omens looked up, Todd was staring at him. The DEA supervisor shifted uncomfortably in his chair.

The boy said, "That information is to be turned over to my father."

Omens shrugged and reached for the fork. "Hey, I'm not asking you to disobey orders. I believe in being a good soldier. Anyway, Frank gave me his word we'd work out something, and that's good enough for me."

Todd pointed to a folded English-language newspaper he'd placed on the table. Omens waved at it. "Garbage," he said to Todd. "Once Frank's network broke the story about his imprisonment, the Filipinos had to put their own spin on things. So they concocted this fairy tale about Frank having invited some bimbo to his room, then getting jumped by three nighthawks. Their story is that Frank was being detained only until all the facts were in. Yeah. Right. I suppose when you're trying to keep foreign businessmen happy, anything goes."

Todd said, "And they still haven't found the person who set the fire?"

"My friend, they are not looking. Far as they're concerned, it's case closed. There's talk about a suspect, some guy who lived with the dead pygmy or dwarf or whatever the hell she was. I suppose Frank was using her to find this guy."

Todd nodded.

Omens looked at Benjy. "You guys have a place near here?"

Benjy grinned. "Never give up, do you?"

"Just asking."

Todd said, "Tell my father I'm glad he's well, and I look forward to seeing him tomorrow. It was good of you to help him."

"Don't forget our mysterious caller, or should I say callers? Wasn't for them, who knows what might have happened to Frank."

Omens sipped his beer and looked through the restaurant window at tourists lining up to visit the ruins of Fort Santiago. Charlie Snake hadn't wasted any time coming after Frank. Two hours after the dago checks into a three-hundred-dollar-a-day suite, he almost gets his ticket punched.

On the other hand, little Todd with the laser-beam eyes seemed to have lucked out. Along with these leftovers from a Chinatown senior prom, he'd managed to elude Charlie Snake's people. You'd have thought these kids were invisible. They'd left Omens in order to touch base with an unspecified individual who'd then given them *something* linking Lin Pao with Nelson Berlin. Had it really been that easy?

Omens said, "You kids run into any trouble? I'm surprised Charlie Sui hasn't tried to move on you."

Benjy grinned. "He has."

Omens raised his bushy, red eyebrows. He couldn't wait to hear the rest of it. And Benjy was about to tell him when a look from Todd made Benjy chill out.

Todd rose from his chair. "We'll see you at the airport tomorrow. Thank you again for your kindness."

Omens, beer glass to his mouth, watched the three youngsters leave the restaurant and disappear into the crowd. *It hadn't been that easy.* They'd run into trouble and survived. They'd had a run-in with Charlie Snake's goons. Omens knew it just as sure as he knew there were mosquitoes in the Philippines big enough to fuck a turkey flat-footed.

Before or after the pickup, the kids had gone up against Charlie Snake and lived to tell the tale. Benjy had been about to spill the beans before little Todd had shot him down with a look. I mean *a look.*

Omens found DiPalma's kid scary. Eight to five, Charlie Snake's people had found him scary too.

In his hotel room, Todd lay trembling on a sweat-soaked sheet. His weeping had awakened Joan, who'd quickly thrown on a robe, then left the room and returned with Benjy. Now both stood over the terrified boy, who no longer knew if he, himself, was asleep or awake.

Shivering, he drew his knees up to his chin and clawed at the sheets. Eyes bright with tears, Joan stepped toward him. Benjy, fighting a growing panic, caught her arm and drew her back. He knew what was about to happen. Pulling Joan with him, he slowly edged away from Todd.

The room, cooled only by a ceiling fan, suddenly turned

freezing. Both Benjy and Joan trembled in the frozen air. Then came the odor, a burning smell so powerful that not even the cold could conceal it. Joan, wide-eyed with fear, began to cough violently. Benjy became sick to his stomach and was sure he was going to vomit.

The room became wintry. A desperate Benjy pulled Joan over to her bed, grabbed a folded blanket, and wrapped it around her. When he'd finished, he pushed her to the floor and under the bed. Quickly dropping down beside her, he shoved himself under the bed as far as possible. His back was to Todd. His body blocked Joan's view of the room. Soon there would be something here that neither of them would want to see.

Across the room, Todd no longer knew if he was asleep or awake, if he was in the grip of a nightmare or a horrendous reality.

*But he was in a man's body. A Japanese man, squat, bearded, and powerfully built, with dark, hairy skin and a hand on the Muramasa sword worn at his waist. He stood only feet away from the man who killed with fire, who was now poised to strike at Frank DiPalma.*

*Todd's father walked toward the fire-man, who waited in the darkness to burn him alive. A fearful Todd attempted to draw his sword, but despite their powerful appearance, his arms were weak. He could not pull the sword from its scabbard. And why was he frightened? He must not—could not—be frightened.*

*Suddenly the Iki-ryo, the ghost of the living, came alive within him. He shuddered as it probed his mind and soul, filling him with its hatred and venom, with its ancient evil and wickedness. The Iki-ryo was again preparing to make him the agent of its depravity.*

"My father is in danger," Todd said. "Save him."

"For him to live, I must live in you," spoke the Iki-ryo. "Tonight I serve you, but soon I will ask that you serve me. Do you agree to this?"

"I agree."

"Then it is done."

*Todd heard and felt the rush of a mighty wind. A heartbeat later his body was consumed by a scorching heat. Body arched against a pain he feared never could be overcome, Todd screamed, a blood chilling cry that forced Joan and Benjy to cover their ears.*

*The heat vanished as suddenly as it had appeared, leaving behind the shocking cold, and Todd saw himself as he once was. He was not a frightened, sniveling boy. He was samurai. He was Benkai.*

It was almost two-thirty A.M. when Leon Bacolod turned his rented blue Toyota right onto a deserted Mabini Street and parked in front of a corner shop selling carved *santos*, statues of popular saints.

He wore a cheap seersucker suit, dark glasses, and blue leather shoes with perforated tips, secondhand stuff bought at Chinatown stalls. His bamboo rosary was around his neck. A yellow rose in his lapel had been taken from a floral offering made minutes ago to the Virgin at Quiapo Church, his customary practice before setting a fire. At the church he'd lit a candle for Huzi and given a priest money to have a hundred masses said in her memory.

After he'd switched off the ignition Bacolod put his head on the steering wheel and wept. Huzi had loved him for what he was. No one else had ever done that. Until she'd entered his life, Bacolod had found it easy to imagine that everyone hated him. Through Huzi he'd discovered himself and liked what he'd seen.

Without her, he once more felt anxious and threatened. He could almost smell his own fear. He hadn't felt this empty since he was a boy in the orphanage. In killing her, DiPalma had killed Bacolod's sense of worth and self-respect. To get it back, Bacolod would have to kill DiPalma.

As the arsonist quietly wept in the front seat of the Toyota, two whores, young and bone-thin, their eyes and teeth green in the garish streetlight, stepped from the darkened doorway of the *santos* shop and strolled over to the car. Both wore white leather minis, long-sleeved blouses, hoop earrings, and wigs. One nervously twirled a pink parasol. The other smoked a Thai stick held between fingers tipped by long, curved, multicolored nails.

Bacolod eyed them with contempt. The broad shoulders, wide hands, and Adam's apples gave them away. Goddamn transvestites. He hated queers; if he had his way, they'd all be in concentration camps. "Fuck off, you goddamn faggots!" he yelled. "I hope you shit-eating bastards die of AIDS!"

His rage sent them back to the doorway, teetering on stiletto heels as they cursed him in English, Spanish, and Tagalog. Bacolod gave them the finger. "Split this between you," he said.

He began breathing deeply, pulling the air in, visualizing it enveloping his brain before forcing the air down to his diaphragm. Deep breathing calms the mind, Huzi had said. She'd done it as part of a twenty-minute yoga routine, performed nude every morning to classical music tapes. Huzi had been a cultured lady.

As Bacolod inhaled, his lungs were filled with the odor of gasoline. It came from a cardboard box on the front seat beside him. The box, bearing a Sun-Gold Banana label, was covered by a ragged blue towel and contained an empty rum bottle, three books of matches, and a half gallon tin of gasoline.

Chin on the steering wheel, Bacolod stared at the Mabini Street station house, located to his right and at the far end of the block. In front of the station house a plainclothes detective leaned against one of three police cars parked at the curb and talked with a trio of female prostitutes. In a few minutes Frank DiPalma would walk out of the station house and Bacolod would burn him alive. Right then and there. If Bacolod died, so what? Nothing mattered except killing DiPalma.

To hell with Charlie Sui, the police, with everybody. Bacolod was going to get his revenge. Let the future take care of itself.

He chuckled, thinking how easy it had been to learn

DiPalma's whereabouts. The newspapers had mentioned the American's hotel, and Bacolod had gone there to find out when he would be coming back. He'd gone at night, when there wouldn't be too many people in the lobby. At the check-in desk he'd flashed his security-guard badge and announced he was a policeman working on the DiPalma matter. Had anyone been around asking for the American?

In minutes Bacolod learned that DiPalma was being thrown out of the country and that two police officers had come to the hotel, gathered his luggage, and taken it to the Mabini Street station. The American would be departing from there at three in the morning. Good riddance, the hotel management said. Mr. DiPalma wasn't welcome here anymore.

The hotel had received more than its share of bad publicity, thanks to reporters, American embassy officials, and American politicians. The plan to quietly remove this troublemaker, Bacolod was told, was a good one. He agreed. It was a good one indeed.

In the Toyota, he suddenly seized the steering wheel with both hands. Several uniformed police armed with shotguns had left the station house and now stood by the squad cars. Four men in suits, two of them Americans, stood on the front steps of the station house and talked quietly. One looked nervously at his watch.

Across the street a small crowd of night people—male and female whores, cabdrivers, beggars—had gathered to behold the show. DiPalma was about to leave. Bacolod could feel it. He licked his lips. His dick started to harden.

Heart pounding, he unscrewed the cap on the half-gallon tin and carefully poured gasoline into the rum bottle without spilling a drop. When the bottle was three-quarters full, he stopped pouring, placed the bottle between his thighs, and recapped the tin, screwing the top on tight.

Then he set the tin down on the floorboard, tore a strip from the towel, and stuffed it into the bottle. The thought of the fire almost made him forget Huzi. When he looked at the police station, DiPalma had come outside. The American was recognizable from newspaper photographs. A big, gray-haired man standing on the steps surrounded by the four men in suits.

Bacolod's plan was simple. Wait until DiPalma steps into one of the cars, then drive alongside, toss the gasoline bomb into his vehicle, and drive away. In Manila, only the fortunate few with air-conditioning closed their car windows. All four of Bacolod's windows were open.

As DiPalma began walking down the steps Bacolod reached for a book of matches. When a uniformed policeman opened the back door of the middle car for DiPalma, Bacolod struck a match and touched it to the strip of towel hanging from the gasoline-filled rum bottle. The cloth flared up immediately.

Suddenly the Toyota's windows shot up and slammed into place. *All four windows were closed.* All the door locks clicked. Someone had locked Bacolod in his own car. What the hell was going on here?

As he looked around his empty car the arsonist found himself gripped by an arctic cold. Then came a stench so overpowering that he felt the hot, bitter taste of undigested food rush to his nose and mouth. Who was playing tricks on him?

His feet felt wet. Sweet Mother Mary. The tin was open and gasoline was flowing out, soaking his feet and ankles and drenching the floorboard. Something bright caught his eye. Flames were now flickering in the cardboard box. *Every book of matches had ignited.*

The cardboard box caught fire quickly, sending flames racing over its sides and toward the gasoline-soaked floor. Bacolod's mind said, *Yank the wick from the rum bottle. Do it now. Then open the doors and flee.* But he couldn't lift his arms. The gasoline bomb, with its burning wick, remained squeezed between both hands, hands he could not lift from his lap. He couldn't move a muscle.

He saw DiPalma step into a car, saw the door slam behind

him and the first police car pull away from the curb. Bacolod shrieked against this final and most painful disappointment of his life. And as he cried out the Toyota became a mighty fireball.

# Eighteen

It was an uneasy conversation that Charles Sui had with the Black General by radio, the Triad's preferred form of long-distance communication. Telephone calls and written messages were easily recorded or intercepted. Radio transmissions were all but impossible to monitor.

Sui dreaded having to bring his godfather bad news. Presented with negative or unpleasant disclosures, the Black General could be levelheaded or stupefyingly cruel. Sui feared these terrifying extremes so much that he refrained from initiating contact with Lin Pao unless forced to do so.

Godfather Pao disliked having things kept from him. It would have been suicidal to withhold news of the diskette that Raul Gutang had turned over to Benjy Lok Nein and Frank DiPalma's young son. The Black General had worked hard to keep his relationship with Nelson Berlin a secret. Anything concerning it must be brought to his attention.

But in bringing his godfather up-to-date, Charles Sui was forced to admit his own failure in not recovering the diskette. This distressing account also included the humiliating admission that he'd lost two men in a fight with Benjy and his comrade.

Sui, a vein throbbing in his forehead, sat rigid in the darkened study of his Forbes Park home and listened to himself being called inept, sloppy, a disgrace to his late father's name. The insults and curses continued uninterrupted for several minutes. Sui felt a migraine coming on.

Lin Pao said, ''You're a well-dressed little shit and not half the man your father was. Thinking—that's what you're good at. But, my dear godson, to think is to do. How many times must I point this out to you? I've said this before: You spend too damn much time on the tennis court and playing the organ. Can't you see what a loss of face it is to allow yourself to be defeated by *children*?''

Lin Pao's fury was not diminished by hearing that Charles Sui had seized the Taaltex computer operator Raul Gutang, then tortured him into a painful state of candor. *Where was the diskette?*

''Do you know how costly it will be to have my relationship with Nelson Berlin exposed?'' Lin Pao said. ''Should Berlin's past be brought to light, even *his* money won't save him from disgrace. Does DiPalma know of this business with Berlin's sister?''

''He does, yes,'' Charles Sui said. ''According to material taken from DiPalma's hotel room and passed on to me by police, he's heard about Berlin and his sister from Gregory Van Rooten. DiPalma has no details, but yes, he knows. Being in jail has prevented him from poking about and asking questions. Mr. DiPalma is a lucky man, having children on hand to do his work for him.''

''Close your mouth and open your eyes. Luck had nothing to do with it. DiPalma's no fool. He planned to use the boys all along. He knew he'd be recognized. In case you haven't noticed, let me point out to you that he's a prominent man. DiPalma elected to play Judas goat and fooled us all.''

''I don't understand.''

''DiPalma saw no one after his arrest. Yet the boys acted with a certain precision. They knew what to do without being told by DiPalma, who obviously worked out his strategy before leaving America. He was always a step ahead of us, an embarrassing thing for me to admit about a West-

erner. You would be ill advised to underestimate this man.
Or the children with him.''

"Godfather, my men tried to dispose of Benjy and his
friend.''

"You're not paid to try. You're paid to succeed.''

Sui wiped a sweaty palm on his thigh. "Godfather, you
know how violent Benjy can be. And I'm told the other
one's even tougher. He's a phenomenon of sorts, this kid.
They surprised my men in the Chinese Cemetery—''

"You're worse than stupid, you're idiotic. How often
must I tell you that explanations do not change facts? Let
me remind you why I ordered numerous women burned to
death two weeks ago. I did it to conceal information that
you have now let slip through your bumbling fingers. And
your only response to this dilemma is to report your defeat
at the hands of two adolescents. If your father were alive,
he would weep with shame.''

Closing his eyes, Charles Sui massaged his temples with
his fingertips. "Godfather, I know where the boys are.''

"And the diskette?''

"I can destroy it and see that the boys do not leave Manila
alive.''

"DiPalma, Van Rooten, and Martin Mackie can tear
down what I've spent a lifetime building in the West. They
could even force me to cancel my meeting with the other
dragon heads. I would not survive such a loss of face. I've
risked much to arrange this conference. At this moment the
secret societies are willing to follow my lead toward compromise. But what happens when they learn that I cannot
rule my own house?''

"Godfather, I—''

"Shut up. Damn you, shut up.''

In the long, uncomfortable silence that followed, Charles
Sui removed his spectacles and massaged the bridge of his
nose with a thumb and forefinger. The old man was in a
foul mood. Trying to please him was like trying to run
without legs. He'd been so edgy lately. Why?

True, Van Rooten had wronged him and Taroko, the

woman they both shared. But Sui suspected that something else was bothering Lin Pao. Something the old man refused to discuss with anyone.

Lin Pao said, "There was a second boy with Benjy, you said. Could this be the same one who fought Ivan Ho and managed to beat him?"

"Yes. He's Frank DiPalma's son."

"What do we know about this little bastard, other than that he believes he's as tough as his father?"

"He's a demon of a fighter, I'm told. The man who survived the fight was terrified. He called the boy odd."

"He's a fucking meddler, that much is certain. Because of him, the Jade Eagles are now out of reach of the Eight Knives of the North. And they know it was I who ordered their deaths. You said he was odd. In what way?"

"He's physically strong," Charles Sui said. "Strikes with extraordinary power, they say. Killed one of my men with a candlestick holder, then half killed another. Calls himself a warrior, this boy. My man tells me the youngster seems to be from another world."

Several hundred miles away in his Taipei villa, Lin Pao closed his one eye and thought of the old priest he'd killed for having made an ominous prediction: You will die violently. The instrument of your death will be a young boy who lives in the West but is of the Middle Kingdom. He is a part of your life and from birth has followed you like a shadow. You will die within twenty-one days.

A dizzy Lin Pao shook his head violently. *It couldn't be.* His hand trembled as he brought a teacup to his lips and sipped twice. After putting the cup down, he picked up the microphone. "DiPalma's son. Is he Asian?"

"Yes, Godfather. The boy is half Chinese."

*A young boy who lives in the West but is of the Middle Kingdom.*

"You say you know where he is hiding?"

"He and Benjy are about to leave the country. But I can get to them."

"Do it immediately."

"On the memory of my dead father I swear to destroy them and the diskette."

Lin Pao's voice was unfeeling, reminding Sui how much his respect for his godfather was based on fear.

"If those boys are alive tomorrow," Lin Pao said, "I shall have your wife killed. It will take her at least a week to die."

In working with his godfather, Charles Sui had long been riding the tiger. The tiger was now hungry.

He clenched his teeth as the migraine struck with full force.

### Manila International Airport

DiPalma fastened his seat belt, then rubbed his sore wrists. Another fifteen minutes until runway clearance, the pilot had said. Meanwhile the half-empty airliner stood alone in darkness on the taxiway. Takeoff couldn't come soon enough for DiPalma. He'd had his fill of boiled eggs.

He looked across the aisle at Todd. The boy lay back in his seat, eyes closed, seemingly asleep. Joan sat beside him, head resting on his shoulder. DiPalma smiled. Could this be the union of two young hearts?

Back at the reservations desk, DiPalma and Todd had hugged each other affectionately, the kid clinging to him as though DiPalma had just returned from the grave. It was disturbing to see Todd so worn-out. DiPalma suspected his son was becoming increasingly weighed down by the despair of four hundred years.

Todd said he was okay, but DiPalma had his doubts. The kid definitely looked worried. Hell, what was there to worry about? They had the diskette and were headed home. Leave the anxiety attacks to Nelson Berlin and the Black General.

Benjy was carrying the diskette, which DiPalma wouldn't access until New York. He'd make copies, put one in a safe-deposit box, and leave one with an attorney. He had Todd's word the information was righteous and that was good enough. The kid had done a fantastic job. DiPalma had never been more proud of him.

DiPalma regretted being unable to dig into Van Rooten's claim that Nelson Berlin had killed his own sister. Police work was common sense and perseverance. You solved crimes through persistence, hanging in there until you found that individual who knew something. A witness. An accomplice. A relative of the perpetrator.

The trick was to knock over one domino and watch the others fall. DiPalma had begun by following the money trail, and he'd ride it to the end of the line. But he'd always be a cop, and nothing would warm his cockles more than solving a forty-year-old murder, then pinning it on one of America's fat cats.

For the past few days something else had been bugging DiPalma besides memories of boiled eggs and roaches in his tea. One name kept popping up in his mind: Taroko, the alluring Chinese singer who had been the mistress of both Lin Pao and Gregory Van Rooten. She'd vanished without a trace. The FBI and DEA couldn't find her, not that they were looking too hard. They had Van Rooten and he was talking. What else did they need?

DiPalma, however, was bothered by her disappearance. He was bothered because he knew Van Rooten. His ex-partner was a man with a king-size ego, a man who hated being humiliated, which from all reports is exactly what Taroko had done. Van Rooten never allowed that kind of put-down to go unanswered.

That's why he'd gone after DiPalma's wife. Shark Eyes always got even.

When DiPalma and Van Rooten had met at Governor's Island last week, Taroko's name had come up in passing. However, Van Rooten had quickly moved on to other things. He didn't want to talk about the bitch. DiPalma had shrugged. He couldn't care less.

But while lying awake at night in various Manila jails, DiPalma had recalled the smirk on his ex-partner's face when he'd dismissed Taroko. There'd also been what could best be described as a winning gleam in Van Rooten's eye. DiPalma had seen it often enough to recognize it in his sleep.

Taroko had done her job, which was to screw Van Rooten in half and, in the process, mind-fuck him as well. As DiPalma's FBI contact put it, when she'd finished, you could have hung a sign on Shark Eyes reading OUT OF ORDER. Supposedly Taroko had left Van Rooten so bent out of shape that he'd taken off for Atlantic City, where he'd attempted to mend his broken heart by pissing away a chunk of the Black General's money. That's what Shark Eyes was telling the world.

But Van Rooten's mouth was no prayer book. The man could lie like a rug. For that reason alone DiPalma couldn't help wondering what had happened to Taroko *after* she'd dumped handsome Gregory.

She hadn't shown up in Atlantic City last week, where a top casino was to have paid her one hundred thousand dollars for three days' work. Nobody gambled more than the Chinese, who flocked to the roulette and crap tables anywhere Taroko was appearing.

DiPalma agreed that Van Rooten's arrest might have spooked her into staying away from America. But what about her appearances in Canada, the Caribbean, and Asia? Taroko was a superstar in Chinese communities around the world. According to the FBI, she made big bucks and was a workaholic. DiPalma couldn't see a woman like that walking away from a hundred grand.

Taroko was also said to be a publicity freak. You couldn't keep her away from newspapers or Chinese television and radio. She'd recently completed a new album and was promoting it everywhere she went. The lady had numerous reasons for remaining in the public eye. In any case, why hadn't she surfaced in Taipei with Lin Pao? The FBI had told DiPalma she'd not been sighted there. *Why had she disappeared so completely?*

Before leaving New York for Manila, DiPalma had discussed Taroko's vanishing act with Jan, who worked with performers and knew them as well as anybody.

"Sounds like the kind of broad," Jan said, "who, if you ain't talking about her, ain't listening. What would make her disappear, you ask? She's off with some guy or she's dead. Nothing else is going to keep that lady out of the spotlight."

Taroko's disappearance wasn't a priority with DEA and the FBI. Van Rooten didn't necessarily have to mention her name. Just let him come up with information of a higher priority and there would be dancing in the streets. Lin Pao, not Taroko, was the target.

DiPalma, however, suspected that Van Rooten knew more about Taroko's fast fade than he'd owned up to. If this were true, it meant that the war between Shark Eyes and the Black General wasn't over two million dollars in stolen drug money. It was over a woman. And wouldn't that be a mindblower!

Philippine authorities had permitted just Barry Omens and one person from the embassy to see DiPalma off. In the Mabini station house, Omens had handed him the envelope containing his passport, wallet, and other valuables. Missing were DiPalma's notes on the Taaltex fire—Lin Pao and Nelson Berlin. Surprise.

The embassy guy had come in handy at the airport. His name was Tyler Dennison, and he was a tall, blond Georgian with excellent teeth and a permanent tan. He'd insisted the Filipino cops refrain from giving DiPalma a hard time and allow him to telephone Jan before boarding the plane.

Jan hadn't stopped crying. She'd been sick with worry, she said, and hadn't eaten or slept since the Filipino version of Frank's problems had hit the American papers. She'd be at Kennedy Airport to meet him and Todd. After saying "I love you" over and over, Jan said, "Frank?"

DiPalma grinned. Shit, here it comes. The zinger. "Yes, Jan?"

"About your little friend, the dwarf?"

"Yes?"

"Was she grumpy or happy?"

For the first time in days DiPalma laughed.

The network had been forbidden to send anyone to the police station or to the airport. But it had left a bottle of Dom Perignon and a message for DiPalma at the check-in counter. "Welcome home, big guy. See you at six and eleven." DiPalma gave the Dom Perignon to Barry Omens.

There'd been a second gift waiting for him at the check-in counter: a large bottle of Perrier and a pair of new *escrima* sticks. The sticks were rattan, twenty-four inches long, and handmade. There was no note.

DiPalma remembered something Todd had said: "Everything in the world is the product of two forces. Positive and negative, light and dark, strong and weak. These constructive and destructive powers play equal roles in making us what we are. The Chinese call this *Te*."

Detective Firlaca could be bought, but he'd also stuck his neck out and saved DiPalma's life. Jan was unfaithful, but she was also a generous and loving wife. Van Rooten was corrupt and a womanizer, but he'd warned DiPalma that Nelson Berlin was tapping Jan's phones. And Todd. There was no finer son in the world. But what about the Todd who was a cold-blooded killer and carried within him an indescribable evil called the Iki-ryo.

In front of the check-in counter DiPalma uncapped the Perrier and lifted it in a silent toast. *To Te*, he thought. *To the best and the worst in all of us.* He drank a third of the warm water, then recapped the bottle and dropped it into Benjy's shoulder bag with the diskette.

The five A.M. flight was less than a third booked. Except for DiPalma, the kids, and a single male traveler, first class was vacant. Once the plane was airborne, DiPalma intended to stretch out on the empty seats beside him and catch up on his sleep.

Benjy sat in front of DiPalma, his seat in a reclining position, which was against the rules, not that Benjy cared. Give him credit for wearing his seat belt, however. DiPalma wondered why Benjy was so jumpy. He hadn't sat still since boarding.

If he wasn't gently knocking his head against the headrest, Benjy was kicking the seat in front of him or cracking his knuckles and staring over at a sleeping Todd. Once, as DiPalma watched, Todd opened his eyes. Before DiPalma could say anything, Todd looked at Benjy, shook his head, then closed his eyes once more. Something was going on between those two, and it had nothing to do with saving the whales.

No sense trying to get any information out of Joan. She wasn't much of a talker; her English appeared to consist of eight words, three of which were *McDonald's, Bruce,* and *Springsteen.* Most of her talking was done in Cantonese and to Todd. She was devoted to him. They lived in a world that was closed to everyone, DiPalma included.

There'd been some difficulty getting the diskette, Todd said. They'd had to kill two of Charlie Sui's men. DiPalma said he'd done what he'd had to do. He didn't ask the details and Todd didn't volunteer. If DiPalma knew his son, the boy wouldn't bring up the incident again.

A Filipino flight attendant, a snub-nosed young woman in a maroon jacket, a nervous smile, and a name tag reading MONTEZ, asked DiPalma if he wanted a drink. At five-ten in the morning? DiPalma smiled. "Too early for me," he said.

Mrs. Montez—she wore a wedding ring—then offered soft drinks to the youngsters, who also refused. Still smiling, she continued forward to the cockpit, where she knocked on the door. When the door opened, she disappeared inside. DiPalma thought, *If I had to smile for a living, I'd fucking starve to death.*

He looked toward the window. The dawn was stealing over the top of the darkened hangars. Catering and fuel trucks were pulling away from his plane, a 707. A baggage loader rolled slowly under the wing and disappeared from sight. DiPalma was going back to New York. He felt good. He turned toward Todd.

The boy was gone. Benjy and Joan were also missing.

Twisting around in his seat, DiPalma looked down the aisle and into tourist class in time to see the explosion.

Joan had locked herself in the 707's rear lavatory, then leaned against the door. She clutched an airline bag to her chest. Seconds later she looked inside the bag and saw the bomb. Plastic explosives, wires, and a timer set to go off in an hour, when the plane was over the ocean and there would be no survivors. The bag was where Todd had said it would be, in the overhead luggage rack near the emergency exit.

She'd closed her eyes and purified her mind, as Todd had directed. The misdeeds of all previous lives would soon vanish. To sacrifice one's life for others was instantly to become one with the gods. If she followed Todd's instructions, Joan would be free from the eternal wheel of birth and death. She need never be born again. She need never suffer again. Her karma would be released. Joan would be ever free.

Opening her eyes, she had bowed her head to the gods, then reached into the bag. Her fingers found the timer.

DiPalma yanked open his seat belt and raced toward the rear of the plane, toward the smoke, the fire, and the screaming passengers. When he reached the scene of the explosion, he began helping attendants to evacuate the aircraft.

Within minutes the evacuation was complete. Survivors were returned to the terminal. Eight had to be hospitalized. Three, Joan among them, had been killed.

Todd and Benjy were missing.

# Nineteen

Rafael Amando's favorite tennis racquet was an old wooden throwback strung with catgut, the kind of racquet that had been out of fashion for years. The label had long worn off, and the string, which turned brittle when wet, had to be continually replaced. Amando, a thin, fiftyish tennis pro with an impish face and a soft-spoken air, had first used the racquet in Wimbledon's semifinals thirty-five years ago.

He owned three Manila shops specializing in tennis gear but refused to be swayed by the theory that the lighter the racquet, the better. His customers preferred steel, graphite, or ceramic-composite racquets because they were both sturdy and light. Catering to the modern consumer was one thing, but Amando had no intention of sharing their tastes. His love for traditional tennis had never weakened.

It was six-fifteen that morning when he sat down to a breakfast of papaya, coconut juice, scrambled eggs, guava jelly on toast, and black coffee. He wore tennis whites and dark glasses, and his thick, graying hair was parted in the middle. As always, he ate breakfast alone in the dining room of his ranch-style home while staring through sliding glass doors at his clay tennis court.

Both his wife and his mother were still sleeping. His

daughter was attending Harvard, and a son was in medical school at the University of the Philippines. Two King Charles spaniels lay beside his chair. Rafael Amando was no longer the frightened ten-year-old who in postwar Manila had supported himself by pimping for American GIs.

After breakfast he swallowed a multivitamin capsule, two vitamin C tablets, and a tablespoon of wheat-germ oil. A maid cleared away the soiled dishes and leftovers, then returned with a shoulder bag, which she placed on the table beside Amando's Smith & Wesson .357 Magnum.

While she stood silently to one side he looked in the bag to make sure that nothing had been forgotten. Wristbands, headband, towel, two apples, a jar of salted mixed nuts, two cans of tennis balls. There was also a vial of salt tablets and a small jar of potassium chloride tablets. Amando perspired heavily and had learned the value of replacing key water-soluble elements in his body.

He zipped the bag closed, handed it to the maid, and nodded, a signal to give the bag to Felipe, his chauffeur and bodyguard. Felipe would then go to the garage, and in minutes the Mercedes would appear in front of the house. Amando's life was an orderly and functional whole.

He rose from the table, took a white satin jacket from the back of the chair, and placed it around his shoulders. Then, after checking to see that the safety was on, he tucked the Magnum in his belt. The last thing he wanted to do was shoot himself in the balls.

Felipe was armed with a Beretta assault rifle, as well as a Taurus PT-92, the Brazilian handgun that fired fifteen rounds. Amando didn't think about the forces behind his country's high crime rate. He knew only that these were dangerous times for a prosperous man to be without protection.

His home was in a small suburb near the U.S. Military Cemetery, which held the bodies of seventeen thousand American soldiers who'd died in World War II. Amando's property, along with that of several neighbors, was encircled by walls topped with broken glass. Two armed guards protected a single entrance. It was Amando's wife who'd said that he'd either spent his life fighting to get money or fighting to keep it.

As he did each weekday morning, Amando was on his way to give Charles Sui a private tennis lesson. The lesson, scheduled for Sui's own court, would begin promptly at seven-fifteen and end an hour later. Sui would then shower, dress, and be at his real-estate office before nine.

The penny-pinching Sui was tighter than the bark on a tree. He paid Amando only half his normal fee, justifying this by saying he considered Amando a friend, and friendship was far more valuable than money. In all his years Amando had never found this to be the case. Friendship was only a word. Money was another kind of blood.

In the end, the former Wimbledon semifinalist did take on the Triad leader as a cut-rate private pupil. Not to do so would have invited a very costly education at the hands of Charlie Snake.

Amando stepped from the front door of his home, wooden racquet in one hand, and shivered in the cool dawn. Felipe was a bit late that morning. Amando had better speak to him before he made such sluggishness a habit.

The weatherman had predicted plenty of sunshine and humidity, but no rain. God, how Amando wished it would rain. Rain meant canceling his morning rendezvous with the austere, unfeeling Charles Sui and instead spending the entire day dealing with his affairs.

Amando's Mercedes, dark blue with dark green tinted windows, slowly entered the gravel driveway and approached the ranch house. When it stopped, he strolled down the short limestone walk with the bowlegged stride that had endeared him to Filipino fans during a highly successful career. As he neared the Mercedes the door opened on the driver's side. Amando's mind was engrossed with the problems of Charles Sui's backhand, which were considerable. He assumed that Felipe would step from the car and open the back door for him, as usual.

But it was someone else who slid from the driver's seat,

a half-eaten apple in one hand and Felipe's Beretta in the other. Someone else threw the apple aside, then yanked the Magnum from Amando's belt.

"In the car or I'll kill you right here," Benjy said. He also wore Felipe's chauffeur cap and dark jacket.

In the backseat of the car a distressed Amando found himself sitting beside a second boy with strange eyes, a boy who stared at him with an authority that left Amando shaken. What kind of young man was this?

The car pulled away from the house and headed toward the enclosure's front gate. Amando's fears multiplied rapidly. Would he ever see his wife again? Why couldn't his great and good friend, Charles Sui, protect him from this? Amando dug his right thumb into the palm of his left hand, a Chinese acupressure technique he often used to calm himself. He was beginning to perspire. Heavily.

He said, "Is Felipe dead?"

Todd shook his head.

"Where are you taking me?"

Benjy looked in the rearview mirror. "Not out of your way, that's for sure."

Todd said, "Do you meet Charles Sui in his home or on the tennis court?"

Amando's eyes widened. "Sui? You intend to go after him? You don't know what you're doing."

Todd leaned toward him. "Answer my question."

Amando felt the perspiration roll down his spine and both sides of his rib cage. Why was he so afraid of this boy? "We meet in a bungalow near the tennis court," he said. "Sui uses it as a changing room. He's a very private person. His house is one of the finest in Forbes Park, but few people have been inside."

Benjy grinned. "I have. Been there twice. Even used the toilet."

Amando said, "Am I being kidnapped for ransom?"

"Tell us about the guards at the entrance to Forbes Park," Todd said.

The Mercedes was nearing the enclosure gates which had

failed to keep out the violence now facing Amando. He felt a tension not unlike a match point at Wimbledon. Would the guards notice that he had a different driver?

He cleared his throat. "The guards—" He stopped. The Mercedes' windows were tinted: His guards would see nothing. Sick at heart, Amando used the sleeve of his white satin jacket to wipe sweat from his forehead.

And why were the gates to his enclosure open? He and his neighbors were paying top money for security. What the hell was going on here? And then, as the Mercedes cruised through the entrance and toward a main road, Amando saw the guards. Both were lying facedown in the grass.

Todd said, "They're alive. Do as we say and nothing will happen to you. Defy me and my friend will kill you instantly. Is that clear?"

Amando, hands pressed down hard on his knees, looked over his shoulder at the home he'd worked so hard to get and wondered if he'd ever see it again. "I understand."

"Tell me about the Forbes Park guards," Todd said.

Twenty-two minutes later Charles Sui reached for the front door of his courtside bungalow.

Benjy opened the door and aimed Amando's Magnum at Sui, who wore a gray robe and sandals and carried two beige towels over his left arm. They stared at each other for several seconds, willing their hatred to grow, no longer seeing common ground but only seeing each other dead. Benjy had instant power, the gun, but Sui had the power of experience and felt himself superior to the boy. Why wasn't Benjy on the plane? Had something gone wrong with the bomb?

With his gun hand, Benjy motioned Charles Sui into the room, then kicked the door closed and stood behind him. Ignoring Benjy, Charles Sui glared at Rafael Amando, who sat on a metal folding chair near a row of metal lockers. The middle-aged tennis pro kept his eyes on his wooden tennis racquet, which he'd taken out of its canvas case and now squeezed with both hands.

Charles Sui now stared coldly at Todd. "You're the one who kills with candlestick holders."

Todd's fingers brushed his belt buckle. "You're the one who burns women to death and plants bombs on planes."

There was a sharp pain in the right side of Sui's brain, followed at once by a slight nausea. Migraine. He tossed the towels aside, not caring where they landed, and jammed clenched fists in the pockets of his robe. "Since you know who I am, then you must know who you should fear."

"I fear no one. Your godfather fears me."

Sui held his breath. Of course. His godfather had been acting strangely lately; this unearthly boy was the reason. They were linked together in some fashion, but how? Perhaps the link also involved the old priest his godfather had murdered, a choice bit of news reported to Charles Sui by a spy planted in Lin Pao's household.

The spy didn't know why the priest had been killed. She only knew that immediately afterward the order had gone out to kill the members of the Jade Eagles: Kill each and every one of them.

Even with Benjy's gun pointed at his head, Charles Sui still enjoyed a feeling of pride. It came from having bested his godfather. The thinker and the organ player had discovered the Black General's secret. The most feared dragon head in Asia was afraid of a boy. Charles Sui intended to destroy this boy and thus earn his godfather's undying gratitude.

He squeezed the beeper in the right-hand pocket of his robe, forefinger tapping the button in a continuous series of silent beeps, the signal that he was in danger. There were armed guards in his home. They should all be at the bungalow within seconds.

Todd stepped in front of Sui, reached into his robe pocket, and removed the beeper.

Benjy grinned.

As Charles Sui clenched his teeth against the growing

migraine, Todd said, "It's not sending. Nor do your telephones work, which I'm sure you've noticed. Since early dawn no calls have come in or out of your home."

Benjy said, "Bet somebody's trying to get through to you now. They just can't wait to tell you about the bomb. It went off, except you didn't kill the people you wanted to kill. I mean, we're here, big as life."

"I don't know what you're talking about."

"Yeah. Right."

Sui sat down on a metal folding chair, crossed his legs, and exhaled. For several seconds he eyed Todd in an attempt to unravel the riddle connecting this boy and Lin Pao. Sui also needed time to regain control. He could not possibly allow himself to be defeated by this odd child.

"Well, little warrior," Sui said, "it would seem you found your way onto my property easily enough. Now let's see you leave without difficulty. Did my dear friend Rafael, here, tell you that after tennis it is my custom to return to the house and shower? And did he also tell you that I am escorted to work by at least two bodyguards? If I don't return to the house, I can assure you my men will come looking for me."

Todd said, "An hour ago your bomb killed a young girl named Joan. It was her karma to sacrifice her life for others as payment for wrongdoing in her past lives. Now you must pay for killing her."

Sui rubbed the back of his neck and chuckled. "I see. And you have come to wash blood with blood, is that it?"

"Before you die, tell me about the murder of Nelson Berlin's sister."

Sui arched one eyebrow. "Before *I* die? Aren't we forgetting something, little warrior? Granted you were able to get past the guards at the walls, but unless I'm seen on the tennis court within the next few minutes, my men will know things aren't what they should be. And that will mean *your* death."

A grinning Benjy stepped to Sui's right side and aimed

the Magnum at his crotch. Sui leaned back in his chair. "You know I'll do it," Benjy said.

Sui nodded. A vein throbbed on his temple. "Yes, I know you will."

Benjy stepped back, Magnum at his side. "Sing your song, big man."

Outside the bungalow an eerie weather change was taking place. It was as if night had fallen. The sun disappeared, and birds, obviously seeking shelter, flew wildly past the small building. A light rain pecked at the windowpanes, followed quickly by a sharp wind that rattled the glass.

On the tennis court the netting snapped loose from one post and trailed across the court like a long, gray banner. Fresh chalk dust rose from the base line and swirled in the air along with dead leaves and bits of paper. Inside the bungalow there was silence as the two men and the two boys stared at the windows or looked up at the roof, now being pounded by an increasingly heavy rain. The bungalow had also grown chilly. Only Todd took the bizarre weather change calmly.

Eyes on the ceiling, Sui said, "Nelson Berlin raped and killed his sister. Happened in China near the end of the war with Japan. My father, my godfather, and the Chinese government arranged the facts to their liking. And to their needs."

"Someone was punished for the crime," Todd said. "Who was it?"

Sui picked an imaginary bit of lint from his robe. "An American missionary named Thomas Service. Just prior to having his way with his own sister, Berlin shot Service. The wound was serious but not fatal. While hospitalized, Service was kept sedated, preventing him from telling what really happened. Both the American government and the Chinese government were seeking a quick solution to this rather messy business."

"My father and godfather devised one that seemed to please all concerned. All, that is, except Mr. Service. One morning he was taken from the hospital, given a trial, then immediately executed. I was told the entire business took no more than five minutes.''

Todd said, ''And Nelson Berlin has worked for the Triad ever since.''

''He was given his life in exchange for providing certain services. Generalissimo Chiang's government and our organization both saw the value in this arrangement. Understand, little warrior, that without our assistance, Nelson Berlin never could have achieved his great success. We are a major investor in his companies. This has helped him as much as it's helped us.''

Todd said, ''You've helped yourselves at the expense of Miss Berlin and Mr. Service.''

Sui shrugged. ''Miss Berlin and Mr. Berlin wanted to serve China. I think you could say they've done that, since our organization is very much a part of China and always will be. Young man, do you seriously believe you can punish Berlin or my godfather for something that happened so long ago?''

Thunder rumbled, then crashed loudly. Lightning flashed in the distance and the rain pounded the bungalow with the force of hailstones. A frightened Amando bowed his head against his racquet and prayed to see his wife again. Even Benjy had stopped smiling.

But he tapped Sui on the shoulder with the Magnum because he wanted to make sure there was someone in the room more frightened than he. ''Guess what, big man? I don't think anybody's going to see us leave here in all that shit. What do you think?''

Sui closed his eyes against the migraine. It was, of course, unthinkable, but at the same time undeniable. DiPalma's son had known beforehand about the storm. He had to. That's why he'd been so self-possessed. That's why even now he had an icy calm that Sui hadn't seen in anyone outside of his godfather.

Sui shook his head wildly. He was going to die at the hands of a child. A fucking child. Ludicrous, yes. Too ironic for words, really.

Screaming, he leapt from his chair and raced for the door.

Todd snatched Amando's wooden racquet from the floor and ran after him. Sui reached the door, yanked it open, and jumped outside. Todd was close on his heels. The stormy darkness swallowed them both.

Benjy and Amando stared at the open doorway as rain poured into the bungalow, drenching the carpet, a rubdown table, and a scale. Two minutes later a thoroughly soaked Todd returned, dragging Sui's rain-soaked, bloodied corpse behind him with one hand. The other hand gripped Amando's wooden racquet, which had blood and human hair entangled in its strings.

Amando spun around and threw up.

Benjy never flinched. He looked at Sui, then at Todd. "Karma," Benjy said. Todd nodded.

With Benjy at the wheel and a nauseated Amando in back with Todd, the Mercedes had almost reached the front gate when lightning struck the bungalow and set it on fire.

# Twenty

That March morning, one week before surrendering to the FBI, Detective Gregory Van Rooten stopped his 1984 BMW on Manhattan's West End Avenue, opened the door on the driver's side, and vomited on a newly planted elm tree in front of a $7,000 a year progressive West Side school.

For a few minutes he kept his head between his knees, wondering if he should continue driving downtown for a ten-o'clock court appearance or return home. At the moment he was groggy, nauseous, and had a splitting headache to go along with his heart palpitations. A cooing pigeon on the sidewalk just feet away sounded like a chain saw running wild inside Van Rooten's head. He was as wasted as he'd ever been.

He'd enjoyed a weekend of drugs and outrageous sex with Taroko, a Taiwanese singer who was staying at his Riverside Drive apartment for several days. She was in her late twenties, a small woman with a wide sensual mouth, long black hair, and lavender spiders tattooed on the inside of both thighs. She also wore blue contact lenses.

They'd been lovers for six months. From the moment he'd seen Taroko, Van Rooten had been determined to have her. But in succeeding, he'd gotten more than he bargained for. She'd immediately become the source of all his pleasure and pain. For the first time in his life he knew what it was like to love and to be hurt.

Last night at his apartment, they'd gotten sloshed on *cachaca*, a Brazilian rum that was undrinkable until mixed with fruit juice. Taroko had brought back four bottles from Rio de Janeiro, where she'd given several concerts before sold-out houses of wildly enthusiastic Asians. The rum was unreal. It had left Van Rooten incredibly energetic, heightening his reflexes and making him feel hornier than he had in some time. He couldn't remember how many times he and Taroko had played hide the salami.

At one point they'd taken barbiturates to calm down. Then it was time for a little freebasing. At Taroko's suggestion they'd filled the water pipe with the Brazilian rum, giving the coke a stunning taste. It was a pleasure that couldn't be described. No woman had ever given Van Rooten the wild ride in life he'd gotten with Taroko.

Van Rooten's father had called him a headstrong bozo, one cursed with an animalistic sex drive. Old Dad had been right. Van Rooten was all of that and more. He was handsome, charming, too reckless for his own good, and impatient with those who couldn't keep up with him.

His father was intense and high-handed, the sort who regarded a free-spirited only child as a bitter disappointment. Each feared the essence of the other. In time that fear developed into a quiet, long-lasting hatred, which they sensed would one day become a major explosion.

Good looks and an easy charm had always made Van Rooten the center of attention, something his father envied and never forgave him for. From birth the boy had gotten what he wanted by manipulating women, whether they were baby-sitters or relatives, schoolmates or strangers. The adult Van Rooten could only feel effective when directing or controlling people. If his manipulation blew up in his face, so be it. Whatever the cost, he had to have his way.

Teri, his second wife, had given him the benefit of her wisdom in this area. "You're a scorpion," she said. "You'd rather sting yourself to death than let somebody else kill you." Right you are, Teri, baby.

His father had been a cold-blooded, money-grubbing prick, and his mother a social snob of a bigot who was obsessed with bridge, charity balls, and right-wing Republican politics. Van Rooten had grown up depending on himself. Meanwhile he'd learned one thing from watching his parents: Men took what they wanted and women took whatever shit you gave them.

Neither college nor the world of business had interested him. The last thing he wanted to do was join the gray people. What he needed was an outlet for his abundant energy. What he needed was a continual challenge, something that would never be dull and would engage his quick mind while offering him constant action and all the women he could ever want.

Which is why he'd become a cop. In time, however, he'd found the underworld even more exciting. He'd always had the ability to shift emotional gears in a second, leaving behind only footprints and a cloud of dust. Van Rooten had done just that upon discovering there was more excitement, freedom, and sex to be found in the underworld.

He wasn't surprised to learn that his father had been washing drug money for years. The old man had always been a full-time hypocrite. Crime was a logical extension of the behavior Nelson Berlin used in business every day.

Van Rooten had been divorced twice, having dismantled both marriages with equal parts infidelity and malicious honesty. Van Rooten's second wife, Teri, hadn't enjoyed hearing him say that being pleasant to the same person day in, day out fucking ruined his peace of mind. Until then she'd believed herself capable of endless forgiveness. Eighteen months with him had cured her of that idea.

As he saw it, marriage killed love. There was simply too much effort required to make it work. He could never be satisfied with one woman, any more than he could be responsible for somebody else's happiness. The pleasure in love was in the variety. Marriage was the open manhole you fell into while looking for love.

Until Taroko he'd seen little difference between women. True, he'd developed a bad case of "yellow fever" before meeting her, chasing Asian women almost exclusively. But Taroko was special and would have attracted his attention under any circumstances. He fantasized about her full mouth doing unbelievable things to his cock. And her stare was so penetrating that it was hard to look her in the eye.

Taroko's hair was unreal. Just looking at it gave Van Rooten a hard-on. Blue-black and stunning, it was a glossy ornament that seemed to be a combination of night sky and sun. Christ, was it long. Van Rooten fantasized about her sitting on his face and rubbing his chest with it, which is what happened three hours after they met. She was even more sexually energetic than he was, and, like him, she followed her first impression. You were either in her life from the beginning or forget it.

They'd met at a party in Chinatown, thrown by Lin Pao's people. As a singer who traveled the world, she was a natural courier for the Black General, who'd bankrolled her career and was said to have been her lover. Pao had a thing for singers, and in this case Van Rooten could see why.

Until Taroko, Van Rooten hadn't gotten in too deep with the Black General. He'd passed on information about witnesses, wiretaps, surveillance, upcoming raids, and trials. He'd done it for the money and the excitement. When Taroko entered his life, she asked him to do more for the Triad. And he agreed, doing it for her and her alone.

He became a courier, carrying Triad money to Europe and the Caribbean. He threatened witnesses and suppressed trial evidence. He also stole intelligence files and murdered Lin Pao's enemies. Van Rooten denied Taroko nothing, for without her he was lifeless. With her he was more alive than he'd ever been. Taroko had him in her grasp. Forget about any idea of right and wrong.

Meanwhile she gave Van Rooten all the sexual excitement he'd ever wanted. When they were apart, he was sometimes unfaithful to her. But he insisted on Taroko being true to him at all times. To her credit, she was up-front on this subject. "I can never be yours alone," she said. "Accept this or get out of my life."

It was too late for him to do that. He wanted Taroko, and when he wanted something, he had to have it. His plan was to hang in there until she saw things his way. So he stayed, refusing even to consider that he might be living on false hope. He stayed and was tortured by jealousy, a new emotion for him.

He hated the thought of sharing Taroko with anyone. When visiting Taiwan, she would stay with Lin Pao, leading Van Rooten to accuse her of sleeping with the son of a bitch. She denied it every time, claiming the relationship between her and Pao was strictly business. Her home was in Hong Kong, but when visiting Taiwan, she found it cheaper to stay with her old patron. Besides, she couldn't insult Pao by refusing his hospitality.

Van Rooten suspected she was lying. But he said nothing, which was the only way to avoid having his suspicions become a conviction. He rationalized by telling himself there was a price to pay for Pao's protection and influence. With her looks and the Black General's power, a trade-off was inevitable. It was a rough world. A gal had to get over any way she could.

On her recent trip to Brazil she said that an eighty-year-old general had offered her a handful of emeralds if she'd sit nude on a bowl of ice cream and shit while he watched. She laughed as she spoke of it to Van Rooten, claiming to have refused the general because of his bad skin. A jealous Van Rooten thought, *Christ, don't let her be laughing at me*.

In the front seat of his BMW, Van Rooten inhaled through his mouth and massaged his temples with his fingertips. *Face it, sport, you just ain't well. You're too sick to go anywhere*. Federal court was a half-hour drive downtown, and when he got there, the scenario was a full day of testifying and meetings with the government prosecutor. No way, Jose.

The court case. He and his partner, Detective Olonzo LaVon, had teamed with the FBI to take down some unwashed, filthy-assed New Jersey bikers and confiscate ten million dollars in amphetamines. During the course of the investigation Van Rooten had fucked the biker president's wife, which had struck LaVon as a bad move.

"Won't help the prosecution's case," LaVon said.

Van Rooten said, "Who's gonna tell? My lips are sealed, and if the bitch opens her mouth, her old man is going to do a lot more than send her ass to the far side of the world. Which leaves just you, partner."

Not that LaVon, a thirty-six-year-old, solidly built Black man with red hair, didn't have his little secrets. He was, like Van Rooten, on the Black General's payroll, which is how LaVon could afford a cabin cruiser. More than a few weekends had been spent cruising Long Island Sound with his teenage Puerto Rican girlfriend while Mrs. LaVon believed him to be out fighting the war against drugs.

In the end, the argument over the consequences of porking the biker's old lady had ended with LaVon giving Van Rooten the Harlem hard-eye and calling him a simpleminded fuck with a death wish. Van Rooten said, "Just because you're not in love, don't throw shit at the moon."

In his BMW, Van Rooten peered into the rearview mirror. Jesus, was he ugly. He looked like he'd been chewed up, spit out, then stepped on. And he felt even worse. Fuck it, he was going back to the apartment and call in sick. Taroko was waiting for him. After he grabbed a few hours sleep, the party could resume.

She was due in Atlantic City the end of the week, where she'd play four days at a top casino for a hundred thou. Taroko was more than a star. The woman was a universe. LaVon could handle the biker case on his own.

Van Rooten wiped his mouth with tissues from the glove compartment, then took his mirrored sunglasses from the dashboard and put them on. Anything to hide his eyes, which looked like boiled onions in day-old piss. That's when he noticed a muscular black woman in a nurse's uniform peering into the car.

She'd been escorting a small, old guy with watery eyes and liver spots on his bald head. The two had been inching along the sidewalk, the old guy holding on to the nurse's burly arm for dear life. Nurse had caught sight of an unhealthy-looking Van Rooten in the BMW and been moved to look in on him.

He grinned, projecting enough genuine warmth and kindness to win her trust, to control her simply because he felt like doing it. He had the power to make her dissolve in his presence, and that she did. She gave him a toothy grin and leaned closer, her regard for his welfare snowballing by the moment. Van Rooten said, "Malaria. Vietnam. On my way to the doc for a checkup." Yeah. Right.

Nurse's square-shaped, ebony face, with its spacious nostrils, turned sad. "Anything I can do?"

Van Rooten shook his head. "Be all right once I get to the hospital. Need a few quinine tablets, that's all. Drugs make the world a better place, I always say."

She giggled, one hand on her sizable bosom while the old guy clung to her and gazed at the entrance to the school without seeing it. Suddenly the pounding in Van Rooten's head made him sit upright. Jesus, the pain. He should be in bed, not out here on the street goofing on some spook with an ass big enough to have its own ZIP code.

He lifted a hand in farewell, then closed the car door and drove home to surprise Taroko.


Van Rooten's apartment was in a russet-colored brick building on Riverside Drive that had once been a nineteenth-century orphanage for black and Indian children. It faced Joan of Arc park, with its statue of Joan in full armor and on horseback, the bronze sculpture sitting atop a granite pedestal containing stones from the tower in Rouen, where she'd been imprisoned and tried.

The apartment had twelve rooms, high ceilings, a terrace

with a small greenhouse, and a view of the Hudson River. Teri's father, a wealthy plastic surgeon from Darien, Connecticut, had given it to them as a wedding present. To insure a quick and quiet divorce, one which would not damage the good doctor's social standing, Van Rooten had been allowed to keep the pad.

He parked the BMW in a garage two blocks from the apartment, then walked to the building. The Indian doorman—his name was Aborpa Joydeep—was missing. Nothing new about that. Joydeep was a good-looking, friendly young dude with curly hair and great teeth. But as a doorman he was nobody's award-winner. He came to work late, left early, and often wandered away from his post to buy Lotto tickets or play the horses at the nearest off-track betting parlor. Joydeep wasn't exactly busting his buns every second of the day.

After taking the self-service elevator to the ninth floor, Van Rooten walked along a parquet hallway until he reached his apartment. It took him a few seconds to find his key, then quietly let himself in. His hangover was brutal; it would take a pound of aspirin to ease the pain. First he'd better let Taroko know he was back.

He found her in bed with Joydeep. Both were too busy to notice Van Rooten.

Eyes closed, a moaning Taroko lay writhing on black silk sheets as the slender, swarthy Indian tongued her navel. Seconds later his head was between her thighs and he was pumping fur. Van Rooten silently watched them for several seconds, then stepped out of the open doorway and leaned against the wall. Closing his eyes, he bit his lower lip until he tasted blood.

Once or twice he and some broad had been caught in bed by her husband or boyfriend, and it had been a joke, something Van Rooten had laughed about. At their second-anniversary party his first wife had found him screwing—her younger sister, no less. A drunken Van Rooten's reply to his dazed wife: "Who you gonna believe, me or your own eyes?"

This shit with Taroko was different. He was the one who'd been cheated on, and it hurt like hell. Because he loved her so totally, the pain and anger were unbearable. His mind raced at warp speed. *I should have distrusted her more. I never should have let her become so important to me.*

She'd been the first woman to create in him a need to love. But the truth was, she hadn't returned that love, and he'd known it all along. Even as he suspected he'd lost Taroko, Van Rooten still wanted her and was frightened by that knowledge. Damn that fucking bitch.

Pulling his .38 Smith & Wesson from a belt holster, he stepped back into the doorway and said, "Knock, knock."

Joydeep's head quickly came away from Taroko's crotch. Almost simultaneously she sat up in bed, shaken at first, then regaining her composure in an instant. Fingers spread, she pulled her long hair away from her face and body.

"How long have you been standing there?" she said.

Van Rooten slowly walked over to the bed and looked down at the Indian doorman. "Joydeep. Well, we've certainly been living up to our name, haven't we?"

The doorman, eyes wide with fear, looked from Van Rooten to Taroko, then back to Van Rooten. "Please, please. I do not want trouble. I go."

"You stay," Van Rooten said.

Taroko dismissed the detective with a wave of her hand. "Grow up, Gregory. I told you at the beginning, you don't own me. Nobody owns me. Besides, we both know I do only what my friend in Taiwan tells me to do. And that includes my relationship with you. Now please put that thing away before somebody gets hurt."

Van Rooten nodded his head. "You're right about Pao. I knew about you and him. At the same time I didn't want to know. I think the word we're looking for here is *dumb*. Meanwhile you've got me in so deep, I couldn't get out if I wanted to."

Taroko brought her knees to her chest. "You don't want

to get out, Gregory. You like doing dangerous things. Besides, you're well paid."

She was right about him being well paid. This weekend, he and Detective Olonzo LaVon were to carry a suitcase of Lin Pao's money down to Panama City, Panama, where it would begin an electronic journey through banks in six countries before reappearing in a Canadian investment firm. Van Rooten and LaVon would each receive fifty thousand dollars for thirty-six hours' work.

Van Rooten said to Taroko, "Why did you have to fuck this skinny-assed fool in my place?"

She smiled. "I like doing dangerous things too. That's what we have in common, remember? Don't take life so seriously, Gregory."

"Want to tell me why Lin Pao ordered you to put the hook into me? I thought the son of a bitch trusted me."

Taroko eyed her left little toe before picking at it with a thumbnail. "You're *gweilo*, a foreigner. An outsider. No Chinese will ever trust you. You might see yourself as one of us, as having been accepted into the club. But you're wrong. My friend doesn't trust anybody. He felt you should be more committed to him than you were. Let's say there's very little chance at this point of your betraying him without betraying yourself."

"I see. So I was being used all around. By you, by him, by everybody."

"Like I said, you were well paid. Besides, you've used people all your life. Women especially. You live by the sword, you die by the sword."

A tic suddenly flared up near Van Rooten's left eye. Man, he hated people dumping on him. Fucking hated it. Payback, he thought. Right here, right now. And there was gonna be plenty left over for the Black General.

He grinned. "You Chinks have another way of putting it. 'You spit against the wind, you spit in your own face.' We say 'What goes around, comes around.'"

Taroko lay back, smiling up at him. "Gregory, get undressed and we'll make it a threesome. I love trios."

Joydeep shook his head. "No, no, no. I must go now. Thank you for having me."

Van Rooten said, "Let me ask you a question, Joydeep. Should I blow your brains out or shoot your balls off?"

"I don't understand, sir. She invited me to come here."

Van Rooten grinned. "I got an idea. Suppose you two just keep on keeping on. Carry on as if I weren't here."

Taroko sat up.

Van Rooten aimed the .38 at her head. "I mean it."

Her face tightened.

The detective nodded. "That's right, princess. I want you and Joydeep here to fuck each other blind. From time to time I'll suggest what I'd like to see you two do. And you'll do it, or I'm gonna get awfully mad."

He backed away to a closet, reached up on the top shelf, and removed a Polaroid camera. "It's showtime, boys and girls."

He ordered Taroko and Joydeep to begin. When neither moved, he stepped to the bed and kicked the Indian in the leg. A tearful Joydeep backed away from him and turned his face to Taroko, who glared at Van Rooten. But she removed a jar of honey from the night table, gently pushed the Indian back on the bed, and poured honey into the palm of one of her hands.

Setting the jar aside, she rubbed her palms together, her eyes still on Van Rooten. They stayed on him while she slowly rolled Joydeep's flaccid penis back and forth in her sticky hands. She turned from the detective, however, when she took the Indian's cock in her mouth. Van Rooten's throat went dry.

But he made them screw each other in every conceivable way, and he photographed it all. Joydeep lost his erection a couple of times, but Taroko's magic tongue brought him back into the game. She performed with a sullen calm, at times acting as though Van Rooten weren't there. Once or twice he came close to being turned on, but he didn't let it happen. It was time to assert himself with the Chinese.

Forty-five minutes later he told Taroko and Joydeep to

stop. By now her anger was barely under control. The Ice Princess didn't take to being humiliated. Well, too fucking bad.

After wiping her mouth with the back of her hand, Taroko threw a pillow at Van Rooten. He knocked it aside and said, "Naughty, naughty." Then he pointed to the photographs of her and Joydeep, which he'd stacked on top of the dresser. "When these get shown around, you are going to be one popular girl. Your phone won't stop ringing. I'll give you one hell of a reference."

Eyes shimmering behind tears, Taroko cursed him. "You and your father," she said. "You're both sick. When Pao learns what you've done to me, you'll wish you'd never been born."

Van Rooten said, "I know all about my father's connection with Pao. That's old news, little girl. Me and my old man, we never speak about it, 'cause we don't speak to each other. Which is the way we both like it."

"You don't know a damn thing," she said. "How do you think Pao ended up owning your father?"

"Money. The same way he ended up owning you."

"Oh, really? Well, I think it's time you learned the truth about Nelson Berlin. Did you know he raped and killed his own sister?"

Van Rooten shook his head, not believing a word of it. "You're lying," he said.

"Am I? How do you think a Chinese can control such an important American businessman? That's your problem, *Mister* Van Rooten. You never want to believe the unpleasant."

Taroko told him the origin of the relationship between his father and Lin Pao. The detective listened quietly, and when she finished, he said, "I knew my old man had done some shit things in his life, but I never figured he'd go that far."

Her smile was slyly triumphant. "There're a lot of things you don't know. The police may be on to you, did you know that? You think you're so clever, so irresistible to women, so special. Well, you're not. You make mistakes. You throw your money around, you insult people, you drink too much, you talk too much. Lin Pao is checking out just how many mistakes you've made, and if he decides the police are getting too close to you, then—''

She drew a forefinger across her throat.

Van Rooten swayed slightly as the dizziness came and went. A pulse was throbbing in his neck. He placed both hands behind him to hide the shaking. Then he closed his eyes, took a deep breath, and opened his eyes. He was calm again. Ready to take care of business.

As Taroko and Joydeep watched, Van Rooten placed the camera on a night table with the pile of photographs, then pulled the .38 from his belt. Picking the pillow from the floor, he held it against the gun barrel. Taroko turned her penetrating gaze on him, and for a second he almost weakened.

Almost.

She said, "You wouldn't dare. Not to me."

Van Rooten shot Joydeep twice in the head. Then, kneeling on the bed, he inched his way toward a whimpering Taroko, until he was treading on her long hair. Weeping, he pressed the pillow against her chest and pulled the trigger three times.

# Twenty-one

DiPalma left his bedroom and entered a small room at the end of the hall shortly after dawn. Through a window he could see the sun starting to rise over the Brooklyn Bridge. March was nearly over. Spring was a week old, but frozen snow remained on the windowsill and a cold wind howled through the street below.

DiPalma switched on the light, then blinked at the sudden brightness. The room's walls were lined with a magnificent collection of samurai swords—*daitos,* long swords; *waki-zashi,* medium swords; *tantos,* short swords. Displayed in small boxes and glass cases were tables of Japanese sword guards, collars, pommels, and hilt ornaments. DiPalma had come there to be alone and to think.

He had regained his strength and the use of his left arm through *kendo.* The way of the sword had become a fixation with him. He had a talent for *kendo* and *escrima,* but he hadn't stopped with mastering techniques. He'd learned the history of the samurai sword, along with the history of the men who'd forged and fought with it.

He'd collected swords and traveled to Japan to research the weapons, producing a book on Japanese swords and swordsmanship that established him as an American authority on the subject. American antique dealers, private collectors, and even certain Japanese asked his opinion on a sword's authenticity. DiPalma was also invited to speak before colleges, businessmen, and other groups interested in Japanese culture. Some called him a sword expert, bringing to mind his father's warning: "When you become an expert, then you've stopped thinking."

In the small room DiPalma shivered and turned up the collar of his robe. He understood his preoccupation with swords and other weapons. He'd spent his life being on guard against deception and betrayal; it was difficult for him to be open with anyone. His suspicion of the world at large made police work a logical choice as a profession. The martial arts were simply an additional method of self-protection.

But in time the martial arts taught DiPalma more than combat. He learned the importance of tradition, of keeping alive the continuity of history and culture, something his father had said must be done with the family's own Sicilian heritage. Through the study of *kendo* and samurai swords, DiPalma came to understand that the past held value for the present. The martial arts taught him the importance of seeking out and using the art and thought of all time.

From a window in his sword room, DiPalma stared down at a police launch slowly cruising New York's empty harbor. Across the harbor, the southern tip of Manhattan remained dark and half hidden by fog. DiPalma grinned. Unnoticed by officers on board the police launch, a sea gull had landed on the boat's starboard bow and was hitching a free ride.

Turning from the window, DiPalma touched a long sword on the way to his right. The weapon, one of his and Todd's favorites, had been forged over three hundred years ago in Japan's Shinto, new-sword, period. This particular sword was deceptive. To the untrained eye it appeared to be an effective weapon. But it had been designed more for display than for combat.

On the blade the smith had engraved flowers and birds instead of Sanskrit words calling for courage and loyalty unto death. The cutting edge was only two feet long, reduced from the four feet found on similar swords forged earlier. The *daito* was more attractive than useful. It wasn't what it appeared to be.

And neither was Van Rooten, now very much on Di-Palma's mind because of the missing Taroko. Shark Eyes had reached out for DiPalma because he owed it to Jan, or so he claimed. Shark Eyes also wanted to destroy his father, which is how DiPalma had ended up in the Philippines and nearly gotten wasted. Now back in New York, and with time for speculation, DiPalma had some questions about Van Rooten's true intentions. Was Shark Eyes running a game on him? Was DiPalma being used to divert attention from the very scarce Taroko?

Shark Eyes was slicker than a greased eel. The guy was a control freak who loved intrigue like a schoolboy loved his pie. The whole world was merely his opening act; Shark Eyes was the star. If Taroko had jerked him around, she'd let herself in for grief. Van Rooten was as sensitive as an eyeball. When attacked, he'd put the hurt on you in a minute.

In the last days of their partnership DiPalma had sought to have him brought up on charges for passing information to the Chinese mobs. Van Rooten's response had been to try to kill him by warning Lower East Side drug dealers of DiPalma's planned meeting with an informant on their turf.

Traveling in an unmarked police car, DiPalma arrived on the Lower East Side late one October afternoon. After parking in front of an abandoned tenement, he stepped onto the pavement and was about to close the car door when the hairs rose on the back of his neck. He sensed-felt-saw the danger out of the corner of one eye. *Kendo* had honed his instincts and he was quick. He leapt clear of the car a split second before an abandoned refrigerator, pushed from a nearby rooftop, hit the car and crushed it.

A few days of asking around, combined with money in the right places, and DiPalma found somebody who could tie Van Rooten to whoever had pushed the fridge off the roof. That somebody was a black junkie and petty thief who called himself Captain Marvel. According to him, the would-be murderers were Puerto Ricans who controlled much of the heroin dealing along Avenue A. And Van Rooten was tight with this crew. Unfortunately Captain Marvel was no hero. He refused to repeat this allegation in court or in front of a district attorney. The attempt on DiPalma's life went unpunished.

He had to be restrained by fellow cops from punching out Van Rooten. For sure, he wasn't about to work with the man again. DiPalma also vowed to drive him from the force. For Van Rooten, this incident was a bit sticky. DiPalma commanded a lot of respect in the precinct. Many cops were willing to take his word that Van Rooten was dirty.

DiPalma was assigned another partner, a comment in itself. A very offended Van Rooten promised payback. And he'd kept his word.

Jan had been preparing to film a romantic comedy on location in Wall Street and had talked the mayor into making a cameo appearance. After reading about the mayor's plans to grace the silver screen, Van Rooten had presented himself at Jan's production office, claiming to be a technical adviser sent by the police department. DiPalma, if he'd been there, could have told her that Van Rooten was lying. But he found moviemaking boring and never visited Jan's sets. To him the process of filmmaking was as exciting as watching flies fuck.

Jan was never borderline about her passions. She was quicker to feel than to think; her emotions were endless. Van Rooten, with a predator's instinct for victims, made the most of her weakness. Later when she'd learned the reason he'd started the affair, they'd had a shouting match in his apartment. She'd broken a two-thousand-dollar mirror, tossed his wallet and badge off the terrace to the street below, then threatened to kill him.

No man had ever used her so blatantly. And who could she blame? She'd stuck her hand in the fire without any prompting. She'd gotten burned badly, but so had Frank. She deserved to suffer; he hadn't.

Jan was never more alive than when serving her passions, but to do so was the greatest slavery and she knew it. The problem was, she couldn't stop herself. What she saw, she wanted, especially if it was a sensual, provocative man. That such men inevitably made her unhappy was an irony not lost on her. "I'm under the illusion that I know what I want," she told Frank.

Both she and Frank knew why he didn't leave her. Without Jan he feared he'd never love again.

In front of one beautiful *daito*, DiPalma reached out and ran his fingers over the sharkskin-covered hilt. He was about to take the blade out of its scabbard when Jan said, "Thought I'd find you here."

DiPalma looked over his shoulder. Jan stood in the doorway, hugging herself against the chill. She wore a red flannel nightgown and fur-lined slippers, and her face was puffy with sleep. He held out his arms and she came to him, burying her face in his shoulder.

"Stomach still upset?" he said.

"It's better. Finally got to sleep a couple hours ago."

"You were dead to the world when I left. Did I wake you?"

"No. You moved with the grace of a gazelle or a bird on the wing, whichever you prefer. Never heard you leave."

DiPalma stroked her hair. "Then how come you're up?"

"Missed you. It's cold in that big bed with nobody to keep me warm. Also, I thought you might be worried about this and that, so I came to ease your troubled mind."

He squeezed her buttocks. "You did that earlier."

She gently bit his chest. "There's more to life than just sex, though right now I can't think of what that might be."

They stood holding each other quietly for almost a minute and then Jan said, "You worried about Berlin?"

DiPalma shook his head. "No. I figure he knows about the diskette. Lin Pao's people in Manila probably clued him in. The information looks good, but I can't use it until I confirm a few things and run it by a half dozen lawyers. The network's going to want ironclad proof, especially about Berlin raping and killing his own sister.''

DiPalma exhaled. ''I figure they'll give me one hell of a hard time on this thing. Once I turn in my report, they'll go to Berlin to get his side of the story. I mean, the man *is* a major stockholder in the network. So the bottom line is, don't look for this thing to hit the airwaves for a while yet. At least a couple of weeks. Which unfortunately gives Berlin time to make a countermove.''

''What about your investigative team? Have they come up with anything?''

DiPalma said, ''Not yet. But I've got them working on it. They've dropped everything to concentrate on Berlin and Lin Pao. They're looking into the Rhoda Berlin killing and her fiancé's execution. They're also trying to get something out of the Department of the Army and the Beijing government.''

DiPalma kissed Jan's hair. ''Charles Sui told Todd that Chiang Kai-shek's government was involved. Nowadays that means Taiwan, but I doubt if we'll get any cooperation out of them. Why should they admit to being involved in a forty-year cover-up that allowed a killer-rapist to go free because he could make money for a Triad?''

Face still buried against DiPalma's chest, Jan slipped her hands into the pockets of his robe. ''Did you learn any more about Charlie Snake's death? Charlie Snake. Where do they get these names?''

''Barry Omens said an autopsy's being performed on the late Mr. Snake. He also said the tennis pro's still missing.''

''Rafael somebody?''

''Yeah. Apparently he showed up for their lesson, then he split right after the storm started. Right after lightning turned the bungalow into a microwave.''

She looked up at him. ''Right after Todd and Charlie Snake had their little talk. Have you had a chance to speak to Todd about Charlie Snake's death?''

DiPalma shook his head. ''No. The kid's pretty exhausted. He slept all of yesterday and hasn't left his room. Benjy's in there with him like some damn guard dog.''

Jan shivered. "Maybe that thing's come back."

"The Iki-ryo?"

She nodded.

DiPalma said, "Could be. I think that's why he's tired. That *thing* takes a lot out of him. He won't talk about it, and who can blame him? Let's say it's possible Todd had something to do with the lightning. He did go to see Charlie Snake about Berlin's sister. At first I couldn't figure out how Todd and Benjy got past Snake's security. Then I remembered Rafael Amando, the tennis pro. Charlie Snake got barbecued early in the morning, around the time of his tennis lesson. So Amando was the only way Todd and Benjy could have gotten to see Snake."

"They told me they were at Sui's place," DiPalma said. "Somehow they got him to admit that Berlin had assaulted and murdered his own sister. Apparently Pao and the Chiang government covered things up. After that Todd and Benjy weren't in the mood to talk much."

"Why would Charlie Snake admit something like that?"

DiPalma shook his head. "I don't know. Yes, I do know. Todd made him do it. One way or another, he made him do it."

"And Joan. Why did she have to die?"

"Karma, Todd said. He'd owned her as a slave girl four hundred years ago. She needed just one act of atonement for the sins of past lives. By sacrificing herself for the people on the plane, she immediately became one with the gods. Todd says she's free now."

"That poor girl. But if it hadn't been for her, the plane would have gone down over the ocean and you would have died. I think that's the real reason she went to Manila with you. Todd didn't mention it because he doesn't want you to feel guilty. You usually come to this room when you're in a mood to ponder the state of the universe. What's bothering you now?"

"Van Rooten."

She tensed in his arms. DiPalma shook his head. "I was thinking about that Chinese singer he went around with. She's missing. I think he killed her."

Jan looked at him.

DiPalma said, "Greg thinks he's smarter than the rest of us. That's one of the attractions the Chinese had for him. He admired their brains and thought he was a match for them. He wasn't. Hell, nobody is, if you want to know the truth. How are you going to beat the oldest civilization on the face of the earth?"

Jan said, "Frank, even if he admits he killed her, he's not going to prison. He's an informant and they need him. You've told me about men who've killed a dozen people and never served a day behind bars only because they were essential in a court case against somebody else."

DiPalma touched the tip of her nose with a forefinger. "Ah, but you're missing the point. Greg gets his jollies putting one over on the rest of us. Right now it's enough for him to know he's gotten away with killing a key player in this little game. He's broken the rules, see, so now he has this feeling of power. Somewhere down the line he'll want to brag about it, but not right now. Right now it's enough that he knows something we don't."

"Tell me something," Jan said. "If Greg was such a shit, why didn't anyone notice it before now? I mean, even I caught on to his act after a couple of weeks."

DiPalma said, "In this town, police work involves a great deal of politics. You have to keep a lot of groups happy. The mayor's office, the governor's office, blacks, gays, Hispanics, Jews. From day one a New York cop's on a tightrope, and God help you if you slip and fall. To survive, you need to be smart, you need to be lucky, and you need friends in high places. Van Rooten survived as long as he did because for a time he had all three things going for him."

DiPalma shook his head. "I saw people close their eyes to all kinds of shit coming from this guy. One reason is, he made those around him look good. Something else: Cops don't give up their own so easily. We're under attack from all sides, so we tend to stick together even when we know a brother officer's guilty as sin. It's us against the world. There are cops who will never think Van Rooten did a thing wrong. To them he's simply being persecuted by commie pinko liberals."

Jan nodded. "It would seem that our boy Greg always had somebody who'd come along and save him from the fine print."

"Until now. I'd like to hit him with this Taroko thing and see his reaction. I'd like him to know he didn't get away with it, that he's not as smart as he thinks he is. It would put a humongous dent in his ego if I could blow his little scheme right out of the water."

"Until I met him," Jan said, "I never knew how much skill was involved in lying. God, if he died tomorrow, I wouldn't shed a tear. He's hurt a lot of people. A lot of people. By the way, how's Martin Mackie doing?"

"Fine, I suppose. He's been in Florida for a couple days. He'll come back to New York before returning to Hong Kong. Since I've returned from Manila we've talked on the phone a few times. He said Angela Ramos would be happy to know the diskette's in America."

"Angela was quite a gal. If for no other reason, Lin Pao deserves to die for what he did to her. Speaking of Lin Pao, why didn't Todd and Benjy continue on to Taiwan instead of coming back here? Don't they have a score to settle with the Black General, as he's called?"

"Todd calls him Kiichi," DiPalma said. "Yeah, they could have gone on to Taiwan, I guess. But if they came back here, there's a reason. I don't know what it is, but there's a reason."

Jan kissed him on the cheek. "Enough of this serious stuff. Know what I feel like doing now?"

DiPalma cupped her breast. "That makes two of us."

"You are wrong, dago breath. That can wait until the bedroom. What I feel like doing now is dancing. Slow, slow dancing."

"Here? There's no music."

"Live a little, sport."

She took his hand, put an arm around his waist, and started swaying. In her low, husky voice she began to sing "All the Things You Are." It was DiPalma's favorite song. He held her close, and as pigeons cooed on the windowsill and dawn crept into the room, they danced.

# Twenty-two

**Taipei, Taiwan**

When Lin Pao and two armed guards left his compound on Yangming Mountain at sundown, they walked slowly toward the mountain's peak. One guard carried a small cage of butterflies. Pao held a blue vase filled with white orchids and plum blossoms.

Near the crest the three men stopped in front of a small bamboo grove that encircled a single pine tree. All trees had been newly planted in memory of Taroko, whose ashes were buried at the base of the pine.

A wave of Pao's hand and the guard carrying the butterflies stepped forward to place the cage under the pine tree. Then, without being told, both guards retreated several yards down the hill, leaving Pao alone. Seconds later he placed the vase on top of the cage and bowed his head in silent tribute.

White orchids had been Taroko's favorite flower. And she'd been an expert on butterflies, something unexpected from a teenage prostitute, her profession when Pao had met her. She'd been born in Sun Moon Lake, where her father had managed the famous butterfly zoo, with its huge wire cages housing hundreds of species of the insects. Pao's nickname for Taroko had been Butterfly.

They'd been lovers, then friends, who forgave each other

everything. Friends who, while they had other lovers, sometimes slept together rather than be alone. She hadn't deserved to die so disgracefully. After shooting her and a young Indian, Van Rooten had placed both corpses in a large freezer, then sent it to Lin Pao in Taipei. He'd also enclosed obscene photographs of Taroko and the Indian. The contents of the freezer and the photographs had caused Lin Pao to weep for the first time in years.

Sending him Taroko's corpse had been a barbarous act. Even the cold-blooded and unfeeling Pao had been startled by it. But then, Van Rooten was an emotional man. If frustrated, he could become spiteful and destructive. He'd been besotted with Taroko, which is how Pao had controlled him.

She'd died because Van Rooten could not live without enjoying power over others. Her murder had been the American's final attempt to go one up on Lin Pao, whose heart had not stopped weeping for Taroko. The Black General now hated everything that was a part of Van Rooten.

To Asians three was the most auspicious of numbers. There were the three worlds of man—body, mind, and soul; there was time's trinity of past, present, and future. There were the heavenly virtues of faith, hope, and charity. Triads were constructed around the triangle of heaven, earth, and man.

Unfortunately calamities also occurred in threes. Violence had claimed Taroko and Charles Sui, two people Pao had loved dearly. Unless the boy Todd died, the third fatality could well be Pao himself. DiPalma's son had made this clear when he repeated the old priest's prediction to Ivan Ho in New York.

Was the boy a devil, or had he learned of the priest and the snow leopard from someone in Pao's household, someone who knew more than they should? As for the names Benkai and Kiichi, they meant nothing to Pao. He understood only that he had barely nine days in which to destroy the boy.

In front of the pine tree, Pao lit three *joss* sticks and stuck them in the earth. As butterflies fluttered in the cage he bowed his head and silently said Buddhist and Taoist prayers for Taroko's soul. A tear formed in a corner of his one eye.

Earlier today he'd gone to the Ma-Tzu, a temple dedicated to the Goddess of the Sea, and lit candles for Taroko. He'd also lit candles for the soul of his godson. Charles had been his last link with Son Sui. Few men were as unmerciful and as savage as Lin Pao, but even he was not above grief. He would miss Charles and Taroko very much.

Charles had been murdered by the DiPalma boy, something uncovered by Pao within hours of its occurrence. Officially Pao's godson had died in a fire caused by lightning. Police, seeing nothing amiss, had ruled Charles's death accidental. An act of God, they'd said. But the highly suspicious Pao, knowing that tennis instructor Rafael Amando had been with Charles, could only wonder why this act of God had failed to carry him off as well.

The results of Pao's own investigation had been quickly fruitful. Both Amando and his bodyguard, Felipe, had been convinced to share information they'd withheld from police. Felipe hadn't accompanied Amando to Charles's estate; he'd been left unconscious in the garage by two boys, who Pao knew to be DiPalma's son and Benjy Lok Nein. Amando then admitted that these same two boys had forced him to take them to Charles. Pressed for more details, Amando had finally admitted that the younger boy had killed Charles with a tennis racquet—Amando's tennis racquet.

Before his death, Charles had been forced at gunpoint to reveal the truth about Nelson Berlin's past. The American businessman's secret was no longer known to only a few.

Pao excused Felipe from any responsibility for Charles's murder. But he was not so forgiving of Rafael Amando. The tennis instructor hadn't participated in the bloodshed, but he'd taken the killer to Charles. And for that he would have to pay.

Yesterday afternoon Pao had ordered his disappearance, an order which had since been carried out. Amando would never be seen again, alive or dead. His wife would also be punished, but not right away. She would be dealt with two or three years from now, when she least expected it, when she and everyone else believed this matter to be forgotten.

For Ivan Ho, who'd been defeated by the DiPalma boy, Charles's death was a final chance to redeem himself. Let him work with the Eight Knives of the North and eliminate the DiPalma boy as soon as possible. Kill Benjy, too, for he was the DiPalma boy's ally and working with him against Lin Pao. Forget the Jade Eagles. Just kill their leader and the demonic young man he now served.

Meanwhile there was the problem of finding another way to move money into the Philippines and into Nelson Berlin's Asian businesses. Information linking Pao to Berlin was now in the hands of Frank DiPalma. So far DiPalma had done nothing with it, but it was only a question of time. His reputation as an investigative reporter was an honorable one.

Four days from now Nelson Berlin would be arriving in Taiwan. He'd had no say about coming. In a telephone conversation that morning, Pao had ignored the egotistical, dictatorial Berlin's protests that he was much too busy to travel. The American had been ordered to Taiwan because he had much to answer for. His son, an unwise and misdirected man at best, had foolishly seduced DiPalma's wife. Berlin himself had then compounded this stupidity by bugging the wife's telephones, giving DiPalma additional reason to go poking around in Triad affairs.

As a result, the Philippines banking arrangement, which had served Pao so well for many years, was no longer practical. Inspector Martin Mackie had conspired to make trouble, but it was Gregory Van Rooten who'd ensured that Frank DiPalma would remain a key player. Let Berlin atone for his son's blunder by providing Pao with a new way of moving his money safely around the Far East.

What Berlin found most disturbing of all was hearing that the truth of his sister's death was now known by Frank DiPalma.

"How did he find out?" Berlin said.

Pao told him about the circumstances surrounding Charles's death. "DiPalma's notes indicate he first heard of this from your son. The next time you and Gregory talk, you might ask him where he got his information. Assuming he'll talk to you, that is."

Pao suspected that Taroko had been Van Rooten's source on this matter. But why mention this to Berlin? Van Rooten was the problem. Let this fact be on the head of the father.

"My lawyers will give DiPalma a run for his money," Berlin said. "We can put a few legal roadblocks in his way regarding the money-laundering thing. But Gregory is another matter. There's just no reasoning with him. He's determined to annihilate me."

Pao said, "Let us take care of ourselves until fate descends upon us."

"Goddamn that Gregory. It would please me enormously if fate descended on him and stopped that little shit from running off at the mouth."

"Karma and shadows follow a man everywhere," Pao said.

"Has DiPalma attempted to contact anyone in the Taiwanese government about the business with Rhoda?"

"To my knowledge, no."

This was an additional reason for Berlin to come to Taiwan, Pao said. He could speak to those old KMT men who'd covered up his sister's murder. A few of them were still alive and receiving a pretty penny from Pao's heroin dealings. These shadows from another time could reassure Berlin that his secret was still buried deep in old files that would never see the light of day.

Meanwhile the Hong Kong conference was presenting Pao with complications. Some of his rivals were having second thoughts about attending it nine days from now. The negative effect of Van Rooten's arrest, no secret in the underworld, had not gone unnoticed by his enemies.

They saw Pao's men in America curtail their activities and even go into hiding to avoid arrest. They saw the confiscation of drugs and money. They knew a few of Pao's regular customers had inquired about purchasing heroin from other importers. Just in case, the customers said. And why had the Black General turned against the Jade Eagles, his own tiger cubs?

Some of Pao's rivals were openly wondering if he was strong enough to protect his own interests. Others wondered if he was in his right mind. Why compromise with a man whose star might be fading? Wouldn't it be wiser to wait a little longer, then take away his empire when he could no longer resist?

Pao now needed that meeting more than ever. It was an opportunity to show that he was still effective and persuasive, that he possessed the power of body and spirit needed to defend what was his. The meeting had to come off on schedule, with him in charge. Pao's empire in the Golden Mountain would be saved by killing Van Rooten. Pao, himself, would be saved by killing the DiPalma boy.

On Yangming Mountain, he turned from the bamboo grove and starting walking down the hill. Below, in the compound, lights were being turned on in the main pavilion and in the connecting courtyards. He heard his tigers growl as they waited impatiently for their evening meal.

A single white orchid in his hand reminded him of how he and Taroko would walk up the mountain at dusk, without guards, the two alone with their memories and questions about the future. She'd begun life as a whore and developed into a great entertainer who'd won the hearts of millions, Lin Pao's among them. Van Rooten may have taken over a million dollars of Pao's money, but in killing Taroko he'd taken more. Much more.

Van Rooten. DiPalma's son. Martin Mackie. All must die as soon as possible. The Englishman had to perish because Pao had promised to kill him, and a Triad leader must be a man of his word.

To fully avenge Taroko and Charles, someone else must be terminated. Someone Pao had decided mattered both to Van Rooten and DiPalma, whose son had murdered Pao's godson. That someone was DiPalma's wife. The Black General's revenge always required the blood sacrifice of a woman.

He stopped to look back at the bamboo grove where Taroko was buried. Seconds later he ordered his guards to precede him back to the compound. He did not want them to see his tears.

# Twenty-three

**New York City**

Nelson Berlin's ironhanded business practices had given birth to what was known as the Nelson Berlin joke.

It seems the devil offered Berlin any business deal of his choosing, for any amount of money he desired. All of the money would be tax-free. Nor would there be any government restrictions of any sort. "But in return," the devil said, "I want your immortal soul."

Berlin thought it over for a few seconds, then said, "What's the catch?"

In real life, Berlin's survival now depended on being more ruthless than he'd ever been in a joke. His life was at a crisis, thanks to his son's ill will. Berlin's successful experience was about to be reduced to a series of embarrassing criminal charges. He could think of nothing worse than having this Rhoda business spread all over the tabloids. Better a quiet death than public disgrace.

Any compromise with Gregory was unthinkable. Both of them had explosive tempers. Both were impulsive and stubborn. In any case, cunning and guile didn't appeal to Berlin. He'd gotten where he was by being strong and decisive. Any solution to this problem with Gregory lay in facing it head-on. Plunge into the battle and go all out to win.

His influence at the television network could delay or

even kill the airing of any investigative report by DiPalma. Lawyers should be able to do that by throwing up legal roadblocks. Berlin felt confident that any network clearance to broadcast a report on him and Pao would be hard to come by.

Gregory was a different kettle of fish. He was presently spilling his guts to the Justice Department, a more difficult group for Berlin to control. Let Gregory tie Berlin to Lin Pao and this could trigger a criminal inquiry that might prove awkward. The U.S. Marshal, Chacon, who was receiving good money to keep Berlin informed, said Gregory's evidence to date had been limited to details on his courier activities and Pao's relationship with Black heroin gangs. Gregory had also admitted to passing on information to Pao. Berlin's name hadn't come up. Nor had there been any reference to Rhoda's murder.

How much did Gregory know about Rhoda's murder? Perhaps he was waiting for proof from DiPalma, with whom he'd clearly cut some sort of deal. Perhaps he was toying with Berlin, deliberately making him suffer by waiting a bit on Rhoda. Anything was possible with that boy.

Immediately after his telephone conversation with Lin Pao, Berlin summoned his security chief, Dave Stamm, to his Rockefeller Center office, which overlooked the granite pools, fountains, and seasonal flower displays of Channel Gardens. Berlin's three secretaries were instructed to hold all calls. The two men conferred for almost an hour.

When they finished, Berlin said, "It's the only solution. Get Chacon in on it. Let that greaseball earn what I'm paying him. There's no other way out for me."

"Risky as hell," Stamm said. He was in his early fifties, a flat-faced, chunky man who wore a gray toupee. He didn't like moving without a plan. And what he'd just heard in this office was too impulsive and dangerous to be a plan. On the other hand, he was being paid a quarter of a million a year, plus bonuses, to do exactly as he was told. So far he hadn't been asked to do anything that had given him sleepless nights.

"Yeah, it's dicey," he said. "But who knows. It just might fly. I take it you haven't discussed this with your Chinese friend."

"Fuck that son of a bitch. I'll be the one who decides what's best for me."

"But you're still going to Taiwan?" Stamm said.

"Afterward. When this thing's over and done with, I'll go. Let's get this thing out of the way first."

"Man's gotta do what a man's gotta do. Think Pao has a plan of his own?"

"I know he does. Goddamn Chinese. They never tell you everything. They could be planning to invade your room and you'd never know it until you woke up and found the mattress missing and your ass lying on the bare floor."

"Chacon's greedy. The bastard might want combat pay for this one."

"Give it to him. But if he becomes a problem, that's your department."

"When do you want to go with it?"

"Right away."

Stamm had his doubts. He was debating whether to bring them up, just to be on record should this thing blow up in their faces. But Berlin said, "I want it done."

The security chief shrugged. "I'll start setting it up *tout suite*. You realize what you're doing."

*"I said I want it done."*

Martin Mackie, cigarette in hand, stood by a window in George Aaron's pocket-size flat, looking across Sixty-fourth Street and Broadway at the ten-story-high Metropolitan Opera House.

Behind him, George kissed his neck and pointed, saying, "Through the main facade of the opera house you can usually see two divine Marc Chagall murals." But not this morning, George added. On sunny mornings like this the curtains were drawn to protect the murals.

It was almost noon. Come two o'clock, Martin Mackie was scheduled to meet DiPalma at his television network on West Fifty-seventh Street. They had a few things to discuss, Mr. Mackie and Mr. DiPalma: the diskette, Charles Sui's death, Nelson Berlin's ravaging of his dear sister, and DiPalma's belief that Van Rooten had something to hide. The TV studio was a short cab ride away, giving Mackie nearly two hours to dally with young George. And dally he would. Mackie was randy and ready.

He'd met George in Miami that morning, on line at the American Airlines check-in desk. George, a slim, blond man in his mid-twenties, delighted in gossip and naughty hearsay. He knew some appalling but delectable details about the sex lives of certain rock stars, professional athletes, and politicians. Like others who claimed not to enjoy gossip, Mackie had found it irresistible.

Describing himself as a photographer-songwriter, George was returning to New York after a brief visit to an uncle in Key West. Mackie figured him for a little queer who'd spent a dirty weekend in Florida with a sugar daddy. Mackie had nothing against bought sex. As he'd grown older, he'd had to depend on it more often than he cared to admit.

George was attractive and amusing. A bit cheeky at times, which was to be expected from an American. His brashness somehow added to his appeal. And he did have rather a lovely bum.

Minutes into their first conversation at the airline terminal, each knew the other was gay. Travelers on the same road indeed. George had the American tendency to confide in total strangers. Mackie, on the other hand, assumed the role of the world-weary businessman who'd popped into Florida to check on various investments. To retain George's confidence, a bit of deception was in order. Gays had good reason to dislike police. Besides, George had become so entranced with Mackie's English accent that no other biographical data had been necessary.

They'd sat together on the plane, passing the trip in ribald and enjoyable conversation. By the time they landed at New York's La Guardia Airport, George had taught Mackie the rude limerick about a girl named Alice in Dallas, who'd never felt of a phallus. Mackie, in turn, told George the true story of a gay Hong Kong investment banker who'd punished a cheating lover by gluing the said lover's penis to the inside of his thigh.

Mackie had also impressed George with photographs of his Key Biscayne home, restaurant, flower shop, and beachfront acreage. George looked up from the photographs long enough to bat his long lashes and smile coyly, indicators that he now believed he'd fallen into the lap of another sugar daddy. Love and money. Man's greatest sources of joy.

They'd shared a cab from the airport into the city, their talk fading away into a silent sexual tension. When George invited Mackie to his flat for coffee, both knew what to expect. Mackie, as they say, had gotten lucky.

In Key Biscayne he'd had things on his mind other than sex. He'd worked hard preparing his home for his forthcoming permanent move there, while at the same time keeping on the lookout for Lin Pao's bully boys. Fortunately he'd had a bit of help there. He enjoyed excellent relations with local police, having contributed generously to their charities and benefit dinners. Florida lawmen visiting Hong Kong had also found him to be an excellent host and guide.

So when Mackie told them he was having trouble with certain Chinese heroin traffickers, the Americans understood. They volunteered to watch his back while he was in Key Biscayne. While he was in Hong Kong, they would safeguard his home and his housekeepers, a Haitian couple who'd been university professors in their own country before illegally immigrating to America.

With that sort of protection Mackie hadn't even felt the need of a gun, probably making him the only man in Florida without one. The state's gun laws bordered on the insane. Down there, a gun was easier and cheaper to buy than a stick of gum. DiPalma would be his host in New York, which should help keep Lin Pao's thugs at bay.

In George's cramped flat Mackie watched the young man put a pot of water on the range, turn on the gas, then spoon instant black coffee into two cups on a sideboard. While the sight of beautiful George was causing Mackie to grow increasingly lustful with each second, the Englishman was not quite as enthusiastic about George's residence.

The flat consisted of two minuscule rooms containing the most insignificant furniture imaginable, some of which George admitted to having picked up off the street. Apparently many New Yorkers furnished their flats in this manner. Mackie found the idea appalling.

One corner of the living room served as a kitchenette. A closet-sized toilet was next to the refrigerator, causing Mackie to wonder how one avoided pissing in the milk. The bedroom, dark enough to grow mushrooms in, looked out on an air shaft, a positively dismal view.

The walls were covered in large black-and-white photographs of George's work, which consisted of shots of high rises, disreputable-looking street people, abandoned dogs, and the ugly faces of various New Yorkers. Total rubbish. And the little bugger actually thought it was art. Mackie decided to concern himself with carnality and not criticism.

He and George drank their coffee side by side on a purple velvet couch with uneven legs and protruding springs. Their feet brushed, their eyes locked, and Mackie felt his groin grow warm with expectancy. In truth, he couldn't believe his luck at meeting someone this attractive. Outside every young gay was an old gay trying to get in.

Mackie was at that age where it was too often no finance, no romance. Cash on delivery, kind sir. Love was on the side of youth, not old nellies. The biggest optimist in the world was a ninety-year-old queen who still shaved his legs.

George wouldn't charge you by the hour, though in the long run he'd undoubtedly prove expensive. Mackie, however, wasn't planning on setting up light housekeeping with the boy. It was going to be wham, bam, thank you, Sam. Mackie was lonely and in heat. A stranger in a stranger land. Just let him lie in the arms of this boy for an hour or so and forget the cares and woes of the world.

He put down his cup, drew George closer, and kissed

him gently, tasting the sugared coffee on his lips. Mackie's heart raced a bit faster and the kiss became more urgent. More demanding. George broke away, smiling. "I think we should settle this argument," he said.

Both laughed. George had told Mackie a joke about two drunk gays at a bar, who'd settled an argument by going outside and exchanging blows.

Rising from the couch, George took Mackie by the hand and pulled him toward the bedroom. The floor of the bedroom was covered with a green oilcloth. Another of George's idiosyncrasies, Mackie decided, immediately putting it out of his mind.

They stripped, kissed, then George gently pushed him away, saying, "I have to brush my teeth. Back in a sec. Don't go 'way."

A nude Mackie sat down on the bed, brushing his feet against the green oilcloth. A rather bizarre carpet, to say the least. Then again, New Yorkers were an odd lot.

Mackie heard footsteps coming toward the bedroom and looked up to see two Chinese standing in the doorway. Both were nude.

One held a chain saw.

# Twenty-four

It was almost noon. DiPalma stood in the doorway of a public telephone booth on Fifty-seventh Street and Ninth Avenue, staring across the street at a white, rectangular slab of an office building, home to the television network that employed him. He wore a topcoat, no hat, and sipped black coffee from a Styrofoam cup. A black messenger on a bicycle recognized him and grinned, adding a clenched-fist salute. DiPalma raised the Styrofoam cup in reply, and that's when the telephone rang.

He picked up the receiver at the start of the second ring. "Greg?"

"Good to see you're doing all right, Frank, like breathing and walking around and shit like that. How was your trip?"

"Let's say I wasn't bored."

"So I heard. Laughed my ass off when I read about you and that dwarf. I fucked a four-hundred-pound-woman once. Wanted to see what it was like. Broad had more body hair than a gorilla. My lawyer said you wanted to get in touch. What's up?"

"I know you murdered Taroko."

There were long seconds of silence. Then Van Rooten said, "Well, shit, man, I don't know whether to kill myself or go bowling. What do you know, Frank? Tell me what you know.''

"You killed her.''

"Did I now?''

"I can't prove it, but my gut says you smoked her. The lady's vanished off the face of the earth. She had eight hundred and fifty thousand dollars in bookings lined up in the next five months and nobody can find her.''

"Know what I think, Frank?'' Van Rooten said. "I think she's off taking a computer course somewhere. That's the big thing nowadays, computers. You learn that, and shit, you can get a job anywhere.''

"You and LaVon played fast and loose with the Black General's money, but that's not why you went crying to the Justice Department. My guess is that things just fell apart after you whacked Taroko, and at that point you just didn't care anymore.''

"Fucking LaVon. We both got stoned that night. The hotel sent four broads up to the suite, me and LaVon being high rollers and all. LaVon he went fucking nuts, all that white pussy in front of him. He just couldn't say no to anything that night. Didn't have to talk him into anything. He just went along with the program.''

"He died because he followed you around,'' DiPalma said. "You killed him as sure as if you'd put a gun to his head.''

"Win some, lose some.''

"Speaking of losers, could be you heard that the FBI and DEA were on to you. So you decided what the hell, might as well give myself up. But before I do, why not get even with Taroko? You knew you could always turn informant and cut a deal that would let you get away with the murder.''

"Frank, Frank, Frank. I deny the allegation and I deny the alligator. Your wife dumped me and I didn't whack her, now did I?''

DiPalma's jaw tightened. "You didn't give a shit about Jan. Taroko was different.''

"That she was, my man, that she was. We wouldn't be recording this little conversation, by any chance?"

"No. What good would it do? The Justice Department wants Pao bad enough to give you almost any deal you want. Far as they're concerned, Taroko doesn't mean squat."

"So why bring it up?"

"Reality's never been a priority in your life. You live in your own little world where you pull strings and jerk the rest of us around. I want you to know you didn't get away with it this time. I'm also hoping that when the Justice Department hears about this, maybe, just maybe, they'll start asking you tougher questions."

There was a new tension in Van Rooten's voice. "Man, don't fuck this up for me. I've got it all figured out. I do the right thing and I get to live out my days in peace and quiet. Maybe they'll send me to one of those small countries where the flag is a paper towel tied to a broom handle and you end up boiling the meat for twenty-four hours, then you feed it to a dog and eat the dog."

DiPalma grinned maliciously at his half-filled cup of coffee. "You holding out on the Justice Department, Greg?"

"What the fuck you talking about?"

"The way your mind works is, you have to feel you know something the rest of us don't. So you're walking around thinking, 'I took out Taroko and everybody's looking for her, but only Gregory Van Rooten knows she's dead.' It's a case of 'Look ma, I'm on top of the world.'"

Van Rooten chuckled. "You're overlooking something, sport. Lin Pao knows where she is. Believe me when I tell you, he knows."

"Yeah, well, he knows you killed her, I'm sure. When I said you're holding out, I meant you haven't told them you killed Taroko. Now suppose they get the idea you're holding out some real good stuff, that you ain't telling all you know. Suppose they start doubting what you're telling them. We both know anybody looking for Taroko's wasting their time. You know she's dead, I know she's dead, Lin

Pao knows she's dead. He'd have to know, wouldn't he? Jesus, that's right. You did her so you could go one up on Pao. Son of a bitch. That's why you did it.''

"Fuck you, man. Fuck you.''

DiPalma chuckled. ''You'd really be in deep shit if they started doubting your word around the Justice Department. Something tells me they'll be pissed when they find out you've known the truth about Taroko all along and haven't told them. Given any thought lately to what life would be like in a federal prison?''

Van Rooten attempted to sound convincing. ''No way you can hurt me, man. No way. I'm crossing the finish line and you ain't even left the starting blocks. I'm a fucking jet plane and you're running on the ground trying to catch me in your bare feet. Can't touch me, dude. Cannot touch me.''

DiPalma sipped his coffee. Seconds later he said, ''I can try. Oh, I can try. I can tell them about Taroko and start them thinking. I can screw up your game plan. When were you planning to let the world in on your little secret? No matter. I'll break the news for you. That should really fry your socks. Somebody mind-fucks you while you try to mind-fuck the world. I love it.''

''I'm warning you, man, stay out of my life. Stay the fuck out of my life.''

''Or you'll what? It's over, dude. One way or another, it's over for you. You've sung the songs and drunk the wine and now it's time to stick a fork in you, because you're done. You are done.''

Van Rooten said, ''It ain't over till it's over. There's things I can still do from here. Things I can still do. I—''

DiPalma hung up, feeling better than he had in a long time.

# Twenty-five

Ivan Ho was an impatient listener. As Yip Woo spoke, Ho leaned against the pool table in the basement of the Elizabeth Street massage parlor, arms folded across his chest, protruding eyes blinking restlessly. Danny Chan, the broad-shouldered Chinese who'd been with Ho the night he'd been beaten in this room, stood on his left. Chan wore the same dark green leather jacket and unpleasant face.

The small Woo, gelled hair and gold teeth glistening in the half-light, spoke rapidly, the words spilling out almost incoherently. Ho was restless, making him a very poor audience. His right leg still pained him, as did his broken ribs, injuries received in this very basement from Benjy's friend. The sooner Woo got his point across, the better.

When he said that Todd and Benjy had been followed to an East Side *kendo* club, Ho nodded. When Woo said that the two boys had left the club through a back exit and could not be found, Ho's eyes blinked faster. His nostrils flared and he began chewing his lower lip. A frown appeared on his forehead and stayed there for quite a while.

When Woo finished, Ivan Ho said, "The guys following them are fucking idiots. They let a couple of kids disappear just like that. Didn't anybody think about following them inside?"

Woo looked down at the ground. "You said not to go inside. You said if we got too close, Benjy would recognize us."

Ho slammed a hand down on the pool table, rattling the balls and cues. "Goddammit, don't tell me what I said. I'll be glad when I can go back to working with the Jade Eagles again. Working with you smart grown-ups is a pain in the ass."

He looked at his watch. Almost nine P.M. Not knowing where Todd and Benjy were was like being in a dark room with a pair of snakes. Being unable to see the snakes made them all the more dangerous. Ho had intended to move against the two boys tonight. Tomorrow at the latest.

He knew where they were staying. And so did the three assassins from Taiwanese intelligence, now upstairs in a top-floor room. But until Ho located Todd and Benjy he couldn't kill them.

As the other two men in the basement watched in silence, Ho removed a small flask from an inside jacket pocket, unscrewed the top, and swallowed a mouthful of brandy. After recapping the flask he returned it to his jacket and stared at the closed basement door. He wanted to kill the DiPalma boy himself but was too afraid. The beating received at his hands had done more than damage Ho's knee and break his ribs. It had broken his confidence, caused him a loss of face in Chinatown, and started him drinking more than he should.

The Black General had given him a second chance. There'd be no third chance. Either Ho got rid of Todd and Benjy, or the Taiwanese assassins, the Eight Knives of the North, would have one more Chinese head to take back to Taipei.

One solution: Send the assassins to Brooklyn Heights, where DiPalma lived, and wait for the boys to return. Sooner or later our two young sparrows would have to return to the nest. Let Ho act decisively, with confidence, and he could still win the day.

There was a knock at the door. Woo walked over and

opened it, expecting to see the receptionist or the bouncer from upstairs. Instead Todd rushed past him and into the room, a *shinai*, a yard-long bamboo stave, in his hands. The *shinai* replaced a real sword in *kendo,* allowing fighters to attack full-force. But in the hands of an expert it could be deadly, especially when used against someone not wearing body armor.

Screaming, Todd charged Ivan Ho and Danny Chan. Chan reached for the fifteen-shot Browning he kept in his belt, a pistol recommended by black drug dealers, who were quite partial to it. Todd, the *shinai* a blur in his hands, struck him in the wrist, forehead, and temple. The crack of bamboo against bone sounded like pistol shots. Chan fell back against a dusty boiler, landed on his side, and was still.

A stunned Ivan Ho watched the room fill up with members of the Jade Eagles. He was too frightened to count, but he guessed a dozen boys were in the basement. Almost all carried guns. He turned to look at Todd.

Todd, eyes on Benjy, nodded.

Benjy barked a command in Cantonese and two Jade Eagles, young, thin boys with grim faces, pushed through the crowd and deposited a bundle on the pool table. One boy placed a chain saw beside the bundle's contents, which were wrapped in green oilcloth. Benjy said to Ho, ''Open it.''

When Ho hesitated, Benjy slapped his face and repeated the order.

Ho turned, pulled the bundle toward him, and slowly unfolded the oilcloth. The contents were revolting. Ho quickly turned away. Staring up at him from the pool table were the bloodied heads of the three Taiwanese assassins. Behind Ho, Todd tossed something else on the pool table. Ho looked down to see the wallets and intelligence IDs belonging to the dead men. His eyes met Todd's. Seconds later Ho looked away.

Todd said, ''You betrayed these boys. So now I give you to them.''

Ho was grabbed, then pushed toward the pool table. He started to scream, but someone shoved a filthy sock in his mouth. And then he was shoved onto the table, flat on his back, hands and legs pressed down by the boys.

He bucked, twisted, and pulled, but his captors held firm. He saw Todd looking down at him, then the boy backed into the crowd. A severed head lay within inches of Ho's face.

Someone pulled the starter cord on the chain saw.

In the changing room of the *kendo* club, DiPalma stood at his locker and removed his *keikogi,* the heavy, handmade quilted cotton jacket worn for protection during fighting. His armor—waist protector, chest protector, and face mask—rested on a nearby wooden bench. His arm guards and *shinai* were already inside the open locker.

He still wore his *hakama,* the divided cotton skirt, and was untying its strings when he saw them. Two clean-shaven Caucasian males in hats and topcoats heading toward him. Aging Troy Donahue look-alikes straight from the Republican National Committee. Processed cheese in polyester. The FBI's finest.

DiPalma continued untying the *hakama.* When they reached him, he had it off and was folding it carefully, making sure there were no wrinkles in it. His arms, back, and legs ached. He hadn't worked out this hard since returning from Manila. He'd needed it to clear his mind. What he did not need was to talk to the FBI.

Which was not going to stop them from talking to him.

DiPalma expected the Feebs to say something about Van Rooten. Or the diskette. His mind, however, was on Todd and Benjy, who'd come through the front door and kept going until they'd gone out the back. DiPalma, busy practicing, hadn't stopped. He'd worried a bit, but he'd continued fighting.

"Mr. DiPalma, I'm FBI Agent Cross, and this is my partner, Agent Schoenstein. Is there somewhere we can talk?"

DiPalma stopped folding his *hakama*, looked at Cross's badge and ID, then said, "Yeah. Over there in a corner."

Had to be Shark Eyes, DiPalma thought. Had to be.

Cross looked around. The corner wasn't private enough, but you took what you could get in this world and made the best of it.

In the corner, DiPalma dried his face with a hand towel and waited. Cross looked around again, took a deep breath, and whispered, "It's your wife. She's in East Side Hospital. They think she's dying. Unfortunately she's lost the baby."

DiPalma froze. Schoenstein never took his eyes from him.

Cross said, "Sorry to have to hit you with it like this, but there was just no other way. They found her and Van Rooten—"

DiPalma squeezed the towel. "Van Rooten and my wife?"

Looking down at the floor, Cross rubbed the back of his neck. "Van Rooten's dead. Looks as if he's been murdered. We'd like to ask you a few questions."

# Twenty-six

At 8:32 that evening DiPalma stepped from the hospital elevator and walked several yards to the nurses' duty station. It was empty. The nurse who should have been there was missing.

Blinking switchboard lights caught his eye. Each light represented a patient calling for bedpans, painkillers, a glass of water, or the duty nurse. DiPalma wondered if Jan was calling for help that wasn't there. He hurried toward her room.

He walked to the end of the empty corridor as rapidly as his bad leg would allow, turned left, and stepped into an alcove containing four rooms. Jan's was the first on the right. DiPalma saw a tall, long-faced woman, hairless from chemotherapy, slowly plodding back and forth with a walker. Outside of Jan's room he saw three bouquets of flowers and a trolley containing covered metal dishes of food. What he didn't see were the two uniformed policemen who were supposedly guarding her.

Heart pounding, DiPalma limped forward, his cane digging into the linoleum-covered floor. The door to Jan's room was open. Her bed was empty.

He entered the room slowly and looked around. The light was on and so was the television. On screen, Bill Cosby was being wonderfully warm and all-knowing. In the closet a clean nightgown he'd brought Jan from home hung beside the coat and dress she'd worn when admitted three days ago. On the windowsill and at the base of one wall were baskets of fruit, vases of flowers, and boxes of candy from well-wishers.

DiPalma, his fear bringing on gas pains, opened the door to the bathroom and switched on the light. He found the cops. One lay in the bathtub, the other on the floor and curled around the base of the toilet. DiPalma entered the bathroom, crouched, and felt the neck pulse of the cop in the tub. He was alive. And so was his partner.

DiPalma found no gunshot wounds, no stab wounds, no evidence of a blunt instrument having been used on the officers. What the hell had happened? He looked closer at the officer in the tub. There it was. A bruise on the left cheekbone.

Both cops had been punched out. Somebody had decoyed these guys, gotten close, and kicked ass. Then they'd grabbed Jan. Sick to his stomach, DiPalma returned to the room and sat down on the bed. Jan had already gone through hell. Why did she have to go through something like this as well?

"He tricked me, that bastard," she'd told DiPalma on her first day in the hospital. "Greg insisted I come to Governor's Island. Christ, I'd never heard of the place. He'd cut through the red tape, he said. Couldn't go into it over the phone, he said. Told me he was trying to save your life, that his father was going to kill you, but that you wouldn't listen. He claimed you hated his guts and wouldn't take his phone calls."

"He was right about me hating his guts," DiPalma said. "But he was lying about everything else. Greg hadn't been in touch with me since our little talk about Taroko."

"I had no way of knowing he was lying. I thought I owed it to you to find out what I could, then report back. Christ, he was so convincing. Said if you knew he and I were meeting, you'd stop it, so don't tell you about the meeting until it was over. All he wanted was to make it up to me for having been such a shit. He really had me going. I knew you'd gotten information from him, so I thought maybe he knew something.''

"What happened at Governor's Island?"

"I wasn't there two hot minutes before I knew he was lying, and you know something? He admitted it. Said he only wanted me here 'just to fuck you over,' is how he put it. Once you learned I'd come to see him, he said you'd go nuts. This whole thing was to get back at you. At that point I just flipped out.''

DiPalma grinned. "So I heard. Your voice carried, I was told.''

"I didn't give a damn. I really let him have it. Called him every name I could think of. Even slapped his face. I carried on like a madwoman. Suddenly I felt nauseous. Then I was on the verge of passing out. Greg gave me a drink, J&B I think it was, and that's all I remember until I woke up here in the hospital.''

"Somebody poisoned the bottle. Greg also drank with you. Obviously he drank a bit more.''

Jan, sitting up in her hospital bed, covered her face with her hands.

DiPalma thought, The baby . . . Not only had Jan lost the child she'd been expecting, she also wasn't sure of the father.

DiPalma took her hand. "Todd told me the child was mine.''

She looked at him. "He said that?''

DiPalma nodded.

Jan used a hand to wipe tears from her eyes. "You tell that son of yours, of ours, that I love him very much. Very, very much.''

"Tell him yourself.''

"I will. Oh, God, what a load off my mind. If Todd hadn't come back to New York, if I had to go through life not knowing one way or another—''

She covered her face with her hands.

DiPalma took her in his arms. After a while she said, "Have you and the FBI finished with each other?"

"More or less. For about ten seconds somebody had the bright idea that I'd done in Van Rooten and tried to get rid of you at the same time. Jealous husband and all that. Eventually cooler heads prevailed."

"And we're paying these people to protect us? Who do they suspect now?"

"Lin Pao. He had a lot to lose if Greg lived. Pao's been hurt a bit by Greg's evidence, but nothing permanent. For the most part, his American operation remains intact. What's more, he can now show up at his Hong Kong meeting with a smile on his face and a gleam in his one eye."

Jan said, "What about Todd and Lin Pao?"

"You know Todd. He keeps his promises."

"And you'll go with him."

"He's my son."

In Jan's hospital room, DiPalma sat on her empty bed and tried to stay calm. She couldn't have been gone long. They'd spoken on the phone a couple of hours ago. He'd visited her each of the three days she'd been here, sometimes twice a day. Jesus, did she hate being in hospitals.

DiPalma reached for the telephone. He had to call the police. Tell them Jan was missing and get the search started immediately.

The phone rang. DiPalma picked up the receiver and listened.

"Hello? Is Frank DiPalma there?"

"Who's this?"

"Hector Chacon. The marshal. I called your apartment and got this number from some kid named Benjy. I told him it was important I speak to you. You and me met when—"

"I know who you are. I can't talk to you now. My wife's been kidnapped. I've got to contact the police."

"I know where she is."

DiPalma stood up. His cane rolled off his knees and onto the floor. "I'm listening."

"She's headed out of the country. Probably gone by now."

"Out of the country? What the hell you talking about? The only way you could know something like that is if you were in on it."

"I had nothing to do with grabbing your wife, but I know who did. You help me, I help you. Somebody tried to kill me once tonight already. I'm pretty sure they're gonna keep trying till they get it right. Like I said, you help me, I help—"

"Chacon, who's got my wife?"

"You're wasting time, Mr. DiPalma, and time's one thing you ain't got too much of. The sooner we get together and work something out, the sooner you learn about your wife."

DiPalma closed his eyes. "When can we meet?"

"I'd say right now's as good a time as any."

Nineteen minutes later, in the back of a bodega on 105th Street and Lexington Avenue, DiPalma stood facing Hector Chacon. Around them were cardboard boxes of pineapples, hairy coconuts, brown-skinned taro roots, and half-ripe plantains. The smell of dried, salted codfish overpowered that of the fruit. Chacon had wanted their meeting to go down in East Harlem, his turf.

The store belonged to his uncle, he told DiPalma. The four male Hispanics with guns and machetes on the other side of the door were cousins. Chacon had bodyguards, but he also feared Nelson Berlin's power and money. He was in the same brown bombardier jacket and black, silver-tipped cowboy boots he'd worn when they'd met on Governor's Island ten days ago. Except now he wasn't so cocky. Now he looked scared shitless.

"Where's my wife?" DiPalma said.

Chacon unzipped his bombardier jacket so that DiPalma could see the Colt .45 in his belt. "On her way to Taiwan by now. One, two hours ago. Lin Pao's people took her from the hospital and put her on a plane. I was supposed to be on that flight with her, which is how I know. And we're talking about a one-way flight, the kind you don't come back from.''

''Why Jan?''

Chacon shrugged. ''Beats the shit out of me. Looks like you did something to Pao, so he's getting back at you through your old lady.''

DiPalma frowned, thinking. Now it was personal between him and Pao. Not Van Rooten and DiPalma anymore, but DiPalma and the Black General. Something very personal. Was it the diskette? If so, why not just come after him? What the hell had he done that would make Pao do something like this? It didn't matter. What mattered was getting Jan back.

DiPalma said, ''What do you want from me?''

Chacon raised his shoulders, then dropped them. ''I want your help in staying alive. Nelson Berlin tried to ice me tonight. Goddamn son of a bitch tried to take me out.''

DiPalma said, ''You know too much about Van Rooten's murder.''

The surprised look on the Puerto Rican's face told DiPalma he was right.

DiPalma said, ''The only thing linking you and Berlin is Van Rooten. Why else would he want you dead? Had to be an inside job. You were fucking stupid to think you could get away with it. How much did Berlin pay you to kill his son?''

Chacon shook his head. ''Not me, man. You talk to Stamm about that. He gave me the bottle. All I did was go in the guy's room, take away one bottle, and leave another one in its place. That's it, Jack. I had no idea what was gonna go down.''

''Yeah, right. You slice meat this thin, you starve to death. You really think anybody's going to buy that bullshit story?''

''I know how the game's played. The guy who gets on board first wins the game. If I can give myself up, like in the next day or so, then cop a plea, I should be all right.''

"You and Van Rooten. A couple of brilliant minds at work. Know what I think happened? I think you saw a chance to start your own trust fund. Whatever they paid you wasn't enough. You got greedy and came back for more."

Chacon looked down at his silver-tipped boots. "Sometimes you gotta go for it, know what I mean?"

"Berlin's the wrong guy to fool around with. But I guess you know that by now."

Chacon reached out to touch a box of coconuts. "I was on the way to meet my woman. She lives down on East Twenty-third, just off Park. Three guys were waiting for me outside her apartment building. Stamm's people. Fucking wiseasses. Said I'd won first prize, a free trip to Taiwan. One way. Me and your wife. They said the crew was all Chinese and that the pilot's name was Won Hung Low. Funny guys."

He grinned. "One thing about wearing boots. You kick somebody and they fucking know they been kicked. Been into karate since I was fourteen. *Shotokan*. Strongest style there is. Got a bad sidekick, I mean *ba-aad*. Those three guys were hustling me toward a car when I kicked one dude's dick through the top of his head. Punched out another one, then took my piece back and aimed it at the third cocksucker. Aimed right at his nose. Man, you should have seen him come apart then. I left him pissing in his pants."

DiPalma's mind was on Jan, not Chacon's martial-arts skills. She was going to die, and there was nothing he could do about it. Nothing. The gas pains were agonizing. He said, "Anything else about my wife?"

Chacon shook his head. "No. My impression was Berlin had nothing to do with it. From the cracks those guys made, it was an all-Chinese operation. Including the plane. At least that's who they were going to turn me over to. Which is strange, because Berlin's leaving for Taiwan tonight. You'd think he'd have taken her with him."

DiPalma's hooded eyes blinked. "How do you know Berlin's going to Taiwan?"

"Stamm told me. He's making the trip with Berlin. Told

me a few days back he'd rather cut off the head of his dick
than go to Taiwan. But he's going, anyway. I think he's
scared of Lin Pao.''

DiPalma snapped his fingers. "Berlin has to be flying out
of Kennedy. Where's the telephone?"

"What about our deal? I want to give myself up to you.
Right now I can't trust nobody. Berlin's rich. Who knows
who that son of a bitch has paid off. FBI, DEA."

"Federal marshals."

"Yeah, well, repo ain't after your car, Jack, and your
landlord ain't threatening to go co-op and put your butt out
on the street if you don't buy."

DiPalma said, "Blow it out your ass, Chacon. You went
over to the other side. No excuses."

The Puerto Rican looked down at the floor.

DiPalma said, "My wife's the only priority I have. You
take me to a phone and I mean now. After I've made a
couple of calls I want *you* to make one. I want you to call
Nelson Berlin."

A wide-eyed Chacon stared at him. "You outta your
fucking mind?"

"If I can bring down Berlin, you've got a chance to keep
on living. That's why you called me, isn't it?"

"Yeah, but—"

"No buts. You get Berlin on the phone and you talk to
him."

"Shit, the man's either at the airport or on his way."

DiPalma nodded. "I know. That's why I need you. I've
got three or four quick calls to make, then I want you to
get on the phone. Stay on it until you get Berlin. And when
you do, I want you to keep on talking. Whatever you do,
keep on talking. You understand?"

In the departure terminal behind a huge cargo warehouse,
Nelson Berlin sat at the desk in the VIP lounge and stared
at the telephone. When it rang, he looked at Dave Stamm,
who sat on a corner of the desk. The two were alone. Berlin

smiled and let the phone ring. After a full minute he picked it up and said, "Yes, Mr. Chacon?"

"You dicking me around, man? Why'd you take so long to come to the phone?"

Berlin, a chunky, sixtyish man with faded blue eyes and a veined nose, gently pulled at a remaining tuft of reddish-white hair near one ear. "You're the one who keeps hanging up, Mr. Chacon. I thought you wanted to come to some kind of agreement."

"Your people tried to kill me, man, and I don't like it. Excuse me if I don't trust your fucking rich ass."

Berlin's smile was still in place. "A minute ago you hung up because you said you were being followed. Were you being followed, Mr. Chacon?"

Stamm shook his head. Berlin nodded, as if to say, *I understand. We have to get our hands on this fool, so let's play his game.*

Chacon said, "I want you to know I ain't that easy to kill."

"So I've been told. Well, let's get down to cases, shall we? You've delayed my flight almost twenty minutes with your on-again, off-again antics. I'm afraid unless we agree on something in the next few seconds, I'm going to have to leave you to your own devices."

"It's about money, Jack. Your money—and me getting some of it."

Berlin pursed his lips and began drawing imaginary circles on the desktop with a manicured forefinger. "Go on."

"I want to be paid for what I did for you."

"You were paid."

"Not enough for what went down. Not nearly enough. A man died while I was supposed to be guarding him, and I figure that's worth a lot more than you gave me."

"How much more?"

"A hundred K."

Berlin's eyebrows crept up toward his bald head. "Well, we certainly value ourselves highly, don't we?"

The anger came swiftly. Stamm almost leapt from the desk.

Berlin, on his feet now, gripped the receiver with both hands. "Listen, you Spic bastard, nobody shakes me down, you understand? I can have you erased from the face of this earth in less time than it takes to tell it, and the world will neither know nor care."

"Better chill out, Mr. Berlin. One way or another, I'm getting mine."

"You don't understand a fucking word I'm saying, do you? Your kind never does. I pay you now and where's the guarantee you won't be back for more? Where's the guarantee that your hand won't go into my pocket and stay there."

"Hey, all I want to do is get over," Chacon said. "I put my ass on the line for you, so now I want mine. Shit, they more or less know it was an inside job. Everybody on duty that day's been interrogated at least twice, and there ain't no sign it's gonna stop. I—"

Berlin's face was bright red. "I'm not interested in your problems. Like I say, you've delayed me long enough. Now you will excuse me. I have some business to take care of."

He slammed down the receiver and looked at Stamm. "You were supposed to have taken care of that little prick."

"My men played him cheap. He—"

Berlin did not restrain himself. He never had. "You're not paid for excuses. If you can't handle this, I'll find someone who can. And that's a promise, mister."

Stamm, feeling lower than whale shit, carefully put his hat over his gray toupee and followed Berlin from the lounge and out into the cold night. He was doing everything except picking Berlin's nose for him, and it wasn't enough. Never take any shit from a man who works for Nelson Berlin. It might be his lunch.

Their limousine was one of three parked in front of the lounge. The area in front of the lounge was deserted. The only people in sight were two uniformed drivers who stood near their cars. One had his back to them; the other was crouched down and examining a front tire on the driver's side.

Berlin's driver hadn't gotten out of the car. Stamm jogged ahead, opened the back door, and watched Berlin get inside. Stamm thought, *The sooner we're airborne, the better.* As they got closer to Taiwan the old man would worry about Lin Pao. Which meant he wouldn't be kicking Stamm's butt.

Stamm got into the car, closed the door, then looked front and saw Frank DiPalma sitting on the jump seat opposite him. DiPalma held a .38 Smith & Wesson in his left hand, which rested on his lap. The other hand gripped his black-oak cane.

Stamm looked over DiPalma's shoulder. There were two Asian kids sitting in the front seat. He recognized one as DiPalma's kid.

The door opened on Berlin's side, and Benjy, dressed in an ill-fitting chauffeur's uniform, slipped into the car. After seating himself on the jump seat opposite Berlin, he removed his chauffeur's cap, threw it on the floor, and removed an Uzi from under his jacket.

Stamm nodded. "Frank."

"Dave. How's the wife?"

"Coming along fine. They found seven dermoids on the ovary. Saved the ovary and that's the important thing."

"Glad to hear it. We'd like to ride along with you and Mr. Berlin to Taiwan, if you don't mind."

Stamm grinned. "Doesn't bother me. How about you, Mr. Berlin?"

Berlin said to DiPalma, "What makes you think I'm going to let you force your way onto my plane?"

DiPalma leaned closer to him. "Because Lin Pao has my wife, and I'll kill you where you sit if you don't do exactly as I say."

Berlin looked at Stamm, whose eyes were still on Di-Palma.

DiPalma said, "Any security on the plane?"

Stamm shook his head. "This isn't a fun trip. We're traveling light. Pilot, copilot, that's it."

He looked through the window to his right at a half dozen Chinese kids standing on the sidewalk staring at the car. One was in a chauffeur's uniform and coat. He positively swam in it. "Yours?" Stamm said.

DiPalma nodded. "All of them."

A somewhat more subdued Berlin said, "DiPalma, even if we allow you on the plane and you get into Taiwan, you're still faced with a major problem. Obviously you're going there to do battle with Lin Pao. Assuming you survive, which is highly unlikely, how do you propose to get out of the country? Or have you looked that far ahead?"

DiPalma said, "Forty some years ago you raped and killed your sister. Couple days ago you killed your own son. I suggest you worry about that."

DiPalma sighed. "On the way out here I kept asking myself why didn't you take Jan with you. Then it occurred to me. You killed a woman and Lin Pao owned you after that. So you figured the smart thing was not to get involved in the murder of another woman and have the Black General dig his hooks into you even deeper."

Berlin's head flopped back against the seat. "You don't understand what it's been like all these years. I couldn't let him do that to me again. I just couldn't."

"Nobody understands but you." DiPalma held out his hand to Dave Stamm, who very slowly reached inside his topcoat. Using a thumb and forefinger, he removed a Beretta and handed it to DiPalma.

Stamm said, "Man's got a point there, Frank. Easy getting in, but a bitch getting out. Sort of like marriage, you might say."

DiPalma opened the door, tossed the Beretta to one of the Chinese kids, then closed the door. "Why don't we wait and see how I make out? What kind of arrangements you have at the other end?"

Stamm shrugged. "We land in a private area of the airfield. No customs, no nothing. The only contact we have is with Pao's people. They have a couple cars waiting for us. They take us to his place. That's it.''

Berlin clutched at Stamm. "Dammit, I'm paying you to to do something. So do something."

Stamm looked down at his hat, which he calmly twirled in his hands. "Mr. Berlin, they say the two most dangerous things in this world are a Jew with an attorney and a Greek wearing sneakers. You can add a third, and that's a man with a gun aimed at you, which is what we have here. You don't fight Frank DiPalma, Mr. Berlin. You get out of his way, especially when he's the man holding the gun."

Stamm chuckled. "You got the Black General on one side and Frank DiPalma and his *Sesame Street* gang on the other. I suggest, Mr. Berlin, that we settle back and watch how this thing turns out. You might find it interesting. I know I will."

# Twenty-seven

**Taipei**

At dawn on the twenty-first day after he'd killed the old priest, Lin Pao sat in the backseat of a black Chrysler and was driven to Ma-Tzu temple. A pair of armed guards were in the front seat. Two cars of armed guards followed the Chrysler.

Inside the temple, three bodyguards trailed Pao as he joined a handful of worshipers in placing offerings before the altars. He was especially generous today, giving a pair of roast ducks, several bottles of wine, sweet cakes, two baskets of fruit, and several cartons of cigarettes. He spent an hour in the temple, lingering before its superb stone sculpture and bronze castings. In that time he spoke to the gods from his heart.

When Pao finished praying, he felt a renewed mental energy. He saw his visions and goals being realized. As he bowed his head amidst wisps of smoky incense rising around him, he'd never felt more capable of pushing aside obstacles that might be in his way. His fighting spirit was strong. The old priest had lied. Pao would live out this day and many days to come.

However, he remained on guard against the DiPalma boy, who was somewhere in New York. The youngster was a flea between a dog's teeth, not easy to catch or hold. The

Eight Knives of the North would soon locate young Todd, however, and separate his head from the rest of him. A dead child was of no importance.

Still, Pao insisted that his estate be kept under heavy guard day and night. Until further notice, any youngster approaching the estate or found on its grounds was to be shot on sight. Adults working on the estate were to keep their children away until further notice.

You will die within twenty-one days, the old priest had said. Well, today was the twenty-first day and Pao was still very much alive. At midnight tonight the prophecy would have officially been proven false. The Black General was subject to no laws but his own.

Martin Mackie's removal from this earth had also been welcome news. Even while taking Pao's money, the Englishman had long been a thorn in his side. Mackie would refuse to perform tasks he deemed too criminal, murder being one. And no amount of threats or pressure could change his mind. Mackie had his dark side, which Pao, as an Asian, could understand. Within all mankind there was *Te,* the power.

A new problem was Ivan Ho, now quickly becoming a liability. He'd begun drinking heavily and seemingly had lost his nerve. It would appear the beating suffered at the hands of the DiPalma boy had crushed his spirit. If so, he was of no further use to the Triad. Apparently he'd disappeared. Most likely he was on a drunken binge of some sort and would turn up later, with profound apologies for his conduct.

More important than the inebriated Ho was today's meeting with Nelson Berlin, to take place at the estate. It was vital that a new Asian pipeline for Pao's money be found as quickly as possible. Then there was next week's conference in Hong Kong with his rival Dragon Heads. Now was the time to conquer new territory. Never before had he felt so capable of challenging those who opposed him.

Before leaving Ma-Tzu temple, he presented it with a sizable cash donation, to be used in repairing the "mountain,'' or roof, of the temple. The spirits dwelled there, which is why the roof and ceiling of any Chinese temple contained elaborate carvings of tigers, heroes, gods, and dragons. Pao requested that additional tigers be carved on the Ma-Tzu roof.

Then he left the temple and returned to his estate, ready to kill Frank DiPalma's wife.

For DiPalma it had gone wrong from the beginning.

As the sun rose over nearby Yangming Mountain, he sat in the backseat of a gray Cadillac parked on a dirt road within sight of Pao's estate. What made him think he could pull this off? He must have been out of his fucking mind. DiPalma and the boys were trapped. They couldn't go forward and they couldn't go back.

Ahead lay Lin Pao's small army, which outnumbered them at least six or seven to one. Behind them and closing in fast were carloads of Taiwanese policemen, who were bringing with them Nelson Berlin, Dave Stamm, and God knows how much firepower. DiPalma had made himself an offer he should have refused.

Ten minutes after Pao arrived home two cars had rolled to within one hundred yards of his lavish home. An edgy DiPalma sat in the back of the first car, arms on top of the driver's seat. In front of him a Chinese chauffeur, a chubby, curly-haired young man, nervously gripped the wheel.

Benjy sat beside the chauffeur, Uzi in his right hand and aimed at the chauffeur's right hip. A hand radio rested on the dashboard in front of Benjy. Todd was in the backseat with DiPalma. Three Jade Eagles and a second driver sent by Lin Pao were in the second car, a dark green Eldorado. Both cars were in plain sight of guards, who unslung their automatic rifles and waited for the vehicles to come closer.

DiPalma had just half of his forces with him. Three Jade Eagles had remained on the plane to guard Berlin, Stamm, and the two pilots. Three others, along with Todd and Benjy, had left Chiang Kai-shek Airport with DiPalma and Pao's two chauffeurs. It was understood that getting inside Pao's estate was to be left to Todd and those forces he'd carried within him for over four hundred years.

Within minutes the shit had hit the fan.

The news had come over Benjy's radio. Airport authorities were forcing their way on board Berlin's plane. The aircraft had to be cleaned and refueled. It also had to be inspected for pests, which was the law. Neither Berlin nor Dave Stamm had bothered to bring this up back in New York.

DiPalma said to Benjy, "Tell the boys not to resist. There's no reason for them to get shot."

A nervous Benjy said, "You sure? Berlin's gonna blow the whistle and we'll have cops all over us. My guys will hold them off if you say so."

In the Cadillac, a silent Todd had looked at DiPalma, who hadn't hesitated. "No resistance," he said. "I'm not going to buy Jan five minutes more—or five hours—with some kid's life. We'll just have to take our chances with Berlin and the Taiwanese police."

He hadn't seen Todd smile.

Meanwhile Benjy had been right. Seconds later a voice claiming to be a Taiwanese police captain had come over the radio and in English ordered DiPalma, by name, to give himself up. If not, DiPalma and those with him risked being shot on sight. When DiPalma had refused to answer, the captain had said, We're coming after you.

In the parked Cadillac, a tired DiPalma rotated his head in an attempt to work out the stiffness. Fear for Jan's safety had made it impossible to sleep on the plane. Fear had also been the reason for not asking Todd about Jan. As long as DiPalma didn't know one way or another, it meant she was still alive.

Benjy and the Jade Eagles had no trouble sleeping. DiPalma decided that the kids could have slept standing up in a hammock. Todd had spent the trip alone in the back of the plane, sitting near the emergency exit, one of DiPalma's medium-length swords resting on his thighs.

He was, as DiPalma knew, mentally preparing for combat. Preparing to avenge that horrible night of four hundred years ago.

On the plane, Dave Stamm had become a devoted Todd watcher. Seeing the respect Todd inspired in the Jade Eagles, Stamm had tried to pump DiPalma about him. DiPalma, however, had refused to be drawn into any conversation concerning his son. "Todd is Todd," he'd said, and that was the end of it.

A testy Nelson Berlin, meanwhile, ignored his fellow travelers. He glared at all who came near him, hounded the already nervous pilots, and spent much of the flight locked in the tiny toilet where he shredded dozens of paper towels in frustration. When his fellow passengers had to heed the call of nature, it had taken a great deal of convincing to get Berlin to open the door.

On the trip, DiPalma's respect for Benjy had increased. The kid was a hood, no two ways about it, but he grew on you. Charisma was an overworked word, but if anyone had it, Benjy did. The Jade Eagles were willing to follow him anywhere. With only a few phone calls he'd gotten twenty-five kids to agree to move against Pao. The possibility of getting killed hadn't seemed to bother anybody. No wonder law enforcement saw Asian criminals as the ones to worry about down the road.

Preferring a small crew, DiPalma had asked Benjy to pick six of his best. A few who hadn't been chosen had cried out of frustration. As Benjy told DiPalma, everyone wanted the chance to get Lin Pao for having killed their comrades. Even if it meant dying, they were ready to go. Win or lose, the kids showed a mind-boggling loyalty. DiPalma hadn't seen anything stronger, not even among policemen.

As for Benjy, he had a sense of humor to match his balls. He'd said to DiPalma, "My idea of teamwork is a lot of guys doing what I say."

In the Cadillac, Benjy listened to the frightened Cantonese-speaking chauffeur, then said to DiPalma, "He says Pao has men in the courtyards, in the gardens, around the main pavilion. He says it's no secret anymore. Pao's afraid of Todd. The man doesn't want to see a kid anywhere on his property.''

DiPalma said, ''And Jan? What about her?''

''He says a *gweilo* was brought to the house a few hours ago. A woman with red hair and wearing a hospital gown.''

The words came out reluctantly. ''Is she alive?''

Benjy asked him, then said, ''He doesn't know. He doesn't get involved in that kind of thing.''

Todd said, ''She's alive. But Lin Pao is about to begin torturing her.''

DiPalma slapped the seat with the palm of his hand. ''Let's go. I can't sit here and let her die.''

Todd put a hand on his shoulder and pointed toward the sky. It had begun to grow darker. It was as though night, and not dawn, were approaching. At first DiPalma thought he was suffering from jet lag. He shook his head to clear it. Then he and everyone else in the car felt the cold wind.

Where seconds ago the weather had been mild, it was now almost frigid. Benjy and the Jade Eagles, who'd taken off the jackets they'd worn from New York, now put them on. DiPalma reached for his topcoat. Only Todd sat still.

DiPalma looked at his son and shivered. Not from the sudden cold but from knowing what was now taking place within the boy. Todd was becoming possessed by Benkai and the Iki-ryo. Eyes half closed, the boy stared straight ahead. His grip on the sword tightened.

Then, without warning, a nightmarish rain began pounding the car, striking the roof with hammer force and totally obscuring the windshield. Placing his hands over his ears, the chauffeur wailed, rocking back and forth, his head coming within an inch of the steering wheel each time. An alert DiPalma kept his eyes on his son.

Ignoring him, Todd looked over his shoulder and pointed at approaching pinpricks of light barely visible in the rainy darkness. The lights shimmered atop a hill a half mile away.

''Police,'' DiPalma said.

Benjy said, ''If they get us, we're dead. I know these

people. They've been covering for Lin Pao for years. The minute they catch us, we are dead.''

"So's my wife," DiPalma said. "Either we get killed 'trying to escape' or, if we're lucky, we're thrown in jail. Meanwhile nobody's around to stop Lin Pao from killing Jan.''

Todd withdrew the sword from its scabbard. And in that instant the sky went bright with lightning. Thunder boomed so loudly, the earth shook beneath the car. Again and again the thunder resounded with the power of cannon. The chauffeur banged his head against the steering wheel in terror. Benjy ordered him to stop.

Todd said, "The main pavilion. The cellar.''

Without waiting for an acknowledgment, he stepped from the car and into the pouring rain.

Benjy pushed the car horn, the signal for those in the second car to come running.

DiPalma left the Cadillac, stepping into rain that hit him with the power of rocks thrown in his face. The mud was up to his ankles. He held on tightly to his cane. The other hand remained in his pocket, gripping the .38. *Jesus, don't let the gun get wet*. It wasn't much against automatic rifles, but it was better than nothing.

Outside in the open, he tensed, expecting gunfire from the guards.

But they were gone.

Meanwhile, ahead of him, there was chaos in the compound. Men and women rushed around madly in the storm, their screams almost lost in the crash of thunder. But not even thunder could drown out the roar of the tigers. The sound chilled DiPalma's blood. It was too close. Much too close.

There was something frightening going on inside the compound. DiPalma sensed it. Feared it. For the moment, however, he had his hands full. Forget the storm, which had drenched him to the bone. He had to keep up in this footrace. The Jade Eagles, hands under their jackets to keep their handguns dry, ran on younger legs. They sped past DiPalma and closed in on Todd. DiPalma, bringing up the rear, looked over his shoulder.

The police cars were closing in on him.

The main pavilion. In the basement, Lin Pao looked down at a naked, weeping Jan, pinned to the stone floor by four men holding her arms and legs. Her torn hospital gown lay near her head. On the floor beside each man lay a long-bladed carving knife. Leaning over, Pao picked up a knife. He'd make the first cut, of course.

For several seconds his attention was drawn to the rain pounding the shutters. Odd. Recent weather forecasts had made no mention of rain. He'd even mentioned this to Nelson Berlin, who'd feared flying unless the weather was perfect. Pao had promised him perfect weather.

Now he looked down at Jan, whose death he had promised to his godson.

Suddenly a woman on the floor above shrieked, then called on the gods for protection. Her cries and frantic prayers caused every man in the basement, Pao included, to look up. Outside, several men raced past the basement window with a desperation that communicated itself to those inside. Someone fired a shotgun. A second blast followed quickly. Guard dogs barked incessantly. Near the building, a man cried out for his life.

Clutching the knife, Pao hurried to the window and opened the shutters.

*The tigers were loose.*

In the main courtyard, DiPalma, Todd, and the three Jade Eagles stood in the pouring rain. None of the five moved. They were living statues, frozen in position. Their lives depended on remaining motionless.

DiPalma, his heart in his throat, had never seen anything like it in his life. And hoped he'd never see anything like it again. He was watching something as terrifying as anything he'd ever seen.

Fur dark with rain, their hooked claws scraping the cobblestone courtyard, over a dozen tigers passed within inches of DiPalma and the boys. The animals marched silently and gracefully, alert green eyes darting left, then right. DiPalma and the boys had raced into the compound and into their midst. *I'm dead*, DiPalma thought. *Fucking dead*.

It was Todd who'd ordered them to stand still. "Don't move! And don't fire your weapons!"

Near the miniature wooden bridge two guards panicked and fired their shotguns at the tigers. They instantly disappeared under several snarling tigers, who tore them to bits. Then just as mysteriously, the bloodied beasts joined the other animals in their march toward the main pavilion.

At the building some of the animals slunk across the veranda and took up what DiPalma swore were guard positions. Except that couldn't be happening. Or could it? Other tigers disappeared into the house. Who'd let them out of their cages? And why had they gone to the main pavilion, DiPalma's destination? Of all the shit luck.

A frightened and frustrated DiPalma turned his face up to the rain. I love you, Jan, he said. I love you.

He heard the auto horns behind him. The police.

Todd walked toward the main pavilion. *Toward it*.

The Jade Eagles hesitated.

Benjy was the first to follow him. The others followed Benjy, slowly at first, then faster. DiPalma, a tight grip on his cane and the .38, limped after them.

At the pavilion Todd slowly stepped onto the veranda, stopped, and looked at the tigers. An Indian albino, sitting near a bamboo settee, growled deep in his throat but didn't move. Todd entered the house.

Moving carefully and not daring to look down, DiPalma and the boys followed. DiPalma was sure he'd wet his pants.

Inside the pavilion they hurried along a narrow corridor lined with Chinese calligraphy. Seconds later they were in a large main room filled with Asian art. DiPalma froze. To his left, a small, dark Bali tiger sat at the base of a Burmese lacquered-wood Buddha. The tiger looked at DiPalma and bared its fangs. Squeezing the .38, DiPalma backed away.

Suddenly three guards armed with shotguns entered the room from the left and fired at the Jade Eagles. Two of the boys went down. Yanking out his .38, DiPalma fired three times, hitting one guard in the head with two shots and missing with the third. Benjy fired the Uzi, killing the other two.

The tigers went wild. Some attacked the downed guards; others moved menacingly toward DiPalma and Benjy.

"Throw away your guns!" Todd shouted. "Now!"

DiPalma obeyed reluctantly. And so did Benjy. Still growling, the tigers backed off. Some, however, continued to tear at the downed guards.

From across the huge room to his right, DiPalma heard footsteps coming from another corridor. And he and Benjy were standing in the open without guns. DiPalma had the cane, but that wouldn't cut it against an automatic rifle.

Light-headed with fear, DiPalma watched Todd back up and flattened himself against a wall, just out of sight of the corridor entrance. The sword was held low and to his right. Seconds later a man in a T-shirt and sandals emerged from the corridor and raced into the room. Todd was now behind him.

The man, who carried a PPK Walther, stopped suddenly. The sight of DiPalma and Benjy so unnerved him that he failed to notice the tigers. Or Todd. The man aimed his gun at DiPalma, who tensed to receive the shock of the bullet.

Todd stepped from the wall and cut off the man's hand at the wrist. As the man screamed, Todd sliced him across the stomach, dropping him to the floor. Turning his back on the fallen guard, Todd entered the corridor. Benjy walked carefully past the tigers. Only when he reached the corridor did he speed up.

A tense DiPalma, looking over his shoulder at the tigers he'd just left behind, caught up to the boys in front of a small red door.

Turning the knob, Todd opened the door and looked down

a narrow staircase. He began descending immediately. Benjy followed, with DiPalma bringing up the rear.

At the bottom of the staircase the three found themselves in a dimly lit, low-ceilinged cellar carved from rock. One area of the cellar contained long-range radio equipment. There was also a boiler, a furnace, and several cords of wood. In front of the wood, four men had Jan pinned down on the stone floor.

Pulling a Beretta from a pocket of his robe, Lin Pao aimed it at Todd. Neither DiPalma nor Benjy moved. For a few seconds Pao frowned in thought, then said, "Ivan Ho said you also called yourself Benkai."

Todd, bloodied sword held low, said, *"Hai."* Hai—yes in Japanese.

"Do we know each other?" Pao said.

"We do. From another time."

"And my tigers. Did you free them?"

"Your karma freed them. They no longer serve you. Nothing you have belongs to you anymore."

Pao looked toward the shuttered window. "My tigers seem to have shifted their loyalty. You walked past them as though they were tamed house cats. You are indeed a special boy. Ivan Ho said you called me Kiichi. Why is this so? I have never heard such a name. I have since learned that Kiichi and Benkai are Japanese names. A Japanese scholar of my acquaintance tells me there was once a samurai warrior named Benkai. Does his soul live in you?"

"That is why I have come to kill you."

"You cannot kill the Black General."

Pao extended his arm, and as he did, Benjy leapt in front of Todd. Pao fired three times, hitting Benjy in the chest. The mortally wounded boy staggered toward the druglord, who backed away, emptying the gun into him. Benjy dropped at Pao's feet.

"Kill the woman!" Pao yelled.

The men hovering over Jan grabbed their knives from the floor. DiPalma charged and backhanded one man in the face with the cane, knocking him into a companion. Next he struck a second man on the left kneecap, sending him spinning toward the stacked wood.

Stepping to his right, DiPalma gripped the cane near its silver knob and drove the knob into the temple of a third man. As the fourth prepared to attack DiPalma from the rear, Todd quickly backhanded the sword across the base of the attacker's spine, dropping him shrieking to the stone floor.

DiPalma turned to see Todd again raise the bloodied sword and charge a terrified Lin Pao, his warrior's cry filling the cellar as he swung the four-hundred-year-old blade in a great arc, sending Pao's shaven head flying from his body.

As a cool drizzle fell on the courtyard Jan, in her hospital gown and DiPalma's jacket, clung to him, the two of them facing Nelson Berlin, Dave Stamm, and several armed Taiwanese police. One officer held DiPalma's cane and sword.

On the veranda behind DiPalma, Todd stood looking down at Benjy's corpse, now laid out on the bamboo settee. Around him lay three dead tigers killed by police. The remaining tigers could be heard in the main pavilion, restlessly prowling back and forth, knocking over antiques and furniture. For the moment the police seemed content to allow them free run of the house.

A grinning Nelson Berlin fingered a tuft of reddish-white hair over one ear, then pointed to the nearby corpse of the third and last Jade Eagle. "A shame. He tried to escape, as you three tried to do and failed. Or so the record will read. Game, set, and match, Mr. DiPalma. I assume you've disposed of Lin Pao."

DiPalma put his arm around Jan. "He's dead."

"Well, you're not going to win any friends around here, that's for sure. I did warn you. Easy to get in, I said. Very hard to get out."

"Did you order the police to kill that boy?" A shamed Dave Stamm pulled his hat low over his eyes.

Berlin glanced at the dead Jade Eagle, then at DiPalma. "Let's just say I don't believe in loose ends. The three you left behind on the plane are also dead. Someone once called secrets ugly things, and I agree. I also feel they should remain private. What you and your friends know about me stays right here.''

DiPalma said, "You're going to kill us, is that what you're saying?"

"Good-bye, Mr. DiPalma, Mrs. DiPalma." Berlin looked at Todd. "And you, young sir. You're quite a handful. I do believe the world will be a better place without you as well."

Dave Stamm stepped forward and took Berlin's elbow. "I think you're making a mistake. DiPalma's not just some schmuck who's going to be forgotten two seconds after he's dead. I think we should talk this over, see if we can work out something with him."

Berlin didn't look at his security chief. "Stamm, you're as spineless as spaghetti. As of now, you no longer work for me. You're a bit too pro DiPalma to suit my taste."

"DiPalma and I are both professionals. We know how the game's played. When you're facing a situation you can't change, you roll with the punches. The solution to a problem doesn't always call for disappearing a guy."

"Good-bye, Stamm. And have a safe flight back to New York."

Stamm looked at DiPalma. "I gave it a shot, Frank. Nothing more I can do."

DiPalma said, "I understand." Then he said to Berlin, "Before you and your goon squad blow us away, I have something I think you ought to look at."

"You have nothing I ought to look at, Mr. DiPalma. I bid you and yours farewell."

"It's over," DiPalma said. "Everything you've tried to hide is going to come out. Everything. You're standing in shit up to your eyebrows and you don't know it."

"Sticks and stones, Mr. DiPalma. And I don't appreciate your pathetic little bluff about my private affairs."

"I don't bluff, Berlin. Ask Stamm."

Stamm stepped forward and looked at DiPalma. "Frank's

a stand-up guy. He's not everybody's cup of tea, but one thing's for sure: He tells you something, you can take it to the bank.''

Stamm looked at Berlin. "If he says you're in deep shit, you'd better reach for a big shovel."

Berlin snorted. "I'm getting soaked standing out here. I think I'll wait in the car and let the police handle it from here on in."

Stamm blocked his path. "Like hell you will. You pay me for my advice and you're getting it, like it or not. Except this time I'm also protecting myself. I want to know what Frank's got up his sleeve because, mister, if you go, then I'm on shaky ground. And I ain't too keen on that, Mr. Berlin. Not. At. All.''

Berlin stared at him for several seconds. "Very well. One minute more won't make any difference. Mr. DiPalma, you have sixty seconds to pull off a miracle. Though the last time that happened, I think it involved three wise men from the East and a virgin. Speaking of which, that wife of yours doesn't exactly qualify as pure and unsullied.''

"If I'd fucked my sister," Jan said, "maybe I'd have grown up to be like you."

Red spots appeared on Berlin's temples. Forcing himself to speak calmly, he said, "Now you have fifty seconds, Mr. DiPalma."

DiPalma said, "Dave, my inside jacket pocket. Take it out for me. I don't want to get shot trying to escape before my fifty seconds are up."

Stamm stepped forward, reached inside DiPalma's jacket, and removed a wallet. "There's an ID that goes with it," DiPalma said.

Stamm reached in and pulled out the ID. "What is it?"

DiPalma pointed to Berlin. "Show it to him."

Stamm returned to Berlin. After examining the wallet and ID, Berlin said to DiPalma, "So you have a wallet and an ID belonging to someone in Taiwan intelligence. Don't tell me you supplement your income these days by picking pockets."

DiPalma said, "That wallet and ID indicates Taiwanese intelligence has a secret operation going in America, and I don't think our government likes it. In fact, I'm sure it doesn't. What this means, Mr. Berlin, is that when our government finds out, the shit's going to hit the fan."

"Ah, but you see, Mr. DiPalma, they aren't going to find out. Not unless your voice carries from beyond the grave."

"I've already told them. And they don't like it."

A red-faced Berlin angrily shook his head. "Means nothing to me. Nothing at all."

"Yeah, well, maybe you'll see things in a different light when the FBI pays you a little visit."

Berlin said, "I suppose your next move is to say that if you're not back in America at such and such a time, your attorney will drop off a letter, etc., etc. Well, buster, I'm not buying that. You're not bluffing me."

"You weren't listening. I don't bluff. There were three Taiwanese agents working this deal, which involved a series of very nasty assassinations. The wallet and ID of the other two are already in the hands of Senator Quarequio. You should be hearing from him or the Taiwanese government any minute now."

"You expect me to believe—"

A radio in one of the police cars started to squawk. An officer in the car picked up the microphone, listened, then called out to a superior. The officer in charge of the detail hurried to the courtyard. No one spoke as he got into the car on the passenger side and picked up the microphone. DiPalma's stomach was on fire. Jan squeezed his hand with both of hers.

Three minutes later the officer walked back and stood in front of Berlin. The industrialist drew himself up, nostrils flaring. "Well?" he said.

"My superiors want to talk to you," the officer said. "You must come with me. These others are to be released and returned to America immediately." He ordered DiPalma's sword and cane handed back to him.

DiPalma exhaled, his head dropping to his chest. Jan threw herself against his arm, her body shaking as she silently wept with relief.

"There must be some mistake," Berlin said. "You don't know who I am." Two policemen now flanked him on either side.

DiPalma put an arm around Jan. Then he smiled at Berlin. The smile had no warmth in it at all. "It's called politics," DiPalma said. "It's the biggest game of all, and you just lost. Been a long time coming, Mr. Berlin, but you just lost."

# Epilogue

## April

Late Wednesday evening, when the first spring shower had stopped, DiPalma and Jan stood in his sword room staring at a rainbow over New York Harbor. Both wore slippers and robes. Jan sipped a Scotch and water. DiPalma drank herbal tea.

They had been standing in silence for a while when Jan said, "You'll forgive me, but I don't have any overwhelming desire to return to Asia."

"You're forgiven."

"Speaking of forgiven, how come Berlin's going to get away with raping and killing his sister?"

"Trade-off. There's a stronger case against him for killing his son and laundering drug money. The Justice Department likes to win, which makes them no different than the rest of us. Bringing back the past just isn't their cup of tea."

Jan looked at him. "But it will come out at the trial, won't it, about what he did to her during the war?"

"No. That's what I wanted to talk to you about. We made the deal today."

"Deal?"

"Me, Quarequio, the Justice Department, and the Taiwanese government. Been working on it since we got back.

Today we finally agreed. It's not the best deal, but it's the only deal.''

"I have a feeling Berlin's going to get away with something."

"As you know, the first deal was three dead bodies for three live ones. The Taiwanese got back their intelligence agents—what was left of them. And their IDs. In exchange, you, me, and Todd got to leave Taiwan in one piece."

"I like that part," Jan said.

"Second, the Justice Department's got Chacon and Stamm pointing the finger at each other and at Berlin. It's pretty certain Berlin ordered his son's death. What's not so certain is who put the strychnine in the booze. Sooner or later the FBI will come up with an answer. Now, here's where it gets tricky."

Jan sipped her drink. "I can hardly wait."

"Before I left for Taiwan, I asked Quarequio to make contact with the Taiwanese, the CIA, FBI, the whole goddamn world, and to do it an hour before our plane was to land."

"Good old Joe."

"We got the Taiwanese to back down and cut us loose, but after that they dug in their heels. I wanted Thomas Service's record wiped clean and the truth to come out about what really went down with Berlin and his sister."

"And they wouldn't do it."

DiPalma nodded. "Flat out said no. It meant admitting they were wrong. It meant tarnishing Chiang Kai-shek's image."

Jan said, "Can't have that, now can we? Why don't you just go ahead and do the story without them? Clear Service's name yourself."

DiPalma shook his head. "Not the same. From what I learned, he loved China. Loved it more than a lot of Chinese did. I wanted his name cleared among the Chinese *by* the Chinese. I also wanted Martin Mackie to be allowed to rest in peace. At this stage, why broadcast the fact that he was dirty and on the take? I owed him."

He looked at Jan. "He didn't die a good death."

"I know," she said. "Some little queen set him up, I understand."

"Right. But to get, you have to give. The Chinese agreed to change Service's record. Officially he's not a murderer anymore. Officially he's now the innocent victim of a socialist conspiracy which the Taiwanese government officially regrets and is happy to make right in so far as it can. Service's name will be clear where it counts."

"And Mackie?"

DiPalma said, "The Taiwanese will use their influence with the Hong Kong police to keep the lid on his private life. Same thing with any money he may have taken. He goes out with a clean record."

"So you got what you wanted?"

"Like I said, I had to give to get. In return, I promised the Taiwanese not to do anything about Berlin and his sister. Fare-thee-well to the story of a lifetime."

He stared through the window. "Todd and Benjy taught me something about loyalty. The word's a lost cause these days. But those two, Christ, every time I think of them I get goose bumps. They showed me something."

"Mackie I understand," Jan said. "But Tom Service . . . what do you owe *him*?"

"You had to read about that guy like I did. Read his letters, read what his parents and Chinese friends said about him. Read missionary records to see the kind of man he was. They don't make 'em like that anymore. He was more than just loyal. The guy was a saint. Somebody's got to stand up and say his life wasn't wasted."

A tearful Jan kissed his cheek. "I love you. And today I understand why."

She frowned. "What's wrong?"

DiPalma pointed. "Down there. Isn't that—"

"My God, you're right. It's Todd. Oh, Lord, he's got a suitcase with him. Where's he going?"

"I don't know."

"Frank?"

He heard the alarm in her voice and turned quickly. She was pointing to a bare space on the wall to her right.

A sword was missing.

DiPalma glanced at the bare space. "The one Todd used to kill the Black General is gone." He looked out the window. "The suitcase says he's left for good this time. Jesus, I hope I'm wrong. I love that kid. God, he's looking up here. It's like he's saying good-bye."

DiPalma tried to open the window, but it wouldn't budge. He screamed Todd's name. The boy turned away from him and walked into the gathering darkness.

Jan whispered, "He's finished what he has to do here. It's over for him. His karma is done, I guess." She buried her face in DiPalma's chest and wept. "Poor boy. Poor boy."

Neither spoke for a while.

Finally DiPalma said, "If his karma is finished, why did he take the sword?"